What
in Vegas…

KATHERINE GARBERA

MILLS & BOON

Published in Great Britain 2013
by Mills & Boon, an imprint of Harlequin (UK) Limited,
Eton House, 18-24 Paradise Road, Richmond, Surrey TW9 1SR

His Wedding-Night Wager, Her High-Stakes Affair and *Their Million-Dollar Night* were first published in Great Britain by Harlequin (UK) Limited.

ISBN: 978 0 263 90562 5
ebook ISBN: 978 1 472 00135 1

05-0813

Harlequin (UK) policy is to use papers that are natural, renewable and recyclable products and made from wood grown in sustainable forests. The logging and manufacturing processes conform to the legal environmental regulations of the country of origin.

Printed and bound in Spain by Blackprint CPI, Barcelona

HIS WEDDING NIGHT WAGER

BY
KATHERINE GARBERA

One brief trip to Las Vegas and **Katherine Garbera** was hooked with endless story ideas and a fascination with that playground known as Sin City. She's written more than twenty books and has been nominated for *Romantic Times BOOKclub*'s career achievement awards in Series Fantasy and Series Adventure. Katherine recently moved to the Dallas area where she lives with her husband and their two children. The only thing she loves more than writing is talking to readers. Visit Katherine on the web at www.katherinegarbera.com.

This book is dedicated to Matt!
Thanks for a fabulous wedding night and
all the nights that have come after!

ACKNOWLEDGMENT

Special thanks to Chris Green who answered all of my Vegas questions and gave me an insider's perspective.

Thanks also to Natashya Wilson and Debbie Matteucci for their editing insight!

One

Long legs, expensive silk hose and the kind of hips that he could sink his fingers into. She had it all. She always had. Hayden still couldn't believe Shelby Anne Paxton was here in his kingdom. He'd never thought to see her again.

Her calves were well formed, tapering down to trim ankles and a pair of stilettos that sent his libido into overdrive.

The Chimera Hotel and Casino was his life. The 24/7 world of Vegas had always been his home. He wouldn't do anything to jeopardize the success of the hotel and casino. He'd sacrificed to make it into one of the premier destinations on the Vegas Strip. And he owed it all to this woman who hadn't believed in him and to his father.

Hayden had made the Chimera the number-one casino in Vegas to prove that their lack of faith wasn't an obstacle in getting what he wanted from life.

His entire operation was first-class, right down to the hotel's own shopping wing, which housed only sophisticated retailers. Always expanding and changing, it was about to add Bêcheur d'Or, a high-end lingerie boutique.

Bêcheur d'Or was on the fast track to the top. It's owners, Paige Williams and Shelby, had been profiled in *Entrepreneur* magazine earlier this year. Apparently Shelby had made more of his money than he'd ever expected her to.

But it had been Paige with whom he'd spoken to cinch the deal, and Paige with whom he'd met to sign the contract. Funny that Shelby had shown up here and now, especially considering he'd never expected her back in Vegas after she'd left him standing at the altar.

A long, low wolf whistle jolted Hayden back to the present and the hallway outside the newest merchandise location at the Chimera. "Well, well, well. What have we here?"

Hayden turned to see the tall, lean, dark-haired form of his best friend stroll up. Pain tightened in his gut. He didn't want even Deacon Prescott to know who this woman was. He'd simply referred to her as the gold digger that one time he'd gotten drunk and talked to Deacon about his marriage.

Hayden glanced at Deacon and fought the surge of possessiveness swamping him. "You're a married man."

"Definitely. But that doesn't mean I'm dead. Besides, Kylie knows I'd never stray."

Deacon and Kylie had been married for almost two years now and things were going well. They were the exception to Hayden's golden rule that marriage was a business deal.

"No, you wouldn't," Hayden said more to himself than to Deacon. Deacon had found something that Hayden would never admit he'd once wanted. His friend had found forever love and happiness. As for Hayden…well, he'd learned his lesson long ago.

Still, Hayden didn't begrudge his friend. Deacon had come a long way from the man Hayden had first met several years ago. A long way from the mob enforcer who'd wanted to go straight, longing for a better life that he didn't know how to find. Now Deacon owned the Golden Dream, a very successful resort and casino that was second only to the Chimera in terms of success.

Deacon had also found love and seemed to buy into the whole illusion of it since his marriage. Hayden knew better then to try it himself.

He wished the ending for his own story had been as happy, but reality had a way of making sure the scales were kept firmly balanced. And to Hayden's way of thinking, if you grew up with every luxury money could buy but a father who couldn't seem to love you, then something had to give. For Hayden it had always been the softer things.

"Are you going to go inside or just stand in the doorway?" Deacon asked.

Normally he'd walk on by, but not today. "I'm waiting for the right moment."

"And that would be when?" Deacon asked.

"When you get the hell out of here."

"You didn't leave me alone when I went after Kylie."

"Hey, we had a bet. I had to keep tabs on you," Hayden said. He'd bet Deacon that Kylie wouldn't marry him. It was one of the few times that Hayden had lost when he'd gambled, but he hadn't minded the loss.

"Want to make another wager?" Deacon asked. "Only this time—"

"I'm not looking for Ms. Right like you were."

"Why aren't you, Mac?" Deacon asked. His friend always called him by that nickname. It was a holdover from when they'd first met and Deacon had needled Hayden about being the "Mac Daddy." The big guy with lots of cash.

"You know I already tried marriage and didn't find it to my liking," he said, playing off the incident as if it were nothing more than a minor inconvenience, instead of a life-defining moment.

"But you didn't make it to the finish line, so to speak," Deacon said.

"I got close enough," Hayden said. No woman was ever again going to get him to stand in front of a church full of his friends and family and wait for her. There were few feelings he could recall as clearly as the humiliation and anger that had simmered in his gut as he'd faced all of his guests and told them that the bride wasn't coming.

Was it getting closer to forty that was catching up with him or was it Deacon's happy union?

"That doesn't mean it won't work with another woman. This one looks fine."

"Deacon, stop staring at her ass or I'm going to send the surveillance video to Kylie."

Deacon put his hands up and backed away. "I thought you might want a little of the good life."

"I think I've already got it."

"Yeah, well, if you change your mind, I'm here and I've got good advice."

"On what?"

"Romance."

"I don't need advice from you, Prescott."

Deacon flipped him the finger and walked away. Hayden leaned against the wall opposite the glass storefront, continuing to watch the lady unpack her boxes. Damn it had been a long time since any woman had gotten to him like this. Why did it have to be Shelby?

He couldn't stand outside her shop forever, so he pushed away from the wall and entered.

She straightened and her auburn hair fell in waves down the middle of her back. She had a phone tucked between her shoulder and ear as she pulled items from the open box.

"I haven't seen him yet. I'll check in on Friday like we planned. Please don't call me again."

She disconnected the call, turned on her heel and froze. Her jaw dropped and he knew she'd spotted him. Her face went pale as she reached behind her and braced one hand on the countertop, on top of her cell phone.

He walked through the room with a long, easy stride that he strove to keep nonchalant. He schooled his features and forced himself to treat her the way he'd treat any other businessperson who'd leased space from him. He wasn't a first-rate gambler for nothing. He knew how to bluff with the best and how to keep his emotions under wraps.

But he couldn't resist slipping his hand deep into his left pocket and rubbing the top of his left thigh where he had a tiny tattoo of a medieval knight's fist wrapped around a bleeding heart. It was his constant reminder that he no longer allowed his emotions to be a part of his sexual relationships.

It took a lot of guts for Shelby to come back to Vegas after what she'd done. It took the kind of gall of someone who had nothing left to lose. And she'd not only come back to his home turf but taken up residence in his kingdom.

She was still the most beautiful woman he'd ever seen. But she'd changed. Before, she'd been kind of wild—more untamed. The kind of woman who'd made his dad crazy because she was obviously eye candy.

God, he'd been an ass when he was younger. He hoped like hell that Shelby hadn't been aware of that part of him. But he suspected she must've been. Otherwise why would she have taken the million dollars his dad offered and left him?

"What are you doing here?" he asked silkily.

"I own this place," she said.

God, her voice was still soft and sweet. Everything

he remembered about her was the same. She still looked twenty-two. It wasn't fair that time had been so kind to her. He'd be able to handle this reunion a lot better if she'd gained weight, had gray hair, something like that.

"I meant in Vegas," he said, leaning in closer and putting his hands on either side of her, caging her between his body and the counter. Ten years had passed, but right now it felt as if she'd just left him. That had been more than enough time to get rid of any lingering anger, but seeing her again had brought it all to the fore. He wasn't ready to let her go.

He'd never forgotten Shelby's voice. The way it sounded when she was happy. The way it deepened when she came in his arms. Or the way she'd sounded on the phone during that hurried conversation when she'd explained that she had to leave.

"I'm working," she said now.

"I remember a girl who used to say she'd never work a day in her life."

"I changed my mind. Money has a way of running out."

"Even the cool million you took from my dad?" he asked.

But when he saw the color leave her face and watched her pupils dilate, he didn't have the rush of adrenaline that he'd thought he'd feel. Instead he felt big and mean, like the bully his father had always been.

"Of course it did," she said. But inside, a part of her was aching. It had been easy to forget the implications of what she'd done while she'd lived on the East Coast. Distance had provided a kind of barrier for her.

Shelby Anne Paxton stared at the man she'd almost married for his money. She'd been looking for a rich boy to marry and Hayden had been looking for a nice-looking girl to annoy his dad. She couldn't explain it even now, but there'd been a connection between the two of them that she'd always thought went deeper than his money and her looks.

He'd changed in the last ten years but not nearly enough. He still had a thick head of dark hair that curled rakishly over one eye. He had bright blue eyes that had always been able to see past her defenses, and thick lips that made her remember how they'd felt on hers.

Damn, where had that come from?

"Did you know this was my hotel?" he asked.

"Yes, I did," she said softly. There was no way she was going to tell him that his father had flown to Atlanta and suggested she bid for this location. *Suggested* was really too nice a term for what he'd done. Alan MacKenzie had practically blackmailed her into coming back here. He'd threatened to leak the information about her gold-digging past to several magazines. Bêcheur d'Or was gaining an international reputation for class, and the last thing she needed was negative exposure. But Alan had also dangled a carrot—he'd offered her anything she wanted, within reason, if she agreed. Shelby knew he expected her to ask for money.

Yes, Alan had pushed her to come back, and she had.

But now that she was here, she wasn't sure she should have listened to him. The problem was, she still had an obsession with Hayden. He was the man she thought of late at night when she was alone.

"Then why are you here?"

"Um…" She couldn't tell him the truth. Would he believe a part of it—that she needed some closure and to pay him back for what he'd unknowingly given her by asking her to marry him? If he hadn't done that, Alan would never have paid her the money she'd needed to get started in business. Her exclusive line of boutiques turned a huge profit and were considered a value-added chain to many luxury resorts around the world. All of that was thanks to this man.

"I'm waiting, Shelby. Tell me why you're here. Are you hoping to strike it rich again in Vegas?"

In ways he'd never understand.

He stood before her, seething with anger. But she couldn't explain why she was back. Or that she couldn't stay away once Alan had approached her.

She'd forgotten about the anger. Maybe because of the way she'd left. Their last meeting had been a joyous one. The night before their wedding. She swallowed hard. She'd forgotten about her own emotions and how hard they could be to deal with.

"When you say it like that—"

"You sound like the gold digger you are," he finished for her.

"Not anymore, Hayden. I'm here because it's a smart business move." She'd left him at the altar. Called him from the airport with his father's check in her hand. How was he ever going to forgive that?

"Nice touch with the boutique name," he said after a few moments had passed.

A brief smile played at her lips. Naming the shop with the French word for "gold digger" had been her idea. After all, she'd always been unflinchingly honest when it came to what she was. She'd grown up too poor to pretend that money meant nothing to her. "At the time it seemed kind of tongue in cheek," she explained. "I mean, you know how I started out."

"With nothing," he said. She realized some of the anger had faded from his eyes and he was looking at her with something akin to lust.

Passion had never been the problem between them. She'd always been the biggest obstacle in their relationship. Only after a few years of therapy was she able to see that they probably wouldn't have lasted together even if she hadn't taken the payoff his father had offered. Hayden had been more interested in having the most attractive woman on his arm, and she'd been too interested in having financial security. Their relationship had been very shallow.

"And now you have this," he said.

His aftershave hadn't changed in all the years they'd been apart. Still a spicy, masculine scent that she knew he had custom blended in France.

"What do you want from me, Hayden?" she asked when she realized he was staring down at her.

He lifted one of his hands and stroked down the side

of her face. His touch was gentle. She stood still, fighting the urge to close her eyes and lean into that hand. Hayden had always been so gentle with her.

Something few other men ever had been.

He'd wanted a wife and she'd left him to deal with their friends. She'd always felt guilty about that. She doubted that Hayden wanted her back in his life. Though now that they were face to face, she was beginning to realize that was something *she* wanted.

"The wedding night we never had."

"Sex?"

He nodded.

Shocked, she didn't know what to say. The same sensual spell he'd always cast around her surrounded her now. She felt the force of his will and his desire. She closed her eyes and opened her mouth, leaning toward him before she realized what she was doing.

In Alan's words she was supposed to bring some closure to Hayden and get him ready to find a nice girl and settle down. Now that he was feeling his age, Alan wanted grandkids and for his son to be happy. But Shelby knew Alan didn't have her in mind.

She scooted away from Hayden but he reached out for her again. The years fell away and she was suddenly that trailer-park girl wanting the golden boy once again. And there was a part of her who still wanted that man.

Since leaving Hayden she'd had two other relationships—both with wealthy men—but things had never really heated up. Her fault. She was the first to admit she didn't trust her passionate side. Because the one time she had, she'd lost her heart.

"Are you really looking for sex?"

He cocked his head to the side. "Yeah."

"Is this only a revenge thing?" she asked. Because she realized she wanted to say yes. She'd like nothing better than to go to bed with Hayden, even with all the years and anger between them.

"I'm not sure."

"Thanks for not lying." But then Hayden never had. From the beginning he'd said he was the spoiled son of a wealthy man. He'd been kind of immature in those days but so had she. Hayden had also seemed like a knight in shining armor. Shelby had known that eventually he'd wake up and realize he'd made a mistake in marrying her.

"I'll save that for you."

This was more what she expected. She wrapped her arms around her waist and backed farther away from him. She bumped into one of the packing crates and almost lost her balance.

Hayden grabbed her arm and held her until she was steady on her feet. She swallowed hard and tried not to flinch from his touch. But there was nothing harsh in his touch. Just a gentle hold.

"Okay?" he asked in that low, raspy voice of his that never failed to send shivers down her spine.

"Yes. Thanks."

They said nothing for a few minutes. Shelby tried to marshal her thoughts. Tried to find her balance in a world that was suddenly out of whack. She glanced around her boutique, her gaze falling on the poster advertising Puccini's *Madame Butterfly* at the Met. Slowly she let the familiar world she'd created soothe her troubled soul.

She took a deep breath and stepped away from Hayden. As tempting as it was to fall into bed with the one man who'd made her feel really feminine, really alive, she knew she couldn't. She'd changed from the girl she was. No MacKenzie man was ever again going to make her feel embarrassed about who she'd been.

She'd been afraid of being like her mom and in the end that was exactly what she'd become. Someone who traded on her looks for money…for security. But she was a different woman now. She made her own way in the world. She was Hayden's equal in every way that mattered.

"We can't be together if you treat me, like…well, like I suppose you have a right to. I'm really not into that kind of pain."

"I don't want to hurt you, Shelby. I never wanted that."

She believed him. Despite his seemingly shallow playboy attitude back then, he'd always treated her like a lady. She couldn't really explain it to anyone who hadn't grown up the way she had, but when your mother dressed like a tramp and you had a rotating stable of "uncles" in and out of your life, people treated you like trash. But Hayden never had.

"It's been ten years, Hayden. Why do we both still feel like this?" she asked, realizing that Alan had done her a huge favor by sending her back here.

"Honestly, I don't know."

She tipped her head to the side and acknowledged that despite the years she'd never really forgotten him. "I came back because of you."

He tipped his head to the side, not saying a word, just watching her with that electric gaze of his.

She spoke again. "I can't…move on until I figure out what went wrong between us."

"Hell, Shelby, that's an easy one."

"Please, don't say it again. I wish I had the money to pay your dad back so that it wouldn't be an issue between us."

He narrowed his eyes and walked toward her. "So what do you say to some sort of compromise? You give me what I paid for."

"What your father paid for," she said.

"I paid for it in ways you can never understand."

But she did and it made her ache to realize it.

"A night of sex? I don't think I'm worth a million dollars."

"What about a week?" he asked.

"Sex and money. They were my mom's downfall. I—I couldn't do that. If we're going to try this again, I want it to be a real relationship."

He nodded. She saw understanding in his eyes and she realized that if she was going to find any kind of peace with him, it was going to be through bonds of friendship. She wasn't sure she could risk her emotions with him. He'd made her feel so vulnerable. And she didn't want to be that woman again.

"Have dinner with me, Shel. Let's figure this thing out."

"I…"

"It's just a meal."

"I have a lot of work to do here and a short time to do it. I need to hire staff, finish unpacking." The words sounded like an excuse to her and she knew they were. It was just that even though she'd planned to come back to resolve the past, now that the moment was at hand, she was afraid.

But her running days were over. And at the end of the day, Hayden MacKenzie was still just a man.

Yeah, right.

Hayden entered his office in the casino nearly an hour later. Kathy, his assistant, was gone for the day. The small desk lamp glowed at her workstation. She always left it on for him because she knew he kept late hours. There were two messages from his dad, and one from the star of his European-style revue, Roxy O'Malley.

He dialed the backstage number for the revue venue and got the director. "Roxy called me."

"She's onstage right now. Want me to have her call you back?"

"I'll stop by after the show. Let her know."

"I will."

"Any problems?"

"A few guys were hanging around after the first show but security took care of them."

"Keep me posted."

He hung up the phone, leaning back in his chair. His office had windows on two sides that showed the Strip out of one, and the Chimera's hotel building out of the other. One wall held a bank of security monitors and Hayden crossed to them.

He took the access remote and keyed in Shelby's store. The lights were on but the place was empty. Had she run? But then he saw her. Standing in the shadows staring at something in her hands that he couldn't make out.

He reached for his phone and dialed her shop. He saw her move from the shadows to the counter near the register and pick up the phone.

"Bêcheur d'Or."

"It's me."

"Hayden."

Just his name softly whispered. He saw her hand go to her throat and her eyes close. What was he doing?

"Are you okay?" he asked at long last. No matter what he wanted from her, no matter that he intended to find some closure from their relationship whatever the price to her, he really didn't want to hurt Shelby.

She put her hand on the counter and straightened up. "Yes, why do you ask?"

"I'm watching you."

"How?" she asked, pivoting to see if he was standing nearby.

"On video surveillance."

"I'd forgotten that part of Vegas. So, am I on closed circuit?"

"Why?"

"No reason. I just want to know who's watching."

He hit a switch and turned off access to her shop at every other monitor except his. "Just me."

"Why are you watching me?" she asked. Wrapping one arm around herself, she looked small, vulnerable. Not a bit like the schemer his dad had called her.

"I was debating something."

"What?"

"What would happen if I took what I want from you," he said.

"What is it you want, Hayden?"

"I thought I told you. Revenge."

He saw her bow her head. Even though he was several floors above her and in a different wing of the hotel, he felt the sadness that swamped her at his words. "I want to give you that."

He was surprised. "Masochism your new thing?"

"No, but reparation is."

"Shelby—"

"Don't say anything else, Hayden. Let's have dinner and talk terms."

Two

Shelby wasn't sure she could do it. She stood in the suite of rooms she'd been given in the Chimera to use until the shop was open. She was only here temporarily until the boutique opened in three weeks, and then she'd be returning to headquarters in Atlanta, where Paige was holding down the fort, until their next shop opened in the fall. Right now she wished she was back in her safe little condo in Buckhead, watching television and eating fat-free microwave popcorn. Safe but boring. Those words described her life and she had to admit she was ready for a change.

So, here she was in Sin City with the one man who'd never been safe or boring. And she was hesitating in front of her closet as if it was her first date. The last time her choices had been simpler. She'd set out to catch herself a wealthy husband. But this time she had no idea what role she was in.

She closed her eyes and tried to find the confident woman she'd been until she'd glanced up and seen Hayden MacKenzie staring straight back at her with anger, lust and pain in his eyes. She'd known then that the dreams that had been haunting her had led her back to this place to do one thing. To find a way to give this man peace in exchange for what he'd unwittingly given her.

She had a successful career and the life she'd always dreamed of. But did Hayden? Seeing how deeply her choice still affected him made her want—no, need—to make up for it in some way. If parts of her dream life weren't exactly perfect, well, that was a price she'd happily pay.

She pulled a brightly colored wraparound silk skirt from the hanger and shed her business skirt and thigh-high hose. The fabric was cool against her legs as she fastened it just below her waist. She shrugged out of her suit jacket and tossed it on the chair in the corner.

She had firm breasts so she scarcely ever bothered with a bra. Tonight was no exception. She paired the skirt with a soft white camisole. She took a quick glimpse of herself in the mirror. She looked the way she always did, cool and polished. She tried to fluff her hair up and then realized what she was doing.

Hayden wasn't really dating her. She closed her eyes, leaning her forehead against the mirror. Then she took a shuddering breath. She was strong, capable, and this was the only penance available to her.

Over the years she'd tried to pay Alan MacKenzie back the money she'd taken. Not in one lump sum, as she'd never had that much disposable cash on hand. But in chunks. And he'd always refused, saying that he didn't want her money; he only wanted his son to be happy.

She didn't doubt that. Alan and Hayden had a complex relationship that she'd never taken the time to understand until it had been too late. She'd realized that Hayden had only dated her to needle his father. But she'd been dating him for his money, so she hadn't quibbled.

She was exactly the wrong type of woman for a man with Hayden's future back then. Hayden would never know how right his father had been. Alan had made it clear that he'd tell Hayden every detail of the life she'd hidden from him if she hadn't taken the money he'd offered.

But now… A lot had changed in ten years. Now apparently Alan thought that she could help Hayden. And in order to pull this off she'd have to keep that secret from the man she'd betrayed.

She was dithering and that didn't fit with who she was, so she pushed away from the wall, put on her strappy gold sandals and left the room.

She didn't look back or hesitate. She'd made a conscious decision when she'd come to Vegas. Facing the past had never been an easy thing. She'd always looked forward because the past— She didn't want to go there. Not now.

She exited the elevator in the lobby and glanced

around for Hayden. She didn't see him at first but then found him standing off to one side talking with an extremely attractive blonde.

Shelby realized that for all she knew, Hayden was involved with another woman and really was just using her for revenge. It didn't matter that she'd said she was doing whatever it took to bring Hayden some peace; she knew in her heart she still wanted him.

Hayden had changed clothes as well, wearing a button-down shirt in midnight blue and a pair of faded jeans. On anyone else the outfit would have seemed casual, but the way he carried himself belied that impression.

He glanced up and caught her gaze, motioning her over. The woman he was talking to had the kind of beauty that made Shelby feel like an ugly duckling. Her long blond hair fell past her shoulders and her makeup, though a little heavy, accentuated her classic bone structure.

Hayden gestured for her to join them. The woman glanced over at her and smiled. It was a sweet, welcoming smile and Shelby felt warmed by it.

"Roxy, this is Shelby Paxton. She owns a boutique that's opening here in the Chimera in the next few weeks. Shelby, this is Roxy O'Malley, the star of the Chimera's top-rated revue."

"Nice to meet you," Shelby said.

"Same here. What kind of shop do you own?"

"Lingerie."

"My favorite kind. I'll have to check it out."

Shelby reached into her purse and pulled out an invitation to the grand-opening party. "We're having a little party to celebrate."

"I'll be there," Roxy said. She glanced over at Hayden.

"I'll look into that matter we discussed," Hayden said.

"I'd appreciate it, Hay. I know he could be harmless, but something about him made me leery."

"No problem, Roxy. I'll let you know what I find out."

When Roxy left them, he turned his attention to Shelby. She felt his hot gaze on her, taking in the length of her bare arms, lingering on the scooped curve of her neckline and then skimming down to her feet in the tiny sandals.

She crossed her arms around her waist but then realized she was projecting her vulnerability for him to see. And Hayden was intimately acquainted with some of her weaknesses. She didn't need for him to know that he rattled her.

"Thanks for joining me for dinner," he said. "Can you walk in those shoes?"

"Yes. They're surprisingly comfortable. What were you two discussing?"

"Jealous?"

She tipped her head to the side. "Yes, I think I am."

He laughed. "Don't be. It was only business."

"She didn't seem like just an employee."

"You're right, she's not."

"Is she your lover?" Shelby asked, though she hadn't gotten that intimate vibe from the two of them.

"No. More like a kid sister. I really try to make the Chimera like a family. So many people come here alone and…"

Hayden knew loneliness. It was one of the things they'd both had in common. Something Shelby hadn't had to lie about when they'd been dating long ago. Her mother had always been working, just like Hayden's dad. It had given them some unexpected common ground.

She tucked her hand under his elbow. "You're a nice man."

"Sometimes."

He escorted her out of the main lobby to the escalators that led to the mezzanine level. "Where are we going?" she asked.

"To the stars."

"We're going flying?" This was the man who'd swept her off her feet years ago. He'd offered her the fantasy of romance and she'd lapped it up without thinking of the consequences. Like those sunset airplane rides in his Cessna. He'd taken things that she'd never imagined she would do and made them happen.

"Not tonight. Last year I had a planetarium built. Well, Deacon and I did."

"Who's Deacon?"

"Deacon Prescott. He owns the Golden Dream. We work together on a lot of projects. I thought we'd have a drink under the stars before dinner."

"Isn't that going to be a little awkward with all your other guests?"

"No, Shel. I closed down one of the theaters. I'd rather my guests stay in the casino anyway."

"More money to be made that way, right?"

"You know that money makes the world go round."

"Yes, I do."

He slipped his hand under her elbow and led her through the mezzanine. He was stopped twice by his employees with questions that he had to take. Owning Bêcheur d'Or made her understand how demanding running any kind of business could be. She'd checked in with Paige early this morning and had a conference call scheduled for tomorrow at 9:00 a.m. with the builders of the next boutique in Washington, D.C.

Finally they entered a long corridor that was sparsely occupied. The piped-in music wasn't some generic Muzak but the sophisticated beauty of Wynton Marsalis playing the trumpet.

Shelby closed her eyes and wondered for a moment if this might have been her life had she made a different choice all those years ago.

"Vegas has changed in the last ten years," she said, though she suspected it was the changes inside herself that made the city seem so different.

"Yes, it has."

"Did you have anything to do with that?" she asked to fill the silence and keep her mind off the uncomfortable feeling that maybe she hadn't changed as much as she wished she had.

"What do you think?" he asked.

She paused and tilted her head to the side to study him. She knew without a doubt that he was on the image committee and the development committees for the Strip. Hayden wouldn't chance leaving any detail that could affect his business to someone else.

"Yes. I like how sophisticated your hotel is, but that doesn't change the fact that one block over, the area is still a little sleazy."

"Everyone is looking for something different in Vegas and we like to say we can accommodate any type of poison."

"What about me?" she asked, wondering what he thought about her was dangerous. *What you think of yourself is the only thing that matters.* But she'd never held herself in high regard.

"What about you?" he asked. He pulled her into a small alcove.

She felt secluded from the rest of the world with the wall at her back and Hayden blocking her front. He stared down at her with an unreadable expression and she shivered deep inside, realizing how much of life she'd been missing since she left this man.

Because she'd never been able to really trust a man enough to let him affect her the way Hayden always had. She swallowed against a dry throat and said, "What's my poison?"

"Only you can say. I suspect that it's a mix between the gritty reality of where you grew up and this." He gestured to the ornately decorated hallway.

"What about you?" she asked, not willing to dwell too much on how gritty her reality had been.

"I'm the center ring, master of ceremonies. Making sure that whatever reason—fantasy or desire—you brought with you gets fulfilled."

There was a husky sensuality in his voice. She looked

up at Hayden, into his deep blue eyes, and realized that he wasn't all show and both of them knew it.

Hayden liked the feel of Shelby's arm under his hand. The lobby of the planetarium was actually between his hotel and Deacon's Golden Dream. They'd funded a wing together last year that would enhance the experience for their guests. He also had a traveling Impressionists exhibit down the hall in the art museum.

Most people came to Vegas for a reason and Shelby's was probably just profit motivated, but his gut said there was more. He wanted to know more about those reasons.

Hayden had asked the head chef, Louis Patin, to send up champagne and strawberries for a predinner snack, and one of the hostesses handed a wicker basket to Hayden as they entered. He took Shelby up the back stairs into one of the VIP rooms.

"Give me a minute to get everything set up," he said.

"Can I help?" she asked.

"No. I've got it." He gestured toward the plush velvet covered seats positioned in front of the low wall. "Enjoy the show."

She sat down and Hayden watched her carefully cross her legs, then shift to find a more comfortable position on the chair. The slit in her skirt widened and he realized it was a wraparound type and that only one or two buttons were keeping that silky fabric in place.

He caught a glimpse of her thigh before she pulled the fabric over her leg, covering it up. He sighed and then turned to open their champagne.

She was watching him as he poured the liquid and handed her a glass. The material from her skirt slipped free of her fingers. It slid down her leg. The woman had great legs.

"Why are we playing these games, Hayden?" she asked, running her fingers along the length of exposed skin. The stars had begun to appear on the planetarium ceiling, and soft classical music began to play.

"I wasn't aware we were. We both like to flirt," he said, lightly touching his glass to hers then moving back to regard her. Her flesh looked so soft and tempting in the muted lighting in the room. His own fingers tingled with the need to caress her. He clenched them and sipped the bubbling drink.

"I thought you were the master of ceremonies. Flirting is where we both try to pretend that we're not still attracted to each other."

"Is that what you've been doing?" he asked. Already his blood was flowing heavy and every nerve in his body said screw talking and take her. She didn't want the niceties he put on when he was trying to be a gentleman instead of the gambler he essentially was.

"I've been trying. And not successfully I might add," she said, twisting her fingers together in a nervous gesture that made him realize that it might not be real desire that motivated Shelby. It was the waiting. Not knowing which way things were going to fall between them.

"Why?" he asked, needing to know more.

"I can't figure it out. There's always been something

about you that makes me feel…I don't know, like I'm about to jump off a cliff. I know that it's going to be an exhilarating ride but I'm not sure my parachute is going to open in time."

It was different for him. He'd spent the last ten years protecting his emotions from the women with whom he got involved. It hadn't even been conscious at first, but the last woman he'd broken up with had said that he was the coldest man she'd ever slept with. White-hot in bed but stone-cold out. And Hayden had realized the truth about himself. The truth that had probably been there the entire time. He couldn't do things by half measures.

"We agreed to dinner," he said.

"I know. But I got nervous when I saw you watching me."

"Wanting you," he said.

He closed the distance between them and bent down on one knee. Up close he could see the smooth, lightly tanned skin.

"Do you want me to want you that way?"

"Yes," she said. "Yes, because that gives me something real to cling to."

He shouldn't touch her. Not now. Yet he couldn't help himself. He reached out, scraping one nail along the edge of the material that covered her leg. She shivered, but didn't pull away.

Her hand fell to his shoulder, holding on to him while he touched her. Stroking her was addictive. Her skin was softer than anything he'd touched in a long time. Her muscles weren't hardened by hours in the gym, but softer. It was a very feminine thigh.

Taking the fabric in his hand, he drew it up over her leg and uncovered her. She dropped her hand to the top of her thigh, lightly resting it on top of his.

"Sit with me, Hayden. Let's talk."

He didn't ask why. He knew that she wanted that sweet feeling that had always been between them. The real reason he could never forgive Shelby wasn't so much because of the money she'd taken. It was because of the lesson she'd taught him.

He'd never been the kind of man who had let anyone inside him. Never let anyone see the real man behind the trappings of the spoiled rich-boy facade. But he'd been tempted to let her in and she'd walked away.

"Why'd you do it, Shel?"

She trembled and lifted her hand from his. She pushed away from the chair and walked a few steps from him, looking out over the railing up toward the stars that were playing across the wide ceiling.

He stood but kept the distance between them. When she spoke it was almost too soft for him to hear, but he could make out the words.

"I needed security."

"That's it?" he asked, sensing she was hiding something. He knew then that subterfuge was a big part of what was going on here and it had little to do with sex. It was all about who they both were and who they didn't want the other to see. "Lay it out for me, babe. Because that just sounds like a line."

"I left because I knew that you were twenty-four-carat solid gold and I was that spray-on stuff they use at fairs that wears off after a few days and leaves a green mark."

She turned her head away from him. "I wanted to leave before I left a mark on you that you'd have a hard time getting rid of."

Hayden led Shelby out of the planetarium to a very exclusive restaurant on the fifty-fifth floor of the Chimera. They were led to a private booth that faced the floor-to-ceiling plate-glass windows overlooking Las Vegas. The view was breathtaking. She slid onto the bench and straightened her skirt, looking casual and at ease.

But Hayden wasn't. Tension rode him like a gambler trying to find a winning streak.

Knowing it tightened the knot in his gut. Why did this woman still have a hold on him? And would revenge be enough to loosen her hold?

His mind warned that logic didn't play a part in his actions here and now, but he wasn't really listening with his mind.

The curve of her neck was looking fragile and vulnerable, and he realized that talking about her past was one of her weak points. They'd never really talked about where she'd come from. Perhaps he'd been too shallow to care or too arrogant to think any of that mattered. But now, with the years between them, he realized that her past very much shaped the kind of relationship they'd had.

"Thanks for showing me the stars tonight," she said.

"You're welcome. Would you like some more wine?" he asked.

She shook her head. "Let's get down to business. I believe you said you want to get what you paid for, right?"

When she said it like that he sounded like a bastard. It didn't matter that they both had been acting true to form in those days. He had been a spoiled young man who'd picked a pretty, shy girl who needed him. He'd liked the way she'd clung to his arm, let him pay for everything and make all the decisions. That wasn't politically correct but he wasn't really a PC kind of guy. Despite the money he'd always had, sophistication had always eluded him.

"Yes. That's what I want."

He saw in her eyes that she knew it as well. Knew that she was sitting across from a man who wasn't quite the gentleman he pretended to be.

"You make me feel very feminine when you look at me that way. And I'm not at all used to it. Most men I date are intimidated by me."

"Why?"

"Who knows," she said, but bit her bottom lip.

She knew. Shelby always knew why people acted the way they did. She made it her business to pay attention to those details. "Just guess."

"Because I'm driven to make my company a success. I made too many mistakes when I was young."

"Like you're old now?" he asked.

"You know what I mean. Sometimes I'm amazed at how immature I was when we were together."

He leaned back, resting his arm on the seat behind her. He wanted to pull her closer to him, to cradle her against his body and protect her. But Shelby didn't need him to do that. He imagined that was what she'd been talking about. That men realized that Shelby was an independent woman who made her own way. It was a bit intimidating.

"You've done really well. I read an article about your company in *Entrepreneur.* The reporter said you were one of the savviest business minds he'd ever encountered."

She shrugged the comment aside. "I think he was just being nice."

"Reporters are never nice. He respected what you'd done." Hayden realized he did, too. She'd taken the hand that life had dealt her and rolled with it.

"Well…" She shrugged. It was clear to him that Shelby wasn't there yet. She didn't really respect herself. Had he played any part in that?

"Let's get back to us. I think your dad paid me off so—"

"No, Shelby. I paid that money to you." He hadn't meant to say it but it was best she knew the facts. He wasn't playing around this game—the stakes were high and he wanted to be damn sure Shelby realized it.

"What?"

"Old Alan wanted to make sure I never forgot the lesson he was teaching. He gave you the money, then made me pay him back every cent." His father had always been real fond of that kind of demonstration—one where the lesson was reinforced by humiliation. It didn't help that Hayden had played on his father's biggest weakness: a woman with big soul-filled eyes and an empty bank account.

"Hayden… I had no idea. I'm so sorry. I took the money…well, I didn't mind taking it from your dad because I knew it was how he kept score."

He said nothing. She'd pegged his father easily. It was how Alan kept score and he'd paid off three wives of his own, so Shelby knew that it didn't bother him. Hayden didn't say anything else but he knew that he'd paid for Shelby with more than just money. He'd paid for her with his soul and now he wanted hers.

Shelby couldn't have been more shocked. She'd never imagined that Hayden had ultimately paid for her giving up their relationship. But then she'd allowed Alan to push a wedge between them. Let him threaten her with revealing the secret she'd kept from Hayden. The one she still didn't really want him to know. She wished there were some way to escape the intimacy that he'd created around them. She didn't want to be sitting so close to him while hashing out the past.

In her mind it was easy to pretend that she was noble and wanted to pay him back—whatever the cost—so that he could find some peace from the past. But the reality was, it hurt. She didn't want to flirt with the only man with whom she'd ever really been honest emotionally.

She didn't want to open up herself and him to the kind of hurt that would undoubtedly come. Because she knew that she wasn't going to be able to just give him a week of sex and then watch him walk away.

Hayden put his arm around her and pulled her against his side. She closed her eyes and pretended that this was something else. Something that she'd done without for a long time. Comfort was easy to take from Hayden. He had big shoulders and a solid chest, and he was more than capable of carrying any burdens.

But that didn't mean that eventually the burdens wouldn't be too heavy for him. She turned in his embrace, put her arms around his waist and rested her head over his heart. His hands moved up and down her back, before settling on her hips, holding her close.

His breathing changed, grew heavier. She felt his body changing under hers as well. There was no getting around the fact that sexually they were like kindling and flame. But was that the kind of fire that could be tamed or would it once again consume them?

He brought one hand up under her chin, tipping her head back. "What are you thinking?"

She struggled against telling him the truth. He already saw more of her than anyone else except Paige. Most people she met were content to see only the surface of who she was—a driven, competent businesswoman. But Hayden...he'd known the vulnerable woman underneath. The one who still wasn't sure of her place in the world.

"I'm thinking this is a mess that I made and it's past time I cleaned it up."

"I think we can both carry the blame," he said, stroking her cheek with a gentleness that made her heart beat a little faster.

"Do you ever feel like life is really a great tragedy? Like the ones in operas?"

He didn't say anything, only continued stroking her back. Shelby wondered if she'd said too much. Her life had never been ideal, but comparing it to a tragedy... She wasn't some scared little miss. She needed to stop acting like one.

"I think that in some ways much of our lives is like opera, how operas show the intense emotions that sometimes influence our decisions. Why?"

This was the man who'd convinced her to take a chance and marry him. This soft poet's soul that she'd scarcely glimpsed since her return to Vegas.

"I thought maybe we were caught at the end of the second act. You know, where all seems doomed."

"And that maybe it was time to move on to the third act?"

She couldn't answer. In one of her favorite operas, *Tristan und Isolde,* the third act had them both dying. But for a love that was so true and right that it captured both of their souls, uniting them even in death. Maybe that was the trailer-park girl deep inside her, but she wanted a man to love her that much.

"What do you want from me?" he asked.

That was the million-dollar question. Alan wanted his son happy and expected her to fix whatever she'd broken when she left. Hayden wanted closure and revenge. But what did she want? Shelby had never really figured that out and it was time to. "I guess a chance to make this real."

Hayden could tempt her into believing that if she showed him her soul he'd reward her with his heart. But she suspected if she did that, he'd take the revenge he so richly deserved. She felt the Sword of Damocles hanging over her. Knew that at any minute the hair might snap.

"How could it not be?" he asked in that deep voice of his.

He was right. There was nothing subtle about the man holding her and nothing tentative in him. He was going to pursue her for his own reasons and she had to decide what she was going to do. She knew with bone-deep certainty that she wasn't going to resist him. He was her secret longing and she'd never forgotten him. So now she had to decide. Was she really going to meekly let him take charge of this? Or was she going to meet him on a level playing field?

"I want you, too, Hayden. And I have an offer for you."

"I'm listening." He traced the line of her spine up her back. His finger circled her neck and toyed with the strap of her camisole.

"Let's make this real. Let's say what this really is. I want a chance to get to know each other the way we never did before."

He pulled the strap of her camisole toward her shoulder and then lowered his head, blowing on the exposed skin. As shivers moved down her arm and back, she undulated in his arms, holding more tightly to his waist.

"Okay," he said.

"Okay?"

She couldn't think when he was this close to her. When he surrounded her with his heat, his touch and his scent. She just wanted to close her eyes and pretend that they didn't have the past between them. Close her eyes and imagine that Hayden MacKenzie really could want Shelby Paxton just for who she was.

"I'll let you try to make me fall in love with you. But honestly, Shelby, I don't have a heart."

"Yes, you do. And I'm just the woman to find it." She promised herself she would. There was no problem she couldn't solve once she put her mind to it. She'd figure Hayden out—find out what made him tick—and slowly work her way into his heart, because she knew from hearing him speak of her betrayed that he still had one.

"You might be right. After all, you were the last one to see it."

She shivered and this time it wasn't from his touch. It was from the coolness beneath his words. She realized this time she may have risked more than she'd anticipated.

"Double or nothing," she murmured, realizing that was exactly the bet she'd made. Both of their hearts united and at peace or once again broken.

"That's the kind of gamble I make every day in business, but this..."

"I'm in if you are, Hayden," she said, unable to keep the challenge from her voice.

"Oh, I'm in."

Three

"The only way to do this is to live together," Hayden said while they were eating dessert.

Shelby choked on a bite of her tiramisu. "What?"

He patted her back and handed her a glass of water. He liked the thought of it now. Her living in his home. Shelby there when he woke up and there when he went to sleep. She said she wanted a chance to know him, to seduce him this time. Living together made the most sense.

"You okay?" he asked.

"Yeah. No. I can't think this late at night. I've had too much rich food."

He smiled at the way she said it, but he knew the truth. She wasn't ready to make a decision. Once she saw his home, though, she'd capitulate.

"Come up to my place and just see it."

She shook her head.

He frowned. In the past, Shelby had never denied him anything. But of course, this wasn't the past. And she was a different woman.

"Why not?"

"Because unlike you I need more than four hours of sleep every night. I need a solid eight and I'm tired."

She had a point. His cell had been vibrating with new messages and he saw Raul, his general manager, hanging around the hostess stand waiting for him. Hayden's reality involved work for almost a solid eighteen hours a day. But that didn't mean he was letting this go. "Are you free for breakfast?"

"Just coffee. It takes a lot of work to open a store in three weeks, plus I have a conference call with Paige and the developers for our D.C. project at 9:00 a.m."

He pulled his BlackBerry phone/PDA from his pocket and checked his calendar for tomorrow. He had an 8:00 a.m. meeting with the gaming commission. Followed by a meeting with his roulette-table staff. And he needed to talk to his head of security about the man who'd been sitting in the front row at each of Roxy's performances for the last three weeks.

"What time?" he asked. He'd move some stuff around if he had to. But his schedule was already tight. Why was he doing this? He didn't question his motives, only knew that if Shelby was willing to work toward something solid, hell, he was, too. It felt right, having her here with him.

She shook her head, her thick hair slipping over her shoulder and down her chest to curl over her breast. "I don't know…seven?"

He remembered how her neck tasted, how soft her skin had felt under his touch, and everything in him went on alert. He wanted this woman. Wanted her naked in his bed. He could see her against his gray sheets. A splash of color in his black-and-white bedroom.

She stared at him.

"What is it? Seven isn't good for coffee?"

He shook himself, but he couldn't push away the image of her lying on his bed with a couple of pillows shoved under her hips. Those lush long legs open, inviting.

"No, that's perfect. I'll have a key card sent to your room. Just come up when you're ready." He was ready now. He didn't know if he could wait. If he could let her set the pace for this reunion of theirs. He wanted to take the lead. Get her into bed and push away the past in the most elemental way. To reassert his dominance over her by making her his.

"Hayden…"

"Yes?" he said. He signed the check and slid out of the booth.

"I'm supposed to be seducing you," she said, joining him.

"Do you think Tristan really waited for Isolde?" he asked, reminding her of the opera she loved, the one that he'd let her talk endlessly about when they'd dated long ago.

She smiled. It was all that was sexy and sweet. Much

like the woman herself. “I’m sure he didn’t, but he was a warrior.”

“Maybe I am, too,” he said, putting his arm around her and leading her out of the restaurant. He’d learned some hard lessons when she’d left him. He’d become a different man because of her. He had realized he was no longer the golden boy who had everything handed to him. Instead, he knew, in his heart, he was a man who’d fight for what he wanted.

“I thought you were a gambler,” she said.

“Can’t a man be both?” he asked, leading her to the bank of elevators. He didn’t really want to dwell on his own shortcomings.

“You tell me,” she said.

“I already did.”

“Where are we going?”

“I’m escorting you back to your room.”

“That’s so sweet,” she said.

He bit the inside of his mouth to keep from smiling. “I’m a sweet guy.”

“Ha. Don’t think you can put the moves on me and I’ll invite you in.”

“Put the moves on you? Give me a break. I’m a little more suave than that.”

They got in the elevator car. There was another couple already in there who got off on the thirtieth floor. Shelby’s suite was on the thirty-fifth. She pulled her key card from her purse when the elevator stopped on her floor.

“Good night,” she said, stepping out.

He followed her into the hall. "Yes, it has been."

"Don't, Hayden. This isn't easy for me."

"I'm not pushing, baby. I'm just seeing you home. Something we never did before."

She flushed a little bit. He wondered at the secrets she hid. Her background wasn't like his, and he hadn't pushed her to talk about it. Maybe that had been part of the problem. He'd easily accepted the personal boundaries she'd set because they'd allowed him to make her into what he wanted her to be.

"About that…"

"Don't say anything more. This is double or nothing. The stakes are high, and as you said, you need some sleep. We'll start again in the morning."

He took her key card from her hand and unlocked her door for her, pushing it open. She paused in the entryway, the glow from a lamp backlighting her.

She looked ethereal, with her thick wavy hair falling around her shoulders. Her skin was soft and pink, and that little white top skimmed her curves.

He bent down to brush his lips to hers. Just a sweet salute to the agreement they'd made. But once his lips touched hers, all that fled and he needed more.

She parted her lips and he tasted her sweet mouth. He touched his tongue to hers as he braced one hand on the doorjamb and buried the other in her hair, holding her head still.

He lifted his head slowly. Her eyes were heavy lidded and he saw the first flush of desire on her face. If he pushed now he could have what he wanted tonight, but he knew that he'd lose ground when tomorrow morning came.

He rubbed his thumb over her lower lip before dropping his hand to his side. He passed her key back to her. "Now it's a good night."

He waited for her to step inside her room and close the door and then he walked away. He wasn't really sure what was going to happen with Shelby. He didn't believe in love. Which might be why he'd overlooked the fact that Shelby had obviously kept a lot of her life from him. But for the first time since he'd opened his casino, he felt really alive.

Shelby had set her alarm for six o'clock but didn't need the buzzing to wake her up. Her sleep had been plagued by fevered dreams of Hayden. He'd always been her guilty, erotic, secret dream man. The one she visited late at night when no one else could know.

His kisses had refueled a fire that had never been extinguished. She was restless and edgy when the alarm finally rang. She hurried through her shower and dressed in record time.

Everything with Hayden was exactly the way she'd always dreamed it could be. But in the back of her mind the thought that Alan had sent her here weighed heavily. She didn't know how to bring up Alan without alienating Hayden once more.

Anxious to see him again, she deliberately hesitated in her suite. She didn't want him to know how much she craved him. She wanted to have a little of the control she'd ceded so easily to him last time, some sort of equality. But she wasn't sure how to find it.

The key card for his penthouse apartment had been delivered to her last night, just twenty minutes after he'd left. She held it in her hand. It was the key to something she'd always wanted. Something she hadn't believed in enough to stick around for the last time. But now…

The phone rang before she could complete the thought. She picked it up reluctantly. Only two people would call her here. Paige, her business partner, or Alan.

"This is Shelby."

"How's our plan going?"

Alan's voice was deeper, scratchier than his son's, thanks no doubt to years of smoking. She hated that he never identified himself. She suspected he did it to prove that everyone remembered him.

"You still there?"

"Yes, I'm here. I…it doesn't feel right. I'm here but that's got to be the end of it, Alan. I don't want to be talking with you behind his back."

"Do you really think that my son is going to accept your past? Do you really think that you can make him overlook the fact that we MacKenzies can trace our ancestors back to the first westward migration and you don't even know who your father is?"

His words hurt and made a wave of shame roll over her. Yes, she did think that. Hayden was no snob, and it was more Shelby's business image and sense of personal privacy that would suffer from the exposure. But she knew she had her work cut out for her in changing Hayden's opinion of her anyway. "I'll do whatever I have to." With those words she hung up on him.

Her phone started ringing again but she didn't answer it. The last time she'd listened to Alan, she'd ended up hurting Hayden. Not this time.

It was exactly seven o'clock when she stepped off the elevator and arrived at Hayden's door. She hesitated a minute and knocked. Despite the key, she didn't feel that she should just let herself in.

He opened the door a few seconds later. He wore a pair of dress pants, a blue shirt that highlighted his eyes and a discreetly colored tie and had a phone cradled between his neck and shoulder. He gestured for her to come in.

"Sounds good," Hayden said into the phone. "Call my assistant and set up a meeting for tomorrow."

He disconnected the call. "Right on time. I was hoping you'd come early."

She didn't know how to respond to that. She'd been so needy before that she was afraid to let him see how much she still needed from him. Still wanted from him.

"I had them set up a light breakfast out on the terrace. I'll give you a tour later, if we have time."

She followed him across the hardwood floors through the living room. There was no video equipment or expensive television, which seemed odd to her for a bachelor. The leather sofa and love seat were situated to face a seascape scene on the wall.

Floor-to-ceiling windows lined one wall and there was a bar along another wall and a small poker table set in front of it. The room was definitely masculine in its decor but so comfortable that she immediately felt at home.

"I like this," she said, stopping to take it all in.

"Good. You can change anything you want when you move in except for my poker area. I host a quarterly poker weekend for some of my friends."

"Tell me about them," she said. She wanted to know more about Hayden. She'd been afraid to meet his friends when they'd been together before. Afraid that they'd make Hayden realize how different she was from his set, how she didn't really belong with the golden boy he'd been.

"Well, I've mentioned Deacon. He's a trusted friend as well as a business partner. Then there's Max Williams—we went to the same prep school. And Scott Rivers—I met him when I was bumming around Europe."

She raised her eyebrows. Former child star Scott Rivers was still an A-list celebrity. She hadn't known he and Hayden were friends.

"When'd you do that?"

"After you left."

"Why?" she asked. She remembered what he'd said about having paid the million dollars she'd taken from Alan. She'd never thought about how he'd earned the money.

"I was trying to make the old man give in and release my trust fund."

"Did it work?" But she knew it hadn't. Alan was a stubborn man and he'd been intent on teaching Hayden a lesson. Unfortunately it had worked better than Alan had anticipated.

"No. It didn't. Finally I ended up on the Côte d'Azur—with no money. I stayed with Scott for a while and then one morning I woke up hungover and out of cash and realized that I couldn't keep living that way. The old man wasn't going to give in. So I went to the first casino I came to and asked for a job."

"Why a casino?"

"I had this idea of showing the old man up."

"Did it work?"

"I don't know if I showed him up, but it gave me an understanding of where he was coming from and eventually it enabled us to have something to talk about."

He led her outside to a wrought-iron table that was set with a carafe of coffee and two plates. "I remembered you liked croissants but I couldn't remember anything else."

"A croissant is fine," she said when they were both seated.

There were also eggs, bacon, sausage and home fries. But she wasn't hungry. She couldn't think about food when Hayden was nearby. She just...wanted him.

"What do you think of the view?"

She glanced out at Vegas. This was the vantage point she'd always wanted to see it from. And knowing that, understanding that she was still that trailer-park girl wanting desperately to escape, she hesitated to say anything else. Because she didn't really know if she wanted to say yes to Hayden because of the view or because of the man.

* * *

Hayden's PDA beeped, reminding him he had to be downstairs in five minutes for his eight o'clock meeting. But he wasn't ready to leave yet.

"What was that?" Shelby asked.

"I've got to go to a meeting in a few minutes," he said. For the first time in recent memory he wasn't ready to go to work. Shelby was more exciting than business.

She pushed to her feet, dropping the napkin on the table. "I need to get to work, too. Thanks for inviting me up for breakfast."

He captured her wrist in his hand, holding her by his side. Her bones felt delicate under his big hand, but he knew that she held all the power. He wanted her. And he'd do whatever he had to do to have her. "I invited you to move in with me."

"I know, but if I do that we'll be in bed together and…I'm not ready yet. I don't want to make the same mistakes we did last time."

"What mistakes are those?" he asked. He'd always figured last time his only mistake was not showering her with presents. But he knew now he'd done other things wrong, too. Frankly, he wasn't sure he'd do them right this time. He wanted Shelby—she was the only woman he'd never forgotten—but he wasn't sure he had forever left in him. His world changed with the roll of the dice or the flip of a card.

"The mistake," Shelby said, "was and would be letting great sex cloud the fact that we don't know each other."

Back then, they'd spent most of their time together naked. He knew he'd been Shelby's first lover and to be honest it had seemed as if they'd been made for each other. He still got hard thinking of the chemistry between them in those days.

"Great sex?" he asked. Maybe he wouldn't have to work so hard to convince her to move in with him after all.

She pulled away from him and wrapped her arms around her waist. That was the second time he'd seen her do that. Why did she? "Trust you to fixate on that."

"It was the only good thing you said." And it was. The sex between them had been great. It had been easy to let sex and lust take the place of friendship and genuine affection. This time he knew she wanted more—but he wasn't exactly sure he would allow it.

"Are you free later on?" he asked.

"For what?"

"A flight over the desert. I recall you liked flying at sunset." She'd never been in a plane before he'd taken her up in his little Cessna. Hayden loved to fly. His plane collection was more extensive now.

She bit her lower lip. "You remember a lot about me."

"Too much sometimes," he said, more to himself.

"I'm embarrassed to say I don't remember the details like you do."

"Why embarrassed?" he asked.

"Because…I was so shallow back then. I was…"

"What?" he asked.

"Fixated on not becoming my mother." She said it so quietly he knew that she didn't want to admit it.

"Are you still?" he asked.

"I think the fear is so deeply embedded in me that I'll never escape it."

He'd never really asked about her family. He'd known that she hadn't had a lot of money—that had been part of her initial attraction for his younger, rebellious self—and that her family wasn't very close, but beyond that he knew nothing.

"What do you like?" she asked at last.

"Pleasing you," he said smoothly. He hoped she didn't realize he was using the same lines and practiced moves on her that he did with all the women he dated. But he knew no other way.

"I don't think so. If we're going to do this…if I'm ever going to move in here, Hayden, we have to have honesty between us."

He rubbed the back of his neck. He was unable to believe she'd called him on his behavior, especially since she had at least as many secrets as he did. "That works both ways."

She swallowed and her face lost color. "Okay, what do you want to know?"

"What did my dad say to make you leave?"

She shivered. He saw her and almost reached for her, but he knew that he used sex as a substitute for real emotions and forced himself to keep his hands by his sides.

"I…um…"

"Just say it. Nothing is that bad. Was it about your mom?"

"Yes. My mom is a stripper."

"Okay. What else?"

"Nothing, just that I don't know who my father is. Mom isn't even sure."

He reached for her then, pulled her into his arms and just held her. She felt small and fragile, and Hayden wanted to take this burden from her. But he knew his dad made a huge issue of ancestry. "I don't care."

She tipped her head back, glancing up at him with those wide eyes of hers. "I do."

He rubbed his hands down her back, not sure what to say. After a few minutes she pulled back.

"Now, what do you really like to do? I want tonight to be to you what flying at sunset used to be to me."

He let her change the subject, lighten the mood because he sensed she needed some distance. "Anything I can gamble on—poker, basketball, skydiving, a fast ride on a desert highway on the back of my Harley, hot sex."

She tipped her head to the side, studying him again. "Wow, that's some list. Let me see what I can come up with. I should be finished in my shop by eight."

Hayden didn't want to relinquish control of her. He knew it was because he'd been burned the one time he'd trusted her. He knew he should let the past go but he couldn't.

She framed his face with her cold hands. Leaning up, she kissed him. There was a lot of emotion, past and present, in her kiss. Her mouth moved over his in a way that was more enthusiastic than practiced. He slipped his arms around her waist and tugged her closer to him.

She lifted her mouth from his and looked into his

eyes for a long moment. What was she looking for in his eyes?

"Let me do this. I want to know the man you've become and show you the woman I am today."

He dropped his arms and turned away, taking two deep breaths to try to get the scent of her out of his nose. But he couldn't. He was inundated with Shelby. Her taste was on his tongue, the feel of her soft skin under his fingers….

His phone rang and he cursed, pulling it out. "I have to go."

"I won't keep you, but what about tonight?"

"I…"

"Hayden, I know that I lost your trust, but let me do this. It's important to me."

He stared at her. "Okay."

She smiled up at him and he felt like a hero. Something he hadn't felt in a long time. But he also felt a little bad that such a simple thing could make her so happy.

"What should I plan for?"

"I'm not sure yet. I'll call your assistant during the day and leave the details."

She turned to leave and then stopped. "You won't interfere, will you?"

"How?"

"By watching me on the security camera or monitoring the calls I make?"

He shrugged. "I can't really monitor your calls."

"And the security camera?"

"I like watching you, Shel."

She blushed then. “I like watching you, too.”

“Say the word and we could move you in today.”

“Not yet. I want you to ask me after you get to know me.”

“I know the important stuff.”

“Like what?”

“That we both like great sex,” he said.

She laughed and they walked to the elevator. The doors closed and he watched her leave but knew he’d made progress in getting her back in his bed.

Four

Shelby's day passed too quickly. She had no idea what to do for Hayden. But she wasn't giving up. She hadn't come from a trailer park to where she was by being easily swayed from her goal. She wracked her brain as she worked, trying to think of a date that Hayden wouldn't expect but would love.

It was harder than she expected. Why couldn't Hayden be like other men? The men she'd dated since she'd left him at the altar all those years ago. A man who was…not important to her, she realized.

Despite the fact that Alan was responsible for her being in Vegas at this time, she wanted Hayden for herself. She wanted him with her for the rest of her life. The thought scared her because it made every action she took more important.

And though she hated to do it, she called Alan for some suggestions. The fact of the matter was, Alan knew Hayden better than she did. Shelby vowed that would change. Alan gave her the number to the marina on Lake Mead where Hayden kept his yacht and said he'd call in the morning for an update.

Shelby made a mental note to turn her cell phone off before Alan called. She longed for a time when she could be with Hayden and just be herself. The first time she'd been too young and too afraid he'd see what she really was. Where she'd really come from.

Ultimately that had led to her leaving him. This time…well, this time she was balancing between keeping him from finding out that Alan had sent her here and just falling for him.

She thought it was telling that Hayden hadn't mentioned his yacht. She wondered if she'd stumbled on to a private thing he liked to keep secret. From running her business she knew how demanding a career like Hayden's could be. Was the yacht his escape valve? His one place where no one could find him?

She hated the out-of-control feeling. But she couldn't figure out how to be herself and keep Hayden. It wasn't that she didn't think she deserved a man like him. It was just that being back in Vegas reminded her sharply of the girl she'd been. And that girl had too many insecurities.

The phone rang and she finished fastening the leather bustier to the headless mannequin before going to answer it. The scarlet garment had a matching thong and was one of Bêcheur d'Or's top sellers.

"I approve of the outfit," Hayden said, his voice low and husky. She smiled to herself.

"Voyeur. I'm wearing jeans and a T-shirt."

"So I like to watch. That's not a sin."

But his voice sounded like one, a carnal sin. This morning he'd been low-key, a man biding his time, but not any longer. Shelby felt restless inside and knew that Hayden had to feel it, too.

She ran her hands down the sides of her thighs. She'd changed into jeans and a T-shirt in one of the dressing rooms earlier. Unpacking boxes was sweaty, dirty work. But she liked seeing the store come together.

"Would you bend over a little and run your hands down your backside?" he asked.

"Is that what you want?" she asked, surprised at how easily his voice and words got to her.

"Baby, you know it is."

She knew that she was playing a dangerous game with Hayden. On a sexual level she'd never been adventurous, never taken any risks. Ha, who was she kidding, she didn't take any risks with her life.

But now, in Vegas this time, she scarcely knew herself anymore but she couldn't help it. She wanted to be his fantasy. Leaning forward, she ran her hands down the back of her legs, then tossed her hair and glanced around to where she thought the camera was located.

"How's that?" she asked, deliberately dropping her voice an octave.

He groaned. "Perfect. Now go slip into that leather number and do exactly the same thing."

The phone was cordless so she moved over to the mannequin and picked up the red leather bustier from the open box. "Have you ever worn leather undergarments?"

He laughed. "No."

"You'd have to make it worth my while," she said, fingering the supple cloth. In truth she liked wearing leather. It made her feel extremely sexy.

"Uncomfortable?"

"Not really, but they don't hide any imperfections."

"What imperfections?" he asked in such a way that she knew he didn't think she had any.

She shrugged. She knew she had them. She spent the majority of her time sitting in an office working. Though she tried to make it to the gym, most days she didn't.

Her thighs were soft, and no matter how many sit-ups or ab crunches she did, she'd always have a slight swell of a belly. Still, she was happy in her body, it was who she was. She just didn't like to see herself in bright light. Didn't like letting anyone see her looking anything but perfect.

"Don't make me say it out loud," she said carefully. Looks had always been important. Her mother had drilled that into her through Shelby's childhood. "Looks are all a woman has when she's poor," Terri Paxton would say. But Shelby had found that brains were better than looks.

"Okay, I won't. Did you make plans for us tonight?" he asked.

Yes, but she was playing her cards close to her chest on this one. "I'm still trying to come up with something you'll like."

He was quiet for a long minute and she could hear only the sound of his exhalation over the open line. "I like being with you, Shel. I always have."

She hugged one arm around her waist and tried not to let the words settle around her heart but they did. She felt a welling of emotion that she hadn't felt in a long time. "You know the right things to say to make a woman buy leather undergarments."

He laughed again and she smiled to herself, pushing aside the deep feelings his comment had evoked. She had to keep her balance here.

"That was my plan," he said.

"I don't know you well enough," she replied slowly.

"I'll show you. Want to spend the night in the casino?"

"I'm not a big gambler. I like to have something to show for my money after I've spent it."

"Like what?"

"Shoes," she said.

"Shoes? An evening in the casino is better than shoes."

She took a deep breath. "Well, maybe one thing is better than shoes."

"Sex?"

"With you," she said, hanging up the phone. She winked at the camera and put the bustier and matching thong in a gold Bêcheur d'Or's gift bag and placed it on the counter next to her purse.

* * *

Hayden spent the day making arrangements for the World Champion Celebrity Poker Showdown. The televised competition would air next month and the producer and her two production assistants were in Vegas for twenty-four hours to get the layout.

Scott Rivers was one of the best poker players in the world and had been a child star of movies and a television show that had run for fifteen years. He'd grown up on TV and Scott liked to say everyone thought they knew him.

But few did. Even after all this time, Hayden still suspected there was a part of Scott that was kept hidden. Growing up in the spotlight had made Scott something of a chameleon. In fact, Hayden had never seen his friend in a situation that he wasn't at home in.

Scott was one of the few people who'd seen him at his lowest. And that had forged a relationship in which both men felt comfortable with each other. Scott was one of his closest friends and Hayden was glad he would be visiting soon. Also, talking with the television people was a distraction. Seeing Shelby this morning, flirting with her on the phone and watching her like some lust-crazed man…well, it wasn't conducive to work.

His cell phone rang as he entered his private elevator. "MacKenzie."

"Hey, Mac Daddy. You up for poker tonight?" Deacon asked.

"Can't. Maybe next month when Scott is here."

"Next month? How about tomorrow night?"

"I'm busy."

"With whom?"

"Why do you suddenly need something to do in the evenings?"

"Ah, let's just say that it's better if Kylie thinks I'm busy."

"Lying to your wife?"

"No. What are you doing? Dating that redhead in the lingerie store?"

Hayden wished sometimes that he and Deacon weren't such close friends, but the truth of the matter was, Deacon was one of the few people Hayden allowed himself to care about. "Maybe."

"Great. Bring her over. We can all have dinner."

"Can't. We have plans."

"Please?"

"What does Kylie have you doing tonight?"

"Dinner with the Vegas Preservation League. A bunch of wealthy do-gooders."

Hayden felt for his friend. Deacon had grown up on the Vegas streets being looked down on by the very people Kylie had invited into his home. "Sorry, I can't help you."

"Page me at eight-thirty."

Hayden laughed. He knew Deacon might want to leave but wouldn't. He wanted to be with his wife. He was besotted with the woman and wouldn't leave her side in spite of the VPL.

"Later, Deac."

"Later."

Hayden rubbed the back of his neck as he stepped off the elevator. God, he hoped he was never so wrapped up in a woman that he was willing to sit through something like that dinner.

Shelby was waiting for him by his penthouse door.

"Are you okay?" she asked.

He dropped his hands, walking toward her. "I am now."

He leaned down to claim the kiss he'd been craving all day. She stood on tiptoe, leaning into his body. He cradled her to him, cupping her face in both hands and angling her head for deeper penetration.

His entire body tightened in anticipation. God, he wanted her. This wasn't a lust thing that could be satisfied with any other woman. He craved her taste on his tongue. Her soft skin under his hands. Her soft curvy body against his muscular frame.

He whispered her name against her skin, skimming his mouth down the line of her neck and nibbling on the pulse beating so strongly at the base. She said his name in a throaty voice.

He bit her gently and she arched closer to him. He licked the spot and then suckled her there. He wanted to brand her as his. To make sure that any other man who saw her knew she was taken. That she already had a man.

She sighed, tunneling her hands into his hair and pulling back from him.

He raised both eyebrows at her. "Please say we're staying in."

"Not quite," she said. Her face was flushed and her lips were wet and swollen. She looked as if he'd done so much more than kiss her. He skimmed his gaze down her neck and was pleased to see the mark of his possession there.

"I figured out something for us to do, but I couldn't catch you before you left your office."

She wore a pair of khaki-colored capri pants and a black tank top. Her hair was twisted up and tendrils curled softly around her face. Her eyes were wide and questioning. Clearly she was unsure if she'd made the right choice.

"Great. What'd you decide? Do you want to take me to a private gentleman's club?"

"Has any woman ever suggested such a thing?" she asked in that haughty way of hers. This was part of the new Shelby. The old Shelby was very pliable. She'd done whatever he said and never stood up to him. But this new woman had a backbone and too much sass.

"I've seen it happen in movies," he said with a grin. She made him happy deep inside where he'd been alone for too long.

"What kind of movies?"

He tipped his head to the side. "Come to think of it, not the kind of movie you'd watch."

"Sex movies?"

"Uh, I'm pleading the Fifth on this one," he said, taking her hand and leading her into his home.

Her deal with Alan had some pluses to it. Shelby had made arrangements to have Hayden's yacht readied for them. Lake Mead was located just east of Vegas and

Shelby had gotten driving directions from the bell stand earlier before going to get Hayden.

Shelby felt a little bit of dread at the thought of someday having to reveal to Hayden that his father was once again behind the scenes manipulating things. She made the decision right then to stop talking to Alan. She wanted to learn about Hayden on her own, not through his father's scrutiny.

She shook off those fears for tonight. The sun was setting and a warm breeze blew through the open windows of her SUV. Hayden had a slight smile on his face.

"Where are we going?" he asked.

"It's a surprise."

"Baby, I've lived here my entire life. I'm not going to be easily fooled."

"I'm prepared for that." She'd spent most of her childhood in Vegas and there was still so much she didn't know about her hometown. Of course, she'd frequented places that Hayden would never have gone to. Places that were saved for the poor and addicted.

"How?" he asked.

She shook off the feelings evoked by her childhood memories and focused instead on Hayden. Focused on the fact that after all this time she was determined to make a relationship work with the man she'd promised herself she'd marry.

She signaled and pulled off the interstate onto the shoulder. The interstate was busy with traffic and she was pleased that Hayden looked a little unsure. She rarely got the upper hand with him.

"This is it?" he asked, glancing at the guardrail and the expanse of desert stretching out toward the mountains. "What could we be doing here?"

To keep from smiling she bit the inside of her mouth as she took the black silk mask from her purse and held it up.

He fingered the silk and when his eyes met hers she saw the heat in them. And shivered. She had the impression that Hayden thought this was the prelude to some exciting sexual adventure.

"Kinky sex on the side of the road. How'd you guess?"

Before she could caution him, he ran the tip of one finger down the side of her neck, his thumb rubbing on the mark he'd left earlier.

"Got anything else in your bag, like a pair of satin lined handcuffs?"

"Maybe. How do you feel about being tied up?" she asked, leaning forward to slip the mask on him.

His pupils dilated, he cupped the back of her head and held her close to him. His minty breath brushed against her. "I'd rather tie you up."

She knew that. He was the kind of man who'd have to be in charge. Her lips were suddenly dry and she licked them.

He leaned forward and traced the line she'd just left with his tongue. Arousal whipped through her body. Her breasts felt full, her nipples tight, and she was so aware that all she had to do was lean forward the tiniest bit and her breasts would brush his chest.

She was shocked at how quickly he'd turned the tables on her. She was the one blindfolding him but she sensed he held all the power. He held her in his thrall and she was helpless.

She bit his lower lip, sucking it into her mouth for a brief second before pushing back into her seat.

"I'm just teasing you. This mask is all I want you to put on for now."

"Ah, baby, if I do this, you're going to owe me."

"Really? What will I owe you?" she asked.

"A dance."

"A dance?"

"Yeah, a nice sexy dance with you in that red leather outfit. Deal?"

She tipped her head to the side to study him, but his words and that sexy tone of voice made her want to do it. "Deal."

He took the black silk mask that she'd brought from Bêcheur d'Or. He slipped it on and leaned back in the leather seat.

The Lincoln Navigator was the same model that Shelby drove at home in Atlanta, so she was very comfortable behind the wheel. Her cell phone rang before she could pull back onto the highway. She glanced at the caller display. It was Paige, and for the first time since she and Paige had opened Bêcheur d'Or, she hesitated, not wanting to think about business tonight.

"I have to get this. Sit tight."

"My pleasure."

She answered it. "Hey, Paige. What's up?"

"Nothing, just touching base to get your take on how the D.C. conference call went this morning."

"I thought it went well. Can I phone you tomorrow to discuss it?"

"Why?"

"I'm kind of on a date."

"A date? With Hayden?"

"Yes."

"Okay, call me in the morning. I want details, and I don't mean about D.C."

She smiled to herself. "Will do."

She hung up the phone and shifted the car into gear.

"Who was that?"

"My partner, Paige. You met her, right?"

"Yes. I like her. You chose well, Shelby."

"Thanks," she said.

He reached over and settled his hand high on her thigh. His fingers traced a random pattern that made her center tighten. She wanted him more than she'd wanted any other man.

"Give me a hint," Hayden said once they were moving again.

"About what?" she asked.

His fingers moved, slipping between her legs and coming teasingly close to her core. She tightened her legs to prevent him from moving any higher.

"Stop, Hayden."

"No. Every time you tease me, I'll reciprocate."

"It's something you like to do."

She shifted her thighs apart, and his touch retreated

but not far enough. She was so aware of his hand on her inner thigh she could hardly concentrate on driving.

"Is gambling involved?"

"No," she said, reaching down with one hand to capture his wrist and move his hand back to the top of her thigh.

"Pretty confident of your answer," he said, turning his hand under hers and lacing their fingers together.

"Yes, plus your sense of fair play."

He leaned his head back. "Don't count on that, Shelby. I'm not always a nice guy. There's a reason I'm a gambler."

"You are so much more than a gambler, Hayden. Don't doubt that."

"Don't let me hurt you, Shel. I'm trying here, but to be honest I don't know how to hold on to something I want."

"Do you want me?" she asked, aware that he wasn't acting at all vulnerable with the mask on.

"Yes, I do."

Her hands shook and she was incredibly grateful that he wore the mask so he couldn't see how deeply his words affected her.

"Then let's make sure we don't hurt each other again."

Five

The soothing scent of the water was the first thing he noticed. Shelby had insisted that he keep the mask on and led him through the parking lot. He felt the wooden planks under his feet and stopped.

How had she known? This was one of his most closely guarded secrets.

"We're at the lake," he said, wondering how she knew about his recent obsession with boating. Not even his assistant knew about the boat he kept at Lake Mead. It was the one thing he'd kept to himself, kept *for* himself and shared with no one. But Shelby knew about it.

She paused next to him. "Are you surprised?"

"Yes. How did you know about this?"

"I can't reveal my source. But it took a lot of time and energy to figure this out."

He pushed the mask up and off, pocketing it for later. He was touched she'd dug deep enough to find this out. "Did you rent a boat?"

"Uh, my source said you had one."

"I do. Follow me."

He noticed she held a picnic basket loosely in her left hand and that large leather bag she called a purse was slung over her shoulder.

He led her to the *Lady Luck,* his thirty-foot yacht. She smiled as she read the name. "Has luck been a lady?"

"More times than not. I always treat her right," he said.

"You do have a way with the ladies."

He helped her on board. Her words echoed in his mind. His way with women had served him well. There had never been a lady he'd wanted that he hadn't been able to date. But the women never stayed. What did that say about his way?

The only constant in his life was the Chimera. He'd spent his life betting on the roll of the dice or taking risks, but that meant that life was constantly changing.

He piloted them out of the marina toward the middle of the lake. The evening was nice and warm and a breeze stirred the short hair at the back of his neck. He glanced over at Shelby, still amazed that she'd taken the time to really find something that he liked to do this evening.

It hadn't been a test for her. But if it had, she'd have passed. That scared him because there was so much he'd forgotten about Shelby. She made the world brighter and more exciting. Even when they were younger, it had been the same. She made him want to take bigger risks—and that was dangerous.

"Ever piloted a boat before?" he asked her. He needed her in his arms, closer to him.

"No. One time Paige and I catered a party for some suppliers that was on the lake."

"Tell me about your business. To be honest, I was surprised when I realized you owned such a successful chain of lingerie stores."

She bit her lower lip. He glimpsed a hint of sadness in her eyes before she turned away.

He scanned the area in front of them. No other sailors. He reached for her, pulling her around to face him. "I didn't mean that as an insult. You just never seemed interested in anything like that when I knew you."

"I know. I was only interested in you and having fun."

"I think it's safe to say we both shared those interests."

She hugged her arms around her waist and stared up at him. "When I left with the money…I thought all my problems were solved. I couldn't believe I had a million dollars. You can't understand this, Hayden, but I never imagined I would see that much money. It felt almost unreal."

"Just because I've always had money doesn't mean I can't understand that. What'd you do with the money?"

"I went on a shopping spree. Then about two days later I realized that everything I'd purchased would be gone eventually and I'd be back in the same boat and…"

He stopped the engine on the boat and dropped

anchor. He couldn't concentrate on Shelby and the boat simultaneously.

"What?"

"I couldn't do that again, Hayden. Whatever else you believe about me, please know that leaving you was one of the hardest things I've ever done."

He traced her jawline with his finger, realizing that in some ways, this strong independent woman was worlds too soft for him. Too innocent. Despite the fact that she'd left him, he knew that he and his father were to blame. When he'd started dating her to get at his father, he'd put her right in the middle of the power struggle they'd always engaged in.

"I know," he said softly. "Tell me how you started your store."

"Well, first I decided to go to college. Since I wasn't going to be using my looks to make money, I figured I'd better use my brains."

"It doesn't have to be one or the other."

"I know that now. But I was only twenty-two. You know, at the time I thought I was very mature. I mean, I knew things about life that other people didn't. But there was still so much I didn't know."

Hayden nodded, realized what she was talking about. He, too, had felt he knew it all as a young man, and in retrospect he realized how little knowledge of life he'd really had.

She walked to the railing, glancing out at the deepening twilight. "I met Paige in college and we were both working in a chain lingerie store at the mall. We had this idea that kind of grew from that. Something more exclusive, more high end. Paige said we needed a French-sounding name because the French know everything about sex."

Hayden laughed at that. Shelby did, too. "Paige is crazy sometimes with the things she says, but she was right. Since we'd both come into our money in unorthodox ways, I suggested calling the shop Bêcheur d'Or. Most consumers recognize the French word for gold and it gave us our brand. Those little gold bags set us apart from other shops, and the rest is history."

"How did Paige come up with her share of the investment money?"

Shelby paused, eyeing him. "She was a wealthy man's mistress for about a year. I don't know the details."

She stared as if she expected a cutting comment, but Hayden had heard it all, living in Vegas.

Hayden was impressed with what she'd made of her life. He was also a little leery of getting involved with Shelby again because she had vulnerabilities that he'd never really explored before. And he didn't want to hurt her again.

Shelby hadn't meant for the evening to get so serious. This night was supposed to be about him not her. They'd had a light dinner and now were sitting on the bow of the boat. She'd removed her shoes, dangling her feet over the water.

"What did you do today?" she asked.

"Meetings and the like."

"Just casino business all day?" she asked, because it sounded as if he was hedging.

"No. I also went to a children's facility that Deacon and I set up."

"What kind of facility? Something for sick kids?"

"No. It's for kids whose parents work in casinos. A place for them to hang out and be safe. Kind of like day care, but for older kids."

"What do you do there?"

"Usually I spend my time climbing on the rock wall. We have a scoreboard that tracks times up and down. A lot of the regular kids like to challenge me."

"Do you let them win?"

"Hell, no. What kind of lesson does that send to kids if you let them win?"

He had a point. "You like it."

He tipped his head and looked her straight in the eye. "I didn't expect to. But yeah, I do."

She'd learned more about Hayden in the forty minutes they'd spent on the water than she had in the weeks she'd spent with him before he'd asked her to marry him. He was a deeply complex man, and a part of her worried she'd never be able to fulfill all his needs.

But she was willing to try. She was falling in love with him all over again. Only this time she knew it was the real thing. Not just a chimera shimmering in the distance. But something real and substantial. An emotion that would last for all time.

Hayden leaned back on his elbows, like some potentate. He was too sexy for his own good. She was still hot and restless from his hands on her in the car. It amazed her how easily he turned everything into something sensual.

"Were there film people in the casino today?"

He arched one eyebrow at her. "Your source is very well connected."

She had to be careful about revealing the things Alan had told her. She wasn't cut out for the kind of intrigue that this type of deception entailed.

"That was the buzz in the buffet," she said, hoping she didn't sound as defensive as she felt.

"I was joking with you. Not accusing you of anything. They weren't film people. The Celebrity Poker Showdown is coming to film here next month."

"Sounds exciting."

"Do you watch it?" he asked.

She didn't really spend much time at home. She was a workaholic who took time for the occasional opera performance and that was about it. "No, I'm really not much on TV. You?"

He shrugged, pushing himself up. "Not too much. I try to watch when I know Scott will be on."

She shook her head at this second reminder of the differences in their lifestyles. "I can't believe you know Scott Rivers personally."

"Should I worry about that? I don't really think of him as anything other than my friend who's very good at bluffing." There was complete honesty in Hayden at that moment and she knew that he didn't view Scott Rivers any differently than he did her. Well, perhaps a *little* differently.

In Hayden's voice she heard the affection he had for the man. She knew from the past and from what she was learning about the man he was today that he had few friends. He was nice to many people but he let few know him.

"Why do you like coming out on the lake?" she asked. He was so at home in Vegas that seeing him out here was almost jarring.

"I don't know. It's just the only time I'm alone. I can kick back and not worry about any of the details I'd have to when I'm at the casino. Sometimes I fish, other times I just drift like we're doing tonight."

"What's it like running the Chimera?"

"Exhilarating, frustrating, fun, a pain in the ass. It's a million things at once but in the end I wouldn't trade it for anything."

"I feel the same about my shops."

He smiled at her. "Are we going to talk business all night? I thought you were supposed to do some wicked seducing."

"Did I agree to that? I think that's your fantasy."

"Let's not quibble about the details."

"Well, I wish I'd planned better. I think swimming in the moonlight with you could be a lot of fun."

"What didn't you plan for?"

"No swimsuits."

"We don't need them."

Skinny-dipping. Despite the fact that she was thirty-two, the thought of it was still forbidden…naughty somehow. And Shelby had spent her entire life following the rules in a game that had always seemed weighted against her.

She pushed to her feet and Hayden stood up next to her. "Did I shock you?"

"Did you want to?"

"Yes. You seem so self-contained, so…untouchable, sometimes I want to shake you up."

He had no idea how much he did. She watched him carefully, her fingers going to the hem of her black shirt. "Will this count instead of the sexy dance?"

"You want to bargain now?"

"Yes."

He scratched his chin. "I'm not giving up my dance, so we'll have to bet on something else."

"What? There's nothing out here but the two of us."

He studied her carefully, gliding forward until no space remained between them. He put his hands on her hips and pulled her fully against his rock-hard body. Each breath he took caused his chest to brush against her breasts, rubbing over her already sensitized nipples.

She struggled to keep him from noticing her reaction. But she could tell by the look in his eyes that he knew she wanted him. He knew she was his for the taking. She pushed against his chest.

He was too used to the power, too used to being in control. Shelby needed to be in charge. Just this once, she thought.

"Last one in is a rotten egg," she said. She kicked off her sandals while tossing her shirt on the deck.

Hayden was a competitor who liked to win so he stripped out of his clothing as fast as he could. Watching Shelby's curvy body emerge from under her clothing slowed him down, however. He knew the moment she realized that he was watching her.

She tipped her head to the side and ran her hands over her breasts and down the center of her stomach. Her fingers toyed with the button at her waistband. "Are you giving me a head start?"

Her voice was deeper than normal, husky almost, brushing over his aroused senses like the whisper of a win in a gambler's ear. The lure was totally irresistible and all he could do was helplessly watch her long legs.

Winking at him, she pivoted away from him and bent at the waist to push her pants off. The thin strip of her black thong pulled tight against the crease in her backside. He clenched his hands at his sides as she straightened.

She glanced over her shoulder at him and pulled her hair free. Shaking her head, she let her hair fall in a cascade down her back. He saw red. A haze came over him and he stepped toward her, but his pants caught at his knees and he almost stumbled.

"I'm going to win," she said, taunting him as she daintily folded each bit of clothing she'd removed. Then she took a leap off the edge of the boat.

Hayden's pants caught on his feet and he kicked them off just before he tumbled over the side, splashing down a scant second before she did. As the water closed over his head, he heard the sound of her laughter filling the air.

Lazily he pushed to the surface, coming up behind her. Reaching for her, he skimmed his hand down her spine. She trembled under his touch.

"I won," he said.

She glanced back at him. "Don't get all arrogant about your victory."

"Why not?" he asked, pulling her closer while he treaded water to keep them both above the surface. The action forced his legs between hers.

"Because there was no skill involved," she said, undulating against him so that her entire body caressed his.

"Then you know that resistance is futile," he murmured against her skin.

She pulled away from him. "Did you say 'resistance is futile'? Isn't that from *Star Trek*?"

"I thought you said you didn't watch TV."

"*Star Trek* is more than TV. But it doesn't seem your cup of tea."

"I went to that exhibit over at the Hilton a few years ago, to see about doing something similar at the Chimera."

"Did the hotel benefit from that trip? Because apparently your legendary charm didn't."

"I beat you once, Shel. Don't make me do it again."

"You can try," she said, and dived. He followed her easily, making out the shape of her white legs under the water.

He caught her ankle and pulled her to him, using a powerful scissor kick to bring them both to the surface.

His skin was too tight and he felt as if he was going to explode if he didn't get inside her soon. But he loved the sensual way she moved. He snaked one arm around her waist and fondled her belly button before cupping her breast in his hand.

"I don't need skill. I have raw talent."

"You've got raw something all right, but I don't think it's talent."

"I'll prove it," he said. It had been too long. Still, he knew he had to take this slow, because despite her teasing, Shelby was still feeling her way in this new relationship with him. And the last time, sex had clouded everything else.

She pushed away from him and dived under the water once more.

Shelby still hadn't surfaced when he felt her hand on his knee, skimming up the inside of his thigh. She cupped him in her hands.

He forgot to tread water and started to go under. Shelby surfaced a few inches from him. "Still going to prove something to me?"

He laughed. This was what had been missing from his life. This element of sexy teasing had been absent in all of his relationships until now. He stroked over to her, capturing her from behind.

She turned in his arms and kissed the base of his neck, nibbling at him and then soothing the ache with her tongue. He tightened his hands on her soft body. He wanted to toss her up on the deck of the boat and bury himself hilt deep inside her. He wanted to bind them so close to each other that they'd never really be separate again.

She lifted her head, her eyes sparkling up at him. "Don't try to tempt me with that smooth voice. I remember it well."

He closed his eyes, inhaling the scent of Shelby, letting the feel of her in his arms totally overwhelm him. He needed her like the air that he breathed and he followed that desire the way he'd always allowed all his cravings to rule his life.

Her wet hair snaked over her shoulders, falling onto his. He liked that feeling, and pulled her closer. He wanted them so deeply intertwined, she'd forget everything except being with him.

Grasping her waist, he lifted her slightly and lowered his mouth to her breast. He traced her nipple with his tongue, lapping at it gently until her nails dug into his shoulders. Carefully he scraped his teeth over her and heard her cry his name. They both sank beneath the water and he realized they needed to get out of the lake right now.

He needed more. He needed it now. And so did she. Holding her carefully with one arm, he swam them both back to the boat and lifted her up onto the platform at the back.

When she would have stood, he stopped her with a hand on her thigh. "Not yet."

Six

Hayden pushed himself out of the water using only his arms. His erection was large and fierce looking.

He scooped her up and stepped over the railing onto the deck of the boat. The remains of their dinner and their clothing still lay where they'd been left.

Shelby was a little embarrassed at her abandon, but there was a sense of rightness about being in his arms that made her realize that they belonged together. A kind of confirmation that she'd made the right decision to come to Vegas to resolve the past and cement the future. She and Hayden weren't finished. Their story was still continuing and she was glad about that.

She wrapped her arms around his neck and shoulders as he strode across the deck of his yacht. His heart beat strongly under her cheek and she closed her eyes, pretending that it beat just for her.

He set her on her feet next to the king-size bed in the stateroom. She was dripping on the carpet but she knew that Hayden didn't mind. He watched her with eyes that seemed to be on fire for her.

"Don't move."

He liked to give orders and she wasn't about to fall into the trap that had plagued their first whirlwind relationship. She followed him into the bathroom area. He bent over to retrieve two thick navy blue towels.

Shelby pinched his backside, then ran her fingers down to cup him.

He glanced up at her. "I thought I told you to stay put."

"I don't take orders well," she said. But she realized that she needed this to be about something more than power. She needed to not get swept away in Hayden but to have both of them get swept away in each other.

"We'll see about that," he said, pushing to his feet.

"Yes, we will see."

She took one of the towels from him. "Stand up and I'll dry you off."

He rose, towering over her. There was a look in his eyes that she scarcely trusted. "I like that idea."

She reached out with the towel but he stopped her with an iron grip on her wrist. "Use your tongue."

She swallowed. Hayden was a dominant lover and she freely admitted that he appealed to her as no other man did. Two could play at this game. He liked to give orders but she knew he wasn't immune to her.

"Close your eyes," she said, softly tracing her finger down the line of hair at the center of his body. The hair tapered down to his erection. She caressed him, coming closer and closer to his erection but making sure she did nothing more than brush it.

She licked the drops of water that still clung to his chest, while he dried her with long, languid strokes of the other towel. She dropped to her knees in front of him, following the trail of water down his strong thighs.

She really wanted to push him beyond boundaries, to push herself further than she'd ever gone before. She lowered her head, letting her breath wash over his erection first. His hands came to her head, rubbing her hair but not holding her or pulling her closer.

She tipped her head back and looked up at him. His skin was flushed with arousal. His breaths were rapid and his pupils dilated.

"Hayden, can I…?"

"Only if you want to."

She definitely wanted to. He felt like satin under her fingers. She lowered her head and ran her tongue up and down his length. Taking her time, she tasted him and discovered the different nuances of him. Reaching between his legs, she cupped his sac, massaging it in the palm of her hand as she took him fully into her mouth.

She sucked him deeper in her mouth, felt his body tighten as she worked up and down his length.

She tasted a salty bit of his essence before he pulled her away and lifted her to her feet.

He carried her into the bedroom, cradled in his big

arms, then slowly lowered her to her feet. She loved the feel of his solid frame against her. He wrapped his arms around her, anchoring her to him with his hands on her back.

He lowered his head slowly and she was consumed by the fire that he effortlessly brought to life inside her. She rose on tiptoe to meet his mouth. She loved the way he kissed her, as if he had all day and wouldn't stop until he'd explored every one of her secrets. She wanted to know him the same way. Reaching up, she took his jaw in her hands and held him still.

She traced the seam of his lips with her tongue, tasting him with small delicate darts. His hands on her back tightened but she didn't hurry. He always seemed so in control. What would it take to rattle him? she wondered.

Slipping her tongue past his lips, she ran it over his. She stroked her way into his mouth before retreating and coming back again.

He groaned and his erection pulsed between them. She felt him growing even harder against her belly and reached between them to enfold him in her grasp.

Not about to be outdone, Hayden placed her on the center of the bed. His hands made long strokes down the center of her body, lingering over her full breasts. He circled her nipples with the tip of his finger. She arched her shoulders, wanting to feel his mouth on her.

"Hayden, kiss me there."

"Yes, baby." He lowered his head and took her nipple in his mouth, suckling at her strongly as she cupped the back of his head, holding him to her.

He rubbed small circles around her belly button before delving lower. His fingers separated her. As he slipped one finger into her creamy warmth, her legs moved restlessly on the bed.

He slid a second finger inside her and brought his thumb down to rub her with a small up-and-down movement that made her want to scream; it felt so good. His fingers thrust in and out of her body and she was arching into him, needing more.

Everything in her body focused on his hand between her thighs and his mouth on her breast. He thrust slowly, driving her up toward a pitch until everything in her body tightened and she knew she was going to come.

Suddenly her entire body clenched and she called out his name long and low. She smiled up at him and she felt a sense of rightness. She wrapped her arms around his head and held him to her.

Hayden waited until Shelby's body stilled before he pushed himself up on his elbows to stare down at her. She smiled at him. Her lips were swollen and still wet from his kisses. Her nipples poked into his chest and though he'd satisfied her, he knew she wanted more.

He needed more as well. Once was never enough for Shelby and him. He freely admitted that only when he was lying between her legs, buried deep inside her body, did he really feel as though he was seeing the real woman. She had no chance to put up barriers then.

He set about arousing her again. Sweeping his hands

down her body. Using his mouth to trace the same path. Slowly building her once again to fever pitch.

She didn't lie passively under him but caressed his back and buttocks. Skimmed her hands over him and then scraped her nails in patterns everywhere she could reach. When he could wait no longer, he kissed his way up her body, lingering at the base of her neck. He sucked against her sweet flesh and bit softly until she was moaning his name.

"Open your legs."

His voice was gruff, guttural even. She'd pushed him past his boundaries. When she did as he asked, he settled his weight over her. Taking her hands in his, he stretched them up over her head, forcing her fingers to curl under the headboard mounted on the wall.

"Don't let go."

She nodded.

He lifted her legs and paused at the entrance of her body. The tip of him slipped inside her. She was so wet and so ready. Her body tightened around him as he entered her. He cursed and pulled out. "Are you on the Pill?"

She shook her head. He didn't want to use a condom; he knew he was free of any diseases and wanted to feel her wrapped around his erection, but he couldn't chance pregnancy.

He pushed off the bed and went into the head and found the box of condoms he kept in the medicine cabinet. He grabbed one, sheathed himself before returning to the stateroom.

Shelby hadn't moved. Her arms were still above her

head, holding the headboard. She was so beautiful to him in that moment, caught up in the feelings he'd brought to her, that he paused to watch her.

"Baby," he said between clenched teeth. He dropped to his knees near the bed. Starting at her neck, he nibbled his way down her body. Lingering over her pretty breasts, he circled the plump globes and left her nipples untouched.

She shifted her shoulders to try to move her nipple to his mouth. He allowed her to get closer, licking the tip before turning his head to her other breast and slowly exploring it.

He slid his hand down her body. Her earlier orgasm had left her body flushed and sensitive to his fingers. She was wet and creamy and he used her juice to coat his fingers, bringing them up to her nipples and rubbing her own moisture on them.

She craned her neck to watch him. He, too, was helplessly fascinated by the sight of his large fingers sliding between her thighs and entering her body.

"Hayden, I can't wait much longer."

"Yes, you can," he said, levering himself on the bed and over her.

He settled between her open legs, taking his erection in his hand and rubbing it up and down her center. He pressed it to her little bud until she tightened her thighs around him and her hips jerked upward.

"Not yet, Shelby. Hold on, baby. Wait for me."

She closed her eyes, breathing deeply, and he knew he'd pushed further than he'd intended to tonight. Putting his arms under her thighs, he lifted her legs, opened her fully to him and entered her. Slowly he filled her until he was seated hilt deep.

Her brilliant eyes opened and she watched him take her. For a moment he remembered the first time he'd taken Shelby. He'd been her first and it had been a surprise. She'd been as openly candid about her appreciation of him and his body then as she was tonight.

Her muscles tightened around him as he pulled back for a second thrust. Her hands gripped the headboard so tightly that he knew she was close. He wanted them to come together this time.

His own orgasm was almost on him. He hurried his pace, thrusting deeper and deeper into her. Finally he felt that telltale tingling at the base of his spine.

"Now, baby."

She came at once, her body tightening around him like a wet, hot glove. He emptied himself into the condom, wishing he'd been able to empty himself into her womb. He wanted to claim her. To stake his claim and make sure that no one—man or woman—ever doubted that Shelby belonged to him.

He collapsed on top of her, spent from the powerful climax. He nestled closer to her breast, idly sucking on one nipple. Her arms wrapped around him and he shifted his weight to the side so that he didn't crush her.

He felt as if he'd found his home. That disturbed him deep inside because he hadn't realized that he'd been searching for one until this very moment.

* * *

Shelby didn't want to wake up. She saw the sun shining across the bed, but the feel of Hayden's arms around her was too good to give up. Even to the reality of morning. How many times had she dreamed of him holding her this way only to wake alone once again?

But she wasn't one to hide from reality. And she knew this morning he was real, not a figment of her hungry soul. But this time she had to deal with her own guilty conscience. Deal with the fact that she had gone behind his back to seduce him with the things he loved.

Her thighs and breasts were pleasantly sore from last night. She was a little scared at the intensity of their lovemaking.

She'd enjoyed herself, no doubt about that, but he'd made her feel vulnerable. She didn't like that. She was a business owner—not exactly an occupation for wimps. She was used to dealing with her fears head-on and would deal the same way with this one, too.

Rolling over and opening one eye, she found herself nose-to-nose with Hayden. His eyes were wide open and the most arrogant male grin split his face.

"What are you smiling about?"

"You, here with me," he said. Leaning down, he kissed her.

It was the slow kind of kiss that didn't put any pressures or demands for more. She felt precious to him. It made her realize how vulnerable she was once again to Hayden. Before, she hadn't really loved him, but this time he was so much more to her than a wealthy man.

Now she was starting to know him, to know that he was constantly going. A moving ball of energy. And that he liked to bet on anything and everything.

She tunneled her fingers through his chest hair, caressing his warm, bare skin. She wanted to snuggle closer. To sink into him until they were just one person and then didn't have to face the day apart.

He lifted his head. "We have to get back. I can't believe I left the casino this long without checking in."

He propped himself up on the headboard and she blushed as she remembered how he'd made her hold on to it until she came in his arms.

He saw her color and shook his head, tugging her into his arms. "Thank you."

"For…?"

"Last night. It was…incredible, Shel. I wish our first time had been like that."

"I don't."

"Really? I've always regretted that I took you too quickly that first time."

"I don't. You were perfect, Hayden. And I don't think we could have handled last night before. We were both…"

"Both what?"

"I can't speak for you but I was pretending to be someone else. Hoping you wouldn't notice."

"Why?"

"Why what?"

"Why were you pretending?"

"Because I wanted a rich boy to marry me and normally you wouldn't have looked twice at the real me."

"Yes, I would have," he said.

"You might have looked but you wouldn't have proposed. I know that firsthand."

"Because of your mom?"

"Yeah. She's never been married."

"Where is she now?"

"Arizona."

"Do you keep in touch?"

"No."

"Why not?"

"She's part of what I was running from when I left, Hayden."

"Aren't you ready to stop running?" he asked.

She couldn't answer that. She thought about her mom a lot. Her mother wrote her a letter once a month and Shelby never wrote her back, but she read those letters over and over and regretted that she'd been so ashamed of herself and the woman who raised her that…sometimes she didn't like herself very much.

Hayden was right, but Shelby didn't know how to bridge the gap she'd forced between herself and her mom. He hugged her closer, his hand coming to rest over hers. He twined their fingers together and then brought her hand to his lips and kissed her.

"Yes, it is time to stop running," she answered finally. "That's part of why I came back here."

"I know you didn't come back because of money."

"Well, I kind of did. The Chimera location is going to make Bêcheur d'Or a lot of money."

"That's business."

"Yes, it is."

The covers slipped lower on his hips. God, she could stare at him all day. She noticed a tattoo on the top of his left thigh. "What's this?"

He covered the tattoo with his hand. "Nothing."

"No secrets, remember?"

He sighed and she realized that though she thought she was coming to know Hayden, he was still a mystery.

He slid his hand away. She bent closer looking at his tattoo. It was a knight's fist, gripping a bloody heart.

Instantly she knew that he'd gotten it after she'd left. She realized that she'd made a huge mistake. But she couldn't decide if sleeping with Hayden last night had been a bigger one than leaving him all those years ago.

Seven

Hayden strode through the main casino two nights later feeling like a gambler riding a streak of luck that just wouldn't quit. Shelby had shown up at the children's facility yesterday afternoon and had given him a run for his money on the rock wall. They'd had a lot of fun and she'd gotten the girls together to compete against the boys.

Last night he'd taken her up in his old Cessna, the same one he'd had when they were dating. They'd flown out over Hoover Dam and Shelby had mentioned that she'd been thinking about going to Arizona to see her mom. Hayden felt as if this time he was really getting to know Shelby.

The sounds of the bells and whistles of the slots and

the rolling of the roulette wheel always excited him, but seeing Shelby standing at a blackjack table, holding one of those small Bêcheur d'Or gold bags, excited him even more.

She still wouldn't move into his penthouse but he contented himself with the fact that she denied him little else. Like tonight. He wanted to show her his world. Wanted her to experience what life was like in the casino and though she said she wasn't much on gambling, here she was. Waiting for him.

She glanced up as he approached, smiling sweetly at him, and it was the sweetness that wrapped around him, stopping him in his tracks mentally. This thing with Shelby was the kind of risk he never took outside of gambling. But he couldn't stop it.

He approached the table and noticed that Rodney, one of his best dealers and longest employees, was the dealer. "Evening, Rodney. You treating my lady nicely?"

"I am, sir, but the cards…not so much."

Shelby laughed a tinkling sound that lit the dark places of his soul and made him want to keep her happy always. "I am the worst player ever. Isn't that right, Rodney?"

He shook his head. "I've seen worse."

"I think he's just being nice."

"Maybe you need some expert help," Hayden said. He took some chips from his pocket and placed them on the table in front of Shelby. She sat perched on the high stool but was still shorter than his six-two frame. Two other players joined the game, but Hayden scarcely noticed them.

He wrapped his arms around Shelby and looked over her shoulder as she picked up her cards. She had the queen of diamonds and a two of spades.

Hayden signaled Rodney for one card, which he dealt faceup. The card was a nine of diamonds. Shelby won.

She squealed and turned in his arms to kiss him. She won the following three hands, still with Hayden standing behind her. "Thank you. I think you're my good-luck charm."

"Ready to try it on your own?" he asked. He wanted to be more than her good-luck charm. He wanted her to move into his house. To sleep with her every night in his bed and wake up with her every morning. He doubted winning a few hands of blackjack was going to sway her.

"Yes. I think I've got it now."

Hayden grabbed an empty stool from a nearby table and joined the play. Shelby lost the first and second hands. Finally she tossed her cards on the table and picked up her winnings.

"Giving up?"

"I don't want to lose all your money," she said, handing the chips back to him.

"They're just chips."

"No, they aren't. I know that you're going to think—I just can't take money from you." She picked up her big leather bag and the small gold lingerie shopping bag.

Hayden pocketed the chips and nodded goodbye to Rodney. This wasn't what he'd planned. He wasn't the most sensitive guy in the world, but he knew that Shelby was telling him something that had to do with more than gambling.

Suddenly all the pieces came together. He realized that while he was dealing with the fact that she'd taken the money and left, she was dealing with the fact that his money, any of it, represented paying her off again.

"Come on." He took her hand and led her out of the casino.

"Where are we going?"

"I wanted to take you to see Roxy's show tonight. We never do anything that's really Vegas."

"Everything with you is Vegas, Hayden."

He tucked his hand under her arm and led her to the theater where Roxy performed. Hayden had a private box where they sat and watched the show. Shelby seemed to really enjoy it, but afterward she was still quiet and he knew that money was still an issue between them. That he'd been insensitive earlier. He still had no idea how to fix it.

"What's next?" she asked.

He had nothing else planned. But he knew that he had to get her away from the casino and taking her back to his penthouse didn't seem right. He needed to get her out of here, to find a way to take that melancholy from her. Somehow he was responsible for it and didn't really know why.

"Let's go someplace a little quieter so we can talk."

"About what?" she asked, but stood and grabbed her shoulder bag once again. He handed her the small gold lingerie bag, not willing to let her leave that behind.

"Luck and Vegas."

"Well, I think we've established I'm not lucky."

"Not at cards," he said, draping his arm around her waist and pulling her into the curve of his body. He shortened his stride to match her shorter one and used his body to protect her from the throng rushing to get to shows or casinos.

He led her out of the casino into the night. The pool and waterfalls were off to the left, but to the right was a small box-hedge maze, and nestled in the far back corner was a padded bench and gazebo.

"Where are we going?" she asked. Her eyes were weary and he knew he didn't want to stare into them anymore.

"It's a surprise," he said, taking from his pocket the black silk mask she'd used on him days earlier. He'd been carrying that damn thing around, tormenting himself with the different ways he wanted to use it with her.

She laughed as he slid the mask over her eyes, fastening it in the back. Leaning down, he brushed his lips over hers. She sighed and opened her mouth for him. She snaked her arms around his waist and laid her head on his chest right over his heart. And he could do nothing but hold her. To make this moment an oasis in two lives that had seen too much chaos and hurt.

The sensation of being blindfolded was difficult to adjust to. Shelby already felt vulnerable from realizing that she was losing Hayden's money in the casino. Sure, she knew it wasn't a lot of money, but still it was the principle of the matter. She'd vowed before she left Atlanta that this time she wasn't taking any money from Hayden. She meant to keep her word—even if it was only given to herself.

After trading herself so cheaply to Alan MacKenzie, Shelby had taken a hard look at herself and her life and she'd promised to never be in that position again. To never be vulnerable to any man. So how exactly had she ended up here—blindfolded with only Hayden's warm hand in hers to guide her through an unfamiliar world?

Panic raced through her. She heard people moving around her and felt as if she was ten again at Meredith Nelson's birthday party. Meredith and the other girls had all disappeared when Shelby had donned the pin-the-tail-on-the-donkey mask. When she'd pulled it off, she'd been left all alone. Standing there in the secondhand dress her mother had purchased on the way to the party. Tears burning her eyes, secure in the knowledge that she wasn't like other kids and would never fit in.

She felt that way again. Being back in Vegas brought all the old insecurities to the surface. It had to be the money thing. Money always triggered that same gut reaction. The blindfold was too much. She reached for the mask.

He caught her fingers, holding both of her hands easily in his grip. "Shh, baby. Don't panic. I'm right here."

"I know I did this to you, but I don't think I like it," she said.

He leaned down and whispered into her ear, "You look so sweet and sexy. I like the fact that I'm responsible for you. I have to protect you. Will you let me do this?"

"I'm a grown woman, Hayden. I don't need a man to protect me."

"Do this for me, please."

He never said please. She nodded her head. She'd try for him, because he'd done it for her without any complaints. But then she doubted he'd ever been in any situation where he wasn't comfortable.

"Are you still upset from the blackjack table earlier?"

She had no response to that. No idea how to respond and still preserve what she now knew was her own illusion that she'd fooled him. The show had been nice but all she felt while she'd been sitting there in the dark was that once again she was in the land of make-believe. Surrounded by people who were pretending their real lives didn't exist.

She felt the warmth of his fingers feathering up her arm, rubbing gently against her skin, wanting her to relax.

"What is going on tonight?" he asked, murmuring his words against the top of her head.

"I don't want you to think I'm after your money," she said, blurting out the words. Then she groaned. She'd never meant to say that.

"Honey…"

"Don't. Let me continue. I'm never going to have as much money as you do. And we'll never really be social equals. But—"

He stopped the wild flow of words with his mouth. His lips moved over hers with surety and strength, making her feel as if everything was irrelevant except him touching her.

He lifted his head but dropped several small nibbling kisses on her neck before taking her hand in his again. "Follow me."

She bit her lip and let him tug her along. She realized that her panic with the mask wasn't only due to the insecurity she'd felt earlier but also had to do with trust. She didn't trust herself. Didn't trust that the woman she'd become was real. Didn't trust that she'd really left behind the young girl she'd been.

Did she trust Hayden? She hadn't when she'd been twenty. But now…? She'd trusted him with her body; she'd set up her shop here based on the success of his casino. Obviously she was leaning that way, but to have the choice taken from her… To have to trust him to protect her while she couldn't see wasn't something she'd been prepared to do.

He stopped walking. She heard him pushing some buttons and then the release of a gate. She was surrounded by the scent of roses and night-blooming jasmine. Hayden wrapped his arms around her waist and pulled her back so that she was sitting on his lap. He nibbled at her neck and she surrendered to the feelings he always aroused in her.

"What's in that little bag?" he asked.

"What little bag?" she asked, turning on his lap so that she rested her head on his shoulder. His aftershave was strong at his neck. She scraped her teeth across the nerve-rich area and felt him stir under her hips.

"You know very well which bag I'm referring to," he said.

His hands roamed up her torso, settling over her breasts. He palmed both of them and she felt them swell and grow heavy under his touch. She reached for the buttons on his shirt, finding them and releasing the top three until she could slip her hand under the cloth and feel his strong, warm pecs. She scraped her fingernail in a random pattern over him and felt his muscle flex under her.

"Stop distracting me. I want to know what's in that bag. I never did get to see you in the red leather."

His thumbs were tracing her distended nipples through the material of her blouse. It felt so good that she couldn't speak for a minute.

"I know. I figured since you were so big on competition, I'd provide you with your own leather."

He groaned. "Damn, woman, I'm not wearing leather underwear."

"Come on. I'll make it worth your while."

"Like you did with the stripping contest?" he asked. His hand was on her waist and then she felt him pulling her shirt slowly up.

She panicked, gripping his wrists. "Hayden, we're in a public place, aren't we?"

He stopped though she knew he was stronger than her and could have pushed her shirt up despite her protests.

"It's time to decide if you trust me or not."

She felt a million things at once—nervous, excited, aroused and a little bit upset that she was so aroused. She shifted on his lap, pressing her thighs together and wondering if she could pretend this was just about sex.

But she knew it wasn't. Hayden wanted her trust and if they had any chance of moving forward, she had to give it to him.

With a sigh, she dropped her hands, knowing that Hayden would always keep her safe. It was him trusting her that had always been the issue. She acknowledged she'd never given him a chance to really trust her because she'd been lying to him. But this time Shelby realized she needed to learn to trust herself and stop lying about what she'd been running from.

Hayden knew they were completely secluded here. The garden was his private place to escape from the busy casino. He'd deactivated the cameras to this section and opened the security gate earlier. They were now in a private section of the maze. She was perfectly safe.

He knew he was pushing her, but couldn't help himself. He wanted—no, needed—to stake his claim on her and he wasn't going to wait any longer. Making love to her two nights ago had made the fact that she didn't trust him into a sharp ache. He knew he'd done little in the past to earn her trust, but this time…this time he was determined to do things right.

She let go of his wrists and he slipped his hands under her shirt. Her stomach clenched as he moved his hand over her. She turned to straddle him, draping her thighs over his, and held him with a fierceness that felt right in his soul.

Slowly, inch by inch, he peeled her shirt up and over

her head. He let his hands trace down the center of her body, stopping to free the front clasp of her bra as they went. She wore a pale pink bra with lacy demi-cups.

"I love your underwear."

She smiled at him and he couldn't resist kissing her one more time. With the mask on, her skirt up around her thighs, her shirt gone and that bra open, she looked like a fantasy come to life.

"Offer your breasts to me," he said.

She ran her hands up her stomach, slowly caressing her own skin, and he realized that Shelby was becoming more comfortable. She covered both of her breasts with her hands, then slowly peeled back the lace to reveal her pink nipples. She cupped her breasts, lifting them toward him. Her hand encircled the bottom and sides but left a small gap between each finger.

With his tongue he traced the gap and felt her hands tighten as he got closer to her nipple. He teased her by outlining the areola first then laved her entire nipple.

He attended to her other breast with the same care. He couldn't stop touching her, needed to caress more of her skin. He loved the way she felt as arousal spread throughout her body. Her hips shifted on the bench. Her hands moved restlessly over her own body, reaching out to hold his head to her as he scraped his teeth down her side.

"Lift your skirt for me," he said, his hands busy at her breasts.

The fabric of her skirt was gossamer light, as he'd noticed when they'd walked through the casino earlier. Ever since then he'd obsessed about it.

Slowly she brought her skirt upward to reveal her thighs and then the matching pink lace panties. Her tight auburn curls were visible under the light material.

He leaned back to study her. Awed that she was his. And she was his no matter how stubborn she was about living with him. Shelby belonged to him. A red haze settled over him and he was determined to prove it to her.

He set about arousing her using every bit of knowledge that he had but couldn't remember where he'd gained it. All other women dropped away. The experiences he'd had with them were only to enhance what he had with Shelby now.

He tugged on her panties, and she obliged by removing them. When she came to him again, he parted her with his thumbs before lifting her to taste the engorged bud he'd uncovered. He suckled her gently, her hips bucking, her hands fluttering to his head to hold him closer.

He brought her to the edge then backed off. He wanted to build a fury within her so that she'd feel the way he did. Out of control.

He kissed her stomach and dipped his tongue into her belly button. He skimmed his hands over her breasts, rubbing them in a circular motion.

Her hips lifted into his chest and he felt her moisture there, realizing he couldn't wait any longer.

"Hayden?"

"Yes, baby?" he asked. Lowering his hands between their bodies, he unzipped his pants and released himself. He slipped on the condom he'd put in his pocket before joining Shelby earlier.

He pulled her forward so that her hips were fitted to his. Now her back was arched and her skirt was still between them.

He grasped her waist and lifted her up. "Hold on to me."

She wrapped her arms around his shoulders, her legs around his waist. Hayden loved the feel of her soft skirt against his stomach and erection. He reached between them, parted her with one hand and guided himself to her entrance with the other.

He thrust upward, going as deep as he could. Shelby's nails scored his shoulders. Her breasts rubbed against his chest. Nothing had ever felt better than the wet heat of her wrapped around him.

She rocked against him again and again and Hayden leaned down, wanting to demand answers from her. But he couldn't. Emotions swamped him as he felt the telltale tingling at the base of his spine signaling that his release was imminent. He slowed his pace.

"Faster. I'm so close," she whispered in his ear.

He put his hands on her hips and thrust up into her as he ground her down against him. He heard her breath catch once and then twice and then a long, low moan as her orgasm washed over her.

He came a second later. He cradled her close to his body, very aware that even if it wasn't wise he was falling for Shelby Paxton, again.

Eight

Shelby spent the next few days in her store readying it for the grand opening tonight. She tried to ignore that more than sex had happened between her and Hayden. They were both busy with work but Hayden made time for her in his schedule. He'd shown up unexpectedly one afternoon after one of her staffers had to go home for a family emergency and helped her unbox the merchandise.

He'd also taken her for a ride on his prized custom West Coast Chopper. He was everything she wanted in a man and more, and she knew she was falling hard for him. Every day revealed another facet of the man and she had yet to see anything she didn't like.

But she remembered Alan and what had brought her to Vegas and worried over that. Not to mention what she'd been forced to realize about herself that night in the private garden. That Hayden already owned her heart and soul. She could try to pretend she hadn't completely given him her heart but she knew that wasn't true.

A part of her rejoiced. After all, she'd returned to Vegas with just that goal in mind. But the other part of her worried. Alan had been out of touch since the night she and Hayden had spent on his yacht, and Shelby worried that Alan was going to show up before she had a chance to talk to Hayden.

She'd tried several times with Hayden to bring up the subject of her return to Vegas. Tried to find the words to make him understand that she hadn't realized how much he'd changed, how much she had. But last night a letter from her mom had arrived and she'd been unable to deal with anything but that.

Hayden had taken her up to his penthouse and they'd sat on his balcony and talked until two in the morning. Talked about their single parents. She'd learned more about Alan than she'd expected to. Realized that once Hayden's mom died when Hayden was quite young, Alan had focused on Hayden, making his son's success the purpose of his life outside the casino.

When Shelby had talked about her own mother, she'd realized that it wasn't her mother she was ashamed of. It was the way other people had always looked at them. She told Hayden about how her mother loved to crank up old Elvis Presley albums after dinner and they'd danced and sung while they'd cleaned the dishes.

She'd forgotten how much she'd loved her mom until that moment. She'd made the decision to call her and set up a time to visit only to have to leave a message on the answering machine when she followed through.

Shelby felt as if all the loose ends in her life were finally being straightened out. She was thirty-two and just starting to get it together.

Last night Hayden had pushed her hard to move in with him, even going so far as inviting his friends Kylie and Deacon Prescott to his penthouse for dinner. Shelby had enjoyed meeting the couple. But more than that she'd enjoyed the feeling that she and Hayden were a couple. A real couple. A happily-ever-after couple.

And that scared her.

She glanced at her watch. 8:50 a.m. She had ten minutes until she'd be addressing her staff. Paige was due in this afternoon and they were having a soft opening by invitation only for the other casino owners in the area and VIPs from each of the surrounding resorts.

A soft opening was a pre-grand opening that was a test run for business owners. Shelby was always nervous at this stage. But as she stood in her office and glanced into the showroom at the gilded shelves filled with unique, sexy lingerie, she felt her confidence return. After all, this was the twentieth store she'd opened.

Her staff had been handpicked and Shelby knew they'd do a fabulous job. She'd decided that tonight, after the formal grand opening, she'd tell Hayden she'd move in with him. And she vowed to talk to him about his dad. To let him know that Alan had blackmailed her into coming back.

She had chosen her clothing for the day carefully, donning the red leather bustier and thong under a long-camel colored suede skirt with a black silk shirt. She'd pulled her hair up into a loose chignon and left several tendrils of curls hanging around her face.

She wore a pair of black heels, and a small gold choker as her only jewelry aside from her watch. Her clothes looked good on her and gave her an added boost of confidence as she exited her office and entered the shop.

Her small staff was already assembled, talking quietly among themselves. Shelby's cell phone rang.

She glanced at the number and saw that it was Hayden.

"Hey."

"Hey, yourself. Will you have time before the opening for a drink with me?"

The day was jam-packed with activities and last-minute details. "Sorry, I don't think so. I'll probably be going over something with Paige."

"How about if I come to you?" he asked.

Nothing would make her happier. She liked that Hayden had made sure his schedule was always available to her so that she could find him whenever she wanted him. "Sure. In fact, I have a little surprise for you."

"Yeah? Is it something I've been waiting for?"

She thought about it. Thought about how long they'd both been together and apart. Thought about their lives and how they'd both used work as a substitute for relationships. And thought about how this time she wasn't leaving. "Oh, yeah."

"Dammit, I'm on my way to a meeting but I want to

come to you. Take you away from all this and just make love to you."

"Stop it. We both have work to do."

"I know. I'll be by around five."

She hung up quietly and turned to her staff. After giving them a pep talk, she walked outside the shop to observe the store, to see it from beyond the gilded gold leaf–inset doors. The window displays looked erotic and sophisticated.

"Nice job."

Shelby froze. Slowly she turned to face an older, more jaded-looking version of Hayden. "What are you doing here?"

"Checking on my investment," Alan MacKenzie said, putting his hand under her elbow and leading her out of the path of the foot traffic.

Shelby took a deep breath and tried to tamp down the sense of panic she felt. Everything was starting to go so well for her and Hayden. "This really isn't a good time. You know this entire casino is wired with security cameras that record everything. I don't want Hayden to get the wrong idea."

"I don't trust you to carry out our plan," he said.

"It's not our plan," she said, pulling her arm away. "Not anymore. I'm not sure I can do what you wanted me to. Please, Alan, just leave this to me."

Shelby turned away determined to leave Alan standing there. She ran into a solid chest and glanced up with a sense of dread in the pit of her stomach.

"Hayden—"

"Leave her alone, Dad," Hayden said, putting his arm around her shoulder and anchoring her to his side. "She's here because of business, not to be bullied by you."

Shelby was shaking and she knew that this moment was going to end badly. She should have told Hayden about his dad's proposition before now. Why hadn't she?

Because she'd wanted to make sure he really liked her before she dropped her bomb. Because she'd always understood that they had to have more than a great sexual bond between them. Because she knew that she needed Hayden's love and wasn't sure she'd had enough time to convince him that what they had would last.

"I'm not bothering her, Hay. I was congratulating her on her store. She's come a long way from the girl we both knew."

"Don't say it like that, Dad. We never gave her a chance."

Hearing Hayden defend her convinced Shelby without a doubt that she couldn't put off the truth any longer. She had to tell him. But she didn't want to spoil this moment. In her entire life, she'd never had anyone defend her the way Hayden was now.

Emotion choked her and she turned her face into his chest, hugging him tightly, trying to tell him without words just what that meant to her.

Hayden was glad he'd gotten down to Bêcheur d'Or as quickly as he had. He'd been in the middle of a meeting when Deacon had called him to say that he'd spotted Alan in the casino. Alan usually visited only twice a year and always caused some sort of trouble with the staff. Last fall Alan had handed out demerit cards to half of Hayden's blackjack dealers for minor infractions, causing distress before Hayden could explain that his father had no power over casino employees.

As soon as his dad disappeared around the corner, Shelby took a few steps away from Hayden. She was pale. He'd never seen her look like this.

"Are you okay?" he asked, lifting her face toward his. There were tears in her eyes, and no matter what she said, he knew his dad had been bullying her.

She blinked and her vulnerability slowly disappeared. "It really wasn't bad. I just know what your father thinks of me. And he makes me feel like…like I'm still a gold digger."

He lowered his head for a kiss, tenderly tasting her mouth, showing without words what she meant to him. He pulled back before he wanted to because he knew she had a busy day. "Well, I know how my old man can be."

Hayden rubbed the back of his neck, not sure how to explain to her about the man he'd become after she'd left. "He blames you for a lot of things, Shelby."

"What does he blame me for?" she asked. She'd put a foot of space between them and had her arms wrapped around her waist.

"Not having grandkids."

"I doubt you've been celibate since I've been gone. There was opportunity, right?"

"I'm not much on settling down. This business is my life. Could you imagine raising a kid here? I mean you've seen the kids at the center. What kind of life is that?" he asked, not sure he wanted her to say no.

"The one you had. You turned out okay."

"I'm a workaholic adrenaline junkie."

"Thought about this a lot?"

"Nah, one of the women I dated called me that."

"She was probably jealous."

"Of what?"

"Of this casino. She probably had just figured out that no woman could come between you and the Chimera. Anyway, your dad raised you here. And you two are still on speaking terms, so it can't have been that bad."

Normally he'd never have left his steering-committee meeting like he had, but here he was several floors away from some very highly paid men and women who were waiting for him. Especially since the dressing rooms of the revue venue had been broken into last night and a nasty note had been left for his star performer.

"No, it wasn't. We get along okay when he minds his own damn business. He thinks he can stroll into my operation whenever he wants and give me tips. The old man still thinks casinos should be run…old school."

Shelby laughed like he wanted her to. He reached out to toy with one of the loose waves hanging around her face. "He has the belief that he's always right, too. He can't believe that people can change."

"People or you?"

"Me," she said, sounding forlorn.

No matter what he said or did, their past would always be between them like an unacknowledged wound.

The past hadn't been healed by years of separation nor was the relationship they were building enough to wipe away the past hurt. He really stunk at relationships and had no idea how to make this right.

The only time he really felt in control around Shelby was when she was in his arms. He walked around behind her and surrounded her with his body, pulling her back against him, wrapping his arms around her waist and bending his head to whisper in her ear. "Don't worry, baby. I'll run interference for you."

And he meant it. The last time, he'd left Shelby on her own to deal with his dad, but now he realized he should have protected her better.

Why hadn't he been able to see that she needed him? He hadn't wanted to acknowledge that they were dependent on each other.

Her hands crept up over his wrists, holding him as he held her. She tipped her head back and looked up at him. He could tell she was searching for something in his gaze and he hoped she'd find it. Frankly, he knew that taking her to bed would go a long way to making him feel better.

"I don't need protecting. I'm a grown woman."

He waggled his eyebrows at her, trying to lighten the tension that lingered in the air like a streak of bad luck at a slot machine. "I've noticed."

"Trust you to turn this back to sex."

"Did I?"

She raised both eyebrows and gave him a very prim look. "You know you did."

He winked at her. "Can't help myself around you."

She sighed and then moved away. "Thanks for coming to the rescue, but I need to get back to work."

"You're welcome. What were you doing out here?"

"Checking out the store from the outside."

"You've checked it out before," he said.

She walked toward her lingerie store and stood out of the foot traffic, watching the action inside. "Sometimes it's hard to believe it's really mine. That this is my life."

"You've worked hard for your success. You deserve it."

"I don't know about deserving all this."

She gestured to her clothing and the shop and him. "I mean, I'm wearing a pair of shoes that cost three hundred dollars. When I was in Vegas before, I bought my shoes from the final-markdown rack."

"I never knew that," he said.

"I would have died if you had. I tried very hard to hide that part of my life from you. The house you picked me up at wasn't really mine—it was the Jenkinses'. I worked there as an after-school maid. Their daughter was two years older than me and Mrs. Jenkins used to give me her old clothes."

He saw now how little he'd known of her real life. Shelby had always looked like a million bucks. He remembered how careful she was of her clothing and shoes. He'd taken it for vanity and appreciated it because she'd made him look good. But now he was beginning to realize that she may have spent all her money on looking good for him. And he'd never noticed.

He told himself he was noticing now, but in his gut he hoped it wasn't too little too late.

Paige closed the door and locked it after the last employee left. Paige was tall, almost six feet, and she wore her jet-black hair in a classic bob. She was reed thin and could have made a fortune as a model in New York if she'd wanted to. Shelby finished cleaning up and stacked champagne glasses on the counter for the catering service.

"I think Vegas likes us," Shelby said. Her entire body was humming with energy. Excitement from the opening warred with sexual anticipation.

"Someone in Vegas certainly likes you," Paige said, pointing to the very large arrangement of exotic flowers that had arrived in the middle of the afternoon.

"I hope so," she said. Paige knew her like no one else, but there were still parts of her life that she'd never shared with her friend.

"I like Hayden, too. I'm glad you decided to come back here and face him."

"Me, too. But I still haven't told him about Alan."

"When are you going to?"

"Tonight."

"Good. You deserve some happiness. Where are you going to stay now that the shop is open?"

"Depends on how things go with Hayden. I'll definitely be at the hotel for the next few weeks."

"Are you moving out here permanently?" she asked. "What about D.C.? You know I don't do openings."

"Chill out. I want to think about telecommuting. I want to give this relationship with Hayden a real chance at working. I'll still do the openings and the traveling."

Paige wrapped her arm around Shelby's waist, hugging her close. "I hate change."

"I know. But nothing is really changing."

"Yes, it is."

"I don't have to stay."

"This is the man you always bring up when we talk seriously about life. I think you better stay. Maybe we can relocate headquarters out here. There's nothing holding us to Atlanta."

"What about Palmer?" Paige's current lover was in the process of getting a divorce.

"He's going back to his wife."

"Oh, Paige. I thought they were over."

"Apparently you and I were the only ones who believed that."

"If you'd seriously consider relocating the business, I think I'd like to be here even if things with Hayden don't work out. You know, since most of our shops are back East, maybe we need a few more out West. I've been thinking of scouting Arizona."

"Like maybe Phoenix?"

"Yes, and the surrounding area," Shelby said, careful not to say more. She'd kept her mom private from Paige, never mentioning Terri Paxton to her partner and best friend.

"We'd have to research the demographics, but why not?"

"Thanks, Paige."

"For what?"

"For making me go into business with you." Shelby hugged her friend.

Paige laughed in that loud way she had. "Hey, I didn't do that. I merely pointed out that the smart thing to do was to work with me."

But they both knew that she had. Shelby pulled away from her friend and started shutting off the lights. "What are your plans for tonight?"

"Uh, hello, it's after midnight, I'm going to bed."

"But you're in Vegas. The city never sleeps."

"Maybe, but I'm a small-town girl and I need some rest. What about you?"

"I'm meeting Hayden in the casino."

They set the alarm and left the shop. Despite the fact that all the stores in the retail section closed at midnight, there was still some foot traffic, but it was lighter than it had been earlier. When they left the shopping wing and entered the main casino floor, Paige said good-night and went up to her room.

Shelby hesitated, glancing through the crowded casino trying to find Hayden. People stood two and three deep at the slot machines and there wasn't an empty seat at the blackjack tables. Rodney the dealer smiled at her as she walked past his table.

"Have you seen Hayden?"

"There was an emergency at the revue. Some kind of security issue," Rodney said.

Shelby headed that way, feeling like she was in a

maze. No matter which direction she turned there were more people and she was starting to feel closed in.

She retreated to a quiet corner of the casino, near one of the exits. She wasn't going to find him in this throng. She'd go back to his penthouse and wait for him.

That idea appealed to her. As she walked to the elevator, the scenario she wanted to create formed in her mind. Hayden had given her so much today. More than he could ever understand. She'd felt accepted and it had been a really long time—maybe her entire life—since that had happened.

Sure, Paige accepted her but that was more from an I-know-your-dirt-and-you-know-mine aspect. Hayden accepted her on a personal level, in a way that made her feel as if she was special to him.

An arm snaked around her waist and she glanced up to meet Hayden's intense gaze. "Hey, baby. How was the opening? I'm sorry I couldn't stay, but we had a major emergency."

"What happened?" she asked. Hayden was tense.

"Roxy was attacked."

"What? By whom?"

"Some crazed fan. He cut her in several places, some deep. They took her to the emergency room and she's having surgery now. Police have the man in custody."

"Oh my God. What can I do?"

"I've got to head back to the hospital."

"I'll go with you."

"You don't have to."

"Hayden, this is what being together is about."

"Thanks," he said.

"No problem."

Ten minutes later they were seated in the hospital waiting room. About five other cast members were there as well. After an hour had passed, they decided to go to the cafeteria to get coffee. Shelby sat next to Hayden, unsure how to help him. She knew that he thought of the Chimera staff as his family and he was taking this hard.

He rubbed the bridge of his nose. "Talk to me, Shel. Tell me about your opening."

She sipped the cafeteria coffee, trying to remember the opening. It seemed as if it was years ago instead of just hours. "It went really well. I can't believe how many people showed up."

"Did Deacon come?"

"Yes, with Kylie. She invited me to have lunch with her."

"Good. I like Kylie."

"Me, too," Shelby said. And it was the truth, though she knew she had little in common with Kylie who had confessed that she'd grown up with her nose stuck in a book. Still, she'd been open and friendly and had said she was glad to see Hayden dating someone with an IQ bigger than her bra size.

Kylie had given Shelby a glimpse of what Hayden's life had become. She'd promised to tell Shelby over lunch all about the infamous bet that Hayden and Deacon had made about Kylie.

Hayden's friendship with the Prescotts was obviously a strong one. Deacon had worked the room and Kylie had hung back, quietly confessing that she wasn't the outgoing person her husband was. She'd also told Shelby not to let being a casino owner's wife intimidate her. But Shelby knew whatever happened in Vegas, Hayden wouldn't ask her to marry him again.

The man in question spoke again, snapping her out of her thoughts. "Did you check out of my hotel?"

"Yes, earlier. I…well, darn, I was hoping to keep that a secret from you."

"Why? Did my dad bother you again? I told him to back off."

"No, nothing like that. I kind of had a surprise for you. But it doesn't seem right to bring it up now."

He put his arm around her and hugged her to his side. "We can have your surprise tomorrow. Tonight I need you to stay with me, baby. I'm trying to go slow and not pressure you, but…will you stay, please?"

Tears burned the back of her eyes and any doubts that she had about staying in Vegas totally disappeared. There was something between her and Hayden that couldn't be denied. And they both knew it.

Reaching up, she cupped his jaw in her hands. "That was my surprise. I'm not leaving your hotel. I'm just moving out of my room and up to your place."

His eyes narrowed. "For tonight?"

"And longer. If you still want me."

He pulled her to him, his mouth finding hers. His hands roamed up and down her back, forcing her more fully against him.

She clutched his shoulders, letting him support her

entire body. Someone at an adjacent table cleared his throat and Hayden lifted his head. But he didn't glance away from her.

She fingered her mouth where her lips still throbbed from his kiss. "I guess that means yes?"

Nine

Hayden couldn't believe the way everything was falling together. Shelby was moving in with him and now Roxy's doctor was giving him a positive report. Roxy had come through her surgery and was resting comfortably. She'd be able to return home in a few days.

Hayden knew Roxy had no family. He'd met her when she was sixteen. A runaway who was out of options wherever she'd come from; he'd never asked. He'd given her a job in one of the restaurants and a place to sleep. The rest, as they say, was history.

He talked to Roxy's doctor and to some of the other cast members of the revue who had agreed to stay with her overnight.

Hayden walked down the brightly lit hospital hallway to see Shelby standing there waiting for him. It seemed almost too easy that she was moving into his penthouse now. God knew that convincing Shelby had been harder than he'd expected.

But there was something right about it happening now. Something right about having her back with him after all this time. Something in his soul said that this hand was playing out accordingly and he should just keep playing the winning cards dealt him.

She slipped her arm around his waist. "Is she okay?"

He nodded. "Let's get out of here."

They were back at the hotel a few minutes later. The lobby was still a beehive of activity even though it was almost three in the morning. Hayden wanted to go up to his penthouse with Shelby but he had to make one more swing through the casino and check in with security.

"Babe."

She arched one eyebrow at him. "Yes?"

"I've got about thirty minutes' worth of work left tonight."

She nodded toward a comfortable-looking chair. "I'll wait over there for you."

Hayden conducted his meetings as quickly as possible and returned to Shelby.

"Where's your luggage?" he asked.

"I brought it up to your place earlier. Was that okay?"

She kept asking him as if she was afraid he'd changed his mind. "Of course. I gave you a key the first night you came back into my life."

She shrugged. "There's a part of me that's afraid to trust this, Hayden. The last time things moved so quickly."

"And they are again. But you have to face the fact that you and I live life at this speed. You wouldn't be able to wait months for me. Any more than I can wait that long for you."

She nibbled on her lower lip as they waited for the elevator and he tightened his arm around her waist. He wanted to stake his claim for the world to see. Yet at the same time he knew he wanted to take his time with her. To make sure that she understood how her action this night had impacted him.

He needed her in ways she couldn't understand. This wasn't the first time one of his employees had been injured on the job. But tonight with Shelby by his side… she soothed him. She gave him someone to share his burden with and he wanted to say thank-you to her without having to actually utter the words.

He shivered a little at the thought. She was the only woman he'd ever let in to his soul. He'd never been able to keep her out—then or now.

The elevator doors opened and they stepped onto the public car. There were two other couples and Shelby chatted to them as they rode to the fifth floor where they'd change cars. When they exited, she wished them both luck and slipped her hand into Hayden's.

"You'll make a good casino owner's wife," he said. The words slipped out without intent.

"Hayden—"

He bent, taking her mouth with his. He didn't want

her to think or explain. He knew it was too soon, but knowing didn't stop him from wanting. And he wanted Shelby. She was what he craved deep in his soul, and he knew he was going to do whatever it took to make her agree to marry him.

He lifted his head. "Let's go home so I can make love to you."

She nodded and was quiet until they reached his front door. Then she stopped, grasping his wrists and holding each one in one of her small delicate hands. Her hands didn't even wrap completely around his wrist.

"Are you sure about this?"

"About what?" he asked, his mind already on the way she'd feel under his body. To finally make love to her in his bed was a fantasy he'd been entertaining for too long now.

"Me and you," she said.

He brought her hand to his body, where he was already hardening, readying to take this one woman who had always been so elusive. "This answer your question?"

She shook her head. "Not that. About me living with you. There's still so much about me you don't know." She *had* to talk to him about Alan. But…not now.

"I know the important stuff."

"This?" she asked, her fingers caressing him.

"Well, yeah, but more than that. I know that you grew up without any luxuries and that you don't like to take money or gifts from others. That you work hard to make your dreams come true but never at the expense of others."

He swept her up in his arms, bending to unlock the door and open it. He entered his apartment, then kicked the door closed behind him.

"I know that I need you in a way I never wanted to need any woman. That when I kiss you, you go up like fire in my arms."

He walked straight through the public rooms of his home, past the poker table and the doors leading to the balcony where he'd had breakfast with her. He entered his bedroom. One entire wall was floor-to-ceiling windows that looked out on his kingdom. His world. Vegas. The 24/7 lifestyle he'd always thrived on.

It paled in comparison with the lovely woman in his arms. He hugged her closer to him, buried his face in the curls at her nape. He inhaled her scent deep into him. Deep into his soul.

"I know that I want you here always. I want to keep you in my bed waiting for me. Ready to make love to every second of every day."

She lifted her head from his shoulders, her hands encircling his neck and her mouth finding his. She kissed him deeply and every part of his being responded. His erection strained against his pants. His chest swelled, his blood flowing heavier in his veins.

"I want that, too. But I couldn't bear it if you had regrets," she said softly.

He let her slide down his body, his hands settling on her hips when she would have moved away. "How could I regret the biggest win of my lifetime?"

* * *

Shelby knew in this moment she'd made the right choice. That all the pain of the past was fading away as she stood next to Hayden in his bedroom. Hayden was a good man with a deep well of caring inside him.

"I'm not good at taking chances," she said. "I worried about your reaction to my moving in here. But no more. Sit on the bed." The bed, she noticed now, was huge, the prominent feature in the dark-walled room appointed sparsely with sleek Danish furniture.

He raised one eyebrow at her. "I don't want to wait."

"Yes, you do. Trust me."

He settled onto the bed, leaning back on his elbows and watching her through narrowed eyes. "Okay."

Even in supposedly ceding control to her, power still radiated from him.

Once he was there watching her, nerves assailed her.

"Shelby, come here."

When she crossed to him, Hayden sat up, widening his legs and drawing her between them. "What's going on in that head of yours?"

She hated that she'd messed this up. "I wanted to give you your fantasy."

"You already have."

"No, something sexy but…"

He raised both eyebrows and brought his hands to the buttons on her shirt. Slowly he opened them, revealing the curves of her breasts where they swelled over the top of a bustier.

He leaned down and kissed the pale white globes.

Her breasts felt fuller under his lips. Holding the sides of her blouse in either hand, he drew the fabric across her skin, rubbing all over her but keeping that layer of material between her and his hands.

The torture was exquisite and she arched her back, tried to move his touch where she needed it. But he controlled her carefully, finally removing her blouse and tossing it on the floor.

He didn't take his eyes from her breasts, and watching him gave her the confidence she'd been lacking. She straightened her shoulders and ran her hands up her thighs to her waist, cinched in by the bustier.

He leaned back on his elbows and watched her. She took a half step away from him, to give herself some more room. She twirled around, feeling the suede skirt slide around her legs.

All day she'd been hyperaware of what she wore under her clothes. Aware that Hayden's eyes would glaze, just as they were doing now, when he realized what she wore. At this moment she knew she'd never been more perfect. More the perfect woman for Hayden, the perfect mate for him. The perfect person she'd always been so afraid of being.

Remembering what Hayden had said when he'd first seen her dressing the mannequin, she unfastened the skirt and partially unzipped it, letting it fall to her hips. She swayed them in time to the music that had been playing in the casino earlier. The slow steady beat of the Marsalis jazz that Hayden loved.

She danced around the room for him. Lost all track

of her body and the imagined flaws she didn't want him to see. Lost complete track of her fears that Alan would somehow ruin what she'd found with Hayden. Lost all of her inhibitions. She offered her body up to Hayden in a slow, sensual dance.

Hayden pushed to his feet. Slowly he unbuttoned his shirt, moving his body in the same rhythm as hers. He danced behind her, his hands coming to her hips and pushing the zipper the rest of the way down. He pulled her back against his erection as he moved with her, each undulation of their bodies inflaming them both a little more.

Her skirt fell farther, stopping just above her knees. She spread her legs, rubbed her backside against Hayden.

He groaned low in his throat, his hands afire on her body as he swept them up and down her torso. He cupped her breasts and pressed hot, wet kisses to her neck and shoulder blades.

Still the music burned inside of her, building to a crescendo in time with the desire flowing through her body. She turned in his arms, pushing his shirt to the floor, fumbling with his belt buckle, finally freeing it. He caught her up in his arms, carrying her the few short feet to the bed.

Tossing her onto the surface, he followed her down, one knee between her legs to keep them open. His hands on either side of her shoulders, he braced himself above her and slowly lowered his chest to hers. His mouth teased hers as his fingers and hands tormented her breasts. He found the pull-away cups on the bustier and ripped them off. He bent to her, suckling her into his mouth with deep, strong tugs of his lips.

Shelby shifted her hips on the bed. Needing more. Needing it now. Not it, him. She needed him deep inside her. She wanted to share with him this feeling that swamped her and made her want to be what he'd said earlier. Want to be worthy of his love.

He pushed her skirt and thong down her legs and freed himself. He fumbled in the nightstand for a box of condoms. She took it from him and opened it carefully.

She took his length in her hand, sliding up and down a few times before she placed the condom on its tip and smoothed it down his erection.

Groaning, he gripped her hips, pushing one pillow and then a second under them, angling her up for his penetration. He held her hips in his hands and stared into her eyes. She met his gaze as he brought himself to the entrance of her body.

"You're mine," he said, thrusting deep inside her.

He set a pace that drove them quickly toward the pinnacle. "Say it, baby. Say that you're mine."

She gasped for breath, felt everything shimmering so close to her. Her orgasm hovered just out of reach. She met his gaze and realized what she'd been waiting for.

"I'm yours, Hayden. Only yours."

They both tumbled over the edge. Hayden's voice echoed in the room as he shouted her name. Shelby clutched him close, realizing that something had changed in the foundation of their relationship and that there was no going back.

* * *

Hayden woke up twice in the night, assured himself that Shelby was still in his bed and made love to her. He was ravenous for her body. He couldn't get enough of the way she reacted to his every touch.

He rolled to his side, propped himself up on his elbow and stared down at the woman who'd haunted him since he'd first met her. Back then he'd been way too young to appreciate her, but there'd always been something about Shelby that quieted his soul and gave him the peace he longed for.

The sheet was bunched around her waist. She lay on her side with her arms curved under her breasts. His morning erection swelled. God, he'd never been this insatiable before.

The alarm buzzed before he could touch her. He shut it off. She smiled sleepily up at him and he felt a sense of rightness with his world that he'd seldom experienced before. Leaning down, he kissed her. She pulled back.

"I'm sore," she said softly, blushing.

He ran his hands down her body, hoping to soothe her aches. "I'm sorry."

"Don't be. I just can't this morning," she said, leaning up to kiss his whiskered jaw. She rubbed her hands over his face and down his chest. "I missed you."

"When?" He hadn't left her side the entire night.

"When I left."

He knew she was referring to their time together ten years ago. "I was so angry."

"I know. That's why I waited until I was at the airport to call."

"Why'd you do it?"

"The money."

"And no trust in me to provide it."

He rolled to his side. He hadn't meant to rehash the past but it seemed inevitable. Neither of them had ever really had their say.

He felt her move behind him, the bed dipping slightly beneath her weight as her arm snaked around his waist. She held him to her, her face buried between his shoulder blades. She brushed a soft kiss on his back.

"I…I needed the money. I'd spent my entire life believing that money would solve my problems. Remember how I told you I didn't grow up in that house you picked me up at?"

Her hand fluttered on his stomach, not caressing but gesturing nervously, trying to explain without saying the necessary words.

He realized anew how much he cared for this woman, and how little he'd known of her before. He rolled over, needing to face her. To see what she was feeling as she spoke. She wouldn't look at him. She dipped her head, tucking her face between his neck and shoulder. "Where did you live?"

She took a deep breath; he felt the warmth of her exhalation against his skin. His body stirred despite the fact that now wasn't the time. He closed his eyes and fought for control.

"In that dumpy trailer park four miles from town, the Silver Horseshoe."

He shuddered. He knew the place. Full of degenerates, drug dealers, prostitutes and other unsavory characters. How could Shelby have grown up there? She was worlds too soft for that kind of life.

"You know it?" she asked when he didn't respond.

"Yeah, baby, I do." Rubbing his hands down her back, he wanted to pull her completely into his body. To vow to protect her from everything, even the dark memories of her past.

He held her, rocking her gently to give her some comfort. He sensed she wasn't really here with him but had traveled back to that place she'd grown up in.

"When your dad offered me a million, I just couldn't take a chance that it might never come again. I couldn't go back to that place. Plus, he threatened to tell you about where I came from. And I knew he was going to cut you off and once you knew I'd lied about who I was… Well, I'm not the gambler you are. I had to take the sure thing."

He heard the conviction in her voice and understood for the first time what it must have taken for her to leave him. To be honest, every time she'd broached the subject of how they'd live without his dad's money, he'd put her off. He knew that he had funds the old man couldn't touch but he'd never shared that knowledge with her. And now he saw that he should have. That maybe he hadn't trusted her the way she'd needed him to.

"God, baby. I'm sorry." He bent his head and rested

his chin on her shoulder. The silky length of her hair fell on his shoulders and he just held her in his arms. She was all that was delicate and feminine. She had always had to protect herself, even once he'd come into her life. He wished he could go back in time and kick his own ass for never seeing beyond her body.

She lifted her face and there were tears pooling in her eyes, but she blinked to keep them from falling. "Don't be. I used you. I knew you had money from the first time you asked me out. I had to pay Christy Jenkins to take me to the country club with her. I was looking for a rich guy and I found you."

He was a little angry to hear her say so bluntly what she'd done. But he'd picked her for precisely the same reason. Because his dad wouldn't like her. He knew that he could screw this up again. That the last piece of the puzzle that was Shelby had yet to be revealed. But he also knew that this woman belonged to him. And if it took a lifetime to figure her out, that was fine by him. He fought to find the right things to say. And knew he'd fail miserably.

"I was just a bonus?" he asked, attempting some levity where there was none. He hated that she made him vulnerable but she did. Because even back then her loss had hurt him more deeply than he'd ever admitted to himself.

He waited for her to answer, wishing he'd kept his mouth shut or just gotten out of bed before their conversation had come to this point.

"No. You were more. I can't explain it but from the beginning I knew you'd break my heart."

Ten

The next week flew by. Hayden and Shelby visited Roxy in the hospital. But the showgirl wasn't always up for company. They went every day anyway. Shelby reminded Hayden a bit of Roxy. Both women had come from nothing to make great successes of their lives.

Each day Shelby's life and his become more seamlessly wrapped together. It didn't matter that Hayden's schedule was hectic. He made time for her in between meetings with the incoming television-poker people, visits to the kids' facility and other casino details.

Shelby, too, was busy with training a manager for her store and phone meetings with the developers of the D.C. project.

Tonight was one of their rare free nights, and they'd

chosen to spend it with the Prescotts, at the penthouse, for dinner and a game of poker.

Shelby sat across the small card table from him. Deacon and Kylie were on either side of them. The room smelled of cigars and fajitas. He had a hard time even calling this a real poker game. The women, having not spent the last fifteen years of their lives living in a casino, didn't have the same experience at the game that he and Deacon did.

By unspoken agreement the men were playing to the women's level.

He glanced up at Shelby and caught her staring at him. She flushed, so he knew the direction of her thoughts. He raised one eyebrow.

Deacon cleared his throat. "I believe it's your turn, Mac."

Damn. How had this happened? He had been determined to claim Shelby again—not to be captured by her. She had always been a fire in his soul and now that she was here and his, it was worse. Some nights he woke and stared down at her sleeping face just to make sure she was really here.

And that pissed him off. He was a cool player. A man of confidence. Not a person easily shook. But she shook him.

He glanced at his hand and tossed two cards on the table. "I'll take two."

Deacon gave him two cards. Hayden picked them up, realizing he had a full house. A pair of aces and three tens. A full house… That echoed in his mind. He'd been a loner for so long, but now he was living with someone. Not just anyone. Shelby.

Could he ever stand at the end of the aisle waiting for her again? He wanted her to stay with him.

She'd rounded out his life, showed him things that had been missing before. She loved every aspect of his life, even gambling, which she was horrible at. He'd never met a person with worse luck at cards than she had.

Kylie's green eyes twinkled as she took one card. Shelby grimaced at her hand. "How many do I have to keep?"

"Two," Hayden said.

She tossed three cards on the table. Deacon gave her three new ones. Deacon sorted his hand out and they all played to see Hayden's hand. Shelby should have folded.

"Baby, you don't have to stay in when your hand is that bad."

"I was bluffing."

Kylie laughed kindly, and brushed back her long brown hair. "Not very well. I'm not good at this either. Deacon has been giving me tips."

Hayden glanced over at his friend and saw him shrug. "What can I say? She thinks I'm an expert at everything."

Kylie scoffed. "Hardly. But you have potential."

"Can you believe the way she treats me? Not married two years and already she's seeing the tarnish on my armor."

Kylie smiled at her husband, reached across the table to take his hand. He rubbed the back of her knuckles with his thumb. "You're still my hero," she said, smiling into his eyes.

Shelby glanced at Hayden and then pushed her chair back. "I think I'll clean up these plates."

Hayden grabbed a couple of plates and followed her into the kitchen.

"I like your friends," she said.

"Yeah?"

"Yeah. They seem so…perfect for each other. How'd they meet?"

"Deacon saw her on a security monitor and said she was the one for him. I bet him he couldn't convince her to marry him, so he went down and found her and asked her out."

She punched his arm. "What were you thinking?"

He rubbed his arm. "Hey, it worked out okay."

"I guess. But why would you do that?"

"Relationships don't make sense to me. Gambling always does. I knew that Deacon wanted her but I wasn't sure he'd really go after her."

"So you gave him a nudge."

He shrugged, and crossing to the sink, he dropped the plates into the sink. Shelby moved around him, cleaning up the remains of their dinner dishes and putting them all in the dishwasher.

Hayden leaned against the countertop and watched her. There was something right about this and he wished there was some way he could not screw this up. But he'd spoken the truth to Shelby. He didn't understand relationships.

The kitchen door opened and Deacon and Kylie

poked their heads in. "We're going to take off. Thanks for the game and dinner."

"You're welcome," Hayden said. Shelby dried her hands and came to stand next to him. He slipped his arm around her waist and together they walked Kylie and Deacon out of the penthouse.

Hayden didn't hear anything they said as they left. He wasn't aware of anything but the feel of Shelby under his arm. When the door closed, he backed her up against it.

He swallowed her gasp of surprise with his mouth. She wrapped her arms around his shoulders and held on to him, let him control the kiss and the embrace. He slid his leg between hers and bent his knee.

He swept his hands down her body, cupping her rump and pulling her lower body into his. She straddled his leg, her hands clinging to his shoulders.

She pulled back to breathe. "What was that for?"

"For being you."

He swept her up in his arms and carried her into the bedroom and made love to her through the night. He hoped it would be enough of a bond to hold her to him for all time.

Shelby sank back into her leather office chair. Everything she'd ever wanted was within her grasp. The new store was more successful than she'd dreamed possible. But then Shelby had remembered the Vegas of her youth, not this new vibrant scene with too much money and elegance.

Hayden was gone for the day, flying some high rollers who had been staying at his hotel every year since he'd opened out over the Grand Canyon in Deacon's helicopter. Shelby had gone to Roxy's house earlier to drop off some flowers for her.

It made no sense in the factual world but Shelby swore she could feel that Hayden wasn't in the hotel and she missed him.

"Ms. Paxton, there's a guy out front asking for you," said one of her staffers, sticking her head into Shelby's office.

"Thanks. Tell him I'll be right there."

Shelby stood and straightened her suit. She'd had five different men seek her out and ask her to personally select an intimate wardrobe for their wives, girlfriends or mistresses. The service was one that Paige and she had offered from the beginning, but usually it wasn't that popular.

She smiled as she exited her office, but froze when she saw that it was Alan MacKenzie. God knew he wasn't here for her professional help.

Her staff was helping a guest near the fitting rooms and Stan, their stock-boy-turned-salesperson, was flirting with a couple of women in their early twenties.

"How can I help you?" she asked Alan. Hayden looked a lot like his father, except in the eyes.

"We didn't get to finish our conversation the other day."

"Come into my office," she said, pivoting on her heel and leading the way. She knew she needed to resolve this. If she'd told Hayden the truth weeks ago, this wouldn't be a problem now.

Alan followed her into her office and took a seat in one of the guest chairs. Shelby went around behind the desk and seated herself. She knew it was petty but she liked sitting behind her big expensive executive's desk. Because in the back of her mind every time she saw Alan she remembered how cold, small and cheap she'd felt when she'd taken that check from him.

"I'm not your enemy here."

But he always had been. From the first time they'd been introduced, he'd always looked at her as if she wasn't good enough for his son. Even when he'd come to her in Atlanta, she'd sensed his distaste for her. Just once she wanted…what?

She knew it was impossible but she'd love to find a way to be accepted by everyone. To find that seemingly easy way that Hayden had of being everyone's equal, be it the croupier, the first-time gambler, his celebrity friends or her.

"I think we both know you never liked me," she said carefully.

"Yes, but my son always has. Why else would I be doing this?"

"I honestly don't know. Thank you for telling me about the shopping wing and suggesting that Bêcheur d'Or bid on the lease here. But that's all this is."

"I think we both know I forced you to come back."

"I would do anything for my company."

He leaned deeper into his chair, crossing his legs and staring at her. She felt the way she imagined a stripper did at that last moment when she was finally naked in front of a crowd. Shelby rubbed her hands up and down her arms.

"You came back for more than this shop and we both know it."

"No, Alan, I didn't. There's nothing more to my being here."

"I thought you were past lying like this."

Shelby flinched. "I'm not a liar."

He narrowed his eyes and Shelby wished she'd never asked him back here.

"Aren't you living with my son?" he asked.

"Yes, but—"

"Are you sleeping with him?"

She nodded. There was no way Hayden was ever going to believe she hadn't been manipulating him. No way. She heard in Alan's voice the same emotionless tone that Hayden sometimes used when he was angry.

"Mr. MacKenzie, please leave."

He pushed to his feet. "Why?"

"Because you are never going to believe I care for your son."

"Do you?"

She bit her lower lip and nodded. He'd never understand how deeply she cared for Hayden. She was sure she did. But she knew there was no way she was going to allow his father to hurt him through her again.

"That's all I needed to know."

"I'm…I'm not sure how to tell Hayden about you and me," she said. Being around Hayden had shown her the value in asking for help…asking for others' opinions. He leaned on his friends when he needed to. Right now she needed to figure out how to fix things with Hayden. And his dad…well, his dad seemed like the only one she could turn to.

"I'll handle that."

He walked out of her office and she sat there feeling shell-shocked. What was Alan going to do? Time was running out for her and Hayden. She had to tell him the truth.

Her phone rang and she hesitated to answer it. She'd been hopeful that she'd left behind that little trailer-park girl, but no matter how far she ran or how much she changed, that girl was still deep inside her.

Finally picking it up and clearing her throat, she said, "Bêcheur d'Or, where your every fantasy is made reality."

"I like the sound of that," Hayden said. His deep voice brushed over her bruised soul like a soothing balm.

"Hayden."

"What's up, baby? You okay?"

"Yes. Just having a busy day," she said. The day was going to get worse, she knew, because she had to talk to him. Not on the phone but in person. And she had to be prepared that he would see the facts and not the feelings behind her actions. "I have to fly to D.C. next week."

"How long will you be gone?"

"Three days."

"You're coming back?"

"Yes. Of course."

"Good, I'm on my way back. Meet me up front and I'll take you away from your mundane life and give you the fantasy one you deserve."

She smiled at that. Hayden was more than a fantasy.

He always knew the right things to say to make her feel better. "Okay."

When she hung up the phone, she took a deep breath. The truth was never easy, but Shelby was determined to set everything straight. Tonight.

The casino floor was buzzing with activity. Hayden was greeted by many people as he moved toward the roulette tables. Shelby's small hand was tucked into his and she followed him quietly.

There was a sadness in her eyes that he couldn't banish. Trying to prove to himself that he could be the man she needed by not taking her to bed was harder than he thought. His gut said to make love to her and get rid of the shadows that way. In bed there was no confusion or doubts between them. Just the kind of white-hot heat that burned away everything and left the two of them with their souls bared.

"The casino is busy tonight," Shelby said.

"Yeah, it is. Damn."

"What is it?"

"Someone is in the casino who shouldn't be."

"Who?"

"A grifter," Hayden said. It didn't matter that he'd known Bart since they were both four years old. Bart's family had lost everything in the early eighties and he felt that the world owed him something because of it.

"Grifter? What is that? Someone like a whale?" she asked.

Hayden didn't really want the grimier side of the casino business to touch her. He pulled her out of the foot traffic behind a row of slot machines.

"No. He's a con man. Can I leave you alone for a minute?"

"Yes, I'll be fine. I'm going to try to figure out roulette."

"Don't bet any money until I get back," he said. He felt bad taking her money. He didn't mind it when others lost in the casino, but seeing Shelby lose anything bothered him.

"Why not?" she asked, teasing him. He was glad to see her smile.

"Because I don't want your money."

"I might win."

"I doubt it!"

He kissed her quickly and walked away. He felt her watching him as he moved through the casino floor. The con man he'd seen noticed Hayden moving toward him. Bart was a regular in Vegas. A grifter who had been in and out of jail more times than anyone wanted to acknowledge.

Bart's family had lived next to Hayden's in Henderson before Hayden's mother had died. And there was a part of Hayden that wanted to help out the kid he'd known back then.

Bart gave him a salute and turned and sprinted through the crowd toward the exit. Hayden keyed his two-way phone and alerted security. He also sent a quick e-mail to the other owners, alerting them that Bart was back in town and looking for action.

He rejoined Shelby but kept scanning the crowd. "Are you ready to play?"

"I'm not sure I understand the game."

Hayden pulled her back against his body, just because he missed holding her. "Everyone is given a different colored chip to buy in so that they don't get confused. Then they place their colored chip on the number they think the ball will land on."

"This isn't very scientific, is it?" she asked after a few minutes.

From what she'd said and what he'd observed, she liked everything to fall neatly into a slot. And gambling wasn't going to do that. In fact, much of Hayden's life wasn't going to do that.

"Not at all. Every roulette player is hoping that Lady Luck will be at his side when he puts his chip on a number. In the U.S. we play with thirty-eight slots. In Europe they play on thirty-seven."

"What's the difference?"

"We have an extra zero spot."

They watched while the eight players placed their bets and the wheel spun. Hayden felt Shelby hold her breath as the ball bounced and then finally stopped.

"Oh, look, there was a winner," she said, though it wasn't she.

"Yes, and several losers."

"That's good for you."

"Yes, it is."

She was quiet again then turned in his arms, looking up at him with those big eyes of hers, their depths fathomless, guarding the secrets of her soul. "I'm not sure I'll ever understand this game well enough to play it."

"That's okay."

"No, it's not. This is your life, Hayden. I want to be a part of it."

"I don't understand everything that you do."

She wrinkled her forehead. "But you do. It's business. And you definitely understand the corporate world."

"So do you."

Hugging her closer to him for a minute, he bent his head and nibbled on her neck. "You fit right here, Shel, and that's all that matters to me."

"I'm just afraid this won't last. That after the bells and whistles fade, we won't have anything solid."

He raised both eye brows at her. "I can't do the relationship discussion thing, Shel. It's not my strong suit. Suffice it to say, we have the important things in common."

"What? And don't say sex."

"Well, we do have that," he said. He led her through the casino and then down the short hallway until they were outside. The night air was warm, wrapping around them. Hayden led her down the path toward the pool bar. "We also have business in common, and similar taste in music. And you make me laugh."

He ordered them both drinks, a sweet Bellini for Shelby and a scotch neat for him. As she perched on the bar stool, he knew there was only one thing to do. Reaching into his pocket, he fingered the ring she'd sent back to him via his father more than ten years ago.

Oh, man, was he really going to do this?

She stared out over the pool. He threw back his scotch and signaled the bartender for another one.

"Hey, Shel. I have something to ask you."

She turned to look up at him, and for a moment everything in his life felt perfect.

Eleven

Shelby took a deep breath, suddenly unsure of what was going on. She'd planned her big confession but now he wanted to ask her something. Apparently after he tipped back his second scotch in just a few minutes.

"What?" she asked. This wasn't like him. She was worried. Had his father already told him? Once again was she a pawn in the power struggle between these two MacKenzie men?

She took a sip of her favorite, sweet peach-flavored wine. It never failed to amaze her that he remembered little details about her.

"Nothing. Don't worry. Let's walk."

She'd barely tasted her drink but she left it behind. She didn't understand Hayden when he was this way.

He always moved through the world as if he owned it. To be honest, that was one of the things that drew her to him. He was always in charge, but tonight he seemed…nervous.

He tucked her under his arm, pulled her up against his body as they walked around the grounds. The moon was full and the night air warm. The scents of the flowers and night-blooming plants filled the air. The distant sounds of voices raised in revelry and assorted casino noises provided just the right background music.

Vegas was alive and the rhythm of it beat through her body in time with her heart. This was Hayden's world and she wanted to become a part of it so that they'd always be together.

"When I built this place I was full of anger, you know. I just wanted to prove to my dad and in part to you that you'd both been wrong about me."

There was no emotion in his words, just a calm telling of what had happened. As if she hadn't ripped his heart out and then coldly left him behind. For a moment, she wanted to go back in time and slap the young girl she'd been. Rationally she knew she couldn't have stayed. Knew that if she'd attempted to, their marriage would have ended in divorce. But she wished she'd found the courage to talk to him. To really show him who she'd been.

"Oh, Hayden, I'm so sorry. It was never that I doubted you." The words sounded almost too pat. They weren't enough. They didn't really explain what had been going on in her mind at the time.

"I know that now," he said, stopping under a large

magnolia tree. He pulled her into his arms, held her gently against him.

She loved the way he did that. Held her like she was precious to him. Like it mattered to him if something hurt her. She couldn't explain, but it made her feel as if she'd finally found a person with whom she could share everything.

"The Chimera is a first-rate hotel and casino." She was filled with pride every time she saw it. She remembered the run-down old hotel that had stood here before. Hayden had taken something that would have made many men bitter and turned it into not only a profitable business but also a community enhancement. He'd given back to Vegas despite the fact that the city hadn't brought him the jackpot he'd been searching for when she'd left him at the altar.

"That's right. But it's not enough anymore. For a while I've been searching for something more but I've done it all. Brought in exhibits many said no one would visit. With Deacon we've upgraded everything you can imagine, from shopping to shows to casino floors. There's nothing left for me to achieve."

He pulled away from her, rubbing the back of his neck. In the moonlight his features were stark, harsh with the emotions she knew he didn't want to reveal.

"I don't know how to say this," he said at last.

She swallowed hard and realized that the idyllic time they'd been indulging in the last few weeks was over. Hayden was a man of action and he couldn't just keep moving along without a plan.

"Say what? Do you want me to leave? Am I making you remember the anger that drove you to build this place?" she asked, wrapping her arms around herself. God, she hated feeling this way. Just once she wanted to be enough for someone. No, not anyone but Hayden. She wanted to be worthy of the kind of kingdom he'd built.

"No," he said. "Dammit, I want you to stay. Not just for a few weeks or months but forever. I want to have you in bed every night. I want to be able to call you during the day and just hear your sweet, sexy voice. I want to spend my nights laughing and loving you."

She took a deep breath. "I want that, too. More than anything. I never expected to fall in love with you again, but somehow I have."

He reached for her, pulled her to him, bending to her and kissing her fiercely. His mouth moved down her neck, pushing her shirt out of his way. He nibbled and suckled against her skin. She knew he was leaving behind a small mark, as he'd done continually since her return to Vegas, and she relished the brand.

He lifted his head and she met his gaze. There was something hot and possessive in his eyes. "Am I branded as yours?"

"Yes. But it's not enough. I want a permanent symbol of our life together. A permanent reminder to both of us that you belong to me."

"Will you have one, too?" she asked. "I don't want to be your possession."

"Yes. I…I want you to marry me, Shelby. But I can't go through the big wedding we planned last time."

She swallowed, realizing what she'd taken away from Hayden when she'd left him as she had. She hated herself for that. She bit her lip and hugged him close to her, burying her face against his chest. Not wanting him to see her own self-loathing.

"So?"

"Of course I'll marry you. There's no one I'd rather share my life with than you."

But she knew she couldn't go to a chapel one more time with secrets between them. She allowed herself this one last night of peace between them. In the morning she'd tell him the truth. Tell him about his father and the deal she'd accepted to return to Vegas and to him.

Arousal flooded his body and he had to claim her. Why the hell had he picked such a public place for this? The ring still sat in his pocket and he knew he wanted to see it on her finger.

This time it meant more than it had the last time. When he'd originally purchased the ring, he'd done so because it was the most expensive one at the jeweler's. Over the years that ring had become his talisman, his way of thumbing his nose at his father and the rest of the world.

Now it would be on her hand again and he couldn't help but feel that Shelby was his good-luck charm. That maybe she had been from the beginning.

"Let's get out of here. I want to make love to you," he said.

She nodded, slipping her small hand in his. He led

them quickly through the casino and to his private elevator. As soon as the doors closed behind them, he took her in his arms, backed her up against the rich walnut-paneled walls.

Her hands slipped to his waist, holding him to her. “Don’t regret this,” she said softly.

As if he could. He took her mouth with his, leaving not one inch unexplored. He caged her face in his hands, tipped her head farther back so that he could go deeper.

He vowed to brand her all over as his. Her hair wrapped around his fingers, tying them together in one more way. He lifted his head. Her eyes were closed, her face flushed, her lips wet and swollen from his kisses.

He lowered his mouth to the slim length of her neck, nibbling at her smooth flesh until he encountered her blouse.

“Bare yourself for me. Show me you want this.”

Her eyes opened. “I always want you.”

Her hands came between them, slowly unbuttoning her silky blouse. He followed her hands, tasting each bit of flesh as she revealed it. He lingered at her belly button and then started back up her body, stopping between her breasts, which were still covered by the ends of her shirt.

“Offer me your breasts.”

She shivered; he felt the tremble that swept over her body. Her hands tightened on the edges of her blouse until her knuckles were almost white. Then carefully she pulled back the edges, revealing first the incredibly soft white skin of her breasts and then her berry-hard nipples.

The elevator bell rang, signaling their arrival at his penthouse. He lifted her in his arms. "Wrap your legs around me."

She did as he commanded and he carried her quickly to his front door and keyed it open. Once inside he went to the floor-to-ceiling windows overlooking the city of Vegas. His city and his woman. He had them both in his arms.

He took her nipple in his mouth, suckling her strongly, trying to quench a thirst that had been a part of him for so long he wasn't sure when it had started. Only that he was still thirsty for her.

Her hands roamed over his back. He wanted her hands on his skin. He set her down and ripped his shirt from his body, tossing it aside. Shelby pushed her blouse off as well. When she reached for her skirt, he stopped her.

"Just take your panties off."

She nodded, reaching under her skirt to remove them. He took a condom from his pocket and quickly sheathed himself. Then he removed the ring, holding it in his fist.

He turned Shelby in his arms, bent her forward, supporting her with his arm around her waist. "This is my life, my kingdom. It means nothing to me without you by my side."

He rubbed his erection against her hot core and she moaned, undulating against him. He skimmed his fisted hand down her body, rubbing his knuckles over her hardened nipples as he bit lightly at her nape.

He slid his hand farther down her body, brushing over the tight curls at the apex of her thighs. He felt her wetness on his fingers, on the tops of her thighs. He loved how hot she got for him.

He slipped two fingers between her legs, teasing her opening. Pushing his thigh between hers, he forced her legs open wider. He held himself poised at the entrance of her body.

"Hayden…"

"Yes?" he asked, teasing her by rubbing in small circles around her core, dipping his fingers in briefly and then pulling them out.

"What are you waiting for?"

"For you to be wearing my ring," he said, bringing his hand up her body and opening his fist.

She caught her breath. "You kept it?"

"I had to," he admitted. He took her hand and pushed the ring onto her finger. Then he brought her hand to his mouth and kissed her. The scent of her arousal was on his fingers and inflamed the lust already straining the limits of his control.

He twined their fingers together and pressed their joined hands against the plate-glass window. "I'm not letting you go."

"Good," she said.

With his free hand he positioned himself at the entrance to her body and anchoring her with his arm around her waist, he plunged deep inside her. Her body tightened around his as he continued to thrust, driving her rapidly toward first one climax and then slowly building her to another.

This time he tumbled over the edge with her. He bit

her lightly on the back of the neck as his orgasm rushed through his body, draining him of his strength. They both collapsed against the window.

Finally Hayden straightened, lifting her in his arms and carrying her down the hall to his bedroom. He'd just claimed her in front of the world—his world, Vegas—and she would be his for all time.

Shelby called her mom—something she hadn't done the last time she and Hayden had planned to marry. Her mother was so happy for her and was driving to Vegas to spend a few weeks with Shelby. Next she called Paige, who promised to fly back for the wedding.

Shelby flew to D.C. for her meetings but missed Hayden horribly. More than she'd thought she would. They talked every night about everything and nothing. And for the first time in a long time, Shelby felt as if she was flying home, to her real home, when she returned to Vegas.

Hayden had suggested they exchange vows in the gazebo in the middle of the maze where they'd made love. She'd agreed.

Everything was going very smoothly—too smoothly. She knew she had to say something to Hayden before his father did. Alan was everywhere, always watching her with that gaze that said she wasn't good enough for his son. She knew it. He knew it. Only Hayden didn't seem to sense the undercurrents.

But she suspected he did. Suspected he was putting all of that down to the past. But Shelby knew that it was more.

And finally, after weeks of anticipation, tonight was her last chance to say something. Her last chance to come clean before the wedding tomorrow. It was the rehearsal dinner, being thrown at the Golden Dream by Deacon and Kylie.

Earlier today Hayden had taken her riding on his Harley out in the desert. She'd planned to tell him then but had chickened out. The day had been perfect, a quiet sharing of their thoughts, the kind of experience that made her realize how much she loved him. How much she didn't want to hurt him.

Now they were back at the penthouse. Hayden was on the phone talking with his security people. They'd found the man who'd attacked Roxy, and Hayden's lawyers were making sure the man went to jail forever. Shelby was dressing—or trying to, at least. Nothing she put on looked right. She'd changed clothes fifteen times.

Finally she just stood in front of the full-length mirror and stared at herself in frustration. Tears burned the back of her eyes and she just couldn't take the internal pressure anymore. She had to say something.

"Baby? What's wrong?" Hayden asked as he crossed the room to her.

He wrapped his arms around her, pulling her back into the shelter of his body. As she stood there, surrounded by him, her fears seemed ridiculous. Surrounded by him she felt as if there was no way he'd ever let her go. Surrounded by him she felt like the lowest person alive. She never should have let this go on so long.

He tipped her head back and lowered his mouth to

hers. He never said he loved her. But in that kiss she felt his emotions. They flooded her and wrapped around her wounded heart, assuring her that everything would be okay.

"I thought you were going to wear that sexy red dress," he said when he lifted his head. He skimmed his hands down the curves of her body. "But I like this dress."

It was a black cocktail number with a plunging neckline. The dress had no back and was held up by a wide band of rhinestones at the neck. The skirt was full, ending just above her knees. She'd pulled her hair up and left a few tendrils curling at her neck and the sides of her face.

"The red one didn't look right," she said. "I'm not sure about this one, either. I want everything to be perfect tonight."

"It will be. Clothing doesn't matter."

"Not to you. You look perfect no matter what you wear."

And he did. Tonight he wore a custom-made tuxedo that he'd special ordered from his Savile Row tailor a few days ago. She was so outclassed and not just by the clothing.

"What are you afraid of?" he asked.

"Everything and everyone. When we walk into that party tonight, once again everyone will know that you picked someone beneath you."

"Shel, no one thinks that. I'm a gambler. Half of the moneyed people in Vegas won't talk to me. The others only talk to me when they're winning. I've been the target of more accusations than you can imagine."

She shook her head at him. "But you're still so…sophisticated. I can't help it, Hayden. I feel like I'm one step away from the trailer park. And that all those people can see it."

"Don't do this to yourself. Your life is a success that few find, regardless of where they started. I'm so proud of you, of what you've achieved."

She smiled up at him. "Thank you. But…there's something I have to tell you."

"You love me, right?"

She swallowed. "More than I thought I could love another person. It's so intense sometimes I have to pinch myself to make sure it's real."

"Don't do that, Shel. I'm here and I'm real."

She wrapped her arms around his, needing to take some of his strength and confidence with her before she told him the truth of their meeting again.

Taking a deep breath, she stepped away and put a few feet between them.

"There is something else I have to tell you."

He turned to face her. With his brooding eyes, she knew he sensed he wasn't going to like what she had to say. For a moment she considered never saying a word but she knew that Alan wouldn't let the truth lie undiscovered for much longer.

The doorbell rang. "Can this wait?" Hayden asked.

She nodded, happy for the reprieve. She watched him leave, already feeling the coldness in the room and in her heart.

Twelve

Hayden crossed the room, grateful for the distraction. Though he'd never admit it out loud, he'd been afraid that something would happen and his wedding to Shelby wouldn't go off without a hitch. Turned out his gut was right—again.

He cursed when he saw his dad standing on the threshold. "Not now, Dad. Really, I'm not in the mood for one of your lectures. And we have to get over to Deacon's."

His father wore a suit by the same tailor as Hayden's. The cuff links that his grandfather had given him shone at his wrists. He was flawlessly dressed from head to toe. Hayden remembered what Shelby had said about clothing and understood what she meant for the very first time.

He'd never really thought about all he took for granted but now he understood that maybe he should have. There were differences between himself and Shelby he couldn't ever really comprehend.

"I'm not here to lecture. I have to tell you something," Alan said, crossing to the bar and pouring himself a drink.

This wasn't good. His dad gestured with the bottle and Hayden nodded. He had a feeling he was going to need the alcohol.

"Not you, too. What is it—confession day?" he asked, taking the glass from his father.

His dad clinked the rims together before tipping his back and draining it. "Who else is confessing?"

"My soon-to-be wife," Hayden said, draining his glass. He dropped it on the bar and reached for the bottle, refilling both of their glasses.

His father stopped him with a hand on his wrist. He seemed almost relieved. "Ah, well then, maybe I'm too late."

"Too late for what?" Hayden asked, knowing that he wasn't going to like the answer. But he hadn't gotten to where he was in business by ignoring the cold harsh facts that life sometimes dealt his way.

"To tell you that I bribed her to get her back to Vegas and take up with you again."

Hayden swallowed. "What did you offer her?"

"That's where I screwed up, son. I told her she could have whatever she asked for."

"Dammit, Dad."

Alan shook his head.

Hayden set his glass down on the bar and crossed to the partially opened doorway of his bedroom. There was no need to ask Shelby if his father's words were true. She was standing there in the shadows, tears running down her face.

She had her arms wrapped around her waist and he knew she was hurting, but he didn't give a damn. How the hell had he allowed himself to be duped by her again? Why the hell wasn't he enough for her? When the hell was he going to learn that money, not love, motivated Shelby Anne Paxton?

"Come on out. Let's hear what you were going to say," he said to her, pushing the door open.

"Not in front of your father," she said, her eyes begging him for a reprieve. But he wasn't feeling generous right now.

"Why not? You seem to have been conspiring with him all this time."

She grabbed a tissue from the box on the dresser and wiped her nose. "There was no conspiracy. Please believe me."

Alan stood in the doorway saying nothing. Hayden wanted his dad to leave. The old man wasn't helping. Hayden knew there was more to what Shelby was telling him than what his father knew. He was angry and he knew that part of it was because of his dad.

"You came back here because of me, remember?" Alan said.

Shelby flinched but didn't look away from either of

them. "You're right, Alan. And you did promise me something if I came back here."

Shelby's voice shook when she spoke. A change came over her and Hayden hardly recognized her.

"I'd hoped this would help undo the mistakes I'd made when you were young," Alan said.

"Looks like you bet on the wrong woman again," Hayden said softly.

He saw her flinch and knew that his words had cut her deep. He felt an answering wound on his heart. Deep inside, where he'd felt safe hiding the fact that he loved this woman.

"I deserved that," she said. "But I'm fighting for our future, Hayden. I'm going to have to demand that you don't make any more remarks like that."

"You're in no position to demand anything," Alan said.

"Don't help, Dad. You've done enough."

Shelby looked away from him and straight at his father. "You said I could name my price."

Money. He'd known that was what she wanted. But a part of him couldn't believe it. This was the woman who wouldn't take any money from him at the blackjack table. The woman who'd fought to get where she was. He knew that his anger was clouding his judgment, that he was missing something really important here. But he couldn't put his finger on it.

He even understood why money was so important to her. But why couldn't she see that he had so much more to offer her? He could be her security if only she'd let him. "Dammit, Dad, you should have left this alone."

Alan stood in the corner, watching like the wily old gambler he was. Shelby watched him as if she wasn't sure whose side he was on. Hayden wanted to warn her the old man was always on his own side.

"What are you waiting for, Shelby?" Hayden stalked to his desk and pulled out his checkbook. "Name your price."

"I don't want a check."

"It's good."

"I'm sure it is. But the only thing I want is you, Hayden. I came back to Vegas for one reason—to reclaim the man I never forgot."

"My father bribed you."

"He threatened to go to the magazines with the truth about how I got the money to start the boutique. Tell them that Paige and I would do anything for money. I couldn't let him do that. But I sold myself once and I never will again. After he left my office, I realized that I'd never stopped thinking about you and…well, it seemed like the perfect chance to come back and take that gamble I wouldn't the first time."

Hayden dropped his pen and checkbook and she saw in his eyes the flame of desire and the hope for the future. "What gamble is that?"

"Double or nothing. Without you by my side that's what I have. Nothing."

"Looks like I won again," Alan said, finally bowing out gracefully, as if he suddenly accepted the inevitable. "Now get busy and give me some grandkids to spoil."

* * *

Hayden was staring at her as if he didn't recognize her. She closed the gap between them, taking his hand in hers. She lifted it to her face and kissed him gently. She knew she'd given him the shock of a lifetime and couldn't bear the thought of losing this man again.

"I appealed to the gambler in you because I know that you like to take long-shot bets. But if that doesn't work, then I'll beg. And if that doesn't work, then I'll simply stay here and wear you down until you can see the truth."

"What truth is that?" he asked, his voice low and husky.

"That I'm not asking you to take this leap by yourself. I'm scared of your world, of not fitting in. I'm scared to stay with a man who doesn't love me. But I'm more afraid of living the rest of my days in that lonely state that my life had become without you."

He said nothing and she couldn't stand the intensity in his eyes. She took a few steps away, reaching behind her to steady herself on the edge of the couch.

"You're wrong, Shel," he said, his voice deep and husky, brushing over her senses like a warm desert breeze.

"Wrong about what?" she asked. She was afraid that it was too late for them and she didn't want to give up hope. Not yet.

"Me not loving you."

"Really, Hayden, you don't have to say it. I know you can never love a woman whom you can't trust. You won't even have a wedding ceremony where you wait for me at the front of the chapel."

He closed the distance between them in three long strides. Grabbing her shoulders and pulling her up toward him, he took her mouth in a fierce kiss that left her battered soul wanting more.

"You're right, I didn't trust you. But I've loved you for more years than either of us realized. And my anger at you and my dad…well, it was due to the fact that I didn't have the courage to go and find you."

"You didn't know where I was."

"I never tried to look. I do love you, Shelby. I meant what I said when I asked you to marry me—you make all of this worthwhile."

Hayden pulled her down onto the couch, but the subsequent pounding on the door pulled them apart. "Go away. We're not available right now," he called out.

"Oh, hell, yes you are. I'm not going back to Kylie and telling her the guests of honor are no-shows."

Hayden cursed but she saw the smile in his eyes. He rubbed away the tracks her tears had made on her face and kissed her gently. "Later, I'm going to make love to you. But for now, let's go celebrate our marriage."

Hayden nervously stood in front of the preacher at the outdoor gazebo in the gardens at the Chimera. The afternoon was perfect, with the sun shining brightly down on them. Deacon stood at his side and Hayden was glad to have his friend there. Scott Rivers and Max Williams were there as well, serving as ushers. The two bachelors couldn't believe he'd given up his single days so easily. Hayden didn't even attempt to explain that life without Shelby wasn't nearly the ride that life with her was.

Shelby's mother waved at him from her seat in the front row, Roxy beside her. The two women had bonded. Terri Paxton needed to mother someone and Roxy needed someone to take care of her as her wounds healed, both mentally and physically. Terri was a stunningly beautiful woman and she loved Shelby. Shelby and Hayden were trying to convince Terri to move back to Vegas, and she was thinking it over.

His dad sat on the opposite side of the aisle, arms crossed over his chest, looking like a man who'd gotten what he wanted. Hayden shook his head thinking about how his father had played him and Shelby. But he couldn't be angry, not anymore. Hayden was grateful his father had interfered for once. Otherwise, he'd still be missing Shelby.

The music started and Hayden turned to wait for his bride. He'd been reluctant to do this again, to wait for her at the end of the aisle with his friends in attendance, but ultimately it was a little gesture that had meant a lot to Shelby and to their life together.

Paige came up the aisle first and then came Shelby. She came to him on her own, with no family to give her away. He felt the depth of his love for her overwhelm him, and tears burned the back of his eyes. Never had he guessed that she would mean this much to him.

She reached his side and he took her small trembling hand in his. Though the preacher was saying words of welcome to the congregation, Hayden bent and kissed Shelby.

She smiled up at him. His heart kicked and his gut tightened. Being married to Shelby was like winning the grand prize.

HER HIGH-STAKES AFFAIR

BY
KATHERINE GARBERA

This book is dedicated to my kids,
Courtney and Lucas, who keep me on my toes
and make every day an adventure!

One

"Hey, sexy lady. Where do you want me today?"

Raine Montgomery bit the inside of her cheek not to respond to Scott Rivers. Every morning it was the same line or some variation of it. It should have sounded like a pickup line but didn't. Instead he made her want to believe she was a sexy lady, even though she'd had enough experience with gamblers to know they never told the truth.

"Can't decide?" he asked, slipping an arm around her waist.

She stepped away from him. "In your chair at the table."

"Honey, when are you going to loosen up with me?"

"When you stop flirting with every woman who walks by."

"Is it making you jealous?"

"No."

Scott laughed and walked away from her as the other players trickled in.

She'd gotten into the film business for one reason and one reason only. She'd dreamed of the moment when she'd be called onstage at the Academy Awards to accept her Oscar for best director. She even had her speech rehearsed:

"I'd like to thank the Academy for recognizing my accomplishments, and I'd like the rest of the world to know that Missy Talbot is a spoiled bitch and my dad isn't a loser."

Okay, so it was a little melodramatic, but she'd been in junior high at the time and it had seemed like the perfect solution to her dismal and dreary life in New Jersey.

But her dream hadn't gotten her to the Oscars; in fact, she wasn't even close to winning a People's Choice Award or even an MTV one. She doubted anyone was going to be giving her an award for World Champion Celebrity Poker Showdown.

The taping ran for four weeks, with three celebrities and three champions from across the country who competed. In each week's episode two games were played and at the end of the show two players were eliminated. When just two players remained, they played two high-stakes games to determine the celebrity poker champ.

The show was essentially a high-stakes Texas hold 'em poker game where viewers could log on to a Web site and win prizes by correctly guessing if the celebrity winner had been bluffing or really held the cards needed to win.

Spawned in part by the reality craze that was sweeping through the television industry, the show tapped into the public's desire to watch celebrities spend their money and their free time. Every four weeks a new group of celebrities and champs were brought in. Then at the end of the season they had a winners-only play-off.

Their show taped a month's worth of episodes in one week. Each person on the show signed a waiver promising not to reveal the results, because viewers had the chance to vote on who they thought was the best and win a myriad of prizes that had been donated by sponsors. The celebrities were playing for charities as were the champions.

Raine had given all the players a wide berth because her producer, Joel Tanner, didn't like her or any of the crew mingling with the players. In fact there was a clear no-fraternization clause in the contracts signed by everyone on the set, both in front of the camera and behind the scenes. Joel wanted to make sure they didn't end up with any kind of lawsuit because of the way the players were shown.

Prizes were given to viewers who chose the winner each week. So how Raine shot and edited the show could influence them. They'd had to fire a cameraman last season because he'd been involved with one of the players and had been giving her more camera time than the other players.

This set of shows was being taped in the exclusive Chimera Casino on the strip in Las Vegas. Still, it was hard work, and Raine rubbed the back of her neck as she headed toward the director's booth. Some people called it the God booth because her voice could be heard but she couldn't be seen. Yet Raine knew she was as far from God as any person could be.

Especially since right now she was having impure thoughts about actor Scott Rivers. She entered the booth and put on her headphones. Since all of the players were miked, she could hear their small talk. The deep sexy tones of Scott's voice came over her headphones and she paused to listen. He was the first guy she'd ever been tempted to break her contract for, and she really struggled to keep resisting him every day. She wished he'd lose.... No, that wasn't true. She knew enough about men to realize that sooner or later he'd stop asking her out, and she honestly wanted to enjoy flirting with him until that happened.

"Shot down again, eh, stud?"

Scott glanced over at Stevie Taylor, the notoriously debauched lead singer for Viper, a heavy-metal band that had been on the cutting edge of music fifteen years ago. Instead of being a has-been, Stevie had the kind of talent and energy that had kept him in the mainstream. He simply changed his style to fit the younger audiences' tastes.

That being said, the man was an ass sometimes, and Scott suspected Stevie was still pissed off about losing to him at the PGA celebrity golf tournament last month in Hawaii. Or maybe it was the fact that Scott had unwittingly been the object of Stevie's third wife's affection.

"Some women take more time than others," Scott said. Especially women like Raine Montgomery. Not that Raine fit into a box or a category. In fact, he knew she'd be ticked off that he'd even thought of putting her in one. "They aren't all impressed with long hair and fast cars."

"I guess that means you have to try harder," Stevie said.

There was an edge to his voice that Scott chose to ignore. Every day was work for Scott. He'd grown up on a soundstage and had learned early on to act the way others found acceptable. With Stevie he acted like a babe magnet always on the prowl, because that was what the legendary rock front-man understood. With Raine he acted…hell, he wasn't doing such a great job of acting with Raine. She made him forget he was playing a role.

"Sure. Everything worth having takes some effort." And Raine was definitely worth the effort. Worth even this job. Not that he was too concerned about getting fired. The producer was a good friend of his, and they went back a long way. He wondered how Raine felt about the no-fraternization clause they'd both signed.

Scott was honest enough to admit that the gambler in him wanted to take a chance on it. The added risk increased the odds that she wouldn't go out with him unless she really wanted to. He couldn't explain it beyond that but knew himself well enough by now to know that there was something appealing about the idea.

"You're working up a sweat and she's barely noticing you, Rivers. What would your fan club say?"

Scott didn't respond to the goad. He didn't have a fan club and Stevie knew it. His child stardom had translated into cult-classic films in his early twenties and two one-offs that had turned into blockbusters. He acted when he felt like it, preferring to spend most of his time working with the charitable trust he had set up with his own money. "I'm not worried, Stevie."

"Some boys aren't meant to play in the big leagues," the other man said.

"Whatever. You know she can't really show that she's attracted to me."

"Because she isn't?" Stevie said with a snicker.

"Because we work together." A man like Stevie would never understand the distinction, but Scott knew that Raine would. That her job and her reputation would be important to her. He understood why.

"I wouldn't let that stop me."

He wasn't going to defend himself like some teenage boy with his first woman. Scott was thirty-eight, and he couldn't believe he'd allowed himself to get drawn into this conversation.

He'd arrived early on the set hoping for some alone time with Raine, and he'd gotten it. He just hadn't expected Stevie to show up.

"What, no glib remark?"

"You're an ass, you know that?"

Stevie laughed. "You're not the first to say it. But that doesn't change the fact that Ms. Montgomery isn't exactly falling for you."

Stevie wasn't going to let this go. No matter what Scott said or did, Stevie was always going to bring up Raine. And Scott didn't want that.

"What would it take for you to drop this?"

"Prove me wrong. Prove you're not out of your element with Raine."

"How am I supposed to do that?"

"How about a little wager?"

"On a woman? Have you been living under a rock for the past twenty years?"

"There's no reason anyone other than the two of us has to know about it."

Famous last words. He glanced around the set. They appeared to be all alone, and so he thought they had the kind of privacy that was something of a luxury on a busy television or movie set.

"What'd you have in mind?"

"A simple bet…you get her in bed before the show wraps."

Scott had that tingling at the back of his neck that he always got before he did something risky. Like sky surfing or kayaking down dangerous rapids. Something that all of his self-preservation instincts said not to do. But he wanted Raine, and he suspected she wanted him, too.

He knew he'd never tell Stevie a single detail of his

time with her, but if it got Stevie off his back, then it might be worth it.

"What's the wager?"

"Fifty thousand."

"You're on."

Raine couldn't believe she'd just overheard Scott making a bet about her with Stevie Taylor. The rocker was as legendary for his kinky sex-capades as he was for his wicked guitar licks.

Why had she activated the microphones when she'd gotten into her booth? Because she was an idiot. This is what happens when you eavesdrop, she told herself.

Raine's hands shook, and she wanted to smack Scott right between the eyes. What the hell was he thinking making a bet about taking her to bed? That was low and mean. And it hurt so much because she'd thought he was different.

She leaned toward the booth's tinted window and glanced down at the floor where the two men stood away from everyone else.

Raine watched both men take their seats at the table and went back to her monitor to watch the screen. But all she saw was red. Having been the pawn in a gambler's game before, she refused to let it happen again.

She wasn't sure how to get the upper hand on Scott. As a child star, he'd grown up in front of America and had charmed everyone by coming into their homes once a week for fifteen years. In the three days they'd been in Vegas, Raine had yet to see one person deny the man anything he asked for—except her.

He was good-looking. Well, only if you liked guys with unruly hair that fell to their shoulders and who wore a goatee. Which, of course, she did.

And she'd been thinking that maybe it was time to take a chance again on a guy before she'd heard his bet. A bet about her. She wanted to sink to the floor and wrap her arms around her waist. But she didn't; instead she pressed the button so that the cast and crew could hear her.

"Places, please."

She hated that she was attracted to a man who seemed to bluff his way through life. She'd been raised by the ultimate con man. A grifter, bar none, who'd blended perfectly into any situation much the same way Scott seemed to. She knew that was what Scott was doing because no one could predict when he was bluffing or really holding a winning hand.

"Action."

She watched him playing his game, the ultimate con man in his environment. His words played over and over in her head. Fifty thousand dollars—that was what she was worth to him. She wished that she could get back at him, do something he wouldn't expect. Maybe run a con on him. Convince him she was falling for him. No one knew how to run a scam like a Montgomery.

And though she'd vowed to never again lie or betray anyone's confidence, it somehow seemed right to her that she do it now. With this man. The one she'd hoped might be different.

"Camera Two, you're out of focus. Camera One, pan the entire table like we discussed."

Raine stopped thinking about Scott and focused instead on her job. If she went through with this scam, there was a good chance she'd be putting her job on the line. Joel wouldn't forgive her if she broke his rules.

"And cut," she said, as the hand was dealt to everyone.

"No one move. Latesha, there's a shine coming off Stevie's forehead. Move Camera One to the left of the table and get ready to resume play."

The East Coast champ, Laurie Andrews, lifted her free hand. "I need a drink of water."

One of the production assistants got her a bottle of Evian and then disappeared out of scene. Raine called action and finished shooting the hand.

So far Scott had fooled them every time. He didn't have any of the "tells," the little signs that the other players had.

She left her booth and went back on the floor to find Andy, her assistant director. He was talking to the NASCAR driver—probably about cars. Andy had a thing about fast cars that bordered on obsession.

She signaled to him that she needed a word and stood a little to the side of everyone else. Scott glanced up from the food table and caught her staring at him. He arched one eyebrow at her in a very arrogant way that made her want to do something really immature like kick his shins.

Her nature was contrary, so she couldn't budge even when he pushed to his feet and sauntered over to her.

"Hey, honey."

"Stop it right now. You're not as charming as you think you are."

"I know that," Scott said with a grin that invited her to share his self-deprecating humor.

She tried to put herself in his shoes. If she'd had people of the opposite sex literally throwing themselves at her, she'd be the same way, right?

She shook her head and turned to walk away. But he stopped her with a hand on her wrist. His hand was big and strong, rough against her skin and totally at odds with his spoiled-rich-boy image.

"Wait. I think we got off on the wrong foot and I'd like to change that."

She still faced away, but glanced at him over her shoulder. There was something in his dark-brown gaze that held her captive and wouldn't let her walk away. Something that made her forget everything except him.

In an instant she realized she'd been using her disdain for the wealthy as a barrier against her attraction to him. Why did she have to pick today to let it drop?

She remembered what her father always said. *You can't con an honest man.* If Scott wasn't trying to manipulate her, then he wouldn't allow himself to be manipulated.

They only had three and a half more weeks of shooting. She should have made it that long. "Since we're on a break, let's get out of here and talk," he said.

"Talk?"

He arched an eyebrow at her. "Unless you had something else in mind."

She shook her head. Maybe before she'd heard him with Stevie, but not now. Honestly, not ever. Think of a con, she thought. Make it about that. But she didn't have a plan. She'd never been good at planning the actions even when she'd been a part of the game. She'd always been the honest one. Her father had said that with her eyes, no one ever expected a lie. "No. I…"

"Listen, I know there's something about me that rubs you the wrong way."

"It's not that." It wasn't fair that he'd be so perceptive when she couldn't get a handle on who he was. But it made an odd kind of sense. Only a man who knew what everyone else wanted would be able to effortlessly change into what they wanted.

"Then what? Because every other player on this tour has seen your smile except me."

"I didn't realize that," she said.

"Sure you did. You didn't care. Why is that, Raine?" he asked her. His voice dropped an octave.

She shivered at the sound of her name on his lips. She tried to remind herself that he was a trained actor, that this was all smoke and mirrors, but the finger rubbing her wrist made it feel like something more. And she remembered the other promise she'd made herself in high school other than getting the Oscar. No gamblers—ever.

* * *

Scott had spent the majority of his life on display, and he'd worked hard at projecting an image that said it didn't bother him. Truthfully, he hated it. Part of the reason he disappeared for months at a time was that he just couldn't stand to be social anymore. He got to the point where he couldn't tolerate anyone around him.

So why, then, was he standing here next to Raine Montgomery, who'd made it perfectly clear she didn't want to have anything to do with him? It wasn't the bet with Stevie. He'd wanted her since the moment he'd set eyes on her in Joel's office.

And she'd looked right through him. Maybe he was a closet masochist. Yeah, right. More likely, the lusty demon in his pants was making decisions for him again.

He wanted her. It didn't help that Vegas was his personal playground. The place that he came when he needed to blow off steam. And they were in the Chimera, the one hotel that he thought of as his home away from home.

The bet was nothing to him. An added bonus to something he'd already decided he wanted.

And there was nothing he liked more than a challenge. Especially one that came in a tempting package like Raine. She was petite but she packed a punch. Gaffers, lighting techs and stage hands all bent to her will.

Everyone joked that her God voice when she was in the booth was straight out of the Old Testament. She was firm and polite but unforgiving of mistakes. She was also lavish in her praise, and he'd seen how well respected she was.

He tucked his hand under her elbow and drew her away from the set through an open door that led to the casino floor. For the television show they were using a high-stakes poker room off the main casino.

"Where are you taking me?"

"To my lair," he said.

She laughed. "Okay, so you're not the big bad wolf."

"Who said that?"

"Stop trying to scare me. It won't work."

"I'm not trying to scare you. I'm attempting to find some common ground."

She pulled to a stop in a small alcove well out of the way of the foot traffic. "I'm not sure there is any."

"I know there is," he said, curving his body in front of hers to block them from the view of passersby.

She stared up at him, and he realized her eyes were a beautiful shade of deep blue. He'd never seen them up close before. Her eyes weren't what he'd expected. With her thick, dark, curly hair they should have been brown.

What else was she hiding?

"Why is this so important to you? I'm sorry I don't smile at you but I'll try to do it from now on."

Scott rubbed the back of his neck. "I want more than a smile."

"I don't date…" She lowered her head, staring at her feet. This woman was different from the director he'd seen on the set. Which was the real Raine?

"Actors? Gamblers? Rich men?" But he knew she meant him in particular. He'd bet half his fortune that she was like most women, who thought if they found some palatable word he wouldn't take it personally. But he knew from the way she watched him that it was Scott Rivers who made her nervous. Not his profession or his money.

"All of the above," she said, glancing up at him.

He stared into her eyes, losing himself there. He'd never admit it out loud but there was something in her eyes that called to his lonely soul. He wanted to explore that, find out exactly what it was. "I don't act anymore."

"That's right, you haven't since…when?" she asked.

"A lifetime ago." He remembered the day with a kind of fondness now. He'd been acting since he was nine months old. To say he'd chosen that profession was a huge exaggeration. He'd learned to act the same way he'd learned to walk and talk. Sometimes he wasn't sure that he knew how to really live.

"What about gambling? Can't deny that. You are being paid to play right now."

"Ah, but that's not really gambling, is it? I'm out there playing for charity and trying to outbluff the other contestants."

"And you always do it."

"Winning's important to me."

"Why?"

"Because losing sucks. Surely you've found that to be true."

"I have. That's why I play by the rules."

"What rules?"

"My rules for safe living. It's not that I'm not attracted to you. Who wouldn't be? But you're not worth the risk."

"Risk? Honey, you're safe with me."

"Don't call me honey. You call everyone that."

"Okay, but don't treat me like I'm nothing more than a list of professions or money. I want a chance to get to know the real Raine."

She shook her head. "I don't have time. And we both signed a waiver saying no fraternization with the cast or crew."

"Live a little, Raine. Take a chance. We both have some free time."

She bit her lower lip, and he realized that he was pushing her. He analyzed Raine and the situation. If he backed down now, she'd never let him get her alone again. But maybe… "I dare you."

"What?"

"I dare you to go out with me. I dare you to see past the flashbulbs and the gossip-sheet rumors about me."

Two

Damn him. That was all she could think as she stood there contemplating the dare.

She wanted to accept it. Not only to get back at him—because it would give her a chance to put her half-formed idea of making him fall for her into action—but also because she liked him. She was attracted to him.

But she wasn't sure what was motivating Scott. Was it just the money he'd wagered with the rocker or did he want more? And was she really willing to risk her job just so she could one-up him? And she definitely was going to one-up this man. Did she really want to take a chance on another man hurting her?

A dare.

Still, it was hard to change her habits. She was a risk taker by nature, and every instinct in her wanted to take him up on his dare. To prove to him he wasn't the hot stuff he thought he was.

A dare.

She'd spent a lifetime tamping down the urges of her wild blood. That was what Grandma Nan had always called it when Raine got into scrapes at school. And in her younger days she'd gotten into more than a few of them.

She'd never been able to resist a dare.

How had this man known? What was it about his dark-brown eyes that enabled him to see past the protective layers others never noticed were there?

In truth she knew it wasn't arrogance. The man had a swarm of adoring people following him around day and night. She wondered how long they'd be alone in the alcove before one of his fans found him.

"What's the matter? Scared you can't handle me off the set where you're not in charge?" he asked in that silky tone of his.

She realized he was so used to getting his way that it never occurred to him she'd turn him down. And it irked her that she was thinking about accepting his invitation. But she was definitely going to make him work for it.

"I think we covered this already," she replied. "I'm not scared of any man."

"Then I'll pick you up in your suite at eight. Dressy casual. Be prepared for the night of your life."

She wrapped her arms around her waist. His words, the delivery and tone, were exactly like her father's. Every birthday he'd called her, promising her the moon, and for eight long years she'd believed him.

"You know nothing about me, Scott. How can you guarantee me the night of my life?" she asked carefully. Maybe going wasn't a good idea, no matter how tempting he was. Actually, because of how tempting he was. She'd forgotten her own rules. No matter what spin he put on it, Scott Rivers was a gambler. He gambled every day on life, taking risks and issuing dares.

"Touché. That was arrogant." He grinned at her.

"Just a tad."

"I'd like to say it won't happen again, but…"

This time she laughed at him. He was very charming, and she didn't care if it was practiced. This was the man she had to be careful around. The one she'd find it so easy to fall for. For just this once, though, she wanted to enjoy basking in his laughter.

"How about a night of getting to know each other?" he asked, propping one hand on the wall behind her and angling his body closer to hers.

The heat of his body swamped her. She struggled to keep her pulse steady, but it had picked up the minute he'd put his hand on the wall next to her head. He captured one of her curls with his fingers and toyed with the strand. "Why is this important to you?" she asked.

He ran his finger down the side of her face, his touch tentative and very gentle. For the first time in her life she felt…special. Not the go-to girl or the can-handle-anything woman. But as if she was actually the one who needed to be treasured and pampered by a man. *He's just playing you*, she reminded herself. But she liked the way he was treating her—which unsettled what she thought she knew about herself.

He leaned even closer to her. She inhaled his spicy aftershave and the smell of his breath mints. Her breath probably smelled like garlic from the scampi she'd had for lunch. This was why she didn't do the fairy tale thing.

"I can't get you out of my head," he said.

She stopped thinking about her breath and stared up at this man who had to be putting her on. "Lust, eh? I'm not really cover-model material."

"No, you're not. You have something so unique. Something that's just Raine."

His words touched her and she had to swallow. She told herself he was a consummate actor, even though it had been a while since he'd tried his hand at that. A part of her wanted to believe him, but another part was afraid. She'd grown up with her father, the accomplished con man who could promise anything and make everyone including Raine believe it.

"Don't say things like that to me. I prefer honesty."

"As you pointed out, we don't know each other. I just want a chance."

"One chance. But no more of those mushy romance lines that you've doled out to a hundred other women."

"Jeez, I'm not sure you'll fit in my car with that chip on your shoulder. And I think we both know I haven't had a hundred women."

"I don't care if you've had a thousand."

"You will," he said. Lowering his head, he kissed her. His lips brushed hers, and when she opened her mouth to breathe, his tongue slipped past her lips and into her mouth. He tasted her with long, languid strokes of his tongue. She tipped her head to grant him greater access.

Still he didn't hurry. He just leaned there next to her, taking his time and exploring the fire that she'd never wanted to acknowledge was between them. Awareness spread down her body, and she relished the taste of him.

The world fell away and she swayed when his hands skimmed down her back and over her hips and he tugged her closer to him. The wall was solid behind her, and he was solid heat pressed to the front of her. She felt trapped and oddly free because the decision was taken out of her hands. This was the most daring thing she'd done in years.

Her pulse raced, and she knew that something she'd caged long ago had broken free. She reached for his shoulders, but he pulled back.

"Eight," he said, and turned on his heel and walked away.

Scott went back to the set, but he was off his game for the rest of the day. He knew no one else observed it but he felt it inside. For the first time in fifteen years he was distracted by someone. He wasn't just focused on his own pleasures. It was an odd feeling and he wasn't sure he liked it.

But the only time he felt alive was when he was doing something risky, which was why he'd made the bet and was pursuing Raine. Who would've thought pursuing a petite brunette would be the challenge he'd been searching for?

Scott almost blew a really big hand, but brought his attention back to the game at the last minute.

They wrapped for the day, and he noticed that Raine stayed far away from him. Even when she came out of her booth, she gave him and the other players a wide berth. Scott finished up the conversation he was having with Stevie and started slowly stalking her.

She glared at him once so he knew she was aware of his presence. He laughed. She was so sassy and spunky that he couldn't help himself. She might prefer safety and routine, but nothing could dampen the innate fire that burned inside her.

Why was she even trying to hide it? He knew then that the secrets he wanted to unlock in Raine were somehow tied to that passion.

She moved toward the exit, and Scott deftly followed her, blocking the one door off the set. He folded his arms over his chest and leaned back against the wall. She tossed her hair and pivoted on her heel, facing away from him.

"You still have that magic touch with the ladies," a droll voice said behind him.

Scott turned to see one of his closest friends, Hayden MacKenzie—the newly married Hayden. "What can I say? I should bottle my charm."

"Well, it is legendary. Does she not know that? Want me to go talk to her?"

"What are we—in junior high?"

"I don't know. I didn't go to junior high," Hayden said.

Hayden had attended an exclusive boys' school back east. Scott had met him in Europe when they'd both had too much money, too much anger and too much time on their hands. The other man stood a few inches taller than Scott.

"So how's wedded life? Still bliss?"

Hayden smiled and for the first time since Scott had met him he saw a kind of peace in Hayden's eyes. "Can't complain. In fact, Shelby and I are having a dinner party on Friday. Can you come?"

"I might have plans."

"You can bring her with you. Max is flying down from Vancouver, where he's brokering a deal. Deacon and Kylie will be there."

"Okay. But it'll be just me. I don't want Max to feel like the Lone Ranger."

"You know Max. He's never alone for long. See you at nine on Friday."

Hayden walked away and Scott watched his friend leave. He wasn't sure he wanted to be surrounded by his bachelor buddies who'd given up the single life. Scott had been alone for so long.

"Is everything okay?"

He glanced down at Raine. "Yes. Why?"

"Hayden owns the Chimera. I wasn't sure if there was a problem."

"Hayden and I go way back. Besides, he'd speak to you if there was a problem, wouldn't he?"

She shrugged. "I guess. Listen, I'm going to have to work late, editing today's shoot. So we'll have to cancel dinner."

He'd never had to work so hard with a woman, and a part of him toyed with the idea of just stopping his pursuit. He could afford to lose the bet to Stevie. But there was something about Raine that wouldn't let him do that.

"No problem. We'll go whenever you can. My plans are fluid," he said, watching her carefully.

She put her hands on her hips and stared up at him. "I'm not sure how to say this…."

"Stop trying to find excuses. I'm not going to ask you to strip naked in front of a crowd of people. It's just dinner."

She dropped her arms and glanced around the set, which had cleared out except for one camera guy, who was still putting his gear away. "I'm not usually like this. You seem to bring it out in me. Are you sure you want to have dinner?"

"Yes. I'm not feeding you a bunch of BS, Raine. Believe me, I wouldn't work this hard for a woman if I wasn't really interested."

There was a hint of vulnerability on her face before she carefully concealed it. "I'm free now. How about something casual?"

"It's a little early for dinner."

"Maybe we could go do something."

"What do you have in mind?" he asked, sensing with Raine it was better to let her take the lead at first. He sensed she was used to being in charge on the job and off as well.

"Minigolf?"

No way. He had a reputation to live up to. "What are we…ready for the retirement home?"

"Well, what do *you* have in mind?" she asked in that quick-tempered way of hers.

"How much time do you have?" he asked, struggling not to smile at her show of temper.

She consulted her watch. "Four hours."

"One round at the roulette table. Winner picks the next activity."

"I don't gamble."

"Why not?"

"I just don't."

"Rumor has it that you were once a big-time player."

"The *National Enquirer* intimated you had sex with an alien on your yacht in the Mediterranean."

"Then you were a big-time player," he said.

She threw her head back and laughed. "Okay, you win. I'll play roulette with you, but only one game. Whoever wins picks the activity."

"I don't lose," he said, warning her.

"Neither do I."

Raine rubbed her sweaty palms against her jeans and stood in front of the roulette table. She was intimately familiar with this game, having grown up a few blocks from the casinos in Atlantic City. She'd spent her childhood on the boardwalk, staring in at her father, who'd spend a few days playing roulette when he couldn't scrape together enough money to stake himself to a poker game.

Just one small bet. That was all she had to do. She wasn't going to become addicted to gambling by placing one bet. She'd bet Scott on this one game and then she'd take him to the Keno diner on the second floor, sit with him in a vinyl booth and bore him to death so he would move on.

Conning him didn't seem like such an easy thing to do just now. She felt as if she was being torn in two, and the balance and serenity she'd worked so hard to find in her life were now gone.

Her heart was beating too fast, and every minute she spent in his presence made her like him more.

"What are you waiting for?" he asked, making her realize that she'd been staring at the rows of black and red spaces for too long.

She scrambled for an answer. She was used to thinking on her feet in the high-pressure world of television. "You have to have a strategy."

"For roulette?" he asked. "Be careful, Raine. This is just chance. Odds or evens, black or red. That's all you have to decide."

"Well, we all aren't you, Mr. Lucky. I need a strategy. Give me a minute."

Turning away from him, she closed her eyes. Coming to Vegas had been a struggle. She wasn't a gambler by profession, but her heart was always ready to bet on something.

Every day she walked past the odds board in the lobby and mentally bet on something, anything. Prize fights, European sporting events, even the outcome of certain reality shows. She was contractually forbidden from betting on their show, but in her mind she bet every time.

She'd watched her father and brother both spiral out of control and into addiction. Right now they were both living hand-to-mouth existences. And she couldn't help them. When she sent money, they only gambled it away, and when she visited, they wanted her to run one more con. A big score so they'd be set for life.

She was being silly. One little roulette bet wasn't going to turn her into an addict. She took a deep breath and looked up at Scott. "Okay, I'm ready."

"What's your lucky number?" he asked.

She didn't have a lucky number, didn't believe that luck came from numbers or rabbits' feet.

"Don't have one?" he asked, putting his arm around her waist and leaning closer.

They were in the main casino, where anyone could see them. She inched away from him. "No. Why should I?"

"No reason. Mine is thirteen. Want to use it this time?"

"No. I'll take fourteen."

"Okay," he said, reaching around her to drop a few casino chips on the table.

"What are you doing?" she asked. What did it say about the man that he had a pocketful of casino chips?

"This is on me."

She shrugged and placed her bet. She put her chip only on the number, not bettering her odds by playing the color.

"You're going for the bigger payoff just like a real gambler would," he said.

He had no idea. She'd watched her father at the roulette table for so long that she'd played the way he would. His words didn't reassure her, and it took all of her courage to stand her ground and not turn and run from the casino. Her hand actually trembled as she saw the croupier begin the play.

Scott captured her hand and rubbed it against his T-shirt-clad chest. "Don't sweat it, honey. This is just for fun."

She looked up at him and felt the waves of reassurance in him. Despite his playboy image and the way he seemed to glide through life unaffected, she sensed a rock-solid part of this man.

"I know."

"When I win, I'm going to take you for a ride on my Harley out into the desert with the warm wind blowing all around us. Then we'll have dinner at my favorite hole-in-the-wall Mexican place."

That didn't sound dangerous. It sounded fun, thrilling. She'd never been on a motorcycle and a part of her had always wanted to ride one. Especially if she was pressed up against Scott's back. She'd have an excuse to touch him and not have to worry about the consequences for once in her life, not taking the same safe route she'd always chosen.

But he had dared her—and she couldn't pass it up. "I don't know what I'll do when I win. Probably something safe and boring."

He smiled at her then. His expression was so tender that the sounds of the casino faded away, and there was only the two of them. "Nothing with you could be boring."

She turned away from the intensity in his eyes and focused on the table. The ball jumped and bounced and finally landed on fourteen. Raine couldn't believe it.

"I won."

"I saw," he said. His arms came around her waist and he held her to him. "Maybe my luck is rubbing off on you."

"I didn't realize that luck felt like a muscled, masculine body."

He dropped a fierce kiss on her lips. "Luck comes in all kinds of packages."

She had the feeling he was talking about more than slot machines and Vegas winnings. "Bad luck sure does."

"Hey, no talk of bad luck," he said.

"I can't believe this. You lost," she said. And she won. After years of carefully avoiding taking any kind of risk, the first time she bet someone, she won.

"I know."

She stepped away from him, fighting the urge to dance around. She won. For the first time she could understand the appeal of gambling. But she realized her euphoria had as much to do with the fact that she was with Scott as it did with winning.

"Does this ever happen to you?" she asked.

"About as often as I make it with my alien lover."

She laughed and felt free in a way she hadn't in a long time. Scott reminded her of what life could be when she let go of the tight control she kept on herself.

"What now?"

He picked up her winnings. "Let's go cash out, and then the rest of the night is up to you."

The glow of victory still hung around Raine as they stepped away from the cashier and she pocketed her winnings.

"So what's the plan? I think we've got a few hours until you have to be in the editing room."

She glanced at her watch, then tipped her head to the side, studying him. "How do you feel about going to Red Rock? They have a nature trail that's supposed to be pretty awesome and it's not that far from here. I haven't had time to check it out yet."

"Sounds good. I'll drive, unless you want to?"

"No, you can drive. I'm sharing the production van with Tim and Leslie."

Just then Scott became aware of a group of three women who were eyeing him. He knew the second they recognized him. They took a few steps toward him, but Scott wrapped his arm around Raine and made for the exit. She shoved her elbow against his stomach but he refused to budge. He suspected she was worried about Joel or someone from the show catching them together, but he liked the way she felt tucked up against him. "You have a choice."

"Of what?" she asked as they left the casino behind and walked out into the warm spring afternoon.

He put on his sunglasses and led her toward the employee parking garage. Hayden kept the top floor of the garage for his own private vehicles and allowed Scott to store his there, as well. Sometimes Scott thought his entire life was just one long travelogue as he moved from one location to another.

"Of how you want to go," he said, leading her to the garage elevator. He pressed the button for the top floor and then inserted his security key to access the parking level.

"I keep a Hummer H2, a Porsche Boxster and a Harley-Davidson Screamin' Eagle V-Rod here. I don't think we can off-road at Red Rock so the Porsche or the bike would be a better choice."

"Your cars cost more than my house does back in Glendale, California."

He shrugged. "It's just money."

She put one hand on her hip and narrowed her eyes. "Not to everyone."

"Is this going to be an issue?"

She said nothing, and he knew it was. He'd dated women with Raine's outlook before. Some women honestly had a problem with the insane amount of money he had. He recognized it could be an issue and he hated that because the money was part of who he was.

"I started working when I was nine months old," he explained.

She dropped her hand. "I know."

"Then you can't expect me to be poor. I spent my entire childhood earning that money."

"Should I grovel for forgiveness?"

Realizing he had his own problems with this issue, he forced himself to relax. "Maybe later."

"I have money issues in general. It was just a shock to hear you rattle off your list of vehicles."

"Can you get over it?" he asked teasingly.

She tipped her head to the side and gave him one of those looks of hers that cut past all the images he'd cultivated over the years and burned straight to the bone. He should probably stay here in Vegas where he fit in. Out in nature he always felt more like the fraud he was. No longer the actor on a set but out in the elements.

"Yeah," she finally said. "I can get over it—especially if you let me drive the Porsche."

"Didn't you hit the security rail with the production van yesterday?"

She wrinkled her brow. "That story was grossly exaggerated. No damage was done to the van."

"I'll think about letting you drive my car on the way back."

He crossed the parking lot to the Porsche convertible. Opening the trunk, he pulled out two baseball caps. "If we're taking this car you'll need a hat. The sun is hot with the top down. You want the Yankees or the Red Sox?"

"We can't ride in the same car wearing those hats."

"Sure we can. You like to fight. This will make people believe we have a reason."

"I don't like to argue. You're the one who's contrary."

"Really? I'll keep that in mind."

"Why do you have East Coast hats? I thought you grew up in L.A."

"I did. The Sox cap is Hayden's. I picked the Yankees just to needle him."

He opened her door for her. She gave him a strange look before sliding into the car.

"What was that look?"

"Most guys don't hold the door."

"Most guys don't have my mom. She's a stickler for manners and men holding doors."

"She sounds like my kind of woman."

"She's…fierce, I guess. She made sure no one took advantage of me when I was a kid. She still watches out for me now."

"What about your dad?"

"He backs her up when she needs him. But he's content to let her lead the way."

"Sounds like they have a good marriage."

"They do. What about your folks?" he asked as he put down the top on the convertible. Once it was down, he backed out of the parking space and headed to the exit.

"My folks are divorced. My mom remarried when I was sixteen. We're not real close."

"What about your dad?"

"He lives on the East Coast so I don't see him."

"My folks live in Malibu. I see them all the time when I'm in Los Angeles."

She said nothing as he maneuvered the car onto 215 and headed toward Red Rock. "Too bad I didn't think of asking you out sooner. We could have applied for a rock climbing permit."

"I think I'd have a heart attack if I tried to do that."

"It's easy."

"Sure it is. Easy to fall."

"What kind of guy do you think I am? I'd never let you fall."

"Stop it. You sound too good to be true. Remember, I'm on to you and your smooth-talking ways."

If only she were right and he were feeding her lines. But there was something too real about Raine. He'd felt her pain when she'd spoken quietly of her lack of parental contact. He wanted to sweep her into his arms and promise she'd never be alone again.

No matter how much she intrigued him, this would be the same as every other relationship in his life. Fleeting and memorable.

Three

A tense silence filled the car as they entered the Red Rock Canyon National Conservation Area. The area had some of the best examples of the Mojave Desert terrain in Nevada. Raine had never been an outdoorsy girl. But there was something so clean about being here now. Especially compared to the overdeveloped Vegas strip where she'd been spending all her time. She closed her eyes and breathed deeply.

"You okay?"

"Yeah," she said, realizing that she was. The bet with Scott, the constant fear she felt being close to gambling, even her own tension about his interest in her dropped away. Within moments there was nothing but the two of them and nature.

"Sure?"

"Yes, I was just thinking how different this is from Vegas. I have to warn you that even though I suggested this, I'm not really a nature girl."

"That's okay. I am."

"You're a nature girl?"

"Ha, nature boy. Seriously, I spend all my free time outside."

For a man who had the world at his fingertips, he spent a lot of his time like any other guy his age.

"I still can't believe this place is so close to our hotel," she said, offering a tentative olive branch to Scott. This was a mistake, she thought. Her gut had said it from the beginning, but she'd foolishly thought she could dip one foot into the world she'd always forbidden herself.

She'd been out of the game too long to pull a con on this guy and she knew it. Besides, her hormones were making it difficult to concentrate on conning him. She wanted to just tip her head back and enjoy being around Scott. This man who'd been acting before he could walk or talk. This man who made his living betting on everything under the sun.

"Me, neither," he said. He pulled into the visitor center parking lot. Turning to look at her, he tugged off his sunglasses, but his eyes still weren't visible under the brim of his Red Sox cap. "Have you been here before?"

His tone was conversational. No more flirting. She wasn't disappointed. Really, she wasn't. "No. I read about it in the area information in my room."

"I've been here a few times. How adventurous are you feeling?" he asked, a hint of speculation in his eyes.

"Moderate." She suspected he was talking about more than the trail. And she'd never been adventurous; she'd always chosen the safe and sane route. Even her career, which was in a field that was constantly changing, had always been stable. Being unadventurous was her one goal in life.

"What would it take to bump that up?" he asked.

"I don't know. Maybe getting to know you a little better?"

He nodded and put his sunglasses back on. "What kind of shoes are you wearing?"

"Why?" she asked.

"There's a trail that involves some climbing and leads to a waterfall. But if you don't have hiking boots on…"

"I don't. Plus I'm not really very athletic."

"Then how about an easy trail?" He pulled a well-thumbed-through guidebook from the side pocket on the door. "Can you do two miles round trip?"

"I guess driving through the park is out of the question?"

Considering he'd only arrived in Vegas a few days ago, Raine thought, he seemed very comfortable and at home here. But then he was a gambler, so he'd probably spent a fair amount of time in Sin City. She had the feeling that he was always at home, wherever he was.

She envied him that. She was still searching to find that kind of peace deep inside herself. And she knew she needed things around her. The same things, the same routines, the same people, to find her comfort level.

He was a chameleon, she reminded herself. He changed to fit all of his surroundings, and she'd do well to remember that.

"Hell, yes, it's out of the question. I really want to do the Ice Box trail but I don't think you're up to it."

"Fine. I can go two miles. I do more than that at the Galleria during the holidays."

Raine went into the ranger station to register them while Scott gathered supplies. She met him back in the parking lot five minutes later and found him talking baseball with two guys.

"There's my lady," he said, leaving the men and joining her.

"I'm your lady?" she asked.

She'd never belonged to any man before. She'd had sex with exactly two men in her life. Her first boyfriend had been in college, and that had lasted one semester. The second guy had been looking for a job in the industry and saw her as the most expedient route to where he wanted to go.

She knew that she was to blame for her love life. She didn't trust men or even want to trust them. She liked her career and got by focusing on that. This current situation with Scott was just a con. She tried to remember that, but it was hard.

"I want you to be my lady," he said, leading the way out of the parking lot and toward the Moenkopi Loop.

She wished he'd stop saying things like that. But it fit perfectly with his bet, and she realized she had to keep her mind sharp. That was another of her dad's lessons—don't forget the end goal.

But Scott was different. He made her want to reevaluate her life. Take stock in where she was—almost thirty and still single. And he made her want to change things, to forget she was very happy with who she was.

"Why are you here?" she asked when they found the trail and walked side by side. Get to know the mark, she thought.

"You asked me to come."

"Ha-ha, smart-ass. I meant, why are you doing the show?" she asked, focusing on Scott and not on how easily the rules of grifting were returning to her.

"I'm friends with Joel Tanner. He needed a name to take to the networks."

Joel was the executive producer on the show. He was riding a string of popular hits on television that threatened to rival Aaron Spelling's golden touch in the eighties and nineties. Raine found him to be a fair man most of the time. She didn't have to deal with him too often, which she liked. He was also her boss, so if this thing with Scott didn't work out, Scott had the inside track on making sure she never worked again. "That was nice of you."

"That's the kind of guy I am," he said, arching his eyebrow at her.

"I think you adjust to being the right guy for every situation." She'd observed it from watching him on the set. Scott was literally the right man in every situation. Just like with those guys in the parking lot, he could fit in with any group at a moment's notice. It was a little unnerving to Raine because she'd never really fit in anywhere.

He stopped walking. The sun was dipping into the horizon, and a nice breeze stirred through the underbrush. "What's that mean?"

She heard something moving through the shrubs and edged closer to Scott. He made her feel safe. For a minute she forgot that she didn't need anyone to protect her and just basked in the warmth of his body.

"Well?"

She should have kept her mouth shut. "That you fit in everywhere. I've seen you with poker players, laid-back and joking. With Joel, serious and discussing business. With those baseball fans, just another guy upset by the steroids scandal."

"I'm well-rounded."

She heard that noise again. "Did you hear that? What kind of animals are out here?"

"Don't worry about them."

"I'm not."

He gave her a skeptical look. "Are you worried about me?"

"I'm not scared of you," she said, forcing her gaze away from the small brush and up to the panoramic view. Nature was nice and everything, but suddenly she just wanted to be back in Vegas where she was dealing with things she could see and understand. Whatever was moving in the brush…that was unknown.

"I'm still waiting to hear what you meant by your comment."

The key to a good con was to act like you believed the situation was real up to the moment you walked away, she remembered. And it wasn't hard to do with Scott because she liked him. Deep inside, a part of her mourned the relationship they could have had.

"I don't know. It seems like you change in each situation. You become exactly what the setting demands. Almost like you're acting."

"Maybe I am," he said. "But that's the only way I know how to be."

Scott eased the car to the side of the road just outside the Red Rocks Park. He'd steered the conversation away from himself after she'd dropped her bomb about acting being his only way of coping. And he'd kept them moving on the path. What would she say if she knew he was doing this for a bet?

What the hell had he been thinking? Stevie really pissed him off, because now Scott knew that he had to overcome those obstacles in addition to the natural weariness that Raine exhibited around him.

He never accurately counted the cost when he took a bet like this one. It didn't matter that he'd dared himself to spend time with Raine long before Stevie had caught him getting the cold shoulder and made it into a wager. The results were the same. He felt wild and out of control. He liked it too much to complain about it.

But that didn't mean he wanted her to see his flaws. He'd carefully cultivated a hip image to make it seem as if he was flawless. He wasn't one of those child stars who'd gone down the road to addiction, because his parents simply wouldn't have tolerated it. And Scott was in his heart of hearts a good guy.

Raine deserved to know that guy. Not the man who'd made a bet about getting her into bed. A stronger man might be able to walk away from Raine. But Scott couldn't. There was something about her that had already gotten under his skin, keeping him in a state of semiarousal all the time.

He shut off the engine as he stopped on the shoulder. Time to let Raine live a little. She was too buttoned up most of the time, and he suspected she was hiding.

"What are we stopping for? Is something wrong with the car?" she asked. She'd had her head back against the headrest but sat up, uncrossing her long legs and pushing her baseball cap off her head.

Her hair was unruly and he liked the way it looked. Her face was flushed from the exercise. He wanted nothing more than to just lean over and bury his face against her neck. Inhale the fragrance of woman and kiss her there.

This was doing nothing to cool him off. But he suspected nothing was going to do that. Raine was a fire in his blood.

"No. I thought I'd let you drive," he said. He wanted more than one afternoon with her. The intriguing Ms. Raine Montgomery was still a mystery to be solved.

"Really?" she asked, her eyes widening.

He leaned back in the seat, crossing his arms over his chest. "Unless you don't want to."

"Of course I want to," she said.

"Do you have any tickets on your license?" he asked, to tease her.

She shook her head, very earnest now, and he ached inside at how innocent she looked.

"Are you kidding? The words *safe driver* were invented for me."

He realized that the bet was going to haunt him, because a woman like Raine was too soft to ever forgive that action. In fact, he wasn't too sure he could forgive himself.

He forced himself to continue the game he'd started. "Hmm. Let me get this straight. You don't have adventures, no tickets, no dating. What do you call that incident with the guardrail?"

She grabbed his hands in hers. "A fluke. Really I'm so safe I usually drive *under* the speed limit."

"What do you do for fun?" he asked because he really wanted to know. Whatever she did, he'd take it up. Even if she said minigolf.

"I have a life," she said defensively.

He'd been teasing her and hadn't expected this reaction. "I was kidding. And hoping you didn't say minigolf."

"I know, but when you say it like that…I seem like

a really boring person who does nothing but work. And there's nothing wrong with minigolf."

In her voice he heard the criticism she must endure from time to time. Like the comments he got about his lack of direction and seemingly unfocused lifestyle. Few people realized the extent of the charitable work he did or that he'd spent the past five years bailing out friends who'd lost it all in the dot-com bust.

"You could be a lady with an exciting job," he said, because he knew she liked her life. Raine wasn't a woman to stay in a job she didn't love.

He slid his hand along the back of her seat, capturing a handful of her curls in his hand. She had the softest damned hair he'd ever touched.

"I think I am. You know, I've wanted to be in show business since I was in junior high school."

He wanted to know every detail of her childhood. Maybe it would help him figure out what made her tick. He already knew she wasn't close to her parents. "Really? Did you always want to stay behind the camera?"

She tilted her head back, rubbing her scalp against his wrist. He changed his grip on her hair so that he could rub her head.

"Yes. I'm not really a spotlight person. And I really like telling everyone what to do."

"I've never noticed that."

"I must be being too easy on you." She turned to face him and gave him a long, measuring look.

"Actually, I'd say the opposite is true. Everyone else gets teased but me. Even Stevie, with his skull-and-crossbones tattoo, gets the soft edge of your tongue, but I see only the…"

"Say it," she said.

"The defensive side of you. What is it about me?" he asked.

"Nothing. Don't project your feelings onto me."

"I'm not. It can't be that I'm a quasi-celebrity."

She snorted. "You're an über-celebrity. But that has nothing to do with my supposed attitude."

"It's not the money thing, either, though we've already established that doesn't earn me any favors."

"I don't know what you're driving at."

"Me, neither, but I'm a patient man, honey. And I'm not going to be satisfied until I figure you out."

"I thought you were going to let me drive."

"I am."

She calmly unfastened her seat belt and opened the door. "Are you sure?"

He climbed out of the car and met her halfway around it. "Stop asking me or I'll change my mind."

She tipped her head to one side. It was something he knew she did when she was pondering something. He'd seen her do it on the set a few times, and earlier before she'd chosen number fourteen on the roulette table. "No, you won't. You don't say things you don't mean."

"How do you know that?" he asked, because he thought he played that one close to the chest. He liked to be the rambling man. The one with no commitments, the one no one asked anything of.

"I've been watching you while we shoot," she said.

That was why he'd accepted Stevie's bet. It gave him an added incentive to stay on this rocky road that led to Raine. He'd realized after the first day on the set that he was interested in her, but it had taken him a little longer to ascertain that she wanted him, too. "Really? And you picked that up."

"Yes. You're a very rock-solid man."

He couldn't help but grin. "Around you, anyway."

"Was that a sex crack?"

"Yes, ma'am, it was. I don't want you to put me into some buddy box. I'm not doing this to be your buddy."

"You're doing this to get me into bed?"

Yes, but he was smart enough not to admit it. "Nah, but I figure letting you drive the Porsche will make it more likely that you'll let me kiss you when we get back to the hotel."

"We've already kissed," she said.

"So?"

"You want more?"

"Don't you?"

"I haven't decided yet. You're a little too…dangerous."

"I'm harmless," he said, and he was for her. He'd never met another woman he wanted as badly as he wanted Raine.

"Tell that to my heart," she said quietly, slipping behind the wheel.

Raine got out of the car at the front of the Chimera, tossing the keys to Scott. She was starting to feel like a manic-depressive. Scott evoked so many different reactions in her. She felt the same sense of panic she always did.

She glanced at her watch and thought she still had forty-five minutes before she had to meet Larry at the editing suite. But she needed a break. A chance to quiet herself and figure out what was really going on here.

"We cut it kind of close. I'd better run."

"Wait up," he said.

"I can't."

She pivoted on her heel and started toward the hotel and then realized that she was running away. She'd promised herself when she left Atlantic City more than ten years ago that her running days were behind her.

She turned back around. Scott was standing by his car watching her. What was she going to say? She knew she had to keep it light. She could do that. Just flirt a little and he'd never guess at the turmoil inside her.

"Let me give the keys to the valet and I'll walk you back to the editing suite."

She nodded and slipped away from the crowd to wait for him near the front doors. She hated this about herself. This thing she'd never been able to control. As a child she remembered countless days standing on the boardwalk while her father played grueling, hours-long poker games and her mother was working two jobs. She looked like an abandoned waif so her father could take money from well-meaning people who took pity on her.

Scott made her feel that way again. Unsure of

herself. She shook her head and pushed away from the wall. This wasn't his fault, but hers. He reminded her of all the tantalizing and forbidden things she liked. And that made her uneasy.

She knew she was losing control of her own con. Especially when she realized two P.A.s—production assistants—were standing on the valet line. Damn. She had to get away now.

"You okay?" he asked.

She pulled the baseball cap lower on her head and walked at a clipped pace toward the hotel door. "I think I see a couple of P.A.s from the show."

"I'm an expert at evasion," he said, pulling her under his shoulder and hustling them through the lobby and into an alcove. He kept her tucked up against his side, blocking her with his body.

"How's that?" he asked.

"Good." Too good, she thought. He was an expert at evasion. Not only of the kind they just did but of the emotional kind. Every time she got close to figuring him out, he danced out of her reach again.

She pushed against his chest, but he wouldn't budge.

"What are you doing?" he asked.

"Trying to get away from you." She bit her lip as soon as the words left her mouth. Great. She wasn't supposed to show him any weakness.

"Why?"

"I'm not used to that kind of exercise. I think you wore me out," she lied, but then made the mistake of glancing up at him. His face was classically handsome, with a strong jaw and firm lips…lips she wanted to feel against her own.

She leaned up and toward him, then realized what she was doing and pulled back. Get a grip, she told herself. You can't kiss him until you have some objectivity back in place. Still, she wanted to.

To hell with her plans. She wanted to feel his mouth moving on hers and his arms around her. Really around her, not just holding her to keep her concealed from prying eyes.

"Thanks for letting me drive your car," she said, praying he'd accept the subject change.

"No problem. Next time I'll get us some bikes so we can do some of the awesome bike trails up there."

She shuddered. She'd suggested Red Rock because it would get them away from the rest of the cast and crew who might see them. But she wasn't sure she could go back and try anything else. "Are you kidding? I can barely make it around the block at my house in Glendale. I'm never going to be able to bike down a trail."

"Well, something else then. Maybe I'll let you take the Harley for a spin sometime, too."

"I don't think so," she said. "I think the coast is clear now."

He glanced over his shoulder and nodded, stepping away. She following him through the air-conditioned luxury of the Chimera's lobby.

He put his hand under her elbow as they walked. She knew it was an old-fashioned gesture, but she liked it.

She also liked the way he slowed his pace to hers. Hell, she plain liked too much about Scott Rivers.

And that was her main problem. She didn't want to like him. Not his friendly smile or his sexy tush. She wanted to not notice those things and find a way back to the adversarial relationship they'd had before this afternoon.

When they reached the bank of elevators, they waited with a small crowd. Raine felt unkempt in her jeans and T-shirt, sweaty from being outdoors, and out of place in the world of the well-groomed people.

Scott slid his arm around her waist and tugged her under his shoulder, holding her protectively.

"What are you doing?" she asked, hoping that he didn't hear the trembling note in her voice. This wasn't like her. But she'd always wanted to be held like this.

"Using you."

Now that was something she was used to from the men in her life. Her backbone stiffened as she realized that her con was the only safe way she could stay around Scott. Otherwise she'd give him too much ammunition to hurt her. "As what?"

"Camouflage. I think those women over there are hunting men."

He gestured toward three women with well-coiffed hair, dressed like Paris Hilton, in haute couture from their scantily covered midriffs to their Jimmy Choo clad feet.

No one could ever mistake Raine as part of that group. She glanced down at her scruffy old Nikes and jeans. "And you're the next target on the list?"

He arched his eyebrows at her. "At the risk of sounding arrogant…yes."

She put her arm around his back and hugged him close to her. Those girls reminded her of Missy Talbot. Immediately she felt as if she was in high school again. Only this time, she was on the arm of the sexiest man in the room.

It was a heady feeling for about a second, before she remembered why he was here. This was his game—but she was playing it to win. She put her arm around his lean waist. "How's this?"

"Slip your hand into my front pocket."

She narrowed her eyes at him. She was physically tired from hiking, emotionally fatigued from the conflict inside her about Scott, and she wanted him too much to keep her hands to herself. "Why?"

"For effect. So they'll know I'm yours and to keep their hands off."

She pushed her hand into his front pants pocket, brushing past the casino chips and feeling the heat of his thigh through the lining.

"Now move it down a little and over."

She snatched her hand back. "Pervert."

He laughed. That deep rumbling one he had that made her want to just bask in it all day. This was why she needed to get away. She was forgetting the lessons she'd learned early in life. A con man wasn't a bad or evil man; grifters were gregarious people with larger-than-life personalities. That was how they lured in their victims.

"What are you thinking?" he asked, suddenly very serious.

"Nothing." Scott was a nice guy on one level and she thought about what she'd do if this was real and not some bet he was trying to win. He wouldn't deserve the baggage she was packing. "I'm thinking that I know better than to get involved with a sex fiend."

"I'm not a fiend. I just like things…earthy."

"You're dangerous to womankind. I can't believe I helped you out. You would have been fine on your own."

The elevator doors opened and he led her into the car, taking a spot against the back wall. No one entered behind them, and once the doors closed they were alone.

She busied herself pressing the button for her floor. She hoped to get a shower before she had to work all night. Glancing over at Scott, she realized he was watching her.

"What? Do I have dirt on my face?" she asked, rubbing her cheeks.

He said nothing, just closed the small gap between them. He took her face in his hands and tilted her head back. "You look wonderful. Too wonderful for a man like me."

"What does that mean?" she asked, afraid she knew the answer. He was, after all, a man who'd made a bet he could get her into bed.

Instead of answering her, he lowered his head and brushed his lips against hers. Her lips fluttered open under his, and his tongue slowly penetrated the barrier of her mouth. She was aware that she was allowing him to use sex to change the subject…but she didn't want to stop him now.

Four

Raine tasted like the wild wind right before a summer storm. He tunneled his fingers into her hair and tilted her head back to give him greater access to her mouth. He framed her face with his thumbs on her cheeks and tasted her languidly with his tongue.

He swept his hands down her back and anchored her to him with his hands on her rump. Shifting around, he leaned back against the wall and pushed one of his legs between hers.

All his plans for a nice and easy seduction had gone out the window. He wanted her too much. When she arched her back, he pulled her more firmly into his body. He lifted his head and noticed her eyes were closed.

Carefully he brushed his mouth over both of her eyelids and then trailed his lips back to hers. He had to taste her again. He had a thirst for her that could never be quenched. A kind of thirst that had always been there. For the first time he felt he might be close to finding what he'd been longing for.

She was shorter than he was and smaller. She made him feel like a big he-man who could toss his woman over his shoulder and carry her off. And he really couldn't go to bed with her without telling her about the bet. He knew he couldn't go back to Stevie and say he'd changed his mind.

She pulled back and stared up at him with her eyes wide. He was pushing too hard and he knew it. The spur wasn't Stevie and that damned bet but the fact that he'd wanted her for so long. And she was still keeping him waiting.

"Still not afraid of me?" he asked. He didn't want her to be. He wanted to be able to figure out what role he had to play to win her. Not because of the money but because he felt good around Raine.

She shook her head and edged away from him. He closed his eyes and searched for that place he always found. That calm oasis that enabled him to forget to be the real Scott Rivers and instead play a role.

But it wasn't working. All he saw in his mind was Raine lying on his bed, her hair spread on the pillow, her small frame naked and her luscious curves bare to his touch.

"Scott?" she asked, her voice soft and pleading.

"Give me a minute," he said. His own voice sounded harsh and almost guttural, but having her in his arms was more than he'd expected. He made himself recite dialoguefrom his last action flick in his head until his body was at least a little back under his control.

"That got a little out of control," he said.

She rubbed her fingers over her lips. "You're right. I'm sorry…I can't do this."

"Do what?"

She shook her head. "Listen, no one on the tour is supposed to get involved, and that goes double for me and someone as high profile as you."

"Joel's not going to give a damn what I do. And I'm not really high profile." He didn't like that she was right. That she had a legitimate reason to back away from him. Why did she keep finding barriers for them?

"He's my boss and unlike you, rich boy, I need this job."

That made him feel like an insensitive cad. He knew he should have considered the implications to her job more carefully. And with Stevie already knowing he was after Raine…the complications were endless. He turned, grabbing her waist and pulling her back to him.

"Don't make me out to be some sort of spoiled celebrity with more money than compassion."

"Then don't act like one. Let me go."

"I don't want to. Not yet. I'm sorry for grabbing you like that but my hands are still tingling from touching you and I'm not ready to let go."

"Scott, don't toy with me. I'm not used to playing in your league and I'm not sure I know the rules."

"What rules?"

"The rules for affairs."

"Do people still have affairs?" he asked, toying with one of her curls.

"Did you want something more lasting?" There was something in her eyes he couldn't read. Something that made him feel like maybe this was a test and he knew in his gut that he wouldn't pass it. This was the normal-life thing he always screwed up.

Because he did want more with her. His instincts said take this woman and hold on to her. For how long he had no idea. But he knew he wanted her for the foreseeable future.

"That's what I thought. I'm not sure I want to risk my career for you."

This time, when she pushed against his chest, he let her go. She started down the hall and he followed her, watching that sexy ass of hers in those skin-tight-oughta-be-illegal jeans she was wearing. Damn, he'd screwed up and had no idea how to make this right.

"Dammit, woman, you need to buy some new jeans."

"What's wrong with these?" she asked.

"They are too damn tight." He had the feeling this wasn't winning him any points. But he knew he wasn't the only man to notice her ass, especially in those jeans.

"Stop cussing. That's a sign of low intelligence."

That stopped him in his tracks. He knew she was right. "I'm smart enough for you."

"I didn't say you weren't. Just that you were swearing too much."

"You bring that out in me."

"Makes me wonder why you're following me," she said, pausing in front of her hotel room door.

"I told you, I can't get you out of my mind."

"Not my problem, Scott."

"I think you're a chicken."

"That's not very mature, just because I don't want to have a… What did you decide we should call it?"

"We'll stick with your word."

"Just because I don't want to have an affair doesn't mean I'm scared."

"No, it doesn't. The fact that you run from everything that doesn't fit in your neat little life does."

She looked like she was going to smack him. He waited for it, knowing he'd pushed too hard and gone too far. But Raine needed someone who didn't accept the boundaries she laid down.

She swallowed and turned her key card over in her hand. "I… You might be right. But I can't deal with you and the possibility of losing my job."

"What if I square things with Joel? I'm doing this TV show as a favor to him."

"No. Please don't mention this to anyone. I think I'd die of embarrassment."

"Don't want to be seen with me?"

She bit her lower lip. "Don't want to be speculated about."

Scott knew then that he'd made a huge mistake in

letting Stevie goad him into making the bet. Raine was intensely private, and in a flash he knew that was why she'd given him such a difficult time. She wasn't sure how to handle him and the baggage he brought with him. No way was she ever going to understand why he'd made the bet. Right now Scott himself didn't understand what the hell he'd been thinking.

He reached out and tugged her into his arms, settling her so that her head rested against his chest. He wanted to make promises, the kind always made in romantic movies, but he knew he wasn't that sort of guy. And he knew that Raine would know the line for what it was.

"Take a chance on me, honey, and I promise you won't regret it."

Taking a chance on Scott was more tempting than she vowed he'd ever know. Tempting in the real sense. Tempting because she wanted to forget that he'd made a callous bet about her and really believe the lines he was feeding her.

She closed her eyes, slid her arms around his waist and just held him. The spicy scent of his aftershave surrounded her. His chest was solid, muscled. Not the chest of a pampered rich boy. She knew then that there was so much more to Scott than met the eye.

Was there more to the bet than she'd observed? She didn't know and in this moment she didn't care. She pretended for a moment that she wasn't the director of a television show that he was one of the stars of. She pretended that she wasn't the daughter of a gambler who knew better than to believe a man in the middle of a heady winning streak. Pretended that for once her luck had changed and this man was the fantasy, not the imitation she knew him to be.

In the distance she heard the elevator car ding. She stayed where she was until she heard voices heading their way. Sneaking around was a pain in the butt, but she wasn't sure enough of anything to risk her job. They couldn't afford to be seen together like this. Forget the con and the game she was playing, her job was on the line.

She pushed away from Scott. "Someone's coming. I've got to go."

She saw Scott narrow his eyes, and it bothered her that he knew she was trying to push him away so she could hide. She wished he'd let her get away with it. She glanced furtively down the hall. "The hiking was nice. Thanks for letting me drive your car."

He shook his head. "I want to finish our conversation and not be rushed away."

The voices were coming closer and she recognized one of them as Joel. "Please, Scott."

He smiled down at her so sweetly she almost believed him for a minute. Almost believed that he was real and genuine. "Anything, sweetheart, when you ask like that."

He ambled down the hallway and out of sight just as Joel walked around the corner with Andy, Raine's assistant director.

"Talk to you later, Joel," Andy said, entering the

room right next to Raine's. Her hands shook as she realized how close she'd come to getting caught alone with Scott. Not that they'd been doing anything. Jeez, did she have a guilty conscience or what?

"Got a minute to talk to me?" Joel asked as soon as they were alone.

"Sure. Come in." She opened the door and let him into the minisuite with separate sitting area.

Joel was in his forties, tall and handsome in a classical way. But underneath that boy-next-door facade she'd heard rumors that he was a bad boy. She personally didn't see it but that could have had more to do with the fact that Joel had always treated her like a little sister.

"What did you want to talk about?"

He took a deep breath and walked over to the plate-glass windows that looked down over the Vegas strip. "I noticed you and Scott in the casino earlier."

"Uh, I can explain."

He held his hand up. "You don't need to. Just make sure it doesn't go any further than flirting, Raine."

She nodded. Joel turned the conversation to business, but inside Raine was in turmoil. She was risking everything she worked hard for and for what? To prove something to Scott.

She wished that were true but she knew she was taking the risk because she genuinely liked him and he'd hurt her. And right then she knew she'd made the wrong choice. Whatever she'd intended, it wasn't worth it. The afternoon spent with Scott had proved that she really did like him, and if she spent any more time in his company she was going to fall for him.

Joel left a few minutes later, and Raine sank to the floor of her room, knees drawn up and her head resting on them. What was she going to do?

Her body still tingled with arousal from Scott's kisses. She wanted that man. It had nothing to do with his bet or her supposed con of him. And everything to do with body chemistry and sexual awareness. She wished for a minute that those reasons were enough for her to go to bed with him, but knew she couldn't do so until the taping wrapped up.

There was a knock on the door and she knew before she opened it that it would be Scott. She pulled him into her room before Andy opened his door.

"Did Joel talk to you?"

"Yes," she said, crossing to the small love seat that faced the windows and sinking down on it.

"What'd he want?"

"Nothing."

"Nothing?" he asked, sitting down next to her, so close she felt the heat of his body through the thin layer of her clothing.

She closed her eyes but that just made it worse. With every breath she took she inhaled his heady masculine scent. He stretched his arm along the back of the love seat and touched her face with just his fingertips.

She opened her eyes, surprised to see the concern in

his gaze as he watched her. "You're not a good enough actor to lie convincingly. I know he upset you. Tell me what he said."

She shook her head. She'd lied convincingly for the first twelve years of her life, and this man looked at her and saw…what? She didn't know. But he didn't see her past, and that warmed her deep inside.

"You can't fool a professional actor."

"I don't want to fool you. I just want to—"

He leaned over and put his fingers over her lips. They were warm and smooth. "Tell me what Joel said."

"He warned me to stay away from you."

"Ah, I thought that might be the case. What should we do? I have to be honest here, Raine, I don't want to let this end."

Because of the bet? she wondered. Was she really worth fifty thousand dollars to him? The thought of money changing hands because of her actions was abhorrent. She should call him on it.

Before she could say anything, he pulled her closer, wrapped his arms around her and just held her. No one in her entire life had done that. "We'll figure this out, sweetheart."

She blinked her eyes to keep from crying at the sweetness of the moment. She felt protected in his arms, something she'd never felt before, and she didn't want to lose that.

This was what she'd always hated about running a con. For her there was no easy switch off of the emotions needed to convince a mark that she was sincere.

And that kiss… Hell, that had had nothing to do with any kind of plan. That had been solely for herself.

That had been the kind of kiss she'd been wanting until she'd heard him making his wager with Stevie.

She looked at him. "Why are you here?"

He framed her face with his hands. She loved the way he did that. Got up close with her and made her feel…like she was special.

"I'm here because you intrigue me."

She pushed to her feet and moved away from him to the window. She stared out at the Vegas strip. Her room afforded her a view of the Golden Dream next door and the huge man-made waterfall that ran every half hour. She watched that, hoping it would make her remember that Vegas was all one big illusion.

Fake waterfalls instead of the real thing they'd seen at Red Rock. Nothing that happened here was real. Nothing that happened here translated into the real world. Even though this was her home for three weeks, next month she'd be in Glendale and back to her normal life.

He came up behind her, just stood there not touching her. She saw his reflection in the glass, noticed the way he watched her. "This is exactly why I came back to your room."

She didn't respond to that. She was used to freezing men out with her cold shoulder, but for some reason that didn't work with Scott.

"It's not going to work," he said as if she'd responded to him. "I'm not going to walk away from you, Raine. I think we have something worth exploring."

She turned to face him. "Then be honest. I'm not willing to risk everything for a guy who won't be honest with me."

Scott froze. Did she know more than she was letting on? Did she realize that he was the kind of man who always pretended to be whatever man would best fit the situation?

"That's easier said than done." He pushed his hands through his hair and took two steps away from her.

"You're asking me to take a big chance with you," she said.

When had life gotten so complicated? This was the first time he hadn't been able to glibly talk his way into what he wanted. His words, always his ally, deserted him. His body was on fire for her and he didn't care about anything but Raine. "I know. I just…"

"Expected to get by on charm?"

He had to smile at the way she said it. Because that was exactly what he'd expected. It should bother him that she knew him so well, but a part of him knew it was right that she did. Because he could see past her defenses, as well. "It usually works."

She smiled back at him, and he was reminded of how much he liked her spunk. "Maybe that's part of your problem. You're too used to getting your own way."

"Hello, pot, it's the kettle calling."

She threw her head back and laughed. His gut tightened, and arousal spread slowly throughout his body. His heartbeat accelerated as he remembered every essence of her kiss and how her body had felt pressed to his.

He wanted her. Whatever he had to do, whoever he had to be to make it happen, he would do it.

She tipped her head to the side, staring over at him. She licked her lower lip, and he wondered if she could still taste him. He wanted to taste her again. To just hold her in his arms on the bed and kiss her until he knew all the secrets of her mouth.

"Scott?"

"What?" he asked, knowing what he felt was revealed in his body. No matter how good he was at acting, there was no disguising his reaction to her.

"You're looking at me like…"

Like he wanted to toss her on that bed and make love to her all night. Even then he had the feeling he still wouldn't be sated. What he felt for Raine was too intense for one night to ever be enough. "Like a starving man looks at a tray of food."

She scrunched her face up and moved away from him, propping one hip on the small table that occupied the sitting area. "I'm not sure that's a compliment."

"How could it be anything else?" he asked, pacing toward her. No matter how close he got to her she was always dancing just out of his reach.

"If you're starving, anything would look good," she said, arching one eyebrow at him as if daring him to argue.

"Well, let's just say I've been in the grocery store, and nothing looks appealing except you."

"Scott, didn't your mama tell you not to say things like that?"

He knew his mom would kick his ass if she knew what he'd been up to in Vegas. He also sensed she'd really like Raine. Scott knew he had to figure out how to keep her, keep their secret and keep Stevie from being the wiser. "All she told me was women need to be told the truth."

"And that relates to the grocery store how?" she asked.

He glanced at his watch, knowing she had a job to do and probably needed to head out in a few minutes. But they had just enough time for one more kiss. "You're the only woman I see who attracts me, Raine."

"I'm not exactly model material."

He hid a smile. That was precisely why he wanted her. He liked the way she looked. She was fresh and unique, not enhanced by Botox or plastic surgery, just one hundred percent real woman. And she didn't act like other women did around him. She didn't treat him as if he was something special.

She treated him as she did everyone else. And that was telling. Unfortunately, she kept everyone at arm's length, but he was determined to find a way around her barriers.

"You are perfect the way you are."

"I wish I could believe you."

"It's easy. Just do it." The best way he knew to convince her that he wanted her—not just any other woman—was to take her in his arms. But he knew that she didn't trust that. That his reputation as a playboy was tripping him up here with her.

"If only I could. But I heard you with Latesha in makeup earlier."

"She's gorgeous and full of life. I love Latesha."

"I adore her, too, but I think your mirror might be off. We are nothing alike."

"Exactly. I'm not like every other man you've met before, honey. I see things differently."

"But how can you? You grew up in the land of the lovely people."

"That's why. I see past the perfection to the shallowness, the emptiness that is usually inside. Not in everyone. But I developed a way of finding out what was real."

"Tell me how you do it."

"Why?"

"So that I can use it on you."

"Honey," he said, moving closer to her. When she said things like that she broke his heart. He lifted her onto the table and stepped between her legs.

He tipped her head back and lowered his mouth to hers. He felt her hands at his waist and struggled to stay in control of his lust.

Her phone rang and she leaned around him to grab the handset. "Montgomery."

She listened for a minute, one hand caressing his chest while she talked. "I'll be right there. Sorry, I lost track of time."

She hung up and glanced up at him. "I've got to go. You cost me a shower, Rivers."

"I wish I'd known. We could have had our discussion in the bathroom."

"I bet," she said, pulling his head down to her. She bit his bottom lip then soothed it with her tongue. "You're not in charge of this."

She hopped off the table and headed toward the door. And like a man he followed her.

Five

Scott had spent the past four hours hanging with Hayden and watching him finesse the many whales in the casino. He'd hoped to find Stevie and call off the bet, but the rocker wasn't to be found. Once Shelby's lingerie shop in the hotel closed, Hayden disappeared and Scott watched his friend go. He'd never seen Hayden happier and more…he didn't want to say it, but alive. It was as if Shelby had given Hayden something he couldn't find on his own.

A big part of Scott wanted that. He wanted what Hayden had found, but he wasn't sure he wanted it forever. Over the course of his life "forever" had proved to be something rather short-lived. Something told him betting about taking Raine wasn't going to be conducive to finding the kind of relationship Hayden had.

He checked his watch and realized that Raine would be finishing up her editing session. Trying to be nonchalant, he cruised on by the editing suite and lounged against the wall, waiting.

Richard Weed, the show's main editor, emerged first. Nodding to Scott, he said, "You were a little off today."

Scott shrugged. He knew it was because of Raine. She wasn't the only one with job security issues. If he didn't figure her out he was going to probably get kicked off the game in the next few days.

He realized he'd made a huge tactical error in coming down here. Now another person from the crew had seen them together. "I need to talk to the director about the shoot tomorrow."

"Whatever, man, I'm out of here." He walked past Scott down the long hallway that led back to the main casino area.

A few minutes later Raine stepped out of the editing suite and paused. She'd pulled her thick hair back into a ponytail, and loose tendrils curled around her face. She had on a pair of tortoise-rimmed glasses that made her look adorable.

She pulled them off and rubbed the bridge of her nose as she studied him. After glancing up and down the hallway, she asked, "What are you doing here?"

"I wanted to see you again tonight. You feel up to a little gambling?"

"Not really, and Joel already caught us in the casino once."

"How about a walk down the strip? Nighttime is when you see the real Vegas."

She slung her backpack purse over her shoulder. "I don't want anyone to notice us."

"I know the back way out of the casino. Follow me."

"I want to see the strip. I'm thinking of including in each episode some live reaction from the people here."

"Good idea. But I was hoping that tonight we could just be Scott and Raine. I want to show you my world."

"Your world?" she asked.

He couldn't read her and he didn't like that. Usually her emotions played close to the surface; it was one of the things that drew him to her. "I spend as much time here as I do in L.A."

"Do you have a home here?"

"I have a place on Lake Henderson. When we wrap I'll probably head over there for a few weeks of down time. Want to join me?" he asked.

He saw her eyes narrow, and something came over her. Her body posture changed, and he knew something important had happened. But he didn't know what. Had he screwed up in that guy way again?

"Maybe. Let's see how these few weeks play out."

"You're very cautious. Why?"

"Growing up I was the sensible one. I guess it stuck."

Soon they were outside and he led them into the flow of traffic. Scott wanted to pull out his quirky guide role and entertain her with stories of his wild youth spent with Hayden MacKenzie, Max Williams and Deacon Prescott. The four of them had cut a wide swath through Vegas, gambling, drinking and living large with the ladies.

But it felt right to just slip his hand in hers and pretend they were like any other couple here. He knew that reality was going to rear its ugly head soon, but for right now, for just one more night, he wanted to pretend.

He also knew that in the morning he was going to confront Stevie and put an end to his bet. He had the feeling that Raine wasn't going to forgive him so easily.

She laughed at some of his stories, reprimanded him for some of them but by the time they were standing in front of the Mirage watching the water fountain show, she had her hand tucked into his and he knew he'd made some progress in wooing this very shy woman.

He ended with a story of how he and his friends had once gotten busted in one of the casino's luxury suites with six girls and too much booze. The story was funny because the women were from a church group in Arkansas and they were trying to reform the four of them. Alan MacKenzie—Hayden's dad—found them the next morning and was not pleased.

"So you got busted by Hayden's dad and then what?"

"He put us to work in the casino as dealers. But we enjoyed it too much so he switched us to the security detail. If you're really good I'll tell you how I busted a ring of dealers who were stealing from the till."

"Define *good.*"

"Hmm, let's see. You could put your hand in my front pants pocket again and we could start negotiating."

"Do you always think of sex first?"

"With you, yes." Because he couldn't be honest with her about Stevie, he felt compelled not to lie about anything else. The only untruth would be that one. He knew it was a big one, but for some reason he felt better knowing he wouldn't lie anymore.

"I think you should have fudged on that."

"Why lie? I think it's obvious I want you."

She smiled at him then, and everything inside him clenched. She wrapped her arms around his neck and pressed her body against his. He felt her mouth nibbling softly against his neck as her hands slid down his back and cupped his behind.

Everything went on point. All day long he'd been waiting for this. Been waiting for her. And now he had her. He knew he had to handle this entire thing carefully because he was beginning to think he was more like Hayden and Deacon than he'd expected. He might be one of those guys who wanted to wake up every day next to the same woman. Not just any woman—Raine.

But that damned bet was going to cause him problems. Plus this was a role he wasn't sure of himself in. But with Raine in his arms he didn't want to think of anything except how her breasts felt pressed to his chest.

He slipped his hands under her T-shirt and felt the satiny smooth skin of her back. He traced his finger up the line of her spine and then back down again. He skimmed his fingernail along the edge of her jeans and wished he'd waited until they were somewhere semi-private before he'd started this.

She tipped her head back. "Was that good enough?"

"That was great. But not enough."

"Not for your story?"

"The story? What story?"

She laughed then, and he knew he was a goner. He was falling for her with each little thing she did.

Watching Scott made Raine realize that gamblers came in different forms. She'd never noticed before that there were different types. All she'd seen was the obsession to play and the fixation on the big score.

Her father was always promising big things when he hit the jackpot, so his gambling was always tied in her mind to money and their lack of it.

Of course, Scott was showing her his best side. But his stories showed her that some men gambled for the thrill of it. For the fun of pitting their skills against everyone else's and coming out on top.

"I want to hear the story about you busting a ring of dealers who were stealing from the casino."

"Ah, that one. Well, being in security is not as exciting as it might seem at first."

"It doesn't sound all that exciting to me."

"When you're a twenty-one-year-old guy it does." There was a sparkle in his eye that told her he'd had visions of being a cool undercover cop like Johnny Depp in *21 Jump Street.*

"Had you ever played a cop?"

"No, and I was ready to."

"Did you get a gun?"

"No, and that was only part of the disappointment. Alan put us all in the laundry area and had us watching over uniforms."

"I'm beginning to think Alan is a very smart man. I bet you all hated that."

"We did. Actually, Max and I talked about leaving. We didn't live in Vegas full-time, so we could have, but we didn't want to leave Deacon and Hayden to suffer alone."

"Why not?"

"Well, it was kind of my idea to try to convince the girls to give up their saintly ways."

"Why?"

"We had some idea of being a modern-day Rat Pack. Drinking, gambling and…"

"Womanizing?"

He shrugged and looked a little sheepish. "Keep in mind I was young."

She shook her head. "You had to pay the piper, so to speak."

"Yes, I did. Besides, Alan wasn't above calling my folks, and they thought I was a good boy."

She laughed. He made her feel good deep inside. And that was playing hell with her emotions. She wanted to be the cool grifter, playing up to him to gain his confidence and his affection and then turn it back on him. But she couldn't because he was unexpectedly more real than she'd ever thought he could be.

Deep inside that made her feel sad at what might

have been if Scott had been a different guy. Because he had something that drew her.

"After three days working in the laundry I noticed a pattern involving one of the baccarat operators."

"What kind of pattern?"

"He'd bring back the same uniform every day."

"Isn't that the point of the laundry?" she asked.

"Yes, smarty. But they were issued three pieces and he never brought back the other two."

"Okay, so now you're suspicious and are about to go all Columbo on him?"

"I was more Rockford than Columbo, honey. When my shift was over I went out on the floor and scoped him out. Just to see if I was right about the uniform."

"Were you?"

"Of course. He was wearing a different uniform. I watched him for a while before realizing that when he was putting the chips in the tray, he was pocketing a few each time."

"Did you make the bust then and there?"

"You're making fun and this was like a *COPS* moment."

"I see that. I can hardly wait to hear how you took down this embezzler."

"It wasn't that exciting. I waited until the end of his shift and confronted him."

"Wasn't that dangerous?"

"Nah, turns out he was a fan. When I told him I was reporting him to Alan, he didn't like me so much anymore."

There was something in his voice she couldn't place. A tone of almost sadness when he spoke. "Fans are fickle."

"They are. But that doesn't bother me. I was totally out of the business by that point. It was something he said."

"What'd he say?"

"That it was easy for me to turn him in because I didn't need the money and I wasn't living on the weekly check Alan was giving me."

That sounded like a first-class con to her. She'd heard her father use a variation of it every time he got busted for a scam. "Did you fall for it?"

"For about a second, but Hayden had seen me leave the floor and he followed me. He stepped into the fray, defending his old man and pointing out that the casino workers were the best-paid on the strip."

She slipped her hand in his and led him down the street toward the Chimera. She saw Latesha and a group of women from the makeup department coming out of the casino and wanted to get away before anyone saw them together. "Was your undercover work what you expected?"

"Yes and no. It wasn't very exciting. I wouldn't do it again. After we turned in the baccarat guy, he rolled over on three other employees who were doing the same thing. Two blackjack dealers and a girl in the cashier's box."

"Why did you notice the baccarat guy?" she asked.

"That's my game. I'm good at poker because I can bluff like nobody's business, but I really love baccarat."

"Why?" she asked, knowing that all gamblers had their game. They picked up skills at other games because they were in the casino all the time. She'd been starting to think that Scott was different because he didn't seem to be like her dad, but maybe she was wrong. Her gut instincts around gamblers were always a little messed up.

"It's complicated, and you have to really think while you're playing."

"Not everyone views it like you do," she said, more to herself than to him. But she easily pictured her dad, who was focused on winning, on the next big score, and only thinking of his strategy to win. Not about the outcome if he lost.

"How can you be sure? You didn't even know how to play roulette."

"I knew. I just didn't want to play. I know more about casinos and games than you'd expect."

He tugged them off the main path and into a quiet area just before the pirates' outdoor water show. "How? I know you aren't a gambler."

"No, I'm a gambler's daughter."

The Chimera had a small grill tucked away on the second floor. Scott led Raine there. Unfortunately, Richard and Andy were seated at one of the front tables, so Scott let go of Raine's hand.

"I'm going to sit in the back and wait for you."

She nodded to let him know she'd heard, and he walked past her, smiling at the hostess. He was seated at his usual table in the back, tucked out of the traffic and secluded.

Raine joined him almost twenty minutes later. She looked tired when she sat down on the banquette. He pulled her against his side. She didn't scoot away from him and instead leaned a little into him.

"What do you want to drink?" he asked.

"Decaf cappuccino, please."

He ordered two of them and a plate of biscotti, then put his arm around her. "Did they notice?"

"Yes," she said. "But I told them I had you show me some of your favorite spots and that I'm going to follow up with the other celebs. So tomorrow night you're going to have go out with the cameraman and show him 'your Vegas.'"

"I don't mind. I'm glad you came with me tonight."

"Me, too," she said, sipping her drink.

"Tell me about growing up as a gambler's daughter. Was it exciting always hanging around high-stakes gamblers?"

"I don't want to talk about it. Tell me another story about your escapades. Do you have any with Joel?"

"Yes, but I don't want to just talk about myself all night."

"Most guys do."

She kept pushing him into a neat little corner with every other man she'd ever met. He wondered why she did that. Was she really not interested in him? Or did she do it to protect herself?

"I'm not most guys. Now, back to you… Was it

Kenny Rogers in *The Gambler*, or *Fear and Loathing in Las Vegas?*"

"Do you use movies to relate to everything?" she asked.

He ignored her question. He did use movies to keep a distance between himself and others. And with Raine that was especially hard to do because he wanted to get it right. Not in the way that Hollywood did with their canned endings, but in the way that millions of people did every day in their private lives. And that was the one thing he'd never figured out how to get.

"What was your childhood like?"

"It's not a pretty story. I doubt that you with your charmed life are going to want to hear it."

He cupped her face in his hand, waited a few moments until he was sure she was focused on him. He couldn't change his past or his life. The truth was he'd known his share of tragedy, and he wasn't going to apologize for the successes that he'd had. The fact that he knew she was striking out at him to keep him from asking more questions about her past didn't mean he was willing to let her get away with it.

"That's not nice."

She turned her face in his hand, rubbing her cheek against his palm. "I know."

"Why'd you say it?"

She kissed the center of his palm. "I'm tired."

"So?" he asked, trying not to be affected by her mouth on his skin.

"I get mean when I'm tired," she said, putting her hand on his thigh.

"That was mean?" he asked. He could barely think with her so close to him. Raine couldn't be mean if she tried. She was too innocent of the real evil in the world. Even growing up with a gambler wasn't enough to taint her.

"Yes."

He cupped the back of her head and lowered his, tasting her mouth with long sweeps of his tongue. He didn't need to know about her past for this. He liked the way she felt in his arms. Liked the way she always opened for his kisses. Liked the way that she seemed to want him just as he wanted her.

He pulled back. Her lips were wet and swollen from his kisses, and her eyes were slumberous.

"Honey, you've got a long way to go to see mean. For the record, my life hasn't been all sunshine and happiness."

"I'm sorry for that, Scott. I was hoping that maybe someone had the kind of childhood that your sitcom portrayed."

"There were downsides to life, as well."

"I know that on a rational level but it's very hard to look at you and not feel resentful. Tell me something bad about being Scott Rivers."

"Why?"

"I want to know something that no one else does."

"If I do, will you tell me about your dad?" he

asked, because he felt her childhood held the key to who she was today.

"I don't like to talk about my dad. My childhood was a combination of *Leaving Las Vegas* and *The Grifters,* only my dad was in the Angelica Houston role."

The dark movie that portrayed a mother-daughter team who ran cons and left the bodies behind wasn't the happy image he wanted for Raine. But it explained a lot about why she kept such a distance between herself and everyone else.

"Being a con man doesn't make your dad a gambler." Con men shouldn't have families, Scott thought. He could easily imagine the hard life that Raine would have had with her father always scamming someone for money and then gambling it away.

"His first love is gambling. Everything he does in life is to make enough money to gamble."

"So you don't trust gamblers?" he asked. Because even though he didn't gamble for a living he had the soul of a gambler. He always wanted to bet on something or take a chance because the odds were low that someone else would. And he'd made a major bet on her.

"No, Scott, I don't."

Six

The next morning Scott didn't want to get out of bed for their 9:00 a.m. call. But he'd built his life around being a professional so he was on the set by 8:45. Raine was in the corner talking with the cameramen and her assistant director. Her hair curled around her shoulders, and he remembered the feel of it in his hands and the taste of her on his lips.

Only five players remained, and this morning he looked over at Brian's vacant chair. The guy had been the best poker player in the Southeast and had won his share of matches on the road, but this game was only for one week, and one mistake had cost Brian his spot at the table.

Scott didn't want to screw up. But his concentration

had been off all day. It was as if Raine had taken over every part of his mind. All he could remember was how right she'd felt in his arms, and he wanted to get her alone again so he could pursue that.

He'd tried to find a moment to speak with Stevie but the rocker was surrounded by groupies and his latest girlfriend, a wafer-thin model from Sri Lanka. She was funny as hell and didn't put up with any of Stevie's usual antics.

Scott tried to be unobtrusive as he watched Raine but walking away from her last night had been hard. And only the fact that he'd made that stupid bet with Stevie had enabled him to leave. What he'd learned of Raine the day before made it impossible for him to go through with the bet. He knew she'd never forgive him if she found out about it, and knowing Stevie, Scott figured the man would get drunk and blab it to the world before too long.

"Scott, you got a minute?"

He glanced over at Joel. "Sure."

Joel led him away from the bustle of grips and props people doing their jobs. There was something very stiff about Joel, and Scott had a feeling he was going to get the same warning Raine had gotten yesterday.

"Is this about fraternizing?" Scott asked before Joel could say anything.

"Yes and no," Joel said as he rubbed the back of his neck. "I know you did me a favor by agreeing to participate in the show, but you have to be careful with Raine."

"Has someone said something?"

"Yes. And Raine's not like the other women you've met in this business."

"You think I don't know that?"

"I'm not sure. All I know is that *you* aren't playing up to your normal game and *she's* distracted."

"Joel, believe me, man, if I could get my head in the game I would."

Joel laughed. "Just be careful. Both of you. This could blow up in your faces."

He nodded, and Joel walked away. Latesha signaled him to come to the makeup area. As he sat in the makeup chair, he thought over what Joel had said. No matter what, he knew he couldn't be the cause of Raine losing her job.

An approaching voice interrupted his thought. "I know you've explained it to me before, but makeup still looks girly to me."

Without looking, he knew it was Hayden. But he didn't feel like joking around with his friend. For the first time in his life things weren't coming easily to him and he wasn't sure of the outcome. He'd never failed when he put his mind to something, but the stakes had never been so high, either. "Are you saying I look like your wife?"

"I shoulda said sissy. Not girly. You can't compete with my wife."

"I'm heartbroken. How will I go on?"

"I imagine you'll turn to your alien lover," Raine said as she approached the two men.

She didn't smile and he wondered if Joel had been warning her away from him again. Probably. Damn, he should have been more circumspect, but he didn't want to have to hide their relationship, and he knew that they had one. Even Raine would admit to that. He couldn't let her go. If that meant he had to leave the show, so be it.

"Mr. MacKenzie, what brings you to our set?" she asked, checking her clipboard for notes.

"I was hoping to watch hotshot here in action."

"We'll be shooting in about forty minutes. You're welcome to stay."

"I've got a meeting but my wife might be free."

"Have Sal put her name on the list and we'll let her in to the taping. She'll have to sign a confidentiality form regarding who wins."

"No problem. Is my assistant taking care of you?"

"Yes, Sal is great."

She glanced over at Scott and he had the feeling she wanted to say something. "Scott, can I see you in the booth when you're done here?"

"Sure thing," he said. He wanted a few minutes alone with her as well.

"Thanks for making us feel so welcome here, Mr. MacKenzie. Scott showed me some of his favorite sights in Vegas last night and one of them was in your hotel. We're hoping to do a montage with that will include a few shots of those locations. Will that be okay?"

"Call me Hayden. My dad is Mr. MacKenzie. I'm sure that will be fine. I'll have Sal assign one of our managers to go with your cameraman."

"Thanks, Hayden. Goodbye, guys."

She nodded and walked away. He loved the way her worn jeans hugged her rump. He remembered the way her hips had felt under his hands the night before and wished he hadn't done the gentlemanly thing and walked away.

Hayden let out a low wolf whistle. Scott elbowed his friend.

"Her jeans are too damned tight," Scott said under his breath.

"No, they aren't. They're perfect. Say the word and Ms. Montgomery can be invited to dinner on Friday." Hayden adjusted the cuff links at his wrists. He had a way of doing things like that and making it look natural. Scott often imitated Hayden when he wanted to look like a real aristocrat.

"Shove off, Hay. I don't need your help with a woman."

"Sure you don't. I helped Deacon get Kylie," he said.

"Liar. You almost broke them up."

"Well, how was I to know women didn't like to be bet on?"

Yeah, imagine that. It was as if he didn't already know that women got royally ticked off when men did stupid things like that. Kylie was soft and sweet, not at all like Raine, who'd probably get some kind of revenge on him if he didn't come clean soon. "Did Kylie take the news hard?"

"You heard from Deacon. She married him and then left him a few days later. That's one mistake I won't make again."

"Did she forgive him?"

Hayden's BlackBerry beeped before he could say more. "Gotta run. I'll be in the casino later tonight if you want to hang out again."

Scott nodded and watched his friend walk away. God, he regretted that stupid impulse that had made him take a bet about Raine.

He went to find her. Seducing Raine without letting the world know what he was doing was going to be difficult. He had a certain reputation that was going to suffer if he played this the way she needed him to.

Scott rubbed the back of his neck as he rapped on the door leading to the director's booth. Losing his reputation was worth it, if it meant he'd get to keep Raine.

Raine wasn't sure what to do with Scott now that he was here in her domain. She'd had a vague plan of coming clean with him. Forcing him to admit to his bet and then maybe starting over with a clean slate.

"Hey, sexy lady, you wanted me?"

"Yes, I do," she said, reaching out and pulling him inside. "Are you miked yet?"

"No."

Good, she thought. She didn't want anyone else to hear their conversation. She'd thought of nothing but Scott all night long and felt restless and edgy this morning. If he lost the game today, then he wouldn't be working on the production any longer, and she could eliminate losing her job as one of the risks of having an affair with Scott.

"I saw Joel over there talking to you. What did he want?"

"Same as he did with you."

"I was afraid of that. What do you think your chances are of winning today?" she asked.

"I'm feeling lucky," Scott said, resting against the back wall of her little room, arms crossed over his chest.

"Like you did at the roulette table?" she asked, arching one eyebrow at him.

"Very funny."

"I thought so!"

He walked around the director's booth, fiddling with the soundboard, noting the monitors and camera angles. "Roulette is chance. Poker, on the other hand, is science. Care to try your luck at the poker table?"

She thought about it. At one time in junior high she'd won enough money during lunch to pay for a trip for her and her mom to New York City. But that was long ago. "No. I don't think I'm going to test my newfound luck. I want to be the one woman who can say she beat Scott Rivers."

"Do you want to see me lose?" he asked.

He stopped messing around with the equipment and turned to face her. She felt as if he wasn't sure what role to take in the booth. As if he was feeling her out to see how she was going to react.

"Not exactly, but it wouldn't hurt your ego to not win once," she said quietly. This was where she knew if she was really running a con, she'd have said something different. She'd have played up to him, making him feel like he was a god among men. Like Scott needed her to do that!

He tipped his head to the side and then said, "I've always been lucky in things of chance."

"What about love?" She didn't know why she asked the question except maybe it had been weighing on her mind. This had nothing to do with conning him and everything to do with the truth of what she felt. She was falling for him whether she wanted to or not. Last night she'd lain in her bed, frustrated and horny from reliving his kisses and wanting him there with her. What kind of lover—not physically, but emotionally—would he be?

"I think it's a draw when I'm dealing with love," he said in that wry tone that told her she was getting close to the truth.

"How so?" she asked, needing to know more. The rational part of her mind cautioned her heart not to get too attached to Scott. Not to fall for his openness and the way he really talked to her. A lot of money was on the line, and he just said he didn't like to lose.

"My folks are great. I have a few close friends who are always there for me. But when it comes to that one special woman…let's just say I've had my heart broken."

"Really?" She was surprised he admitted to it. She didn't know if she'd be brave enough to tell him about Raul Santiago, the young actor she'd had an affair with right out of college. She'd thought she finally had her life on track, with a new job as assistant director on a hot new television series, new boyfriend, new life. But Raul had really only been interested in her contacts, and once he'd gotten access to them, he'd moved on. No hard feelings, he'd said.

The sad thing was she hadn't had any feelings of remorse when he'd left. Maybe she was more like her father than she'd ever thought. He'd never seemed upset when he'd hurt her, nor when she'd left him the last time and told him she wasn't coming back. Of course, she'd still sent him money, so maybe he didn't care that he wasn't seeing her.

Scott replied to her question. "Yes. Want the gory details?"

Yes, she did, because she wanted to know what made him tick. Wanted to be sure she wasn't in over her head with a playboy who was really only romancing her for the money. "Would you really tell me? Aren't you afraid of looking like a loser?"

He laughed and smiled at her. "Honey, you keep a man humble."

"With you it's a real effort," she said. But it wasn't. He was a very natural guy.

"If you want to know about my heartbreak, I'll tell you. But only you. And maybe you'll feel sorry for me. I'm doing it for sympathy, not to seem pathetic."

"Ah, now I understand. Sorry, but I don't want to know about your past lovers."

He moved closer to her. The spicy scent of his aftershave teased her senses, and she wanted to breathe a little deeper so she'd always remember what he smelled like. She wanted to cuddle close to him and feel his arms around her again. The only time she'd ever felt safe was when he held her—and she knew that was dangerous.

"What about you? You ever get your heart broken?" he asked in that quiet way of his.

She didn't want to have this conversation. Not now. Not with him. She wanted him to believe she'd always been this calm, cool person he saw on the set. "Yes, more than once."

"Really? You strike me as someone who'd never let a man break her heart more than once."

"I'm not sure I like the sound of that. But you're right. It was only one man. The other times were my dad and my brother. You'd think I'd learn."

"Learn what?"

"Not to believe their promises."

"What do they promise?"

"To quit. To go straight. To live a normal life. You name it, my dad has probably promised it to me."

"So basically you've learned not to believe any promises a man gives you?"

"Basically."

"Well, then, I won't make you any promises," he said.

She couldn't respond, because she knew she wanted to believe the sincerity in his voice, the earnest look in his eyes that said he wanted to protect her: the promises that she wanted to weave around that unspoken one he'd just given her.

"What's the matter, honey?" he asked.

"Nothing," she said, not to annoy him, but because she didn't know how to say what she was thinking.

He closed the distance between them, wrapping his arm around her waist. She liked how he always touched her. She didn't analyze it, just snuggled closer to his solid chest. Closing her eyes, she pretended that they weren't on a television set and that this moment was real.

Seven

Scott held Raine in his arms, trying to remember that he could be a gentleman instead of a raving sex maniac. But he wanted her. Having her in his arms, feeling her curvy little body pressed against his was inflaming him. Driving out his good intentions.

Somehow he had a hard time reconciling good intentions and the bet he'd made. It would just take a few simple words to end his torment, but at this point he was in too deep to stop the train.

"I prejudged you because unlike Stevie, you don't have a real job."

He had a real job, but he kept it quiet. He knew it was better if everyone believed he was nothing more than a playboy. It enabled him to do his work without a lot of outside interference. "I run a charitable foundation."

"Really? I didn't know that. What do you do at the foundation?"

"I'm the CEO. That means I run the day-to-day operations."

"From a sound stage?" she asked in that snarky way of hers. She liked to push his buttons, and he was the first to admit he didn't mind it most of the time. But he was sensitive about his work.

"Or from my yacht or wherever I am in the world. I have a crack assistant who makes sure that I'm always up to date on whatever project we're working on."

"What are you working on now?" she asked.

He fiddled with the buttons on the soundboard in front of him. "A children's hospital in Orlando for low-income families."

"I'm impressed," she said, moving next to him and plugging in a pair of headphones.

He said nothing since this was the first time she actually sounded interested in something he did. Being a CEO was respectable. He knew it essentially involved being a number of characters rolled into one, based mainly on his friend Max Williams, who'd been running his own company since he was twenty-two.

"Nothing to say to that? I think I'm beginning to know you, Scott. You talk a lot when you're feeling… cocky, but if I get too close, you clam up."

"I think I know you, too," he said, not wanting to dwell on what she'd revealed.

He captured her wrist and held her hand against his chest. She scraped her fingernail down the buttons of his Oxford shirt. "I know you're a sleeping beauty, and it's going to take more than a kiss to get you out of your castle."

"Do you believe in fairy tales?"

"Yes, what about you?" he asked, because right now he had one in his head that went beyond a chaste kiss at the end.

"I guess. I'm surprised you do."

"What can I say? My mother is a literature teacher and she read me all kinds of stuff growing up."

"Including fairy tales."

"Hell, yes. And all kinds of women's fiction and nonfiction. She's a liberal feminist." Who'd be outraged if she knew her son had bet on a woman.

He turned away so that she couldn't read the guilty thoughts going through his head. He fiddled with the buttons on the panel again and accidentally pushed one this time. Voices filled the sound booth.

"Last night I saw them come into the restaurant together but then they separated." He recognized Andy's voice.

"I think it's kind of sweet if they are getting together."

Raine gasped. "Oh, my God. They're talking about us."

Scott hit the button again, tuning out the talk, and turned to face her. "How was that possible? Andy's not miked, is he?"

"The entire room has microphones in it, so we can

pick up different audio tracks and edit out what we don't need."

Had she heard him that morning with Stevie? He glanced over at her, watching carefully. He should tell her now. Apologize before things went any further, and make sure she knew he'd never meant the bet to be anything other than a bit of fun.

"Have you ever heard anything you wished you hadn't?" he asked, not sure how to broach the subject of his bet.

"I just did," she said. "I knew this wasn't going to work out."

"Why not? They were just speculating. We haven't done anything to be ashamed of."

She pushed past him and out of the booth and looked at that button and then down on the floor. Andy was standing right where he and Stevie had been the day they'd made their bet. The tightening in his gut said she had to know.

Nothing went right on the set once the entire cast and crew were there. Laurie Andrews kept throwing up, and the doctor they brought in ruled out food poisoning, telling Laurie instead that she was pregnant. The news was a blow to the woman and she asked for the rest of the day off to adjust to the news.

To top it off, Scott's discovery in the booth early this morning was just what she didn't need. Now she knew he had to guess she'd overheard the bet. Or maybe he was hoping she hadn't. But the time for silence was coming to an end. She needed to say something, and soon.

They were on a tight schedule that allowed for no extra days, and after a quick chat with Joel it was decided that they couldn't just give her the day off. Raine did, however, call a cut to taping and asked everyone to return after eight this evening. Laurie was okay with this as were most of the other players.

She spent an hour with the crew giving them some additional direction for things she wanted done this evening. She asked one of the cameramen to go get some exterior shots of the hotel. Once Sal got clearance from Hayden, which took another twenty minutes, she sent Stevie with the cameraman to show him some of his favorite okay-for-television spots in Vegas. Then finally everyone was gone and she was alone on the set.

For the first time in her life being alone felt lonely. She wished that she could go find Scott and spend some time with him, but people were talking about them and she knew she had to nip any gossip in the bud. She shrugged on her backpack purse and headed out toward the lobby.

As she neared the front door, she noticed Scott talking to a group of people. He broke away from them as she approached.

"What are you doing?" she asked as he approached her. She glanced around.

"Waiting for you."

Maybe she wasn't so alone anymore. He was starting to like her, and a big part of her knew that it was good for her con to sucker him in. But her heart treasured the fact that he seemed to like her for her.

"If you don't have plans, I'd like to take you for a ride on my Harley."

"I'm not sure that's such a good idea."

He nodded as if he understood some great universal truth. "Are you nervous about being seen or being alone with me?"

"Why would I be nervous about that?"

"Because we're not going to be around the casino where you're distracted and we're interrupted. I'm talking about you and me alone for the day."

To be honest it sounded like heaven, and for the rest of the day she was just going to try to forget about bets and men and gambling. "You can get a little tedious, so maybe I should think about this."

He snagged her close with an arm around her hips. "That sassy mouth has just landed you in a boatload of trouble."

"Wow, really? What are you going to do, spank me?"

"Maybe," he said, taking her hand and leading her out of the lobby and to the garage.

Her mind was full of images of herself over his lap while his hand came down on her naked backside. It was a little kinky and nothing she'd ever done in real life but it definitely aroused her.

He took her backpack and put it in one of the saddlebags on the bike and handed her a helmet.

She took it as she climbed on the bike like it was

second nature. Like he hadn't just thrown down a gauntlet she wasn't sure she was ready to pick up. But Raine knew better than to show any sign of weakness.

Normally she knew better. With Scott she just wanted to stop hiding who she really was.

"Want to see my place on Lake Henderson?"

She knew he was asking for more than just a trip to see his place and she took a deep breath and acknowledged that she was way beyond running a con on this man. She wanted him with the kind of soul-deep intensity she'd hidden from all her life. She was so afraid to believe in Scott.

So afraid that the pattern of her life would repeat itself. So afraid that she was going to look like a sucker who knew better than to take the sucker bet.

"Honey, what can I say to make your answer the one I want to hear?"

"Tell me that this isn't just some easy lay for you."

He cursed under his breath and turned away from her for a minute, on his head bowed. She knew that her words had affected him—more deeply than she'd intended.

"Dammit, woman, you are more trouble—"

"Than I'm worth?"

He turned to her. "Did I say that?"

"No, but I know I'm a bit of a shrew."

"Honey, I know better than to agree with that. No matter what you might have heard I'd never treat you that way."

Was he talking about normal gossip or hedging his

bets in case she'd overheard him and Stevie? It was too difficult to figure out, and since she wasn't supposed to know about the bet, she had no idea what to say to him. He stared at her for a minute before turning away again.

She climbed off the bike and walked over to him, put her arms around his waist and rested her head against his shoulder. "I'm not good at these kinds of things. I want to go with you but I'm not sure I'm ready."

His hands settled over her wrists, his callused thumbs rubbing over her skin. "Honey, I'll take whatever you're ready to give me. Hell, I'm more turned on by the thought of you riding pressed against my back than I am by the thought of taking any other woman."

She squeezed him tight. "Then let's go see this house of yours."

She dropped her arms and struggled to get the helmet on. Scott took it from her and put it on. "There. Now you're ready and no one will recognize you."

She was touched that he'd remembered she didn't want anyone to see them together. It was probably nothing to him but it meant something to her. He put on his own helmet, and then they both climbed on the bike, heading out of town, leaving the artificial world of Vegas behind and heading into the real-life world of Lake Henderson.

Raine clung tight to Scott's back and let her mind drift away from reality as she knew it. It had been so long since she'd just let herself go and relaxed with a man she truly liked. She was claiming this day for herself. She knew there'd be a price to pay later. But for now she was going to simply enjoy being with Scott.

Scott's house was built to take advantage of the view of the lake offered by his property. The entire back of the two-story structure was made of wood beams and glass. There was a deck leading to a pool and then a walkway down to the lake. He had a small boathouse where he kept a Bayliner, two Sea-Doos and a catamaran.

Raine had said little on the drive here and now that they were standing in his living room he wasn't sure what to say to her.

"I like this place. It seems a little rustic."

"Thanks. This is my place. I don't let anyone else come here."

"You brought me to your retreat?"

"Yes. We needed privacy, and no one has ever found me here."

"Thanks, Scott."

"Anything for my lady."

"My entire house would fit in your living room."

"I bet it's cozy."

She laughed and he smiled to hear it. "Point taken. I wasn't expecting this."

"What were you expecting?"

"I don't know…some cold, aesthetically pleasing house that looks like no one lives in it. But this is comfortable. I could sit in here, put my feet up and not feel out of place."

He was glad. He wanted her to relax and to drop her guard, which she never did. He opened the glass doors, pushing them into the pocket so that they were open to the outdoors. "Want to take a walk?"

"Just a walk? Isn't that too tame for you?"

"Keep talking, honey, that mouth is going to do you in."

"I don't think so. You like it when I tease you, because everyone else takes you too seriously. They're always trying to please you or flatter you to win your favor."

"But not you," he said.

"No, not me. I'm not wowed by your fame or your millions."

She made a circular route around the living area, stopping to study the pictures on the wall. Two of them were by an artist friend of his who was just starting to make a name for himself in the art world. They were bold landscapes that reminded the viewer that Mother Nature—not man—was still in charge of the earth.

"Who is this?" she asked. She reached out to touch the canvas but stopped.

"Thom Jenner. We're not in a museum. You can touch it if you want to."

But she didn't reach out. She kept her hands by her sides, very much the cautious woman she'd always been. "I've never heard of him. I think I'm afraid to touch it. The storm looks so real."

Scott walked over to stand next to her. "You will be hearing Thom's name soon. He's starting to make it big.

I picked up the *Grand Canyon* when I was in Denver last year." The *Grand Canyon* showed New York City being buffeted by a massive storm. The storm was definitely what drew your eye.

"Why do you have his work in here?" she asked. "What drew you to it?"

He considered her question for long minutes, studying the painting, trying to pick through his true reactions and decide what to tell her. Baring his emotions didn't fit with his role this afternoon—leading man in a romantic comedy. Light, sexy, funny. But Raine always reacted to the unexpected.

"You have to promise not to leak this to the media."

She held her hand up. "I solemnly swear."

"Well, I like that it takes symbols of what we consider successful and makes them seem small. It reminds me every time I see it that there's a lot more to the world than just big cities and—you'll love this—money."

She slipped her arm around his waist, sliding her hand into his front pocket the way he'd asked her to do that day in front of the elevator. "That's—"

"What?"

"Deeper than I expected of you. I think I glimpsed the real Scott under the role you've been playing."

He wrapped his arm around her shoulder, holding her to him as they stood under the painting. "I don't know if there is a real Scott."

Her eyes softened and she looked up at him like he was some kind of hero. And he never had been. He wanted to warn her that there wasn't any substance to him. That he'd always been an image on celluloid. Nothing more.

"There is. He's a nice man."

"Nice? I brought you here to seduce you."

"And that's not nice? Are you going to have your wicked way with me?"

"Yes. And then I'm hoping you'll have your wicked way with me."

She slipped her hand deeper into his pocket, edging it toward his inner thigh. She stroked her fingers against him, and his body responded. He tried to adjust his stance, glancing down at her to see that she was watching him harden in response to her touch.

Her other hand came up to lightly rub over his fly, and he groaned deep in his throat. She toyed with the tab of his zipper, glancing up at him.

"Can I?"

He was so hard and ready for her touch. "I think I'll die if you don't."

She popped the snap at the waistband of his jeans and then slowly lowered the zipper. She pushed her hands into his pants and ran her fingers over his length, still encased in the fabric of his boxer briefs.

"I'm ready to be seduced," she said, running her fingers over him.

Her hands were cool, her long fingers slipping inside his underwear to wrap around him. A drop of moisture leaked out, and she rubbed her finger over it, smoothing it into the head of his erection. He groaned at how good she felt with her hands on his body.

He realized he'd already been seduced by Raine in a way that had nothing to do with sex and everything to do with acceptance. He pulled her hands from his body, scooped her up in his arms and carried her down the hall to his bedroom.

This was where they both belonged. Far away from the bright lights of Vegas with its spinning wheels, gamblers and games of chance. Far away from the prying eyes that would threaten her career. Far away from everything except the real world he'd never thought he could really live in. But with Raine in his arms, he felt real, and that was enough for now.

Eight

Scott lowered her to her feet next to the bed. Raine realized that her con had ended probably that first afternoon on the desert trail in Red Rock. She knew herself well enough that she had no doubts about being here with Scott now.

"Take off your shirt for me, honey."

Her fingers trembled as she brought them to the hem of her shirt and lifted it to expose her belly button and the bottom of her ribs. "What makes you think you're in charge?"

He scratched his chin, studying the smooth skin she'd revealed. He reached out and rubbed his palm over it, and she shuddered at his touch, wanting more of it. She wanted his caresses all over her body.

"You're always in charge on the set. Don't you want to let go now?"

She did, but not because of that reason. She wanted to let go because she was afraid she'd do something to ruin this wonderful moment. That somehow with the same bad luck she'd always had she'd say the wrong thing and drive him from her.

"No, I don't want to be in charge," she said, her voice sounding husky to her own ears. The last time she'd had sex had been hurried and a way of saying goodbye to Raul. It had been emotionally painful. She hoped she wasn't setting herself up for a bigger heartache with Scott.

"Do you want to be mine?"

She thought about it, forgetting everything except the two of them together now. She remembered the feel of his body in front of hers on the Harley. She remembered his hand in hers at Red Rock. She remembered his face in front of the Bellagio hotel. She nodded.

He cupped her face in his hands and kissed her, his mouth moving tenderly over hers, his tongue dipping inside to taste her. "Say it out loud so there will be no doubts later."

"I want to be yours."

He ran his thumb back and forth over her lower lip. "And you'll do whatever I ask of you."

She hesitated. She wasn't really adventurous when it came to sex. "I'll try. What are you planning? I think you should know I'm strictly a missionary-position girl."

"We're going to expand your horizons a little. But only if you agree to do what I ask."

This was it. She took a deep breath and nodded. "I agree."

He kissed her deeply and quickly and then stepped back. He crossed his arms over his chest and surveyed his room. The windows had no coverings and looked out over the lake. She realized as she studied them that they were actually sliding doors that opened onto a deck.

"Does exhibitionism excite you?"

"Not today."

He nodded. "Then come away from the windows. Now, take your shirt all the way off," he said, walking across the room to the ladder-back chair in the corner. He moved it to the center of the room and sat directly in front of her.

She pulled it the rest of the way off and tossed it on the floor at his feet.

"Pick up your shirt, fold it and place it on the dresser."

She arched one eyebrow at him but did as he asked. She felt more vulnerable than she'd expected being almost naked from the waist up. She took heart in the fact that his jeans were unfastened and she could see his hard length through the opening.

"Now you," she said.

He considered her request for a moment then stood up and unbuttoned his shirt, revealing his sculpted chest. He had the best chest she'd ever seen. And the fact that he was here in this room with her—hers to touch and caress—made her wet.

She stepped closer and ran both of her hands down

his chest. The light dusting of hair was tingly against her fingers.

"Who said you could touch me?" he asked in that dominant tone of his, but his pupils were dilated and his pulse beat visibly at the base of his neck, so she knew he liked it.

"I can't?" she asked, skimming her fingernail down the center of his body. His stomach clenched and she slid the tip of her finger into the waistband of his briefs, touching the tip of his erection.

He put his hand over hers, moving her hand down his length and wrapping her fingers around him. He tightened his grip almost painfully on her hand and then drew her touch from his pants.

"Not yet. Take off your bra."

"Scott—"

"We both agreed I was in charge. Remove your bra so I can see your pretty breasts."

She reached behind her back and slowly removed her bra. Scott's breath caught in his chest and she watched a flush spread over his chest. His erection strained against the front of his underwear and his hands were clenched at his sides as he waited to see her.

Teasingly she tossed the bra at him. He caught it and put it on the dresser behind him.

"Offer your breasts to me, Raine."

A shiver of excitement pooled in her belly. She ran her hands upward from the waistband of her jeans to her breasts, cupping them. Watching Scott for his reaction. He groaned and unclenched his fists.

He reached out and ran his forefinger along the edge of her hand, right where her fingers cupped the globes of her breasts. Her nipples tightened, begging for his attention. He circled her aureole with just the tip of one finger.

He leaned down and licked the tip of one breast, sucking her deep into his mouth. She let go of her breasts and held his head. Held him to her.

Wrapping both of his arms around her waist, his mouth never leaving her nipple, he picked her up. He bit lightly at her nipple and let it go. It tightened painfully when the cool air touched it.

She shivered, staring down at him. He lowered her until the tips of her breasts rubbed against his chest. She sighed at the feeling. She wanted more. She wanted his mouth on her again.

"Wrap your legs around my waist."

She did, adjusting her body over his hardness and then rocking against him. He felt so good, and it had been a long time since she'd had sex. Everything in her focused on that contact through their jeans. His erection and her wetness. She held his shoulders and rocked harder against him.

"Wait," he said, holding her still. He set her on her feet, unfastening her jeans. He pushed her jeans and panties down her legs. He knelt at her feet to remove her shoes.

"Lift your feet, honey," he said in a deep rasp that she made her body clench.

She lifted first one foot than the other and soon she was standing naked over him. He ran his hands up the outside of her legs, his fingers slowly caressing every inch of her.

"Spread your legs."

She stepped her feet apart.

His hands moved to the inside of her legs, starting slowly at her ankle, lingering behind her knee and then sliding up her inner thighs. Her own moisture coated the very tops of her inner thighs; he rubbed his finger in the wetness there.

"Want me?" he asked.

"You have no idea."

He teased the opening of her body, circling his finger just at the rim, not entering her. She canted her hips forward, hoping to force him inside. But he moved his fingers away.

"Part yourself for me."

She did as he asked and felt his warm breath and then the brush of his tongue on her most intimate flesh. She trembled as he continued to caress her, and then her legs gave way. Scott supported her with an arm wrapped around her thighs and continued his intimate kiss until she was shuddering in his arms as her climax approached.

"I'm going to come," she said.

He pushed one finger into her body and then a second, thrusting them in and out of her while he scraped his teeth along her body. Everything inside her centered there where he was touching her, and her orgasm rocked through her. She grabbed his shoulders, held on to him while the world tilted and drifted away from her.

He lifted her and carried them both to the chair. He

sat down and she straddled his hips. His jeans abraded her inner thighs. She reached between their bodies and freed him from his underwear.

He was hot and hard in her hand. A drop of fluid glistened on the tip. She soothed it with her finger, rubbing it into the head of his erection, then lifted her finger to her lips and licked it.

"Did you like tasting me?" she asked.

"As much as I'm going to like taking you," he said. He set her on her feet for a minute then shucked his jeans and underwear in one fluid movement.

But they got caught on his boots. Raine eyed his erection; he was bigger than she'd realized.

She touched his shoulder and he looked up at her. She'd never wanted a man's body inside her as badly as she wanted Scott's at this moment. He pushed to his feet and sat on the chair. He had a condom packet in his hand.

He tore it open and donned it quickly. "Come here, honey. I need you."

She climbed on his lap and immediately felt too intimate with him. From this angle they were face to face. His eyes were open, staring into hers. His erection pressed between them, hot and hard, ready for her. And she was ready for him.

She closed her eyes and grasped his shoulders as he positioned himself between her legs. His hands moved to her hips and then swept up her back, cupping the back of her head. She opened her eyes and found him watching her.

"Ready?"

She nodded. Despite being in the position of power, she felt powerless. It had nothing to do with Scott and everything to do with her. She didn't like it.

The tip of his body was lodged in hers, and she bit her lower lip and slowly sank down on him. He groaned deep in his throat.

She held on to his shoulders and rocked against him. He let her set the pace. His mouth trailed over her shoulders and down to the curves of her breasts. She held him to her, scored his skin with her nails and rocked a little harder against him. But she wanted to see his weakness. She wanted to arouse him and then hold him at the point of orgasm.

She wanted to make sure that he was at least as vulnerable as she was in this affair of theirs.

The chair creaked as she increased her thrusting. Everything was building inside her to that glorious slide once more. Scott braced his feet on the floor and started thrusting up into her. His hands were no longer caressing but held her still for his thrusts. She found his mouth with hers.

She thrust her tongue into his mouth as his hands tightened on her hips and he grunted with the force of his orgasm. He thrust into her two more times and as her own climax rolled through her body, she sank deeper onto him.

She wrapped her arms around him and laid her head on his shoulder. He felt right in her body, holding her tight to him. She felt as if she'd found something she didn't know if she could ever give up.

That scared her because she knew that she wasn't running a con. In fact, she now saw she hadn't been from the beginning. What she'd been doing was trying to avoid falling for a man who could hurt her.

Why was she having this revelation now?

Scott carried Raine to the bed and set her under the covers. She rolled to her side, her eyes sleepy looking as she watched him remove his boots and then his pants. He went to the bathroom to dispose of the condom and then returned to his bed.

"When do I get to have my wicked way with you?" she asked, trailing her fingers down his chest. She slipped her hand between his legs and cupped him.

"What'd you have in mind?" he asked. He had a driving need to possess her. To ensure that she didn't take a breath that wasn't filled with his scent. That she didn't lick her lips without tasting him. That she didn't close her eyes without seeing his face.

"Well, since you were so big on orders I thought about ordering you around a little," she said. She stroked her hand up and down his erection in just the right way, squeezing him at the tip, then caressing down to his root and lightly teasing his scrotum with her fingers. She repeated the caress until he was harder than he'd ever been.

He raised one eyebrow at her. He toyed with the edge of the sheet, pushing it down her body until all of her curves were revealed. "I'm not sure that's a good idea."

"Why not?" she asked, still stroking him.

He could hardly think. He wanted to push her legs apart and thrust into her, but he wasn't sure she was ready for him again. "Because I like to be in charge in bed."

"So?" she asked, moving her hand to his erection. He sucked in his breath, painfully aroused and past the point of thinking.

He pushed her thighs apart and dipped one finger into her body. She was wet and hot, ready for him. He fumbled in the nightstand, finding a condom and handing it to her.

"You rode me last time, I'd say you were in charge."

She ripped open the condom packet and rolled it down his length. "Yes, but you were the one giving the orders."

He rolled her gently to her back and settled himself over her.

"Just like you're in charge this time?" she asked, bracketing his hips with her thighs.

"Exactly," he said. He reached between their bodies to adjust himself, then slid into her body. She felt so good around him; he wished he didn't have the condom on so he could feel her heat on his flesh.

She skimmed her fingers down his back as he thrust lazily into her body. She cupped his butt and moved lower, teasing his scrotum and pressing into the flesh beneath. His erection throbbed. He needed to get deeper. Now.

He crushed her mouth under his and started to thrust

harder, deeper. She continued her teasing play between his legs, and he realized he was going to come in a few seconds. He reached between their bodies and found her bud, stroking it with a few touches until he felt her body begin to tighten around his and he gave over to his orgasm.

Sweat coated both of their bodies, and he rolled to his back, tucking her to his side and holding her tight. The condom needed to be disposed of but for this moment he needed to hold her.

"Wow, I guess you showed me who was boss."

He leaned over and kissed her hard on the lips. "You have my permission to do that any time you want."

She laughed and he held her for a few more minutes before getting up to deal with the condom. When he returned to the bedroom she was staring out the windows at the lake.

"That was incredible. You are one hot lady."

He liked seeing her there, his blue sheets tucked around her bare limbs, her hair loose and hanging to her shoulders as she watched him and teased him. Raine was so perfect for him sometimes it scared him. She was yin to his yang and he didn't know if he could ever let go. He also realized there was a very real possibility that she might leave him when she found out how callously he'd behaved before ever really getting to know her.

He had to bind her to him. He'd use sex and charm, everything he had in his arsenal to make her fall for him before he had to tell her the truth, because this was the kind of thing that was going to hurt.

She was the first woman he'd had at this place. She was more precious to him than he could ever explain. Even thinking about it made him feel edgy. When he was with Raine, he never found the right role to play.

Being submissive to her will wasn't one he could slip into. It went against his grain and his true personality. He could pretend to be congenial with everyone else but not with her.

"Well, I do have my reputation to consider," she said and glanced away from him as he climbed in beside her.

He realized he'd said the wrong thing. "Dammit."

"What?"

"Just when I think it's okay to be myself I screw it up."

"What are you talking about?"

He rolled over, settling her underneath him. "When I'm not playing a role, I don't say the right things."

She reached up to run her fingers over his face. Though her touch was so light, he felt it all the way down his spine. It was the kind of caring touch he seldom experienced in bed. Most women were after the playboy Casanova and not a gentle lover. But with Raine he felt she really did see him. Both the good and the bad parts.

"Everyone screws up. That's what makes us human and real. This affair of ours isn't a Hollywood script."

"I know that," he said, settling beside her on the bed once more. That was the thing that scared him. He had a hard time creating lasting bonds away from the set.

He had no idea how to be the real Scott Rivers, and for Raine he wanted to be a good man. A real man. The kind of man she'd never had in her life. Not a gambler or a rogue, and those were the roles that came easiest to him.

He knew that the easy things in life weren't the ones worth having. Hadn't his parents said the same thing to him many times? Only now did he understand what they'd meant.

Nine

Back on the set Raine concentrated on work. Scott had left her at the garage elevator, and she'd gone back to her room to shower and change. Her assistant director, Andy, was already on the set when she got there.

"How's Laurie?"

"Good. Her boyfriend is flying out and they're going to get married at the end of shooting."

"I'll talk to Joel about taping it. Maybe we can get the show to pay for part of it."

"I thought you'd say that, so you're meeting with Joel tonight after taping. I also spoke to Sal on the QT and he said the Chimera would do something for her, as well."

"Great. Sounds like a nice bonus for our viewers."

They finished their discussion and Andy left to check on the players over in makeup. Raine went back to her booth to watch everyone taking their seats. Scott smiled up in her direction but did nothing else to even hint that they'd spent the day together.

By the end of the night, Junior McMillan, the NASCAR driver, was eliminated from play. It was almost eleven and Raine still had her meeting with Joel as well as post work to do.

When she exited her booth, she saw Scott in a corner speaking quietly with Stevie. She wished she could hear what they were saying. Was he collecting his bet?

She felt small and vulnerable thinking about it and as she turned to hurry away, she walked straight into the man behind her. His arms steadied her.

"Thanks," she said, looking up into the steel gray eyes of her executive producer and boss, Joel.

"You're welcome. You okay?" he asked.

"Fine. I just remembered something I'd forgotten. I was on my way up to see you," she said, needing to get the topic to business and not her dismal personal life.

"I thought I'd save you the trip upstairs since you'd probably be back down here editing when we were finished."

She smiled at him. "You know me well."

"We can talk in the edit bay," he said.

She led him out of their temporary sound stage and away from Scott. They walked down the short hallway to the room they'd set up as their editing bay while they were in Vegas. They discussed Laurie and her impending wedding and decided that they couldn't pay for any of it because they didn't want to seem as if they were partial to one player.

"We can shoot some of it and air it if she wins, but only after the fact. Maybe in the postmortem at the end of the episode," Joel said.

Each player had one-on-one camera time to discuss why they thought they'd lost the game.

Joel continued, "If she loses we can play the angle of how she might not have been lucky in cards tonight but she struck gold in love, marrying her longtime sweetheart, blah, blah, blah."

"Sounds good, except you're not the type of guy who can carry off 'blah, blah, blah.'"

"I know, I'm too stuffy."

"I wouldn't say stuffy."

"Not to my face."

She laughed. He was very different from Scott and for a moment she wondered how the two men had met and become friends. "That's right, not to your face."

With a hand on her elbow Joel drew her to the side and looked around. His expression grew serious, and her stomach sunk. She knew she wasn't the type of woman to sleep with a man and not have it get out.

"Was there something else?" She was almost afraid to ask.

"Yes. One of the stringers I know at the *Enquirer* said that a woman was photographed at Scott's Lake Henderson house."

She blanched.

"I wanted to let you know before it leaked out."

Did he know she was the woman or was he trying to save her some heartache? "I know."

"You were the woman." He said it without question in his voice.

"Yes."

"Dammit."

"Do you want me to resign?"

"Let's wait for the pictures and see if you can be identified."

"Why?"

"Because I like you and you're good at your job. And I think maybe you and Scott could be good for each other. To be honest I've never seen him this way with a woman before."

It was on the tip of her tongue to ask if he'd ever known Scott to risk fifty thousand dollars on a woman. But she didn't. Instead, they parted ways. Joel had a late-night game with some friends.

She drifted through the casino but didn't want to go up to her room yet. She didn't want to close her eyes and dream about Scott. She wasn't sure which Scott to believe. The one who'd held her so close to his naked body or the one who'd been in quiet conversation with Stevie.

She exited the hotel and walked on one of the many garden paths around the pool. There was a maze with a gazebo in the middle of it and she thought she might try to find that and…hide. But she couldn't hide from herself.

"Is this a private walk or can I join you?"

Scott. He was standing quietly in the shadows behind her. She couldn't see his features or anything except for his jeans-clad legs. She wasn't sure she was ready to talk to him.

She should have called him on the bet a long time ago instead of playing a game with him. Shoulda, woulda, coulda, she thought. You can't go back and change the past.

"I don't think that's a good idea," she told him. "Have you talked to Joel?"

"No, why?"

"He heard that the *Enquirer* is going to be running a picture of you and an unnamed woman taken at your place on Lake Henderson."

"Damn. I'm sorry, Raine. I never meant for that to happen. I'll call my lawyers and see if we can get the photo pulled."

"Can you do that?"

"I'm sure as hell going to try."

The grounds were mostly deserted; all the serious gamblers were inside the casinos playing their hearts out. The tourists were in their beds sleeping, since all the late-night shows were over. She felt as if she and Scott were the only two people here. But she'd thought that at the lake, too, and it had proved to be wrong. It was too late to just walk away. The damage had been done to her career. If anyone recognized her, she'd be fired from the show.

She wished they were really the only two people here. But instead she remembered seeing him earlier with Stevie, and she found that little girl deep inside her who'd learned how to play the game of the grifters. She knew what she had to do—hide her aching heart and lead Scott down the primrose path. Lead him to his own destruction.

"Do you believe me?" he asked softly.

She knew he'd do his best to stop it but with a sense of inevitability she knew it was too late. "I don't know what to believe anymore."

"I wish we were still at the lake where that wouldn't matter."

"Me, too," she said quietly, meaning it. If they'd never left she could have continued in the dreamlike state that Scott had evoked in her when they'd been together. He slipped his arm around her waist and pulled her to him. She closed her eyes and held him to her, pretending once again that the con was real. That Scott was real. That she hadn't made a huge mistake by sleeping with him. Because she knew she couldn't sleep with a man just for sex. Scott meant more to her than she'd realized.

Everything crystallized in her mind. Seeing Scott and Stevie talking together had reinforced what she already knew. She couldn't trust him. She couldn't trust gamblers. She couldn't trust Scott Rivers.

But why then did she feel as if he was the other part of her soul? Why then did his arms around her feel like the home she'd never had, the home she'd always searched for? Why then did she, who'd made it her life's goal to be honest and real with herself, want to pretend she'd never heard of his bet?

* * *

Scott held her in his arms and knew that everything was spiraling out of his control. He'd ended the bet with Stevie, telling him that Raine had shot him down for the last time and that Stevie had won. Stevie had ribbed him about losing but said he'd been frozen out by Raine, as well.

When the pictures hit the paper, they would be the end to Raine's career as well.

Scott could understand that she wouldn't want him then. He hoped one day she'd meet a man who could give her what she needed. What he wanted her to have. He already knew that he couldn't be that man.

Still, he couldn't help but try.

He couldn't get her out of his head. After making love to her all day, he'd hated the fact that they'd had to return to Vegas and go back to work. Go back to being with other people. He'd wanted to keep them both naked at the lake house for weeks, maybe months.

He wanted them to spend their days and nights just talking, teasing and making love. He knew his hold on her was fragile.

He'd already called his accountant and made arrangements for the money to be wired to Stevie's bank in the morning. The loss of the money didn't bother him. Now he had to get on the phone with his lawyers and he should do it now, but he had the feeling that if he let Raine go, he'd have a hard time getting her back in his arms.

He just hoped that she didn't know about the bet and that he could confess things before it got worse.

Stevie wasn't the kind of guy that Scott could ask to keep a secret. All in all that wasn't one of his better decisions—taking the bet. He'd only done it because… well, his ego was feeling a little bruised by the way she'd kept ignoring him. Now he felt like an idiot.

He'd cleared the way to confess to Raine. But not tonight. She seemed almost fragile tonight, which didn't fit with the woman he'd come to know.

He didn't know how else to bind her to him except to give her all the things women liked. Picnics, romance, jewelry, chocolate. But were those things enough to keep Raine? She wasn't like other women. She saw the ruse he used to keep everyone at bay.

"I have a surprise for you tomorrow afternoon," he said, rubbing his hands down her back.

She tipped her head back and looked up at him. "What makes you think I'm available?"

"Are you going to be difficult?" he asked, tracing one finger down the side of her neck and along the ribbed edge of her T-shirt.

She nodded. "I don't want to be like all the other women you've known."

"You aren't. You keep me on my toes."

"Someone needs to."

She was sassing him and he liked it. There was something low-spirited about Raine tonight and he couldn't figure out what it was.

"Okay, if you don't want to have the adventure of a lifetime."

"Whose lifetime—yours or mine?"

"Both of ours. It'll be a first for both of us."

"What is it?" she asked.

"A flight in Deacon's helicopter to Hoover Dam."

"Who's Deacon?"

"One of my buddies, remember, the other trouble-maker."

"Oh, that one. You've never flown in a helicopter before?"

"Yes, I have, but not with you. I thought we'd take a picnic with us and have dinner before coming back to the hotel."

He led her away from the stone path and into the maze. The night air was filled with the scent of jasmine—his mother's favorite plant. He kept Raine tucked up under his shoulder as they moved through the maze.

She bit her lower lip and wouldn't really look at him. "I'm tired."

"Tired of me?" he asked. That was his real fear. That by being himself, he'd somehow bored her. He could play a more exciting role, be anything she needed him to be.

She stopped then. "No, Scott. Tired of me. Tired of replaying the same things in my head."

"What things? Maybe I can help."

She shook her head. "I have to do this myself."

"Can I take you upstairs and make you forget about your troubles?"

She turned to him then. The moonlight fell softly over the planes of her face. "Yes. I think I'd like that."

He bent and kissed her. He couldn't get enough of her mouth, and when she looked up at him with her eyes filled with some indefinable emotion, he needed to. He wanted to wipe away the sadness he sensed in her and replace it with…what? He couldn't be responsible for another person's happiness, no matter how much he wanted to be.

He slipped his key card from his pocket. "My suite number is 2435. Go on up. I'll meet you there."

"What are you going to do?"

"Call my lawyers and take care of that picture. Then I'll be up."

"Thanks," she said.

"Honey, I wouldn't do anything to hurt you."

"Really, Scott?"

"I wouldn't lie to you, Raine. I know that we haven't known each other long, but you're too important to me for me to lie."

She stepped away from him. "I'm glad to hear that. I don't think I could ever forgive a man who lied to me."

She walked away from him, and he felt the weight of his actions and his words fall heavily around his shoulders. He knew he was going to have to tell her about Stevie's bet. But he also knew he needed time to bind her to him. And romantic dates weren't going to be enough. He needed to bind her to him first with her body and then hopefully her heart and soul would follow.

Raine let herself into Scott's suite and waited for him. His suite was larger than hers and overlooked the hotel's waterfall and pool. It was made up of two rooms and a small balcony. She walked through the two rooms and steeled herself to continue playing the role she'd selected for herself. The role of a woman falling in love with a man who was too good to be true.

If only it were a role and not the real thing. She knew she was going to have to push aside those doubts. That very real feeling of being betrayed by a man she'd let herself care for. She'd been doing a better job of it before—no, she hadn't. And she refused to lie to herself. She'd been falling in love with Scott since the moment she'd met him.

The room was opulently appointed and though she knew Scott would feel comfortable in this room, she now knew this wasn't the real man. The man she was coming to know was more comfortable in a relaxed setting. She trailed her fingers over the leather love seat in the sitting room before opening the French doors leading to the balcony and stepping outside.

That was the hard part. The glimpses she'd had of the real Scott Rivers all added up to a man who really wouldn't be able to make a bet about getting a woman he cared for into bed.

She wished he'd just confess to her what he'd done. That way she could try to figure out if he was sincere in his pursuit of her—which, her heart told her, he had to be—or whether he'd just been playing one of those kinky games that bored, wealthy men sometimes played.

He was out of her league on so many levels. But

were they only surface things, as she wanted to believe, or were they things that went bone deep?

She curled her fingers around the cold wrought-iron bars that lined the balcony and stared blindly down at the fantasy world of the Chimera. A world designed to entice its visitors to forget about the mundane details of everyday life and indulge themselves in their fantasies. To forget the consequences of their everyday world and just live for the moment.

She heard the suite door open but stayed where she was on the balcony. She didn't want to face Scott yet.

She heard his footfalls on the carpeted floor as he came toward her. He paused on the landing just before stepping out on the balcony, where she was.

"My lawyers are taking care of the pictures. I think we got to it in time."

She didn't turn around and look at him. She needed to pretend that this was real. That here in the land of the ultimate illusion they'd found something to believe in.

"Honey?"

She didn't want to talk. She wanted to lose herself in his arms once more. To feed the fantasy that was so believable until they'd returned here.

"Make love to me out here."

He stepped out onto the balcony, his arms closing around her from behind. His hands skimmed down her body, lingering to cup her breasts and to tease her nipples through the layers of her T-shirt and bra. She laid her head back on his shoulder, turned her head so she could kiss his neck.

He lifted her shirt, pushed her bra out of the way and cupped her breasts. He held them up, and she noticed him staring down at her exposed body. Her nipples were beaded and hard from the combination of his touch and the cold night air. She shivered and undulated against him.

He plucked at her nipples until she moaned his name. She needed him. Turning in his embrace, she leaned up on her toes and kissed him. She thrust her tongue deep in his mouth and rubbed her aroused breasts against his chest.

She wedged her hands between them and ripped open his shirt. The buttons fell to the floor and she pushed the shirt off his shoulders. She needed him now. She wanted to feel his warm, naked skin on hers.

She rubbed her breasts against his chest and heard him moan. She felt his hands skimming down her back and cupping her butt, pulling her more fully against his erection.

She adjusted her body against him so that he was rubbing right where she needed him to be. He lifted her up and suckled her nipple, biting lightly at her flesh and then soothing it with his tongue. She wrapped her legs around his hips and rocked against him.

He suckled her other nipple into his mouth, pulling so strongly at her that she felt her womb clench. She wanted him inside her now.

She slid off his body, undoing her jeans and pushing them down her legs. "I need you now."

"Me, too, honey."

He turned her around, put her hands on the wrought-iron railing. "Don't let go."

She couldn't have if her life depended on it. She felt his mouth at the nape of her neck then the scraping of his teeth down the line of her spine. Then he returned to her nape and traced his tongue down her back.

She shivered with each touch of his mouth on her skin. Her entire body was extremely sensitized, and she felt as if she was going to peak at any moment but held off the inevitable because the waiting felt so good. And she wanted him deep inside her when she had her orgasm.

His fingers traced the crease in her buttocks, then she felt the nip of his teeth on each cheek. "You have such a nice ass, honey."

She bit her lip as his fingers dipped lower, found her wet and ready for him. As always his fingers were firm, his caresses arousing her so much that in a meeting she'd seen him shake hands with Hayden and had immediately felt his fingers on her skin.

The way he rubbed his hand over her belly just before he entered her. The way he caught her wrists in one hand while he thrust into her. The way his callused hands aroused her to the point of no return.

Then he was pressed against her back. His jeans felt rough against her, his erection prodded at the small of her back. She reached between their bodies, caressing him and freeing him from the confines of his jeans. She was surprised to feel him naked under his pants.

He thrust into her palm and she cupped him, held

him while he moved against her. "I wanted to be ready for you this time."

"Condom?"

"One minute."

She heard him opening the packet and glanced over her shoulder to watch him put it on.

"Open your legs a little wider."

She did and he bent his knees and entered her from behind. He held himself just inside her until she squirmed and pushed herself back on him. He slid all the way home and she felt her body quiver. She knew it wasn't going to take more than a thrust to push her over the edge. He slid his hand down her body, his fingers finding that little bud between her legs.

"Come for me, Raine," he said, circling it with his finger as he started thrusting deep inside her.

She did and then again before he finally found his release inside her. He held her carefully in his arms, both of them spent. He separated their bodies and carried her inside, making love to her again in his bed.

Ten

The next few weeks Scott dedicated himself to keeping Raine happy. The *Enquirer* had caught three more photos of him, but he'd been careful to stay away from Raine in public. He didn't like it, but he'd had to sneak into her room, or her into his, late at night. He'd won his week of matches and now had one more week of shooting with the three champions from the other weeks.

Raine had been in Vegas the entire time and he stayed in the background during her time on the set. He flew his parents in to meet her and they'd spent the weekend at his lake house. Raine had gone there with Kylie and Shelby to visit and then later Deacon and Hayden had arrived so that there was no way a picture of just Raine and him could be taken.

His mom adored Raine and told him if he let her get away, she'd never forgive him. Scott needed some solid advice, and his dad was the kind who would be able to help him out. But in the end Scott, who'd always been the good son, couldn't tell them that he'd made a bet about Raine and ask for some suggestions on how to break that news to her.

But tonight that would end; tonight he planned to tell her everything at dinner. Hayden was waiting for him in the lobby of the Chimera. He liked his friend but didn't really want to see him right now.

"There's a major problem," Hayden said.

"What do you mean?"

"We've got a pack of paparazzi waiting outside that door for you and Raine."

"Both of us, why?"

"Gossip on the set was leaked to the press and the *Enquirer* ran that picture you suppressed a few weeks ago. Then one of the players speculated you've been sleeping with Raine to continue being on the show. And Steve let slip you bet him 50K you'd get her into bed."

"What's it like out there?"

"Crazy. Sal is running interference and I've called Deacon and few of the other hotel owners to see if there is anyone bigger in town who can take the heat off of you two."

"Any luck?"

"No. They latched on to your story because it's a slow news week."

Scott wanted to put his hand through a wall. He'd

waited too long to come clean with Raine, and now it was going to be too little, too late. This was why he'd stuck to relationships built on movie screens or television sets. He sucked at real life.

"What the hell were you thinking?" Hayden asked him. "You know Stevie can't keep his mouth shut."

"I wasn't thinking. I knew I wanted Raine and nothing would stop me from having her…so betting on it didn't seem a bad thing."

Hayden clapped his hand on Scott's shoulder, and though no words were spoken he knew his friend would do whatever he could to help him. He swallowed hard.

"I managed to catch Raine before she walked into the lobby."

"Where is she?"

"In my office. I've got the monitors on so we can keep an eye on the paparazzi."

When they reached his office, Hayden pushed open the door, but Scott didn't enter. Raine sat huddled, sipping some kind of hot beverage. He'd never seen her look so small or fragile as she did in that moment. He started to really hate himself when he saw her. He knew that he'd convinced her to play for high stakes. And she'd lost.

He'd never allowed himself to think there would be anything but a happy ending for them. After all, it was what he was used to. But now he was standing a short distance from the press who all wanted to take photos of a woman he'd bet fifty thousand dollars that he could take to bed.

Shelby was there with her but still Raine kept to

herself. Scott didn't know what to do. He'd always been the press's darling. He liked them; they liked him. He'd never done anything that would sell papers like this story would.

Joel was en route. They both knew that Raine would be losing her job and there was a fairly good chance Scott wouldn't be playing in the championship this week. He didn't give a crap about that.

What pissed him off was that he'd ever made the bet. A big part of him acknowledged it was because he was so used to winning, so used to getting his own way, that it had ticked him off when she'd kept turning him down.

"Can we have a moment, Hayden?" Scott asked. He just wanted to make this right.

"Um, I'm not sure how to say this, but this is the wrong time for you to be alone with your woman."

He knew Hayden was right. But he didn't care. This was what happened when he tried to be himself. When he stopped playing the roles he knew how to play. And he had to fix it.

"Will you get the press assembled in a room? Tell them I'll release a statement."

Hayden made a few calls and put the entire thing in motion. Raine still hadn't glanced up at him or said a word to him. Shelby, Hayden's sweet wife, was also there, glaring daggers at him.

"I'm not leaving," she said.

Scott barely nodded at her. Raine still wouldn't look at him, and he knew he needed to do some fast thinking if he wanted to make this right. He stepped back out of Hayden's office and called his folks. His dad was still up watching the late news.

"I need you and Mom to come to Vegas tonight."

"What's the matter?"

"I screwed up, Dad. Big time. And I hurt Raine. She…doesn't have the kind of family we do, so will you and Mom come here?"

"Tell me what happened," his father said.

Scott did. Not sparing himself or Raine in the telling, he just explained his stupid bet. And then ended with the paparazzi camped in Hayden's hotel.

"Get her out of there. We'll meet her at the lake house."

"Take my plane, Dad. I've got them readying it."

They hung up a few minutes later, and Scott was aware that his parents were disappointed in him. It was the first time he'd had to call them to bail him out of something stupid he'd done, and he didn't like it. He liked being the golden boy. He liked the kind of life he had when he was golden and not some kind of schmuck. He'd wager that Raine was thinking the same thing.

Deacon pushed through the door at the end of the hallway. "Hayden called me. Kylie's out front with the Mercedes and she's volunteered to get Raine out of here."

"Thanks, Deacon. She's pretty mad at me—"

"Say no more. I'll go talk to her. Hayden's got them distracted. I'll take care of your woman."

Scott's heart skipped a beat. If only she were still his woman. But he had a feeling when he sorted this mess out, she was never going to talk to him again.

Joel walked in a few minutes later, and a bold photographer pushed his way past Hayden's security guards to snap pictures of Scott in the hallway. The guards grabbed him and forced him back into the casino.

"This is a hell of a mess, Rivers. I'll need to see Raine privately, then you. Don't go anywhere."

"I'm not leaving."

Joel had left her alone after terminating her contract. He wouldn't bring legal action, because as he said, the ways of the heart didn't give a damn about legal obligations. His words echoed in her mind as she sat in the passenger seat of Kylie Prescott's Mercedes, riding through the night toward Scott's lake house. Shelby sat in the backseat.

Raine felt a certain sense of comfort from the other women. They were both so indignant on her behalf and upset with Scott. She felt almost guilty about it. They didn't know that she'd run her own con. That she'd played Scott and herself in a dangerous game involving both of their hearts. Now she was jobless and she had no one to blame but herself.

"I know how you feel," Kylie said into the quiet.

"I doubt that," Raine said. She honestly didn't think any other person understood how she felt. They couldn't possibly unless they'd had a glimpse of the kind of life they'd always longed for. One filled not only with a job they loved, but with the kind of man who she'd never imagined could exist.

"You're angry, hurt, you can't believe that you could fall for a man who'd think making a bet about you was a good idea."

She glanced at Kylie. "That sounds like the voice of experience."

"It is. Hayden bet Deacon he couldn't convince me to marry him. I didn't find out until after we were married." Kylie shook her head at the memories. "Deacon had some idea about marrying the perfect woman."

Raine studied the woman. Kylie was pretty and obviously in love with her husband. And she was kind. Nice and quiet in a bookish sort of way with her horn-rim glasses and her conservative clothing. It was hard to think she was the ideal woman for a gambler like Deacon.

"Scott wasn't looking for the perfect woman. He was looking to prove he could thaw my ice-queen image."

She felt a little raw when she thought about it. What he'd thought of her and how he'd acted.

"Who'd he bet with?" Shelby asked from the backseat. "I know Hayden and Deacon both learned their lesson from what happened with Kylie. And I don't think Max would bet on a woman."

"Stevie Taylor."

"Scott should have known better. Stevie spends more time on the cover of the tabloids than he does onstage."

Raine said nothing. She couldn't fully blame Scott, because she'd known about the bet and could have walked away. She should have, but there'd been something about him that enticed her. "I knew about the bet. I conned Scott into falling for me so I could push him away."

Kylie took her eyes from the road, her face illuminated in the dashboard lights. Raine felt like her father's daughter in that moment. She wondered how he ever got used to that feeling that came from knowing you'd used someone for your own good.

"But you fell for him, didn't you?" Shelby asked.

Raine had never had any girlfriends and wasn't sure she liked talking about her feelings, but there was something so easy about these women. "Yes, I guess I did."

"To be honest, these guys are good men, they just make error judgments. With Deacon it's because he grew up without any parental supervision. He learned to scheme and con to get everything he wanted. It never occurred to him not to wager on me."

Raine leaned deeper in the seat. Scott didn't have that excuse. "I think Scott is so used to playing roles that he doesn't always think about the consequences until after he gets into the part he's playing."

But Scott had soon stopped acting around her. She wished she'd met him at a different time. Like now, when she had no job and lots of time on her hands.

They arrived at the lake house. Kylie handed her the key that she'd gotten from Scott before they'd left the Chimera. "You don't have to stay," Raine said.

"Yes, we do. You might want to talk."

"I'm really not that type of person."

"Well, if you change your mind we'll be here," Shelby said firmly.

Raine opened the door and they turned on the lights as they entered the house. Raine felt Scott's absence keenly.

Shelby came to stand next to her. "Listen, Raine," she said softly, "I also have been where you are—"

"I don't think so." Shelby owned a very successful chain of lingerie stores, Bêcheur d'Or, so Raine highly doubted that the sophisticated woman standing next to her really had ever been where she was.

"I married Hayden for his money," Shelby said bluntly.

"What?"

"I took a million dollars from his dad to leave him at the altar when we were both too young to be married. So believe me when I say I know what you're feeling."

Shelby explained how she'd come back to Vegas to make up for her past with Hayden and ended up falling for him again. Only this time they both were honest with each other.

Raine stared at her. Maybe these two women did understand her. "I can't forgive myself for trying to fool him like that. I mean, I know he didn't start out with the best intentions, but I still shouldn't have played him like I did."

The other women watched her for a minute and then gave her a hug. For the first time ever, Raine felt it was okay that she was flawed. These women weren't perfect and their husbands hadn't always done the right thing, but they'd made their relationships work. So maybe there might be hope for her and Scott.

Later that night as she lay in Scott's bed, she replayed the day in her head and realized that she now had a clean slate. A chance to go to Scott as a woman in the open, not lying to him, not hiding from him and not hiding from herself.

His parents had gone up to the lake house, and Shelby and Kylie had returned to town. Scott had avoided them, not really wanting to know that there was no hope left for him and Raine. So instead he'd made a public apology on every entertainment news program who'd have him on. He took out ads in *Variety, Premiere, Entertainment Weekly* and *USA Today* apologizing formally for his crass bet. Stevie had done the same thing at Scott's insistence.

It turned out Stevie had made an offhand comment about the bet to one of his bandmates and this had been overheard by a tabloid journalist who'd been in town to cover Paris Hilton's latest party.

Scott knew that Raine had been used in her life by her father and her brother. He also knew that the one thing she'd always counted on—her job—had been taken from her because of him. He'd hurt her on so many levels that getting her back was going to involve more than just candy and flowers.

He racked his brain for something that would

convince her that he wasn't a schmuck and that she should take him back. Finally he figured out what he had to do.

He approached Joel and since Joel had been rooting for them from the beginning, he agreed to do something a little unorthodox. It took a lot of planning and finessing but at last every detail was in place.

He had Joel call her back to Vegas to say he had a few questions for her about the show. Then he waited until she was back in the hotel. Hayden had offered him the use of the penthouse garden-side balcony and Scott took him up on it.

He was going to ask Raine to be his wife. He was going to come clean with her, then apologize and make love to her.

He held the bouquet of stargazer lilies in one hand and a small bag from Bêcheur d'Or in the other and waited in a private lounge for the elevator to arrive. He'd sent the invitation for dinner to her room. He had no idea if she'd show up, but Hayden and Deacon had both promised to watch the monitors for her.

His cell phone rang. "Rivers."

"It's Hayden. She's on her way."

"Thanks," he said, then hung up.

The elevator opened and she stood there looking up at him wearily. "What are you doing here?"

"Coming clean." He handed her the flowers. "Have dinner with me tonight."

Scott had ordered Italian food because he knew that Raine loved it. And she'd been eating from craft services for the last few weeks. Between Hayden and Deacon they had the most accomplished chefs in Nevada on staff. He'd asked for dishes he knew would keep well. He hadn't wanted servers or anyone else in this paradise he'd created.

He'd studied for this role carefully. In his experience every woman wanted a man with a three-part combination that included the suaveness and sexiness of James Bond, the intelligence and wit of Robert Redford in *Legal Eagles* and the safety and security of Michael Keaton in *Mr. Mom.*

He led them to a satin-draped table where candlelight sparkled off two Waterford flutes. He pulled out her chair, and before he sat he poured them both a glass of champagne and took a deep breath. Now that the moment was here he couldn't remember any of the performances he'd studied. He nervously felt under his chair for the ring box. It was exactly where he'd secured it with gaffers' tape earlier.

He snapped it open and felt the diamond ring waiting there. It was his great-grandmother's ring. An antique platinum setting. His father had been happy to give it to Scott, ready for his son to settle down and very happy with the woman he'd selected.

Now if only she'd have him. Scott knew there was a big chance she'd say no. Raine didn't make snap decisions. And she wasn't one to do anything without weighing the consequences.

He finally found his voice. "First I want to apologize for not making sure those photographers stayed away from you. And for not taking the threat to your job as seriously as I should have."

"You weren't the only one to blame," she said carefully, but she wouldn't look at him and that hurt. Had he killed every bit of feeling she'd had for him?

He cleared his throat and lifted his champagne flute. She lifted hers as well.

They both took a sip. She moved to set her glass down, and Scott realized the time was at hand. He needed to…just do it.

He pushed to his feet, startling her and bumping the table. He shoved the ring into his pocket and tried to recall the smooth moves he'd studied to get ready for this night.

His mind drew a blank.

"Scott?"

He came around the table to her side, then leaned one hip on the edge of the table, facing her. His hands were sweating. Dammit, he never sweated. Not even when he'd debuted on Broadway at the age of twelve.

He wiped his palms on his pants. "I have something…to say. Those weeks we spent together were the best of my life. I've always had a rich life, I'm not denying that, but you've added a new dimension. One I didn't realize was missing until you stepped onto the set and gave me direction. And I know that I screwed up majorly, but I hope that this will help make up for it."

She tipped her face back to look up at him. In his mind's eye he saw her the way he wanted her—her lips swollen from his kisses, her eyes soft and wide, her skin still a little flushed—and he wanted her again.

He wanted to say the hell with all these trappings of romance and take her back to his suite. He wanted to lay her in the center of his bed and make love to her, and when she was limp with exhaustion from his loving, he wanted to slip the ring on her finger and make her his forever.

"Are you okay?" she asked.

He realized he was standing over her just staring at her. "Yes. I'm trying to tell you that you gave me something I've never found with anyone else. With you I don't have to be 'on' all the time. With you I have the luxury of being myself and I'm finding I actually like it."

"You might believe that I gave you that but it was already there. You're a very generous man and a loyal friend. I had nothing to do with that." Her words weren't reluctant and he saw she was sincere.

"Yes, you did. You made me comfortable in my own skin. Made me want to be better than I've ever been before."

"Well, you've done the same for me. I think I would have continued on, carefully keeping all men at arm's length for the rest of my life, if you hadn't pushed your way closer."

"You were just waiting for the right Prince Charming."

"Now you're an animated character. Really, Scott, is there no end to your talents?"

"What can I say? You lucked out when you met me," he said.

"And hardly any ego."

"You're right. I should have said I lucked out when I met you. I really did, Raine. My life…well, let's just say you've given me purpose."

She bit her lip. "I swear if you say I complete you, I'm not going to be responsible for my actions."

"Dammit, woman. I'm trying to tell you something important."

"Then stop trying to be whatever you think I want. Just lay it on the line. Why am I here? So you can make amends before you jet off to your next exciting locale?"

He dropped to one knee in front of her. "No, honey. Never. What I'm trying to tell you is that…"

He couldn't say the words out loud. He realized now that he always just said "Me, too," when his mom said them to him. Always just settled for a gruff hug with the old man when it came time to say goodbye.

"What?"

And here was Raine. A woman who needed the words from him. As he looked up at her, he knew he needed to say them. To make this moment as real as it could be. To know that this wasn't just another memory he thought he had that turned out to be a scene from a play or a TV show.

"I love you," he said.

Her eyes went wide and jaw dropped. "Scott, I don't know what to—"

"I'm not done yet. I want you to marry me."

She swallowed as he pulled the ring from his pocket and held it up to her. "This was my great-grandmother's ring. It was one of the only possessions she brought with her from Italy when she came to the U.S." He slid it on her finger. "It would give me a great feeling of honor and pride if you'd say you'll marry me and wear this ring."

Eleven

Raine looked down at the antique ring on her finger, unable to believe what she'd heard. What he'd asked her. She wanted to say yes. She wanted to somehow find a way to make what they'd shared real enough that they both could spend the rest of their days together.

"Raine?" he asked, still on his knee in front of her.

His hand felt big and warm around hers. Safe in a way that she wanted to be for the rest of her life. But he was more than safety. He was more than she'd expected, and she knew that she'd been falling for him. "I…I don't know if I can."

"Why not?" he asked, pushing to his feet.

She tipped her head back to look up at him. Marriage was unexpected, though she'd had an inkling he'd been thinking of long-term with her when he'd brought her to meet his parents.

It had been obvious from that weekend where the "real" Scott came from. His parents were retired teachers who had a strong sense of self and community. To be honest they were the kind of parents she'd always craved for herself. And Scott was the kind of man she'd dreamed of having by her side, except for his penchant for adventure and gaming.

"I haven't been thinking of us in those kinds of terms."

He went back to his seat, reached across the table and took her hands in his. "How can you not be? I know that feelings this strong can't be one-sided."

Tears burned the back of her eyes. "You're right, but how do we both know that it's not just this wonderful setting?"

"Hell, I'd feel the same if we were in your hotel room or at Red Rock or riding on the Harley. It's you, Raine. You're the one I want to spend my days and nights with. The one I want to hold in my arms and make love to every chance we get. The one I need by my side."

His words moved her. She saw the truth in them and it scared her. She did love Scott. There was no doubt inside her that she loved him. But was it real? She was so afraid to believe it.

They'd both spent their entire relationship in Vegas not living real lives. They'd also both spent the entire time lying to each other, and she was the one who knew it. "Honey, I swear you won't regret it."

"It's not that I fear I'll regret it."

"What are you afraid of?"

"That this isn't real. You're a gambler not only by luck and skill but by design. Everything in your life is a risk or a challenge or a dare."

He shook his head.

"Our first date was a dare. That's how you approach life and how you live it. I'm not like that. I have dreams about marriage, Scott. Dreams of what I think a husband and wife should be."

"I can make them come true," he said. "You say that I live for a dare or a challenge. Tell me what you want and I'll make that my challenge, wrapping you in my love and keeping you happy all the rest of our days."

How could she say no? How could she not reach out and take what he was offering her? He offered her the fulfillment of the secret dreams she'd always held.

"Let's make our dreams come true," he said.

And she flashed back to her father saying the same words to her so many times throughout her youth. She knew that Scott wasn't her dad. Knew he had money… now.

"Dreams aren't what life is about," she said, slipping the ring from her finger.

"What are you talking about?"

"I'm not the right woman for you. You need someone who is willing to play your games, someone who is happy living from moment to moment. And I'm not that woman."

"You could be," he said, taking the ring and holding it in his hand. He took her wrist with his other hand, brushing a kiss against the center of her palm. "And I could be the perfect man for you."

She closed her eyes against the truth she saw in his. This was what her life was going to come down to. This one moment when she either had to take a chance on Scott—take a chance on falling for her own con and knowing for the rest of her days that she had tricked him into loving her—or walk away and spend the rest of her days alone.

"I'm so afraid that this won't translate away from Vegas. That once you see me in the real world, you'll realize all the reasons you don't want me as your wife."

He shook his head, kissing her palm one more time and then her wrist. He placed the ring in the center of her palm and closed her fingers gently over it. "I could never do that, honey."

"You say that now when things are going well. You've been winning on the show and at the tables here in Vegas. But what if your winning streak ends? Then what will happen?"

He said nothing and she knew he couldn't. She was bringing him down and hadn't intended that. She should have ended things a long time ago, before either of them had to be hurt. And she knew Scott was hurting, as well. But she couldn't marry him. She just couldn't.

She opened her hand, stared at this family heirloom that he'd been willing to give to her. "I'm sorry, Scott, but I can't marry you."

She handed him back the ring and walked away from the magic of the night, the magic of the man, the magic of love. Because Raine Montgomery knew that magic was just an illusion.

Scott watched her walk away, unable to believe that this night was going so wrong. He pocketed the ring and ran to her, stopping her before she could get on the elevator.

"You can't just walk away."

"Yes, I can." There were tracks from her tears running down her face, and it was like taking a body blow to the gut.

He pulled her into his arms, not wanting to see her hurt. He hadn't meant to hurt her with this. He wanted to resolve their affair. To make it more than a temporary thing. Having fallen in love for the first time, he wanted to show her to the world.

She sniffed and he found his handkerchief in his back pocket and handed it to her. She wiped her eyes.

"Thank you." She neatly refolded the handkerchief and handed it back to him.

"There's no reason for this, Raine. We can have a long engagement if you need time to come to terms with marrying me."

"It's not just that." She took a few steps back, putting some distance between them, wrapping her arms around her waist.

"Then what the hell is it?" he asked, frustrated that he couldn't get her to see what their lives could be, that she wasn't buying into his vision of their future together. She was standing in the exact same spot she'd been in earlier, when everything had been going smoothly. Earlier, before his carefully rehearsed evening had gone to hell.

"I…can't trust you," she said, biting her lower lip.

"You did before the press showed up and ruined everything."

"I mean with my heart," she said quietly.

"Dammit, I'm not your father, Raine. I'm not going to make promises, get your eyes shining in anticipation and then never deliver. Don't you know that by now?" he asked. He knew this romance thing would backfire. If he had her in bed…but they couldn't spend their lives together in bed. Sex obviously wasn't a problem between them. What had he missed?

She shook her head and he realized that being the kind and caring suitor wasn't getting the job done. "Don't make me pay for your father's sins."

"Is that what you think this is about? Some payback for all the times any man has wronged me?"

He shrugged. He had no idea what was going through her mind right now. "It seems to me that you are still running. I'm not going to dare you to marry me. This is too important to me. You are too important to me.

"You need to take a leap of faith and trust that I'll be here to catch you. But until you're ready to do that, we don't have anything." He held his arms open, inviting her back into his embrace.

"Trust works both ways, right?" she asked, not moving.

He dropped his arms to his sides. "Of course it does."

"How does lying fit into the entire trust scheme?" she asked in a silky tone that made the hairs on the back of his neck rise.

"What are you talking about? I'm not lying to you."

"You already have done that, Scott." She dropped her arms to her sides and took a step forward, no longer vulnerable but angry.

"When?" he asked, afraid she was referring to the bet.

"When you made a bet about getting me in bed and then seduced me by being the man of my dreams."

He didn't attempt to deny it. "I'm trying to make it right by asking you to marry me."

"Don't try to explain. I might start to believe in this fairy tale you've created."

"How did you hear about it?"

"I overheard you that first day."

"Why didn't you say something that day in the booth?"

"Why didn't you?" she countered. "I was so angry with you. Believe it or not I'd started to weaken and was thinking about maybe going out with you after filming was over."

"But then, like an ass, I made that bet," he said. Having come to know Raine and fallen in love with her, he realized that he'd done something she'd never be able to forgive. He'd known that for a while now but had thought he could tell her about it after they were a couple, when he could convince her to forgive him.

"Exactly," she said. "And I got angry."

"What do you mean?" He didn't know the woman standing before him now. The softness and the caring he'd come to associate with Raine were gone. Her eyes, which usually broadcast whatever she felt, were cold.

"I mean you really pissed me off. And I decided to see if I still had it."

"Had what?"

She walked right up to him, ran her fingers across the stubble on his jaw. "The ability to run a con."

"What kind of con?" he asked, because he needed to know how deeply they'd both played each other and themselves.

"The perfect con, the one to make Mr. Charming fall in love with me."

"Are you trying to tell me this has all been an act?"

She nodded.

"I don't buy it. You might have started out planning to make me fall for you, like a first-class grifter, but it changed, didn't it? You fell for your own con."

"There were times I was tempted, but then I'd remember—this is a man who's got a lot of money riding on making me fall for him, and that's not something I can love."

This time she walked away and he let her go.

Raine was shaking as she entered the elevator car. Everything had gone horribly wrong. She felt ashamed of herself for what she'd done to Scott. It didn't matter that he'd been lying to her. All that really mattered was that she wanted to get away.

She'd lost Scott and a little of her self-respect in the process. She wrapped her arms around her own waist and leaned against the back door of the elevator car. When the door opened, she tried to wipe her tears. She was surprised to see Scott standing there.

She realized she'd never selected a floor, so the car had stayed where it was.

"Oh, honey, come here."

She shook her head, but he came to her and pulled her into his arms. She couldn't hold back her tears, and she fought not to sob out loud at how right he felt wrapped around her. A part of her wanted to say to hell with cons and bets and just start over.

But trust wasn't easily won from either of them. He stroked his hands up and down her back, and she just clung to him, hiding in his strength one last time.

"I ended the bet with Stevie, told him he won and paid him the money. I don't want you to think that I would sleep with you for the money."

"If you did you overpaid," she said, because she wanted to hurt him, maybe even wanted to hurt them both. This wasn't easy. She didn't think it ever would be. A part of her wished she'd never told him she knew, so then she could have continued the ruse forever.

"Don't do that. You are so sensual, willing to do whatever I ask of you. I swear, woman, I'll never get enough of you in my bed."

She felt the same way. Scott had unlocked a hidden part of her soul that she'd never thought really mattered. Sex had always been something she did when she needed to feel close to another human being. When she needed to be held, she'd date a guy a few times, have sex with him and then move on.

But she couldn't move on now. She knew it. Scott had changed something inside her, and while she might have been trying to con him into falling for her, she knew she was the one who'd been conned. Conned into forgetting about the circumstances of her actions.

"Come back and let's finish our champagne," he said, taking her by the hand.

She allowed him to lead her back to the table. She followed closely on his heels and took her seat. She sipped the champagne, but the magic of the night was lost in the reality of what they both were.

She wondered if Joel would want to make a reality show based on gamblers and con artists and how if they both mixed it would be to their detriment.

"What are you thinking?" he asked. There was an edge to his voice that had never been there before.

"That we can never trust each other. Aren't you thinking the same thing?" she asked. She knew it had to be true. They'd both been playing with each other. Was their love a by-product of the games or was it the real thing? To be honest that was what scared her—that she'd think it was the real thing and wake up one morning to the truth.

He put his flute down. "I'm trying not to. Just let it go, Raine."

"Don't want to marry me anymore, do you?"

"I didn't say that. But I do realize we don't know each other as well as I thought we did."

"Or maybe we know each other too well. Maybe the fact that you fell for a woman who was acting is too eerie for you."

"I don't think you know what you're talking about."

"Actually, I think I've finally figured it out. We're both actors. I'm pretending that my life can be normal, and you're pretending that your life's not one big play written by someone else's standards."

"If you want to be down on yourself, that's one thing. But I was raised by real people, not someone who taught his daughter to prey on men's emotions for her own gain."

His words hurt, cutting deep into the very heart of her. Part of her knew he was right, but that didn't stop her from getting mad.

"Yeah, your parents must be really proud that you bet on getting a girl in bed."

"What bothers you, Raine? That I made the bet with Stevie or that we both know I won it?"

She pushed to her feet. Gone was the emotional fragility she'd felt earlier. Now she was just angry. Angry enough not to care that she might regret this later. How could she ever have felt she was in love with him?

He was a gambler, a daredevil. All the things she knew better than to fall for.

"I'm sorry, Raine," he said, catching her in his arms before she could leave. "If you're not ready to be my wife, that's okay. I'll wait. But know that I'm ready to be your man."

"I need some time."

He nodded, but he knew time was the last thing she needed. She needed to realize that she trusted him and that he was worthy of that trust.

"No, you don't. You need your man to take control."

Twelve

"How do you plan to do that?" she asked.

His smile was bold and wicked. And he kissed her with all the passion and emotion she'd been afraid to believe he felt for her.

"I'm going to have to blindfold you so you will focus only on me."

She arched one eyebrow at him. "Okay."

From his pocket he took a long, smooth piece of silk he'd gotten from Bêcheur d'Or here in the Chimera. "How do you feel about fur-lined handcuffs?"

"On you?"

"Pink's not really my color. But if you wear them for me, I'll wear them for you."

"That's what I like about you, Scott," she said as he

fastened the blindfold over her eyes, carefully freeing a few strands of her hair.

"What do you like?" he asked.

Her breathing was a bit more rapid. Her skin had a healthy glow to it, and her lips were parted. He leaned forward and stroked his tongue over them, dipping inside to taste her mouth. He was addicted to her mouth. He could spend all night kissing her.

When he pulled back she licked her lips, as if wanting to hold on to the taste of him.

"What do you like about me, honey?" he asked again.

She shook her head. "The fact that you're into kinky things but always play fair."

"Play fair?"

"Yes. I think of it as equal-opportunity bondage."

He threw his head back and laughed. This was going to be the best night of his life. If he had any doubts about asking Raine to spend forever with him, they quickly disappeared. She was everything he wanted in a woman.

He led her to the elevator and put the key card in for the penthouse floor. When the car stopped and the door opened, he bypassed Hayden's apartment and opened the door to the balcony overlooking the garden some fifty floors below. Everything was as he'd planned. Twinkle lights sparkled in the trees, and a table was set with fine china. He bent his head, kissing Raine one more time.

Raine leaned up into Scott's embrace. She loved the feel of his arms around her. He made her forget the worries of her day, forget the emotional doubts that plagued her when they were apart. Like a junkie with her favorite drug, she needed the sweet bliss that being in his arms gave her.

She slid her arms around his waist, then lower, cupping his butt as she canted her own hips toward his.

She pulled her head back, wishing he'd removed the blindfold so she could see where they were. She strained her ears and heard nothing but a light wind and soft music.

His thumb stroked over the pulse at her wrist. His scent surrounded her, and she tipped her head to the side, waiting to see what he had planned for her.

She felt him move around behind her, his breath hot on the nape of her neck. She'd struggled with her hair and finally gotten it up in a fairly decent chignon. His mouth at the base of her neck banished all thoughts of her hair.

He sucked on her skin there. Shivers radiated down her shoulders and arms, spreading over her breasts and down her body. He scraped his teeth along the edges of her bare shoulders.

"Do you like that?" he asked, brushing his lips over her ear.

"Yes."

"You'll like what I have planned next even more."

She felt something smooth run along the neckline of her dress. It was soft, like his mouth on her skin, but cool. A faint flowery scent teased her senses, and she realized it was a rose. He traced the lines of her face with the flower, teasingly drawing it around the edges of the blindfold.

He trailed it down her neck and down the edge of the bodice of her dress. He skimmed it over her arms and then brought it back again to her neck.

"Untie the fastening at the back of your neck."

She hesitated. He kissed her again, this time fiercely, showering her with his masculine skill and power.

"Do it for both of us," he urged.

She lifted her hands and loosened the knot that held the halter dress up. As soon as it was untied, she lowered her arms. The zipper at the side of the dress ensured that the top stayed up.

Scott lowered the front of her dress until she felt the air on her naked breasts. Then the heat of his breath as he traced random patterns over her entire chest with his tongue. She stood there in her heels, blindfold on, breasts exposed, quaking and wanting him.

Then she felt the petal softness of the rose over her skin. With his tongue he followed the same pattern, completely devastating her with the thoroughness of his touch. Her nipples were hard, tight, begging for his attention.

She felt the rose swirl over first one nipple then the other. He repeated his caresses between her two nipples until she was ready to scream. She reached up and grabbed for his wrist, catching only two of his fingers.

"Enough, Scott. I can't take any more."

Her breasts were so sensitive she felt like one more brush of that rose and she'd lose it. He twisted his fingers in hers, capturing her wrist and bringing it around to the small of her back. She felt him fasten a bracelet of some sort to her wrist. It was soft, like some kind of fur. A second later her other wrist was surrounded by an identical bracelet. "Am I wearing the handcuffs?"

"Yes. Are you comfortable?" he asked, his concern genuine.

She laughed out loud. She was standing outside with her breasts bare, her wrists behind her back in furry pink handcuffs and wearing a blindfold and, honestly, she'd never felt safer.

"I'll take that as a yes."

"I thought we were going to have dinner."

"In a little while. I'm still working on broadening your horizons beyond the missionary position."

Scott had made love to her two or three times a night when they'd slept together, which was nearly every single night since the first time. He always pushed her sexual boundaries further than she'd have felt comfortable with any other man.

That was what scared her the most about Scott. He wasn't content in just knowing her surface personality. The Raine everyone else thought they knew. He liked to push past those barriers and find…her heart.

"Are you excited?" he asked.

"What do you think?" She didn't like to make things easy for him.

She felt her skirt rise and then his hand on the left cheek of her buttocks. She was wearing a thong, and he traced the back of it down between her legs. "Ah, I'd say yes."

He tugged the fabric to the side, circling his finger

around her pouting flesh. Her legs trembled and she swayed, and he put an arm around her waist, holding her up as his finger entered her.

He continued to touch her intimately until she hung on to her sanity by only a thread. Then she felt the heat of his mouth on her nipple, biting lightly.

"Scott."

"Hmm," he murmured against her skin. He suckled her deeply in time to the thrusting of his fingers inside her. Colors danced behind her eyelids as everything in her body clenched and her climax washed over her. She dug her fingernails into her palms.

He kept his touch between her legs until her body stopped clenching. He kissed her gently on the lips, then refastened her bodice, removed the handcuffs and her blindfold.

She stared at him with a dazed look on her face. His erection pushed against the front of his dress pants but he led her to a round table set on a bed of rose petals and lit by twinkling lights strung in potted trees.

"That's just the beginning of the surprises I have in store for you tonight."

She swallowed against the love she felt rising up in her for this man. Feelings that threatened the belief she'd always held about men, and made it a lie.

"You trust me, baby. You trust me with your body and your heart. Sooner or later you're going to say the words."

After they ate, he lifted her in his arms and carried her around the corner of the balcony to the tent that he'd had set up and the bed of silk pillows he'd made inside. He'd borrowed it from one of the sheiks who frequented the casino. Ali liked to take the tent out into the desert for a week after gambling.

Scott wanted this night to be romance and fairy tales…all the dreams that Raine had ever dreamed made true by him.

He'd saved the hardest task for last. Not that convincing the woman he loved to forgive him was a task, but it was the hardest thing he'd ever done. He'd read books, watched movies, asked advice, and in the end he'd realized that the actions that worked for other men wouldn't work for him.

Because Raine was unlike any other woman. He'd hurt her, caused her to hurt herself and left them both extremely insecure where love was concerned. And to be honest, neither of them had started out believing that love was real.

But the pain in his heart, the gut-clenching fear he felt when he thought of Raine never forgiving him, was real. He settled her in the middle of the mattress.

"What are you doing now?" she asked. Her lips were swollen, her eyes slumberous, and he knew that his making love to her had reminded her of the good things between them.

He took the large canvas bag from the corner. A warm breeze stirred through the open tent flap. On the silk pillows, she shifted onto her side, holding her head up with her hand, her thick hair hanging in waves over her shoulders.

He cleared his throat. He tried to read her eyes to see what she felt at seeing him, but he couldn't read any emotion there.

"What's in the bag?"

"A surprise."

"I hope it isn't anything else kinky. You've worn me out."

"Have I?"

"Yes."

"I'm sorry, Raine. I want you to know that." He knew she understood his meaning.

"Me, too. I should never have tried to play you the way I did. All my life I've hated my dad for doing just that sort of thing."

"I don't think you played either of us."

She took a deep breath. "You might be right. I kept pretending I was only letting you think I was falling for you, but that wasn't true."

He leaned forward and captured her hands. "I'm glad to hear that."

She smiled. "You would be."

Her smile faded as she continued. "My life is a mess, but I realized that my own actions made it this way. It had nothing to do with you, no matter how much I wanted to blame you. I realized I took the risk with my career, the risk with my heart. And I…I think I would again."

He pulled her to him, kissed her hard and deep. "Me, too."

"So what's in the bag?" she asked.

"Apology gifts."

"Flowers and chocolate à la every romantic leading man."

"You know me well…but I'm trying to be more with you, Raine."

"You don't have to try so hard. You are more. I was teasing you."

"I know. But I really spent the last few days going over movies and television shows in my head, trying to figure out which guy to be. But in the end I realized you'd never pretended to be anyone else with me—even when you were trying to."

"I used to be much better at the con."

"Maybe, or maybe I was the first person you cared about."

"Maybe you were, Scott. That's why it hurt so much when I tried to leave."

"Tried to?"

"Well, I'm an out-of-work director. I can't go too far."

"I fixed things with Joel. Stevie and I both took the blame for what happened."

"I'm not blameless. I signed a contract and then I fraternized with one of the players."

"I'm so glad you did, Raine."

He realized that they both were in better places today than they were a few nights ago. He reached into his bag and brought out a small box.

He handed it to her. "Raine, I really love you. I'm not sure you're ready to hear that but it's the truth."

She took the package from him but set it on the pillow without opening it. Instead she cupped his face in her hands. "I love you, too. More than I thought I could. And these last few days apart have convinced me that what I'm feeling is real. Not an illusion I was trying desperately to believe."

She kissed him. Her lips were soft and tender on his. A slow embrace that promised a lifetime together. A life of taking the biggest gamble of all—marriage, children and family. But with Scott by her side those things seemed like a dream come true.

* * * * *

THEIR MILLION-DOLLAR NIGHT

BY
KATHERINE GARBERA

This book is dedicated to two of my cousins—
Annette Queck, who is like my mom's twin!
And Michelle Griffin, who is like my sister. Thanks for making my summer trips to New Jersey so memorable. First as a teenager when we spent tons of money on the midway rides in Point Pleasant. Then as an adult when we went gambling in Atlantic City and certain ones of us had to lie about our ages. Finally as a parent when we sat on the beach huddled in sweatshirts (us Floridians aren't used to a cold breeze at the beach!) watching our kids play together in the surf.

One

Roxy O'Malley stared critically at the body in the mirror. For the first time in her life she was embarrassed by how she looked. She skimmed her gaze and her hands down the tight Spandex running bra that ended just below her 36DD breasts. That part wasn't bad.

Always when she got this far, she wanted to stop. She wanted to pretend that the last three months had never happened. Pretend that when she glanced lower all she'd see was the smooth skin of her midriff and stomach. Pretend that her life and what she knew about herself were still true.

She closed her eyes for a brief second, her hand going to her stomach. The ridges of the scars weren't rough against her fingers, but she thought they should be. The texture was different—foreign—and Roxy O'Malley, who'd once been called the most gorgeous bod on the Vegas strip, glanced down at the three scars. Three of them. One would have been bad enough, but three?

"Hey, sexy lady! Admiring the view?"

Roxy glanced over her shoulder at her boss and friend Hayden MacKenzie. She forced a cheerful note into her voice. "Hi, Hay! What's up?"

Hayden was a tall, good-looking man with dark hair and piercing blue eyes that always made Roxy feel like he could see straight to the heart of her vulnerabilities.

Quickly she dropped her hand and picked up the T-shirt she'd left draped on the back of the weight machine. She couldn't look him in the eye until she covered up. She would have turned away from him for privacy, but her back was worse than her stomach. Alan Technety had made sure of that. Because she'd broken up with him, he'd decided to make sure no other man would want her.

He'd also ensured she'd never dance again by cutting her so deeply on her left leg that he'd damaged the muscles and tendons. She couldn't even walk without a limp, which was worse than having the scars. Her body, which she'd always counted on, the one thing in her life that she'd always been able to control, was now out of her control.

Alan had done better than he could have expected. He'd made it so she didn't even want herself anymore. And her face had never been her vanity—Alan had known that and had focused instead on the lean dancer's body that she'd kept honed and in top form through careful diet and exercise.

"I need a favor, but only if you feel up to it," Hayden said.

"Okay, what do you need?" She walked to the small refrigerator in the employees' gym that held bottles of sports drink and water. It was only five o'clock in the morning. Normally Roxy was completely alone in the gym. She was surprised to see Hayden down here so early. The newlywed was besotted with his new bride and everyone in the casino knew Hayden and Shelby had a ritual breakfast every morning.

"Well, I want you to stop dealing," he said.

She froze. For the last month, since she'd been off on medical leave, Hayden had assigned her to work at the blackjack tables. Dealing wasn't really her thing, but she could do it—and she couldn't go back to headlining the European-style revue in the main theatre of the Chimera Resort and Casino. Being a dealer was a bit of a struggle, because she was on her feet all day and thanks to her leg injury, standing was a pain. Literally. But there was nothing else for her to do at the casino and living off charity—even

Hayden's disguised charity—by taking an extended leave of absence was something she couldn't tolerate.

"I can't dance. You know I can't have another surgery for six months..."

Hayden put a hand on her shoulder and turned her around to face him. "I'm not asking for that, Rox. I want you to be one of my VIP hostesses. Entertain the high rollers, keep them happy and in the hotel."

She glanced up at him, feeling like a fool. She never reacted the right way. It was just like old Ms. Wiggins had said back at the group home. Blood always tells. And Roxy O'Malley's blood, much as her name implied, didn't include a pedigree worth mentioning.

She stepped away from Hayden, walking carefully so that the limp wouldn't be obvious. He was always treating her like she was his kid sister, and there was a part of her that *wanted* to be his kid sister.

"When would I start?" she asked, grabbing a towel from the floor and draping it over her neck.

"Tonight."

"Who will I be accompanying?"

"Max Williams. He's a good friend of mine and I think you'll enjoy his company."

"That doesn't really matter, Hay. I'm going to be working with him, right?"

Hayden shrugged.

"Please tell me you're not setting me up with him."

"I'm not. This is a legit job. But if you like him…"

"Hayden MacKenzie, matchmaker. There's something very wrong with this picture," she said. But deep inside, she was touched. "I think I'll stick to the job."

"Okay. I'll have Kathy send you his information. I'll need to see you in my office at three. We'll meet Max in the lobby when he arrives."

She nodded and Hayden started for the door. "Does he know about me?"

Hayden paused. "What do you mean?"

She wanted to chose her next words carefully but the only ones in her head were blunt and honest. "That I was a topless dancer who was attacked by a crazy man."

She knew her words came from old criticisms that she'd thought she was past. But her new scarred body had left her vulnerable in a way she hadn't realized she could be.

Hayden came back to her, put his hand on her shoulder again and didn't speak until she looked up and met his clear steady gaze. "Roxy, you were the headliner in a highly regarded show. I don't gossip about my employees."

She saw something more than the truth in his eyes and it warmed her in a way that she couldn't explain. But no man had ever really offered help to her and she didn't trust it. "I know. But I also know Max is your friend."

"Even to my friends."

She nodded and he left. She slowly made her way out of the gym and into the employee locker room. She couldn't shower here. Couldn't take the chance that another woman would come in and see her scars. She always went back to her condo on the other side of town to clean up. When she'd been the star of the revue, she'd had a private dressing room with her own shower. But not anymore.

She thought about what Hayden was offering her. It was a good job. One that would require her to be charming, funny, entertaining—all the things she used to be, but wasn't sure she was anymore.

Max Williams was tired and frustrated with the businessmen he was dealing with. Each time he negotiated with them and came close to sealing the deal, they came up with another item that had to be settled before they would sell to him. The latest hiccup appeared to be the fact that he was a bachelor and married to his job.

Duke, his right-hand man, had suggested that Max take a break, leave Vancouver and go to Vegas for a few days and let him handle this latest setback.

Max had agreed, even though Vegas didn't hold the same charm for him that it always had. With two of his closest friends recently married, Vegas was no longer the bachelor playground that it used to be. At least not for him, the only single guy in a group of besotted fools.

Every time he turned around lately it seemed that marriage surrounded him. It was the reason Harron was stalling on closing the merger deal, and it was the reason his friends were no longer available for all-nighters.

His father, the five-times-married Harrison Williams, IV, had said marriage was the ultimate match in the man-versus-woman game. And only the player with the most cunning survived. Max wasn't interested in negotiating as hard in his relationships as he did in his work, so he'd always steered clear of those types of entanglements.

The limo pulled to a stop in front of the elegant facade of the Chimera's hotel. Max made no move to leave the vehicle. He scowled and cursed under his breath, then forced the social mask he always wore into place, that mix between interest and confidence that his mother said every successful person should always portray in their smile. He forced that look onto his face just as the chauffeur opened the door. Max stepped out and walked confidently past all the tourists, gamblers and celebrities milling there.

A rock guitarist stood in the middle of a group of fans, minor celebrities and photographers.

As soon as Max entered the air-conditioned comfort of the lobby, Hayden MacKenzie strode over to him. They shook hands and then hugged each other quickly. Max let his smile drop and a bit of his frustration show on his face.

"Glad you're here. Shelby is, too. You're invited for dinner tonight."

"Thanks. I think I have an appointment in the high-stakes gaming room, so I'll have to pass."

"When are you going to have time for anything besides business and gambling?"

Max rubbed the back of his neck. "Not any time soon."

Hayden put his hand on Max's shoulder and Max let the bond of their long friendship ease some of his tension. "So where's Jack?"

"I've got someone new for you this time. She's really great and I think you'll like her."

"Does she have a nice personality? Am I supposed to bring a rose so she'll recognize me?"

"She's your hostess."

"Then why does it sound like you're setting me up?"

"I don't know. Maybe I am. I like both of you, and you're both…"

"Don't go there. I'm here to gamble and that's it."

Hayden nodded. "I thought you'd feel that way. Let me introduce you to Roxy O'Malley."

Hayden turned and gestured to a stunningly gorgeous blonde. She was the embodiment of everything that was feminine and seductive. She took one step toward them, carrying herself with grace. Her second step faltered, and he noticed she had a limp.

He also noticed the frustration that passed briefly over her face.

"Roxy, this is Max Williams. Max, Roxy O'Malley."

Max reached out automatically to take her hand and forced his genial smile back onto his face. He'd been told by his second stepmother, Andrea, that he had the sweetest smile. Duke assured him that was not the case unless one was blind. There were too many teeth in Max's smile to miss the resemblance to a shark. But then, Duke wasn't a woman.

"Pleasure," he said. But the rest of his words stuck in his throat. Her hand was smooth and cold in his. And when he glanced into her eyes, he saw how nervous she was. She was stunningly beautiful and her body was built to make a man think of long nights and slow loving.

He held her hand longer than he knew was polite, rubbing his thumb over the back of her knuckles until a faint blush stole over her cheeks.

"Nice to meet you, Mr. Williams."

"Call me Max."

"Max. I'm Roxy."

"I'll leave you two to it then," Hayden said and then left.

She tugged on her hand and he let her go. "Your luggage is being taken up to your suite. Do you want to stop up there first or head straight to the casino?"

"I want…" *you*, he thought. But knew better than to say it. He didn't understand it, this wild attraction to her. And it *was* wild. He didn't *do* lust at first sight. He had never had any problems controlling his reactions to any woman. Why her?

"Yes?"

"To head to the casino," he said at last. Other than sitting in the boardroom and negotiating a takeover, there was nothing else he liked as much as playing the odds at the poker table.

She smiled at him. "Then let's go play."

"What do you think my game is?"

"Poker. And it was your game long before the current Texas Hold 'Em craze that's sweeping America."

He was surprised she'd guessed it. But then he knew better than to judge a book by its cover. How many times had he been mistaken for a rich brat of a man who never worked a day in his life? Okay, so, not often, but it had happened.

"Don't be impressed. I read your file before you arrived. You won close to $50,000 last time you were at the poker tables."

"What else did you read about me?" he asked, wondering what was in his file. He wasn't concerned.

Hayden kept stats on all the high rollers who came into the casino, even his friends.

She tipped her head to the side and her long hair brushed against her neck. He wondered if it was as soft and silky as it looked. "I can't tell you that. You'd know all my secrets."

He caught her hand and pulled her to a stop. Damn, she had the softest skin he'd ever touched. "All of them? I doubt that. I'd only know the ones about myself. And technically, those aren't yours."

He was flirting, and he hadn't done that in a long time. The fatigue that had dogged him for the last few weeks melted away when she smiled and slipped her arm through his, leading him into the poshest section of the casino. The dinging bells and whistles of the main casino floor faded as they stepped into the high-stakes room.

She paused in the doorway, and Max realized that she must be new to the VIP hostess thing, because she pulled them into a quiet corner instead of urging him to the table.

"Do you really want to know my secrets?" she asked, her voice dipping low and sounding sensual, husky.

Yes, he thought. But didn't say it out loud. He didn't know why he was reacting so strongly to her but knew that he wasn't himself and he needed to get back on track. He wasn't looking for another affair.

In fact, he was damned tired of them. And right now he needed just to play.

When he said nothing, she flushed and moved away from him. "Sorry if that was too personal. Let's get you to a table and I'll get you your favorite drink."

She started to walk away with her limping gait and he almost let her but didn't. He stopped her with his fingers on her shoulder. She glanced back at him, and he saw that damned vulnerability in her eyes again. "I do want to know your secrets, Roxy."

He walked past her and seated himself at a table with a few familiar faces. But instead of concentrating on the cards and the game, he saw only the surprise in Roxy's blue eyes in his mind.

Roxy tried to remember everything that Hayden had said, especially the part about being friendly but never forgetting that business was the focus of her assignment. Keep the gambler happy and at the tables.

Max made that hard. Every time she dropped off another drink for him, or inquired about his needs, he flirted. And for the first time since she'd wakened in a hospital bed, scarred for life, she felt like flirting back.

He played and won for almost four hours before pushing back from the table. Since this was her first hostessing assignment she had no idea if she should try to make him stay longer.

"Are you sure you want to stop now? You're on a winning streak."

"I'm sure. I want to take my hostess to dinner and see if my luck stays."

"I don't know if I'm allowed to do that," she said, knowing she wasn't lucky but not wanting him to know it. Every time she got close to grasping the brass ring of what she wanted from life, it slipped away. So she knew luck wasn't with her.

"You're supposed to keep me happy."

She wanted to laugh at the way he said it. But didn't. "Then I guess I'm going to dinner with you. Where do you want to go?"

"I'll take care of the arrangements," Max said. He pulled her out of the flow of traffic and reached for his Blackberry.

Immediately she knew she had to keep her head in the game with this man. This was a job. She couldn't forget it, no matter how tempting it might be to do so. This new assignment was much better than dealing and she didn't want to mess it up. "No, you won't. That's my job."

"And you take your work seriously?" he asked, arching one eyebrow at her.

She sensed he was teasing, but she couldn't joke about work. Anyone who'd ever lived off the charity of others learned pride at a heavy cost. "Of course I do."

"I thought you were new here."

"New to hostessing. But I've worked at the Chimera for almost ten years now."

"What did you do before?" he asked.

"Danced," she said. She heard the longing in her own voice and cursed herself for it. She should have been prepared for the question. But most people she encountered either knew her story or didn't care about her personal life. Max was the first stranger to ask about her since…

"Why'd you stop?" he asked.

A simple little question. She closed her eyes for a moment. Years of practice and discipline gone in a few short minutes. Gone because she'd judged a man and his intentions badly. *Don't do it again,* she warned herself.

"Injury," she said. The lie fell easily from her lips and she hated herself for it. She'd grown up in a world where lies were traded and accepted for the truth. She was becoming her own mother. Something she'd promised herself she'd never do. "But that's old news. Give me a minute and I'll get us a table for dinner."

She turned away from Max and took out her cell phone to call the VIP office. Thirty seconds later everything was set up, and she and Max were on their way to the exclusive five-star restaurant on the fifth floor of the casino.

"Have you eaten here before?" she asked, hoping

he'd say no so she could slip easily into her role of tour guide. She led Max past the crowd at the front of the restaurant to the maître d', very aware of his quiet presence behind her.

"Yes. In fact, the chef/owner is a friend of mine."

She smiled at the maître d', Henry, whom she knew from her years at the hotel. Henry winked at her and she relaxed a little. This new job was not what she expected. Or should she say that Max Williams wasn't what she'd expected. "Mr. Williams and I are ready to be seated."

"Certainly, Ms. O'Malley. Follow me."

Max put his hand on Roxy's back as they moved through the restaurant. She tried to ignore the heat from his large palm, but she couldn't. It made everything feminine in her pulse into awareness. That long-sleeping part of her, the part that had been dormant even before her accident started to awaken. That scared her.

She was grateful when they reached the table and took their seats. Max asked for the wine list and the sommelier came to their table.

"Do you have a preference?" he asked after the sommelier suggested some wines.

"I usually buy my wine by the gallon in the supermarket," she said. Then flushed as she realized how that sounded. "I mean—"

Max chuckled. "I have cousins who own a vineyard in the Napa Valley. They'd be outraged to hear that anyone in the U.S. still drinks cheap wine."

"Sorry," she said.

"Don't be. Have you ever tried South African wine?"

"Does Gallo make one?"

He laughed. "We'll have a bottle of the Thelema Chardonnay 1998, Stellenbosch."

The sommelier left and Max turned his attention to her. She felt uncomfortable under his intense stare, as if she was naked but not in a sexual way. His gaze was probing as if he were trying to fit together all the pieces that made up Roxy O'Malley. She desperately hoped he couldn't, because Roxy O'Malley wasn't sure who she was anymore. Not a dancer, not a hot body, not any of the things she'd always been.

Finally she couldn't stand it anymore. "What?"

"What, what?"

"Why are you looking at me like that?"

"Because you are a beautiful woman."

His words hurt in a way he couldn't understand. Because at one time she'd have tossed her hair and given him a smile that would have brought him to his knees. "Not anymore."

She couldn't believe those words had escaped. "How long will you be in Vegas?"

"Long enough to convince you that you are beautiful."

"That's not why you came," she said, telling herself that he was here for the Vegas allure. The mindless flirting, the hours of gambling. The vacation from reality and real life.

"My plans have changed."

"Well then, you won't be needing my company anymore. I'll let Hayden know."

He took her hand in his, his thumb stroking over the backs of her knuckles as it had when they first met. "I'll still require your company, Roxy."

She tried to tell herself that things hadn't turned personal, that she was still objective and just his hostess. But she knew she wasn't.

There was a promise of something in Max's eyes that she wanted to claim for herself. Something elusive and tempting, and she couldn't quite make herself ignore it.

Two

After dinner, Max excused himself to return several business calls. Sitting in his suite, he was aware of what his life had become. He was forty and successful but alone.

Alone by his own design, granted. But still alone. No mistress—he'd learned the hard way that even couching an affair in business terms didn't mean a clean break when things were over.

Harron had made several comments about the fact that Max was lacking a wife, a family. But Max had his family. They were paid employees and a small core group of lifelong friends.

There was a knock on his door. He hoped it would

be Roxy, but knew it wouldn't be. Instead it was the bellman with a FedEx box containing paperwork from his office.

He took the papers with him to the minibar and poured himself a Scotch. Looking hard at his life made him realize that in his quest to make sure no one thought he was riding his father's coattails, he'd created a vacuum. A place where no one existed except for himself.

Ah, hell, he was getting morose. He signed the papers, dropped them in the return envelope and then swallowed his drink in two long gulps.

He wanted Roxy.

He wanted to spend more time with the beautiful woman who could be charming until she remembered herself. Then she was awkward and shy. And he wanted to know why. He really did want to uncover her secrets, but he sensed she wouldn't share them. Not yet.

He also couldn't compromise her job. He made a quick call to Hayden and asked that Roxy's job be changed, explaining very little to his friend, but then Hayden was a man known for being quick-witted. "I'll be taking her out of the casino tomorrow for the day."

"Don't allow my business to get in the way of your personal plans," Hayden said.

"You are the one who extolled her virtues."

"That's right. I did, but I didn't count on your interest interfering with my business."

"I won't."

Max hung up the phone then dialed the front desk and asked for Roxy, knowing that even though it was almost midnight she'd be available. Everyone was always available to him in Vegas. To be truthful, wherever he traveled he was seldom turned down. He waited while he was connected to her.

"Hello?"

Her voice was soft and sweet, husky with fatigue, and he knew that if he were a nicer man, he'd just hang up and let her get some sleep. But he wasn't feeling particularly nice tonight.

"It's Max."

"Did you decide what time you wanted to start in the morning?" she asked, her tone warming a little.

Gambling was no longer the reason he was in Vegas. But he knew he'd have to keep that to himself a while longer. "No. I'm going back to the high-stakes room tonight. I need you there."

She hesitated and he wondered if she'd tell him no. "Oh, sure, Max. Only, I went home so it'll take me at least a half hour to get back to the casino."

"Why aren't you staying at the hotel?" he asked. He'd assumed she'd get a room while he was there. That was what his usual host, Jack, did.

"Hayden didn't ask me to. Actually, it never occurred to me you'd need me in the middle of the night."

If she only knew how much he needed her.

"Pack a bag when you come back," he said.

"For what?"

"To stay here until I leave."

"I'm not sure my job covers—"

He didn't want to discuss the fact that her job description had changed. "I'll cover it."

"Max, are you okay?" she asked.

Her voice sounded sweet, but he heard the underlying pique. She didn't like to take orders. And for the first time since he'd met her he had a glimpse into the fact that she was more than a pretty, smiling hostess. Her annoyance wasn't unexpected because most people didn't like to be told what to do. But Max had found the easiest way to get what he wanted was to do just that.

"Fine. I'll see you in the lobby in thirty minutes."

"It may take me longer than that."

"Why?"

"I have to shower and then pack an overnight case."

"What were you doing?" he asked. Jealousy pricked the back of his mind. Had she been with a man? *He* was her job.

And he was the one who was thinking this could be something more than gambler and hostess. He hoped he didn't turn out like his father, desperately seeing a relationship where there wasn't one.

He rubbed the back of his neck. It wasn't personal,

he reminded himself. But he knew that the reminder came too late. He felt something for Roxy whether he wanted to or not.

"Working out."

"What about your injury?"

She hesitated and he knew that she wasn't at peace with it yet. Was it recent?

"It's fine."

But something in her voice said it wasn't. "You never said what type of injury it was."

"I'm not going to, either. I'll meet you in the hotel lobby in an hour, okay?"

"Why won't you answer me?"

"Because it's private and personal. Isn't there something in your life you don't talk about?"

There was a lot, but he had always had a knack for getting people to open up. It was one of the reasons he was so good at takeovers. He could find out exactly the qualm the other CEO had and reassure them that he'd take care of it.

"Max?"

"Yes, I have things I don't discuss. But I'm asking about an injury, not asking you to bare your soul."

"I wish that were true, but my injury changed who I am."

He wished he was with her so he could read her expressive eyes instead of having to rely on the phone line to figure this out. Not being able to dance must be tied to her sense of self. He'd met dancers before. Knew that they'd usually spent their entire life practicing. Living at the dance studio and keeping their bodies in top shape.

"Tell me about it," he invited.

She said nothing. The silence lengthened, but he knew she was still there. She was waiting him out, trying to see if he'd simply give up and hang up. But Max had made patience a priority when he was ten years old and had never forgotten it. His impatience at age ten had cost him time with his father. Something that had been rare in his childhood, and he'd never forgotten that had he waited an extra thirty minutes he could have gone on an extended weekend with his dad instead of spending time at the arcade with his boarding school pals. Nowadays he could wait for days—even weeks—for what he wanted.

"I'm not going to go away."

"Yes, you will, Max. I can't do this right now. I'm just your hostess. I'm not willing to be your vacation fling. That thing you did in Vegas that *has to stay here* because it's a dirty little secret."

He cursed under his breath. "You know nothing about the type of man I am if you think that I'd pursue a woman just to have a tawdry thrill to bandy about in the boardroom."

"You're right. I *don't* know you."

"Come to the casino with me tonight. Let me show you the man I am."

She agreed and hung up the phone. Max left his suite and headed for the busy casino floor, hoping that by surrounding himself with people he could dull his need for Roxy.

It didn't work.

Roxy had three dresses and four approved pantsuits that Hayden had sent to her to wear for this assignment. But they weren't her style and she hated the feeling she got when she put them on—as if she was pretending to be someone she wasn't.

She took the pants from one of the suits and paired them with her favorite silk halter top. She now had to wear flats instead of heels, and she hated that. Grabbing her overnight bag, she left her house without a backward glance.

She drove the same car she'd had since she'd made headliner. It was a sweet BMW Land Shark convertible. And for the first time in a really long time she didn't have that sinking feeling in her stomach that stemmed from things lost. Instead she put the top down and let the cool summer air whip her hair around her head. She pumped up the music on the stereo, slipping in her favorite Dave Matthews CD when she couldn't find a song she liked on the radio.

She sang at the top of her lungs to "Ants Marching" and refused to let her mind dwell on the joy that had come from…a man. It had come from Max.

His phone call. She never slept at night. *No one knew that.* His call had rescued her from tortured hours of trying to force herself to sleep. Trying to close her eyes and not see images of Alan's face. Or worse, images of herself on stage performing the way she used to before the audience gasped in horror seeing her bright red scars.

Her foot slipped off the gas. Why had she let her mind go down this path?

She pulled into the parking lot of the casino and parked, but couldn't make herself get out of the car. Suddenly everything was there. Every emotion and fear that she'd been running from, every damned thing she'd thought she'd left at her small house was in that car with her.

She put her head forward on the steering wheel and tried to recapture the joy, but it was gone. Dave Matthews kept singing, but now she felt that bittersweet emotion that came from hearing something happy when all you felt was sad.

She switched off the radio and forced herself from the car. She put the top up and locked the doors before walking toward the shimmering lights of the Chimera. The ultimate illusion, she reminded herself. She'd learned early on that illusion wasn't bad. And the Chimera offered her an illusion of herself that she easily embraced.

She forced herself into the lobby, a smile firmly in place. She could do this. In fact, she had done this every minute since she'd come awake in the hospital. She'd learned that most people were fooled by a smile and a quick assurance, because most people didn't like to dwell on things like her attack.

"Roxy."

She stopped and looked at Max. He held a cigar loosely in his left hand and watched her with eyes that seemed troubled. He looked sophisticated and urban. The trappings of success fell easily on his shoulders and in the glittering crowds of Vegas she saw him for what he really was.

There was no illusion in Max Williams. There was only a solid core that made her realize he was the real McCoy. He was successful and sophisticated. She crossed to him and stood, unable to think of what to do next.

Then she remembered the old Roxy, the one who'd been so bold in life. What would she have done? She'd have wrapped herself around his arm and said something flirty. No matter what she felt inside.

"Roxy?"

She shook her head to clear it. She needed to get her emotions under control. Hayden was counting on her to make sure that Max stayed in the hotel and gambled. And she didn't want to let her friend down. "Sorry, Max. Let's hit the tables."

"Not yet," he said, cupping his hand under her elbow and leading her out of the hotel and into the lushly landscaped gardens. There was a box-hedge maze that was illuminated by the light of the moon and subtle horticulture lighting.

"Where are we going?" she asked. She hung on to her illusion of happy Vegas girl by a thread.

"Somewhere quiet."

"Why?" she asked, closing her eyes as she inhaled the aromatic scent of his cigar mingled with the scent of jasmine. For a moment she felt as if she were somewhere else. Someone else. But who?

He stopped and trailed his fingers up her bare arm, leaving gooseflesh in their path. She shivered, opening her eyes and looking into his clear gray gaze.

He was watching her with an intensity that made her hyperaware of herself. Of her femininity and his masculinity. Of the elemental differences between the two of them. She put her hand on his biceps and felt the solid strength in him.

This was a man who could handle everything life threw at him. She wondered if she could learn how he did it. If she could figure out what made him tick and use that knowledge to help herself. Yeah, right, she thought. The main reason she wanted to know what made him tick was that she wanted to know *him.*

Wanted to lean up and kiss him. To see if the fire in his eyes would be matched in his embrace. To taste his kiss and see if it would be as exciting as she knew it would be. But he was still a stranger, and she was wary of letting any man too close too quickly.

He ran his finger down the line of her cheek and traced it over her lower lip. "We are out here because I want us to be. And you are supposed to cater to my every need."

His every need. "I'm not sure what you're insinuating. But I've never been that type of girl."

"I know that. I'm not insinuating anything. I don't want you to be my hostess, Roxy."

She swallowed. "Okay."

"I want to be free to spend my time with you. To take you out of the hotel and away from the gaming room."

She didn't know what to say. She only knew that this job had lasted only one day, and she had no desire to go back to dealing. She was going to be out on the streets. She'd have to sell her car.

"I want us to get to know each other," Max said.

She shook her head. She'd have to find another job. "I'm not ready to date."

"Yes, you are," he said. His breath brushed against her face and she leaned into his body, wanting to kiss him. Wanting to feel his lips on hers and see if it would be the intense experience she sensed it would be. She realized that she was falling for the Vegas fantasy. Rich man, beautiful woman, whirlwind romance.

She pulled back, turning away from him and walking toward a bench a few feet away. "You're too bossy."

He didn't follow her, just stood in the middle of the path, taking a draw on his cigar and watching her with enigmatic eyes that saw too much. "I'm used to being in charge."

"This isn't your boardroom and I'm not one of your employees."

"No, you're not. But that doesn't mean that I'm not going to take control."

Max was pushing and he knew it so he backed off. He really did want Roxy by his side, and not just here in Vegas. She was the right woman at the right time. He needed a fiancée and, well, she fit the bill.

Even as the words echoed in his mind, he knew he was walking on thin ice. She wasn't just an accessory he could pick up in Vegas and return with to Vancouver.

"Come with me to the casino. You can be my lucky charm, and then I'll take you to breakfast and we can discuss this further."

"I've never been anyone's lucky charm," she said.

"Maybe you just didn't realize it," he said, steering them through the crowded casino floor toward the high-stakes poker area in the back. Now he hardly noticed her slight limp.

"I think I'd know if I was lucky."

"Maybe your luck is with things you take for granted," he said, knowing that his luck came from making things happen. From never sitting and waiting but getting up and taking action.

She stopped walking. "I think you might be right. I mean, I wanted to win the lottery but didn't. I wanted to keep on dancing and can't."

"I didn't mean to bring up bad memories."

She shook her head, shaking her honey-colored hair against her shoulders. Her hair looked like silk in the casino lighting, and he knew he should be concentrating on her words but instead just wanted to bury his hands in her hair and hold her head still for a soul-deep kiss.

"I just realized that I am lucky in a million little ways," she said.

He took a deep breath and reached for the concentration that he was known for. Then he took her by the wrist and led her away from the noise and the crowds to an alcove tucked away in the corridor. "What are those things?"

She bit her lower lip and his concentration almost flew out the window. What would her mouth taste like?

"It will sound silly," she said.

"I just called you my lucky charm, I think we're already into silly."

"Did you mean it?" she asked.

"Yes."

She smiled at him then and her expression was so…tender that his heart almost broke. "That wasn't silly, Max. It was very sweet."

"Ah, hell, God save me from being sweet. You're supposed to look at me and think, What a sexy guy. Not a sweet man." But he liked that she thought of him that way. No one had ever seen him in that light before. They'd called him ruthless, determined and successful, but never sweet.

"Can't you be both?"

"I don't know, can I?" he counted.

He wrapped his arm around her waist and pulled her closer to him. Her words—that she wasn't ready to date—echoed in his mind as he held her. Hell, neither was he, but holding her soothed that bit of loneliness that had been echoing through his soul.

"I'm not sure this is on the approved list of acceptable activities between a VIP and his hostess."

"Your boss is one of my best friends, so I think I know how to make this right."

"For you?"

He realized again that he was moving too fast. Her comment still ticked him off because he'd always been the kind of man that others respected. "No,

Roxy, for you and when you know me better I'll expect an apology for that."

"I'm sorry. I'm much better at light social talk, or performing up on the stage where I can't say the wrong things."

"You didn't say the wrong thing."

"Yes, I did. I offended you."

"I get offended daily."

"How?"

"Usually from investors of rival companies. Or the board of directors of a company that I want to take over. Sometimes from my second in command, but he says that's to keep my ego in check."

"He's your friend, then?"

Max thought about Duke and nodded. "Yes. He saved my life once."

"Did you repay him?" she asked, with a shrewdness he wished she didn't have.

"Of course I did. I couldn't let that kind of debt languish."

"Have you ever let any debt languish?"

"No, I haven't. I like to keep things even," he said lightly because he knew that he really preferred to keep the balance tipped toward him. To make sure that he was the one who did just a bit more in a relationship.

"But you're bossy. So I'm guessing that you like to be in charge all the time."

He shrugged his shoulder. "What can I say? I run

an international conglomerate. I have to lean toward the type-A personality."

"Just in business?"

He shook his head, uncomfortable pursuing this topic. "You were going to tell me what you were lucky at."

"I was?"

"Yes, you were."

"Is that an order?"

She was sassing him. And he liked it, but he gave her a quelling stare. One that always made the office staff jump through hoops for him.

"I'm not intimidated," she said. "But I will tell you what I'm lucky at…."

She paused and he waited for her to continue.

"I'm lucky in being alive. Now, if I can just remember how to live."

Three

Max played for four hours straight, insisting Roxy stay close by. She enjoyed being with him but the combined cigarette and cigar smoke was giving her a headache.

"I need to step outside for a few minutes. Breathe some fresh air."

Max nodded. "I'm going to play one more hand and then we'll go get some breakfast."

Since it was almost six o'clock, it would be an early breakfast but she didn't mind. She doubted that he'd only play one more hand.

Most of the men she'd dated had been gamblers. She'd met them all in a casino, and they never left any table or game after just one more hand or roll.

Six months time had made a huge difference in how she spent her days. Normally she would have been arriving at the casino about now and heading to the rehearsal hall for an intense dance workout and review of the previous night's show.

Instead, she was fetching drinks and keeping a man who didn't need the incentive in the casino. She hadn't felt this lost since she'd turned eighteen and realized that she no longer had a place to stay at the group home in which she'd lived. Two months left until high-school graduation, and she'd been on her own.

"Rox?"

She glanced over her shoulder and saw Tawny and Glenda crossing the casino, heading toward the rehearsal hall. Glad to see her old friends, she tried to smile. This feeling of envy, jealousy and embarrassment was exactly why she'd been avoiding them. They were still doing something she no longer could, and she felt a weird combination of envy, jealousy and some joy every time they visited her.

"Hey, girls. How's the show?" she asked. Both of them were still fit and pretty. Roxy looked at them and didn't feel the same sense of belonging as she used to. She shifted her weight, trying to feel as if she could still fit in if she wanted to.

"Not the same without you," Glenda said. "Roger has been really mean lately. One small slip-up and he reams you a new one."

"Well it's his butt on the carpet if the show isn't good," Roxy said. Roger's temper was legendary, but he usually only exploded if the chorus was loafing. And she couldn't imagine Glenda or Tawny loafing. They took dancing as seriously as she did… had.

"I didn't see you at the blackjack tables earlier. I hoped that meant you'd be backstage," Tawny said.

"Not yet. I still have a few more surgeries before I'll be ready." But that wasn't the truth. She'd never dance again. The combination of the strenuous show moves and the weight of some of the headdresses they wore would be too much for her body. The doctor had told her after her last surgery that dancing in Vegas was out. A showgirl no more.

"Get well soon, girl," Glenda said, giving her a hug before the two women moved on.

Roxy leaned back against the wall for a second. She really wanted to sink into it and become invisible. Then she remembered she was in public and straightened up, forcing herself to head for the exit.

The warm touch of a man's hand on her back startled her. She jumped a little. But she knew that touch. The feel of that palm had been embedded in her memory already. She glanced back at Max.

"You okay?"

"Fine," she said.

He rubbed his hand down her arm, linking their

fingers together, and led her away from the casino floor and out of the hotel. "Who were those women?"

"Friends of mine," she said.

"Dancers?"

She nodded. She wasn't ready to talk about that part of her life. Not that he was probing into it. She knew her reaction had a lot more to do with the fact that she didn't know how to deal with seeing her best friends than any question Max asked. "Where are we going?"

"For breakfast. I think I mentioned we'd eat after I finished that hand."

She flushed a little, remembering she hadn't thought he'd really get up and leave the table after one hand.

"Uh-oh, what's that look?"

"What look?"

"That sheepish one."

"I didn't think you'd actually leave after one hand."

"I'm a man of my word," he said, pulling her to a stop in the middle of the path.

She tipped her head back to stare into his eyes. He patiently let her look at him and she sighed deep inside realizing that she'd never met a man like Max before. She doubted she ever would again. He was solid through and through. He wasn't part of the illusion of Vegas.

"Sorry. Most gamblers can't leave."

"I really just do it for fun and to relax."

His fun had a much higher price tag on it than hers did. She could have bought a new house with some of the jackpots that were won and lost while Max played cards.

"Tell me about your job," she said.

"Later. We have to get moving to make our breakfast."

"Are we leaving the hotel?"

He nodded, steering her down the path that led to Hayden's private garage.

"We have some really nice—"

He held up his hand. "I know. I've already talked to Hayden about moving you to be someone else's hostess."

"You did?" she asked. She couldn't believe his gall. Did he think he owned the world?

"Now don't get mad."

"Too late. Do you think that you own me? I'm not sure that you listened when I said I don't work for you."

"I heard that. That's why I spoke to Hayden. I have other plans for you and I, Roxy."

She shook her head. "Maybe I don't want to be a part of them."

He didn't force her closer, but she felt surrounded by him. "I'm not like this normally, but there is something about you that draws me."

"Lust?"

"Yes," he said with a devilish grin. "But more

than that. If you don't feel the same, then say the word and this ends here."

"What is *this?*" she asked, unwilling to admit that she found him attractive. She knew he was out of her league.

"I have no idea, but I don't want to let you go. I want to spend the next day with you, exploring the attraction between us."

His words combined with the fire in his eyes melted her resistance. She knew that this was going to lead to heartache. They were so different. But she wanted to spend more time with him.

Santa Barbara, California, was perfect for his needs. Roxy was quiet as he drove them to the private airport and his waiting Learjet.

"Okay, where are we going?"

"For breakfast on the beach. I want to watch the day begin with you."

He could tell by her expression that she was overwhelmed and that pleased him. He'd been overwhelmed by a need to be with her ever since they'd met.

"The sun rises in Vegas, too," she said vaguely.

"Trust me, this is one you don't want to miss."

"Is this a normal thing for you?" she asked as they boarded the jet.

"Welcome aboard, Mr. Williams and Ms. O'Malley," Lourdes said.

"Roxy, this is Lourdes, our pilot. She's been working for me for five years now."

"Nice to meet you."

"You, too," Lourdes said. "Buzz me when you're ready to go, Mr. Williams."

He nodded. Lourdes went into the cockpit and left them alone. Max crossed to the bar and poured a glass of California sparkling wine and orange juice for each of them. Roxy stayed just inside the jet, her gaze sweeping over the plush carpet and leather seats. She took a step inside and then stopped completely.

"This is not going to work," she said.

He knew she meant the two of them, but Max had already felt that irresistible pull toward her and knew that for him to walk away was impossible. Even if the only thing between them was this heat, then he'd be happy to explore it. But he sensed there was something more. The restlessness that had become a part of him was gone—at least temporarily.

"Give me this morning and then we can discuss our differences on the way back. I think you'll find we have a lot in common." He set the champagne flutes down and pulled her into his arms. She inhaled and held her body stiff. He rubbed his hands down her back, enjoying the feel of her in his arms.

"That's kind of presumptuous."

"Sometimes my instincts get the better of my manners. Please come to breakfast with me."

She nodded.

"Have a seat and I'll let Lourdes know we're ready to go."

He spoke to the pilot via an intercom and returned to Roxy's side. He handed her a glass of the sparkling wine and O.J., and relaxed deeper into the leather seat as they took off.

"Most people go to the Grand Canyon for quick flights."

"Have you been there?" he asked. He wanted to analyze her as he would a company he was thinking of taking over. He needed to figure out what her strengths and weaknesses were. Then he'd figure out how to make her his completely. That one brief kiss wasn't enough.

If he played it right, she could also give him the edge he needed in his merger with Harron. Roxy would dazzle the businessman and Max could finally close the deal. He knew she'd dazzle Harron, because she'd dazzled him without even trying.

"Yes. I met a gambler one time who came to the show and saw me dance and then won five hundred thousand dollars. He took me on a helicopter flight to the Grand Canyon."

Max was doubly glad he'd chosen the beach. He didn't want to be lumped together with some gambler. "And you said you weren't lucky," Max said, not liking the jealousy he felt at her story.

She gave him a wry smile and took a sip of her sparkling wine. "I'm not, really. When we returned he asked me to accompany him to the craps table and he promptly lost the rest of his money. He definitely didn't think I was lucky anymore."

Max reached over and ran a his finger down the side of her face. He couldn't explain it, but her luck stemmed from things that couldn't be won or lost in a casino. "Maybe you weren't lucky for him."

"But I'm lucky for you?" she asked in a throaty little voice. She tipped her head more fully into his touch and he cupped it, loving the feel of her silky cool hair on his skin.

"Something like that. You were in the show at the Chimera?" he asked, wanting to piece together an understanding of her life. He had never been to any of the shows. When he came to Vegas he played hard, and watching shows had never figured into his plans.

"Yes, I was. At that time I was a lead dancer, but not yet the headliner."

She tensed when she talked about it. He put his glass down and took her hand in his.

"That takes a lot of discipline, I imagine."

"Yes, it does, but then dancing is my life. *Was* my life. Now, hostessing is."

"Really?"

"To be honest, no."

"Tell me about your injury."

"Um…it's not that bad. I'm going to have a few more surgeries and then I'll be good as new."

He didn't think so. There was something in her eyes when she talked about dancing that told him she wasn't sure about that part of herself any more.

"What about you? What's it like to be a CEO?"

"Well, for one thing, when I give an order it's usually obeyed," he said, arching one eyebrow at her.

"You need someone to defy you. You're too used to getting your way."

"Maybe so. It's very challenging. I've been at the helm of Pryce Enterprises for more than ten years."

"Why Pryce and not Max or Williams Enterprises?"

"Pryce is my middle name…my mother's maiden name."

She encouraged him to talk about his company. As he did so he realized that he was glad to hear that she was at a crossroads. It made his plans for her and the future easier to achieve.

They took a limo to the beach and Roxy was overwhelmed by the luxury that Max seemed to take for granted. Someone had set up a low table in the sand, and large cushions were provided for seating. There were hanging candles on the canopy that covered the dining area.

The table itself was topped with a large, cut-glass vase full of light-pink and white roses. There was also a small blue box tied with a white ribbon. She'd never received anything from Tiffany & Co. before.

He was seducing her carefully with romance. And it wasn't the kind of romance that she'd ever imagined existed. This was big-time fantasy romance, and she couldn't ever forget that it *was* a fantasy. Max was used to throwing money around on things. For goodness' sake, he had a Learjet.

This was more than breakfast, whatever he said. He wanted more than just a chance to get to know her on the beach. She might not be the savviest woman when it came to men, but she knew a setup when she saw one. The thing was, this setup was straight from her dreams.

"What is going through your head?" he asked, in that way of his that made her feel as though he could read her mind. As though he could see through all the barriers she'd thought she'd erected.

"We are never going to make this work," she said at last. No way could she ever fit in this world. She was flashy and brassy, not sweet romance. She was… not his kind of woman. Was that what he wanted? Some kind of tawdry affair?

"Why not?"

"We are literally from two different worlds, Max. Why can't you see that?"

"I already do. I want the chance to show you that

we have more in common than you think. I'm not going to pretend that this isn't my way of life."

"Flying somewhere for breakfast?"

"It's a mode of transportation. I bet you've driven places and met people for meals."

He wasn't going to let this be an issue and she wanted it to be one. She wanted to somehow convince him—and, okay, herself—that it was money that made the difference between them, and not her own fears that were holding her back. Her fears were responsible for that block of ice in her stomach. A block of ice that had started to thaw in his embrace.

"That's hardly the same thing," she said.

He arched one eyebrow at her. "We'll talk about this some more after you've changed."

He gestured toward a canvas structure that was the size of a dressing room. She was amazed at how much he'd accomplished in such a short time. She'd seen him on the phone before they'd boarded the plane, so she knew he'd made a few calls. She tipped her head to the side and studied this man who was able to make things happen so quickly.

"I didn't bring anything else."

"I've provided everything you'll need. Go," he said, putting his hands on her shoulders and urging her toward the changing area.

She entered the room and saw two boxes from Saks. She opened them both. One held clothes for her, the other clothing for him. She sank down on the wooden bench that was inside the structure and closed her eyes.

What was she doing? What did this mean? She should be at the casino in the gym working out. She should be trying to claw her way back to where she'd been before Alan had taken her life away from her. She should be more leery of being with Max—but she wasn't.

But she was tired of living with the fear that she'd never be fully alive again. Tired of pretending that nothing had changed when everything had. Tired of being scared because she'd never allowed herself to be before.

She stripped out of her clothing and opened the box. Her new clothes were wrapped in tissue and she pushed it aside, sorting through them. There were a pair of capri pants in signature Burberry plaid that hung low on her hips, bisecting one of her scars. The pants only covered part of it.

She dug deeper and pulled out the shirt, which was a cute T-shirt trimmed to match her pants. She pulled it on, but the T-shirt ended an inch above the pants. Her hands shook as she realized that her scars would be visible to Max.

She couldn't do it. This was just one of many things she didn't want to let Max see about her. He might be able to ignore the differences between them, but she couldn't. He was physically perfect—she didn't have to see his naked body to know it.

"Does everything fit?"

She grabbed her silky halter top and held it up to her stomach, trying to make the shirt cover her. But it didn't.

The flap opened. Max stood there on the sand, his shoes removed, his shirt collar open and the sea breeze blowing in his hair. There was a slight chill to the morning and she shivered.

"I can't wear this."

"Okay."

"I mean, it's not that I don't appreciate the gesture but it's—"

He put his fingers over her lips again. Rubbed his thumb carefully against them and she closed her eyes, wanting to lean more fully into him. Wanting to pretend that all the things she didn't like about herself wouldn't matter to him.

But she knew they would. Because her scars mattered deeply to her.

"There should be a sweater in there."

She hadn't looked deeper. She sat on the bench and looked up at Max.

He came and sat down next to her, wrapping his arm around her and pulling her into the side of his body. She was tempted to rest against him. But didn't.

She froze when she felt one finger trace the edge

of her shirt to where the fabric ended and her skin was bare. She knew the moment he encountered the first scar. He didn't pull back or flinch away, just let his fingers continue caressing her, but she couldn't go on.

She pulled back, wanting to run away. To find some place to escape to.

Max lifted his head. "Let me change and then we'll have breakfast."

He wasn't going to say anything.

Grateful for the chance to escape, she stood and left. He knew her secret now—and she wasn't sure she wanted him to.

Four

Max watched the canvas door drop back into place and clenched his fists. Now he knew more about her *injury* than she'd wanted him to. What the hell had happened?

He could call Hayden and get all the details. Hayden treated the staff at the Chimera like family, and Max knew that his friend would have the facts. But he would rather have Roxy tell him.

He changed quickly, barely noticing the clothing, and exited the dressing room. Roxy wasn't waiting at the table but instead was standing close to the water, watching the waves cycle.

She turned as he approached, her face still, as if

she were afraid of what he'd say or do. And his heart ached for her. He realized in a flash that she needed something…someone who could make her forget her scars and the life she'd once had. She needed him—or maybe he could convince her that she did.

No one should ever feel the way she did. And he knew that she felt alone and in a kind of emotional pain that couldn't be expressed. Knew it because he'd felt it himself. Of course, that had been long ago before he'd started taking steps to make sure he'd never be dependent on anyone again.

"Isn't this better than the Grand Canyon?" he asked, striving for a lightness he wished he felt.

"It's definitely one of a kind."

"Well, I try. Want to take a walk? There's a big surf point at the end of the beach. I don't know if the waves will be breaking but if they are, well, it's awesome to watch."

"I'd like that. Do you surf?"

"Not big waves, but some in Waimae. You?"

"No. I can't chance—couldn't chance an injury."

Dancing. He finally started to understand the impact of not being able to perform anymore. "Were you always going to be a dancer?"

"Yes. My mom wanted me to be one."

"Was she living through you? My dad wanted me to row because he'd been on a champion team."

"No, it wasn't like that. She died when I was

four, and it's one of the few things I really remember about her.

"She'd sit in the front room at the dance studio and watch me."

Max slipped his hand into hers as they walked down the beach. He was aware of each step she took and made sure that he kept the pace slow so she wouldn't stumble.

She told him more about her life and he realized that until recently dancing really had been her everything. Listening was the key to his success in business, and when he'd been in his early twenties he'd realized that he could apply those same techniques to personal relationships.

But it was hard to focus on social skills when he wanted to pull Roxy back into his arms. He wanted to have her in his bed where he could remove her clothing and see her scars for himself. He wanted to lave them with his tongue and sooth away the lingering hurt they'd left deep inside her.

"What?"

He realized he'd stopped walking and was staring at her. Staring at her waist. "Nothing. Are you ready to head back?"

She took a deep breath. "I know you felt my scars."

"Yes, I did."

She said nothing else and he wasn't sure how to proceed.

"I just want a chance to get to know you, Roxy. You don't need to tell me anything, any of your secrets. Keep them for now."

They arrived back at their picnic spot. Max seated Roxy and then himself.

"How did you arrange this so quickly?"

"I have a well-paid staff that knows how to make things happen."

He signaled to the caterers, who were waiting patiently nearby to start serving breakfast.

He picked up the Tiffany box and handed it to her. When the caterers had left and they were alone again, he said, "Just a little memento for you."

"You didn't have to."

She held the box loosely in her hands as if it were a time bomb.

"Open it."

"Stop bossing me around," she said, but a smile flirted at her lips.

"No."

She stuck her tongue out at him but slid the ribbon off the box and then carefully opened it. She pulled the necklace from the box, and held it up. He stood and walked to her side of the table. Dropping to his knees behind her, he took the platinum chain from her and fastened it around her neck. The pendant was a diamond-encrusted sea branch.

Unable to resist the smooth length of her neck, he

dropped a kiss there. Her skin tasted so good that he wanted to nibble on her. But she shifted to her side, her hands coming up to frame his face. She turned until they faced each other.

Their breath mingled, their eyes met and Max felt something shift in his soul. Something he hadn't been aware he'd been missing or searching for until this very moment came into focus. And he realized that he wasn't going to let Roxy go.

"Thank you."

She kissed him then, nothing tentative in her embrace, but like a woman who knew what she wanted. Her tongue traced over his lips before sliding into his mouth, tangling with his own tongue. Tasting him with leisurely strokes of her tongue. Strokes that set flame to his entire body.

He angled his head, forcing hers back until he was in control. Control of the kiss and the woman in his arms. She made soft mewling noises in the back of her throat and he swallowed them.

Roxy forgot about the fact that she didn't know who she was. Forgot about the strangeness of this experience that was unlike anything she'd ever known. Forgot that she had a body she no longer liked.

Instead she let herself live in the moment. She felt the crisp linen of Max's shirt under her fingers and how that contrasted with the muscled body underneath. She felt the passion in his mouth as it dominated hers.

She felt the swarm of lust rising in the pit of her belly and overcoming her. She moaned deep in her throat and felt him move.

He stood up and walked back around the table. She touched her lips as he settled onto his cushion.

Every other man she'd ever dated would have pushed her for more. Would have taken the invitation she hadn't meant to issue with her kiss. She wasn't sure if it was Max who attracted her or the fact that he was looking beyond her scars to the woman beneath. Making her feel once again like a sexy, vibrant woman and not handicapped.

If he'd taken advantage she would have known how to handle him. She would have frozen him out because she could barely stand her naked form, how could she let anyone else see it? Even Max.

"It looks lovely on you," he said.

"The flush from your kiss?"

"That, too."

She tried not to be charmed but she already had been. Her cell phone started to ring and she pulled her purse into her lap, trying to mute the sound of the song she'd downloaded as her ring tone.

"Is that 'Dancing Queen'?"

She groaned. Every time she heard it she wanted

to pretend her life hadn't changed even though she knew it had. "Yes, please don't tease me about it."

Now that the cat was out of the bag she might as well answer her call. "Hello?"

"Hey, Foxy Roxy, it's Hayden. Wanted to let you know I've got you scheduled to start working tomorrow morning with the spouse of one of our high rollers. Basically you'll entertain her and keep her busy in the casino."

Hayden was all business and she wondered if Max had ruined her relationship with her boss with his high-handed manner. She needed to make sure that Max knew dating was one thing—were they even dating? Did she want to?

She took a deep breath and turned away from Max. "Is that okay, Hay? I know that Max asked you—"

"Everything's fine. I'm glad to see you and Max enjoying each other."

"It's not like that," she said, wanting to explain but not sure where to begin. There was no other man she'd have gotten on a plane with and flown out of Vegas just for breakfast.

"Whatever you say. I'll see you tomorrow."

Hayden disconnected the call and she turned to face Max. He watched her with that intense gaze of his that made her wish she could read his mind.

"Everything okay?" he asked.

She thought she heard genuine concern in his

voice but that could just be wishful thinking. He'd said he wasn't after a vacation fling and the necklace he'd given her—her memento of the day—cost more than her mortgage payment. So what was he expecting from her?

"Yes. Just Hayden telling me about my new assignment."

"Is it to your liking? I can have him change it to something else."

"You have to back off that. I'm used to being in charge of my own life."

He shrugged. She noticed he was more relaxed than she'd seen him since they met. In the casino there'd been an intensity to his face as he'd gambled. But not here.

"I'm not trying to take over, I promise. I'm only making the way smoother so that we can do things like this."

"I can't do breakfast tomorrow."

"Lunch?"

"I don't know. But my job is important to me."

"I can appreciate that. But I'm only in town for a short time."

"I mean it, Max. I grew up on charity and I have to work. This is important to me. Don't do something like this again."

He nodded. "I'm sorry. I'm used to making things happen."

"You're used to getting your way. But I'm a working girl and I'm not easily managed. You have to ask me before you rearrange my life."

"I can do that," he said.

"You seem different here," she said, before he could comment on the fact that she'd been staring.

"How?" he asked.

She felt silly; she'd never intended to bring the subject up. "I don't know exactly—more relaxed."

"I am in the company of a beautiful, charming lady and we're alone on the beach. What more could anyone ask for?"

"I'm thinking, fewer of those clichéd lines."

"Hey, that wasn't a cliché."

"Beautiful and charming…I know I'm not either of those things."

"How do you know that? Maybe you've never been told before."

She leaned forward, hearing the words of Madame Tremaine in the back of her mind. Her level-three ballet teacher had made sure that Roxy knew her limits. *You're too homely to be the lead without having the skill to keep the audience's eyes from straying to your face.*

The words echoed in her head, and for a minute she was that twelve-year-old at that awkward stage between girl and woman. "I was told by an expert that I shouldn't rely on my looks."

"No you shouldn't, but that doesn't mean you should dismiss them, either."

She didn't know what else he wanted from her. But he didn't stop watching her. "What?"

"I'm trying to figure out what you see when you look in the mirror."

Those words struck fear into her heart and she wrapped her arms around her waist.

Max had no idea how to deal with Roxy. Usually his words had a golden quality to them and people took them to mean more than he ever intended. But he'd never had someone look at him the way Roxy was. And he felt like a jerk.

She was hyper-sensitive about her body and he struggled to understand that. To him she was a woman who worked out and took care of herself. He could tell that she spent time on hair and makeup, yet she didn't have the confidence he would have expected.

He hadn't meant to hurt her but somehow he had. Maybe he should buy her something. Except he knew that money wasn't the solution. He'd learned that at a young age when he'd watched his mother wither from expensive gifts but a lonely life.

Roxy definitely liked the beach.

"Do you want to go to Hawaii for a few days?" he asked. He had a place on the Big Island of Hawaii, which would probably be crowded since it was summer and the height of family-vacation season. "We can get away from Vegas and really have a chance to get to know one another."

She shook her head but the sadness had left her eyes and he felt better. He wasn't even sure what he'd done to make that happen. "I have to start a new job tomorrow, remember?"

She was pretty cagey about that job that she wasn't even sure she liked. But he could respect her need to work and pay her own way. Those were the very two things that had driven him to start his own company, Pryce Enterprises, and not go to work for his family.

"Hayden won't mind waiting a few extra days for you," Max assured her. He was confident that he could pay the wage of a temporary employee so that Roxy's job would be waiting for her when she got back.

"I can't. Why would you even offer such a thing?"

"You seem to like the beach."

She tipped her head to the side, studying him, and he hoped she found whatever it was she was searching for in his gaze. Hoped that whatever was there wouldn't scare her off. He tried not to think about how her breasts had felt pressed against him when they'd kissed. Or the fact that he'd been able to feel her nipples harden. He wanted to touch and taste them.

"I do. But why a sudden trip?" she asked.

He couldn't remember what they were talking

about. He was imagining them both naked in his tropical paradise retreat.

"Max?"

Something about why he'd offered to take her to the beach…he remembered suddenly that it hadn't started out as a sexual thing but more of an emotional one. He'd wanted to stop her from hurting.

"Blondie, you had a look on your face…" How could he say it without upsetting her again. Damn, this was exactly what he wasn't good at.

"What look?" she asked, shifting her legs under the table.

"Never mind, I thought you needed a distraction and it was either offering a trip or kissing you."

"So you opted for the trip?"

"If I kiss you again I don't think I'll be able to stop until I'm buried in that sexy body of yours. And I have the feeling public displays of affection don't rank too highly with you."

"They used to."

"Really? Well, don't let me be the reason you stop."

She laughed. "God, you are so sophisticated I forgot you were a guy."

"What does that mean?" he asked. No one had ever said anything like that to him before. But to be honest, that was true of just about everything that Roxy said. She was a breath of fresh air in his world, which was filled with the jaded and cynical.

She winked at him. "Just that I thought you were too cool for lust."

"Think again." Obviously he'd been a little too gentlemanly in stopping earlier. He should have followed his primitive instincts and made love to her on the cushions.

"I am," she said, with a blush that revealed more than she probably realized.

"So what's your hang-up with public nudity? I think together we can get you past that."

"I don't think so," she said, the humor dying in her as she scooted back away from the table and stood up.

He pushed to his feet and went around to her. Signaling the caterers to start cleaning up their picnic, he put his arm around her shoulders and led her down the beach to a rocky outcropping.

"I did it again. I said something that made you close up. What is it?"

"You're moving too fast, Max. I'm still getting used to the new me. I'm not ready for a man to notice me yet." She moved so gracefully, he could see years of dance training in her posture and in her body. There was no hesitation to her movements today. Her injury, whatever it was, didn't seem to be bothering her.

"How were you injured?"

She looked out at the sea. Suddenly he realized that she must have done something to her body that would require cosmetic surgery. That the surgeries she was referring to were aesthetic.

"Look at me."

She glanced over her shoulder at him and he saw the tears in her eyes. Saw the way she clenched her jaw from saying too much. He stepped up on the rock next to her, easily finding his balance and pulling her into his arms.

He slipped his hand under her shirt at the small of her back, remembering the way she'd frozen earlier when he'd touched her there.

Carefully he brushed his fingertips over her back and felt the ridges left by scar tissue. He lifted her shirt to her midriff and leaned down for a closer look. The scars were still red, still healing, and they were vicious. He heard her gulp in a huge lungful of air and then felt her shaking in his arms. He dropped the edge of her shirt and pulled her into his arms, wishing he knew how to make this right.

Five

Roxy was glad to be back on the jet and headed toward Vegas. She wanted to go to her small house and hide. No matter how attracted she was to Max, they were from two different worlds, and she didn't want to fall for a man who'd be leaving in a few days time.

She especially didn't want to bare her soul to someone who might only be interested in her while he was here. Max hadn't said anything else or asked any more questions, but she saw in his eyes that he wanted to. That he needed to know what had happened.

Lourdes smiled warmly when they stepped back on the plane. Roxy took a seat close to the cockpit and questioned the pilot about her job while Max sat in the back returning phone calls and receiving faxes. Finally it was time for takeoff and Lourdes shut the door, leaving Roxy with no choice but to turn and face the man who saw too much.

She'd found the sweater he'd left in the box of clothing for her and donned it. She didn't think she'd take it off around him again. Not that it would matter if she stripped naked. Now that he'd seen the ugliness she carried around with her he wouldn't want her to.

"Stop looking at me like I'm the Marquis de Sade." He didn't even glance up from his paperwork. She knew he was busy, had heard his phone ring several times when they were on the beach, but he hadn't even glanced at it until they'd boarded the plane.

"I'm not. I wasn't thinking you wanted to have kinky sex with me."

He looked up then, arching on eyebrow at her. "But I do."

His words made her mind jump to images of the two of them in bed, maybe with her hands tied above her head. Max was so dominant outside the bedroom she couldn't imagine him being any other way in it. "Stop teasing me. We both know I'm not the woman you thought I was."

"You say that as though I just discovered you were a transvestite."

"Please stop trying to make light of this," she said around the lump in her throat. She couldn't joke about her body. Not yet. Maybe never.

He caught a strand of her hair in his hand, rubbing it between his fingers. "I don't know how else to deal with this, Blondie. It's either joke with you or give in to the anger that someone would hurt you."

"I used to love my body," she said, because Max was the first person she'd met whom she didn't know from before the accident. "I was more than a little vain about it, and I was mean about people who didn't take care of themselves. I've been struggling with the fact that maybe this is some kind of cosmic payback for that attitude."

He shifted the papers on his desk. "I don't believe in things like karma. I think we make our own. No matter where we start or what kind of baggage we are dragging with us, it's how we handle the present that defines us."

"I hope you're right. But I'm struggling, Max. You're the first man to look at me and make me forget that I'm not who I used to be. And that frightens me, because we both know that this isn't ever going to go beyond an affair."

Max left his desk area and joined her on the low couch toward the front of the plane. She didn't have a magazine and thought about pretending to go to sleep but knew Max wouldn't fall for it. She wasn't surprised when they reached their cruising altitude and he unfastened his seat belt and hers.

"Take your sweater off."

"No."

"The only way you're going to get past it is to stop viewing your body as something abhorrent."

"I don't think seeing it in broad daylight is going to help."

"How about seeing it through my eyes?" he asked, stretching his arm behind her and drawing her into the curve of his body. He was big and strong. Solid in a way so few men in her life ever had been.

She stared at Max, afraid for a minute to trust him. Okay, she was afraid to trust herself. She'd been serious when she mentioned the fact that all they had between them was the possibility of an affair. Max wasn't a forever kind of guy…at least not for her.

"Trust me," he said.

Strangely she wanted to. She'd never have left Vegas with any other man she'd known only twenty-four hours. There was something very trustworthy about Max Williams. "I think I do. But the last man I trusted…"

"Did this to you?" He slipped his hand under the layers of her clothing and traced over her scars.

"I'm not sure about this," she said, grasping his wrist and trying to stop him from moving any farther up her body. From discovering the extent of her scarring.

"Tell me what happened."

She took a deep breath. No one knew the whole truth. She'd been too embarrassed ever to utter the words *My ex-boyfriend is stalking me.*

The words appeared in her head—*A guy I dated over a year ago never got over me. And one night when I went into my dressing room, he was waiting. We had a fight and he...he...stabbed me. Several times. He left my face alone because he said it was my body that I loved and worshipped.*

But they made her feel dirty and guilty and she couldn't say them out loud. Especially to Max, who was all that was sophisticated and polished. For God's sake, the man took her to breakfast in another state. How could she say that her own vanity had driven an ex-boyfriend to come after her?

She couldn't. She liked Max. She wanted him to like her, to think that she was worth this trip to the beach on his Learjet.

He framed her head with his hands and leaned down, kissing her with exquisite gentleness and making her doubts fall away. She wrapped her arms around him and laid her head on his shoulder. Then quietly told him the story of the night that had changed her life.

Max knew that it would take more control than he had at the moment to conceal his anger from Roxy. The quiet rage that had grown as she spoke in that soft, hesitant voice. He held her in his arms and made plans. If it was surgeries she wanted, he would see that she had them.

He'd make sure that Technety never saw the light of day again and that the other women in the show were protected. Because she worried about that as well. He didn't question or understand why what he felt seemed magnified. He only knew that it was, and he couldn't tolerate anything other than fixing this problem.

"You're quiet."

"I'm quiet because I'm trying to find a way to speak around my rage. And no, you haven't disappointed me."

She tipped her head back against his shoulder and looked up at him. "That's the sweetest thing anyone has said to me."

"Ever?" he asked, lowering his head so that his lips brushed against hers. He wanted to make the physical part of the relationship all-powerful so that she wouldn't notice the fact that his emotions were kept hidden away. And he was going to keep them locked away because Roxy made him feel things more intensely than any other woman had, and there was danger in that. Whenever he reacted from that raw emotional place everything in his neatly ordered life fell apart.

"Ever," she confirmed.

He hardened and groaned. He wanted this woman.

He wanted to strip her naked and then take her. Make her forget about the imperfections which seemed so large in her mind.

He pulled his mouth free and dropped kisses down the length of her neck, sucking on the sweet spot at the base. She smelled so womanly, all fresh air and sea breeze, but more than that, her scent was the essence of Roxy. Sassy and shy. Tasting her was addictive.

"You are so beautiful," he said, framing her face in his hands and looking into her eyes. They were fathomless and he couldn't read what she felt there. That bothered him, because he'd thought she would be easy to read. What else was he missing about her?

"Don't talk, Max. I don't want to think—just feel, okay?"

But he couldn't after that. He didn't want her to kiss him because she wanted an escape from her life. He wanted her to want him with every part of herself. He rubbed her back and knew that he was going to regret being noble. Not taking what he wanted went against the grain. But Roxy wasn't just an object to be acquired. She…she was getting to him.

She was quietly illuminating parts of his soul that had been dark and dusty for too long. And he knew that he wanted to be more to her than just a means to forgetting her reality.

"I ruined the mood, didn't I?" she asked, slipping off his lap and back into her seat.

"No, you didn't. I was rushing you and I'm sorry."

"Well, I'm not. Rush me some more. That way I don't have to think about how different we are."

He was tempted. But he'd learned early in life that all the good things were worth waiting for. And he didn't want to make love to Roxy for the first time on the jet. He wanted to do it in his bedroom where he could stand her in front of a mirror and make her see the woman she really was.

"When you're ready for me, the differences won't matter."

Roxy had never been so glad to be back in a casino in her life. She felt unkempt, exposed from her time on Max's plane. She just wanted to escape and find a quiet place to regroup. She stood awkwardly in the portico in front of the hotel while Max tipped the valet and gave him the keys to the Jaguar that had been waiting for them at the airport.

"I guess this is goodbye. Thanks for breakfast."

She turned and started walking toward the employee parking area. Max caught her arm. She felt the steel in his grip and knew that he wasn't happy at the way she'd tried to dismiss him.

Well, she wasn't happy, either. She couldn't look at Max right now, because she was still embarrassed that she'd confessed so much to him.

"We're not through yet."

"I'm tired, Max. I need a break. I know that I owe you an apology for what happened on the plane."

"No, you don't. I really don't mind waiting. When we do make love I want to take you in a bed, where I can stretch you out and really worship that luscious body of yours. But I want it to be about more than sex when we're together."

She warmed inside, where the real Roxy had always lived. The shy dancer who just wanted to lose herself in the movements. She knew the image she projected was of an outgoing woman who could come through anything. But deep inside she'd always felt insecure, still the awkward adolescent who'd been dropped off at a group home.

Max, for all his worldliness, had seen past the facade to the woman beneath.

A group of Japanese tourists were headed straight for them and Max used his body to move her out of the flow of traffic. He backed her up against the sun-warmed wall of the casino, his tall muscular body surrounding hers and caging her.

"Have dinner with me tonight," he said, rubbing his lips over hers. His breath was minty and warm.

She opened her mouth, hoping for a deeper kiss, but he only nipped at her lower lip and lifted his head.

"I'm waiting."

"Are you asking me?" She knew he wasn't. He was so used to having his way.

"Only if I have to. I think there's something between us that deserves to be explored."

"Shouldn't you be playing poker? That *is* why you came to Vegas."

"I think I've hit the jackpot already."

She started to close her eyes against the charm she saw in his, but then she forced them open. She made herself look up and down the strip. To see the fake Eiffel Tower and pyramid. To remind herself that this was Las Vegas, baby. The place where sinful behavior was indulged in. Men like Max came to Vegas for one reason and one reason alone.

But the way he held her didn't feel as though he was looking for a cheap thrill. And he'd stopped earlier, on the plane, when she was willing to go further. "What do you want from me?"

"A chance."

"Why?"

"Because it's been a long time since anyone has interested me as much as you do. I love the contradictions of you. The mystery of what makes you tick. And I want to solve it."

She leaned forward, breathing in the scent of his aftershave mixed with the salt from the sea breezes. "Max, I'm not worth all this effort."

"You are to me. I'll pick you up. Does eight sound good?"

"You're not going to listen to me are you?" she asked.

He gave her a half smile. "I always listen. It's just that sometimes you say things you don't mean."

"How can you know that?"

"Because I've held you in my arms and looked deep into your eyes. I'm beginning to know what makes you tick."

"Then maybe I should pass on dinner. If you figure me out then I'll have no place to hide."

"You don't need to hide from me."

"What about you?"

"I'm not hiding from you."

But she knew he was. He was dazzling her with fancy plane trips and expensive trinkets. He was keeping the focus on her and she was letting him. "What about from yourself?"

"I'm forty, the CEO of an international conglomerate and I've lived a full life. There's nothing to hide."

She tipped her head to the side studying him. She knew he had secrets. Real secrets, the same as she did, and she wanted to know them, because she already liked him too much. She was very afraid that before too long, liking would turn to love. And, as he'd said, he was a sophisticated, successful man. The kind that didn't marry a former topless dancer.

Six

Max spent the rest of the afternoon in the casino. Hayden and Deacon showed up during one of his winning hands and then enticed him to play with them. Deacon Prescott was one of Max's oldest friends. A hell-raiser who'd grown up on Vegas's mean streets and worked hard to make himself into the man he was today. The owner of the Golden Dream Casino was every inch the family man and casino owner. Since they were two of his oldest friends, they played a little dirty, deliberately distracting each other. It was fun, and Max relaxed around the men for the first time since Hayden's marriage.

He didn't analyze it too closely and refused to answer any of Deacon's and Hayden's prying questions about Roxy. He took great pleasure in beating them both and walking away from the table with his friends' money in his pockets.

But as he fastened his tie in a classic Windsor knot, staring at himself in the mirror, he realized that he was doing what he always did. Trying to fix Roxy's life.

Since he'd been eight years old he'd always followed that pattern. As an adult he'd realized that part of the problem was his mother's demand for perfection. She wasn't an uncaring woman; she just had very high standards. And Max was very much her son. But he was also his father's. And if he'd learned perfection at his mother's knee, then he'd learned compassion at his father's—and also how to move on.

The course of his life had been set when he'd befriended Hayden at boarding school. When the two boys had met, they hadn't hit it off at all. Hayden, in fact, hadn't gotten on that well with anyone, spending all his time alone until one night Max had overheard a conversation between Hayden and Hayden's father. The conversation reminded Max of the many he'd had with his mother. And he'd seen that the arrogant boy who no one had liked was really a lot like himself.

Max blinked. Damn. He was still trying to fix people. Hayden had called him on it more than once, but Max couldn't change. He knew that much about himself.

But fixing Roxy in this instance could help him with business. There was no doubt that he wanted her, but he was thinking of her in terms of permanency, and he'd never thought of any woman that way before. Was it simply the effect of having his pals settle down? Did he want a wife because it would make his negotiations easier? Or did he want Roxy tied to him because of emotions he'd rather not acknowledge?

When he arrived in the lobby Roxy was waiting with the two friends he'd seen her talking to the day before. As soon as she spotted him, she smiled and held up her hand, telling him she'd be right over.

He didn't wait for her to come to him. It was simply a power thing, but he didn't want to lose control for a minute. He slipped his arm around her waist and pulled her back against him.

"Hello, Blondie."

"Max," she said. "These are my friends, Tawny Patterson and Glenda MacIntosh. Tawny and Glenda, this is Max Williams."

Max shook hands with both women, who eyed him speculatively. "It's a pleasure to meet you both."

"Right back at ya," Tawny said, winking at Roxy. "We've got to be going. We'll talk to you later."

Roxy groaned as her friends walked off. "They are

not going to be happy until they've pumped me for information on you."

"What will you tell them?" he asked, leading her toward the escalator to the shopping and dining level. The resort was crowded. Now that night had fallen the casino was starting to really come alive.

Max breathed in the sights and the sounds. The feel of the woman in his arms and the sound of her soft voice enhanced the night.

"I'll tell them…I'm not sure, Max. I think I want to keep what I'm feeling for you a secret."

Not, he suspected, just from her friends, but also from him. She was such a blend of blatant sexuality and shyness. It turned him on to watch her go from confident woman to reserved, because he knew that when he touched her, he could make her lose her inhibitions.

"What are you feeling?" he asked, keeping his hand at the small of her back. Her sundress had a deep V in both the front and back.

He stroked his finger along the fabric and watched her body react. Her skin flushed a little and then goose bumps spread up over her shoulders.

"Lust," she said.

"How could you be around me and not experience that?" he said without blinking an eye.

"What an ego you have."

She leaned back into his touch as if she couldn't get enough of his hands on her, feeding his ego in a way that no woman had done in a long time. She tipped her head to the side when he spoke, really listening to his words. And she showed him the real woman behind that perfect face and knockout body. The real woman, with all her faults and fears. That was a bigger turn-on than she could ever realize.

"Hey, you're the one who brought up lust. The way I feel around you, it would be impossible to deny our attraction."

"Impossible?" she said, blinking at him.

"Oh, yeah. You're not going to try it, are you?"

"How can I argue with a crazy man?"

He laughed and realized that he was more relaxed here with her than he'd been at the poker table. That the game which had always been his release valve wasn't working the way it was supposed to.

When they reached the dining level, she paused and glanced at the row of restaurants that would impress the most jaded gourmet. Max was glad that the all-you-can-eat lobster buffets of the past were gone. Now, five-star restaurants and celebrity chefs were the norm in Las Vegas.

"Where are we going?" she asked.

"Dinner, remember? Is that lust thing messing with your mind?"

"Yeah, like that'd ever happen. I meant, where are we going for dinner?"

"I promise you, before our night is over I will

make sure you are totally out of your mind with lust," he said, lifting her hand to his mouth and brushing a kiss along the back of it.

Their dinner was a five-course affair at a themed casino restaurant—the Chimera's Applewood Vineyard of Sonoma—the vineyard sponsored the restaurant and they'd sampled a different wine with every course. She felt very mellow and relaxed as Max led her out of the restaurant and up one more level to one of the smaller clubs on the entertainment level.

While they waited outside for the doors to open, she saw the line to get into the main club revue. *Her* show. Not her show anymore. She'd left that behind…at least for now.

"Is that where you used to work?"

"Uh-huh." She felt butterflies in her stomach as she recalled how it felt each night to wait backstage for the house doors to open. She remembered how they'd all tease and laugh to hide their nerves, but even the fact that they went out on stage every night hadn't dulled the magic that dancing and performing had always held for her.

"Roxy?"

She realized he'd spoken, said something. She pulled her gaze from the crowd of people and looked into his gray eyes. He was watching her with that intense look that was half lust and half something she couldn't read.

"I'm sorry. I haven't been up here since the… accident." She flushed as she realized she'd mentioned something relating to her injuries.

"Do you want to go into the show? Would that help?"

"No. I'd rather go into the jazz club."

The doors to their club opened and people slowly filed in. Max and Roxy waited until the crowd had lessened, and then approached the ticket taker. Max handed over their tickets, and they were seated at an intimate table close to the stage.

Her hands were shaking and she didn't understand why. She looked up at Max, a sense of panic closing in on her. "Talk to me, please. I need some kind of distraction."

"About what?"

"Your job. Are you on vacation?"

"No, I'm here to take a break from some tense negotiations."

"For what? I don't even know what you do."

"I run an international company. We're trying to merge a travel agency into our conglomerate. But the owner of the travel agency isn't too sure he wants a man like me at the helm."

"A man like you?"

"A bachelor. They are very family-focused, and

Harron wants to be assured that I won't let that focus slip."

"You don't strike me as a family man," she said, carefully.

"I guess I'm really not. But that doesn't mean I can't see the value in being one."

She tipped her head to the side. "I've never had a family. Just the girls in the show."

"Will you be able to dance again?"

She shook her head. "Not at the same level, and I'm not one of those people who will settle for second best."

He scooted his chair closer to hers and wrapped his arm around her shoulders. Leaning in close, he whispered directly into her ear.

"Are you wearing a bra?"

She glanced up at him, startled. "I'm a 36DD, what do you think?"

He ran his finger down the V at the front of her dress to the cleavage revealed there. He slipped his finger under the material. She shivered from his touch. His finger was big and warm. Gently caressing her. Moving slowly lower, his finger encountered the lace edge of her demi-cup bra before brushing her areola.

"Ah, yes, you are."

Her nipple had hardened at his first touch. They were secluded close to the stage in an alcove where no one could see them. But the fact that they were in a public place heightened her excitement.

He drew the tip of his finger lazily back and forth across her nipple. With his free hand he stroked her neck, urging her to tip her head back onto his shoulder. She did, and he lowered his mouth to hers.

His tongue teased hers before dipping deeper, thrusting into her mouth in time to his finger strokes across her breast. She squeezed her thighs together as she felt an answering pull in her center.

He lifted his mouth from hers. "Are you wearing panties?"

"A thong," she said, feeling dazed by the sensuality he wove so easily around her.

"Take it off."

She'd never done anything like this before. And it made her feel exciting and daring. "I'm not—

"Please."

No other word would have made her react, but that one did. There was a fire in his eyes that answered the one he'd started in her body. She'd expected him to remove his hand, but he kept stroking her breast and nipple as she lowered her hands to her lap.

The table was draped with a cloth that fell to the floor, so there was no way anyone could see her. She attempted to glance around, but Max stopped her with his hand on her chin.

"No one is looking. There's just you and I and the music. No past or present. But it's up to you…do you want to do this?"

She swallowed hard, staring into his eyes. She nodded. Speaking would break the spell he'd cast around her.

"Lift your dress to your waist."

She did as he asked, pulling the fabric up slowly. His eyes were on hers the entire time. And what she saw in them egged her on. Made her want to be the sexy woman he thought she was. The sexy woman she'd known she was before her attack.

"Is your skirt up?"

"Yes."

He glanced down and his hand tightened on her breast. He breathed a little more heavily, lowering his hand to her thigh. She glanced down as his hand moving higher, slowly, toward the apex of her legs.

"May I touch you?" he asked, again directly in her ear."

She nodded again. He slipped his hand into her thong, his blunt fingers caressing her, slipping lower to find her wet and ready for him.

She inhaled sharply as he slipped one finger into her while at the same time scraping his fingernail over her nipple. She had to bite her lower lip to keep from crying out. Just then the house lights dimmed even further and the jazz combo took the stage.

The tempo of the music was mellow and smooth. But the tempo in her body raged out of control—like a Stevie Ray Vaughan guitar riff that went on forever.

His mouth found hers as he teased her body, driving her closer and closer to a climax. A second finger slipped inside her, driving deeper. He continued to play with her nipple and his tongue matched the thrusts of his fingers. She gripped his thigh with one hand then slipped it between his legs, finding him hard. She stroked him in time with his stroking of her body. Her fingers bit into his thigh as he pressed his thumb to the nub at her center and drove her over the precipice to orgasm.

She felt him lower her skirt over her thighs and he pulled his hand from her breast with one last caress. His erection still strained against his zipper, but when she tried to open his pants and bring him some relief, he stopped her.

During the second set, couples left their tables for the small dance floor. Max watched Roxy watching them, a look of envy flitting briefly across her face.

"Let's dance," he said.

She hesitated. "I'm…"

"Scared? I promise not to step on your feet."

"Not of that. You're poetry in motion."

He arched one eyebrow at her. "No one has ever said that before."

"Well, I'm sure they've thought it. You move like a graceful predator."

"A predator?"

"Not that you're looking for the kill. You're just very confident, very sure of yourself and very aware of where everyone else is."

Since he knew that he was always aware of others, he wasn't surprised to hear her description, but he was surprised that she'd noticed. She seemed to see more of him than others did.

"I want to hold you in my arms, Blondie. I want your luscious body against mine, teasing us both. I'll catch you if you stumble. Trust me?"

She licked her lips. "Okay."

Max escorted Roxy to the floor and held her in his arms. Something he'd been craving since…he realized that he had no idea when the urge had begun, only that he *needed* her in his arms.

Her skin was flushed, and the remembered feel of her warmth on his fingers kept him in a state of arousal. But he wasn't ready to end the anticipation and take her back to his suite. He wanted to keep the tension building between them.

"You're a good dancer," she said.

She held on to him as they moved. Roxy's dance training was obvious to him as they swayed together. Her posture, which was always very good, was even more so here. And every beat of the music came alive in the way she danced.

"Thank you."

"Is there anything you don't do well?"

Yes, but he wasn't about to tell her. He was horrible at cooking no matter how many lessons he'd had. "My mom made sure I knew the basic ballroom steps. My dad has to be coerced onto the dance floor."

She rested her head on his shoulder, shifting closer to him as they danced. And he had a flash image of her underneath him. They'd be a perfect fit in bed. He slid his hands down her back to her hips.

Her mouth was at his neck, kissing him as her hands slid up and down his back. She bit him softly and he reacted immediately, hardening further against her lower belly.

One of her hands was at his nape, her fingernails scraping over the skin there. His breathing deepened, his blood flowing heavier in his veins, pooling in his groin. He knew he'd have a problem when it came time to leave the dance floor, but for now, it felt good to have her tease him.

This was the first time she'd taken the lead, and he savored it, knowing he was starting to unlock the real Roxy, the woman who'd been frozen by the cruel attack.

He lowered his head and breathed in the summer scent of her hair. His hands lowered from her hips. Her butt was full and curvy, and he flexed his fingers against her. She shifted her hips, rubbing her mound against his erection.

He heard her breath come in quick and sharp. Her full breasts rubbed against his chest and he wished he'd left his jacket at the table so he could feel her against him. In fact, he wished they were both naked.

She was toned and in shape. Everywhere he touched renewed the lust he felt for her body. But every touch of hers on his body renewed the affection in his heart. He liked this woman. Liked her in a way that he didn't understand or want to analyze.

The tempo of the music changed, but Roxy didn't seem to notice and he didn't want to either. He maneuvered them away from the center of the dance floor to a corner near the stage where the low lighting didn't reach, and they continued to sway together to a beat that could only be heard by the two of them.

"Let's get out of here," she said.

"Give me a minute."

She skimmed her hand between their bodies, running her fingers over his erection. "I think it might take more than a minute."

He grabbed her wrists and pulled her hands behind her back, then lowered his head till his mouth nearly touched hers. "If you keep that up, it will."

She shifted in his arms, undulating against him. "When we're alone, you're going to pay for that."

"Promise?"

"Oh, yes."

He reached between them, adjusted himself as

best he could and led her back to their table. She grabbed her purse while he tossed some bills on the table to cover their tab. He put his hand at the small of her back as they walked from the club.

Outside, he wrapped one arm around her waist, putting the other under her chin, tipping her head back and kissing her until she softened against him. After a long moment, he lifted his head.

"Come back to my suite."

"Yes," she said. And he took her hand, leading her toward the bank of elevators.

Seven

Max's cell phone rang while they were waiting for the elevator. He took one look at the caller ID and cursed savagely under his breath. "I have to take this call."

She nodded and started to move away, but he held her close, unwilling to let her go. She held his hand and stood patiently at his side. Though it was only ten o'clock in Vegas, it was after midnight in Atlanta where Duke, his right-hand man, was calling from. So he knew that this had to be some sort of emergency.

"Williams."

"It's Duke. Sorry to bother you so late, but I just got a call from MacNeil. He has another objection to the merger that only you can satisfy."

Max was sick of Harron MacNeil. The man was making what should have been a beneficial corporate merger a living hell. Max was ready to change his bid on the company and just take it over regardless of what MacNeil wanted. “What the hell is it now?”

“He wants another face-to-face meeting—tomorrow afternoon.”

No way. MacNeil was assuming a lot of bargaining power from the fact that Max wanted the man’s company. Too much. “I can meet with him on Friday.”

Duke chuckled. “I had a feeling you’d say that. So I scheduled a Friday lunch meeting and he’s coming to you.”

“Thanks, Duke.”

“Hey, that’s why you pay me the big bucks.”

“Then why did you have to call me tonight?” Max asked. The elevator car came, but he held Roxy by his side. The elevators had really poor cell reception.

“MacNeil is bringing his wife. Just a heads-up. Any chance you found a lady in Vegas who will convince Harron you’re a family man?”

He glanced at Roxy, but said nothing to Duke. “MacNeil is going to have to take me as I am.”

“No? I have the feeling he’s going to be on the phone to you here tomorrow morning as soon as the office opens. Which means either I get up early or—”

“You take care of it before you go home to Cami,” Max said. Cami also worked for Max. She and Duke had met when Max had assigned them to work together. Cami never hesitated to take him to task for working Duke too hard.

"I'm already home and she's not too happy. I've been on the phone all night."

"Would a bonus make her happier?" Max asked. He knew that the key to a successful company was happy employees.

"Nah, you know Cami. I think a vacation will satisfy her."

"You can have two weeks at my place in Fiji as soon as MacNeil signs on the dotted line."

"I'm out the door before the ink dries," Duke said.

"Anything else?"

"His latest offer should arrive by courier tonight."

"Thanks, Duke." Max pocketed his cell phone.

"Everything okay?" Roxy asked.

"Just business."

She wrapped her arms around her waist and stood awkwardly by his side just staring at him. She seemed…unsure.

He realized too much time had passed and she was thinking about her scars again. He knew it only because in the jazz club he had glimpsed her totally relaxed and wallowing in her feminine sexuality. Now she wasn't. "Changed your mind about going up to my suite?"

She shrugged her shoulder, but she'd dropped his

hand and had her arms wrapped around her waist. "I'm not sure."

The elevator cars opened again and Max knew that if he pushed now he would lose whatever advantage he had with her. But he was physically on the edge and waiting was not going to be easy.

Touching her had a pronounced effect on his body. Going dancing was out of the question. They each needed a distraction, Roxy from whatever fears had crept into her mind and him from the ones that hadn't left his.

"What would it take to make you sure?"

"Could we leave the lights off?"

"No."

She bit her lower lip and once again the elevator car left without them. "You didn't even hesitate."

"I know that I want to see you—all of you."

"I don't think I'll ever be ready for that."

He realized then that his usual take-charge style wasn't going to get the job done. Roxy needed understanding. He'd be understanding if it damn well killed him, and he knew he wouldn't die from not having sex.

"Let's get out of this place."

She blinked at him. "Where will we go?"

"I don't know, but we need to do something active, something that requires me to use my brain."

"Thinking is a turn-off for you?" she asked, with just a little bit of the sassiness he'd come to expect from her.

"With you around, I don't think anything will work."

She took a deep breath and let it out slowly, her hand reaching for his. She led him back to the elevator alcove. And shocked him. "Let's go up to your room."

They stepped on the elevator and he felt the trembling in her body and noticed her hand shaking as she clutched her handbag. They were the only ones in the car.

He put his hands on her waist and held her loosely between his body and the wall of the car. She glanced up at him, her blue eyes wide, but not with fear. Instead he saw desire.

"What?"

He bent his head to hers and took her mouth in the gentlest kiss he had in him right now. Then he lifted his head and stared down at her. "Just wanted to make sure you were still with me."

He lifted her into his arms as the elevator arrived on his floor and carried her down the hall to his room.

In Max's arms there was no room for self-consciousness. Roxy forgot everything except the taste of him on her tongue, the feel of his strong shoulders under her hands and the emotions he drew effortlessly from her.

No man had ever tempted her more than he did. In the jazz club, she'd simply forgotten they were in a public place and found that the world had narrowed to just the two of them. She'd asked him to distract her because her own thoughts had been starting to scare her. And Max had given her a refuge that was so totally captivating and exciting that her fears had melted away.

She closed her eyes and tucked her head against his neck. No man had ever treated her the way Max did, with his demanding sexuality that was at times at odds with the concern he showered on her. He really paid attention not just to how she reacted physically around him, but also her emotional reactions. She suspected it was due to his time in the boardroom. He just knew how to read people. Especially her, and that made her more than a little nervous.

He made her feel needy and she was used to standing on her own. For tonight, though, she would put those fears to rest and enjoy her time with him.

He set her on her feet at his door and opened it with the key card. "Still sure?"

She nodded, not voicing any more of her body concerns. He made her want to stop hiding in the shadows of her former self—her former life—and step back into the land of the living.

She took his hand and tugged him behind her into the room. She stumbled over the carpet and reached out blindly to catch her balance. Max slipped his arm around her firmly holding her in place.

"Okay?"

No, no. But she wanted to be and Max was the one man to offer her that chance. As soon as the door shut behind them they were surrounded by the darkness. She knew that if she let Max take the lead, she'd be standing in a fully lit room with all her imperfections on display.

The only way she was going to come through this in one piece would be to take control now. She'd rarely done that in her relationships. She wasn't aggressive outside of dancing. But dancing was gone, and with Max she…she felt different than she ever had before. She wanted her actions to be distinctive to this man and this relationship.

So she pushed him back against the wall and leaned up to catch his mouth with hers, kissing him deeply and with all the passion she'd been waiting to shower on him since he'd brought her to a climax in the middle of the jazz club.

She sucked his tongue into her mouth and when he tunneled his fingers in her hair and tilted her head to a better angle for him, she nipped his tongue.

"Convinced?" she asked.

"I'm not sure. I might need a little more persuasion," he said, turning on the light.

She froze, then pushed her fears down. This was about Max and what he made her feel. She'd ignore the light for now—distract him—until she could turn it off.

She loosened the knot in his tie but left it dangling. Then she tugged his shirttails from his pants and slowly unbuttoned his shirt, taking her time with each button, leaning down and kissing each new piece of skin that was revealed.

His nipples were hard by the time she had the shirt unbuttoned and his erection strained against his zipper. She smiled to herself at how he reacted to her. It made her feel very much like a woman. Very much in control of this man who made sure he was always the one in charge.

She lifted his collar and slid his tie over it to rest against his skin. The differences between them slipped away and there were only Max and Roxy in this moment. It didn't matter that he had more money than Midas and she'd been a showgirl.

She removed the cufflinks at his wrists and put them in his breast pocket before pushing his shirt off his shoulders and onto the floor.

Undoing the knot and holding on to each ends of his tie, she drew the soft, silk material over his nipples. His breath hissed out through his teeth.

She continued to brush one nipple with the tie while she bent and licked delicately at the other one. Then, when his hands clutched at her shoulders, she bit very carefully at his nipple.

He groaned and his hips jerked toward her. She smiled and switched her mouth to his other nipple while continuing to move the silk over his body. She kissed her way down his chest, following the line of hair that disappeared into the waistband of his pants. She let go of his tie and reached for his belt buckle.

He had six-pack abs that had to have come from working out. She traced her finger over the delineated muscles and watched them ripple under her touch. "Do you work out?"

"Yes. Another thing we have in common," he said in that husky voice of his.

Maybe the only thing they had in common. Doubts surfaced, but she pushed them aside. She wanted Max, and to be honest there was little she'd wanted in life lately.

"May I?" she asked, stroking her fingers over his belt buckle. The metal was cool in comparison with his hot stomach.

"Yes, you may," he said, in a voice that was little more a rasp.

She unbuckled his belt and pulled it through the loops. Once it was free, she doubled it up in her hand and snapped it. "Have you ever had your hands tied during sex?"

"Why? You think you can dominate me?" he asked.

She waited a heartbeat and then two before looking at him from under her eyelashes. "I know I can, and I don't need this leather belt to do it."

He arched one eyebrow at her and leaned back

against the wall. He looked like a decadent pasha from an exotic land who could have his pick of glamorous women, and for a moment she faltered. Max could have any woman…why her?

But as she looked at this man, she knew that tonight he wanted only her. She dropped the belt and unfastened his pants. Slipped her hand into his loosened waistband and was surprised to encounter nothing but warm male flesh.

"Commando?"

He shrugged. "I don't like to be confined."

She stroked his length, exploring him with her fingers before reaching lower to cup him. He shifted his stance, spreading his legs farther apart. She scored him with her fingernails, scraping carefully against his sensitive flesh.

He cupped her head and brought her lips to his. His tongue thrust deeply into her mouth before he pulled back and stared into her eyes. He pushed lightly on her shoulders and she knew what he wanted. She lowered herself slowly, not kissing her way down his body but keeping her gaze fixed to his as she sank to her knees.

She leaned forward, letting her breath brush over his erection before twirling her tongue over the tip. Before she could go further, he held her head in both his hands and gently guided her back up until their eyes met. She felt a shift deep inside her and knew that she was falling for this man.

* * *

Max lifted Roxy into his arms and carried her into his bedroom. He placed her fully dressed in the center of his bed. He toed off his shoes and socks and then pushed his pants off before he turned on one of the bedside lamps. The room was cast in soft light and shadows. His tie still dangled around his neck but otherwise he was naked.

She rolled to her side to watch him, the skirt of her dress moving up to her thighs, and she shifted on the duvet. When she noticed how much skin she'd exposed, she stiffened and drew the skirt down her legs until they were covered again. Part of his heart was sad at the way she'd covered herself. Roxy was a woman who liked sensual things and that world had been taken from her when Technety attacked her.

He was determined to give her back that world. To reintroduce her to the pleasure of sensual delight and to her own body. He wanted—no, needed—to make her come apart in his arms.

He approached the bed. "I think you convinced me that you want me."

"Did I?" she asked, a candescent light in her eyes as she watched him.

"Yes. Now, it's my turn to convince you," he said, knowing he had to take it slowly for her but unsure of his ability to do so. He wanted to claim her, to thrust inside her body and make her admit that he was her man.

"How are you going to do that?"

"You'll see," he said. Since she was on her side, he sank down next to her and lowered the zipper at the back of her dress. She rolled onto her back, her honey-colored hair spread out on the comforter and he felt that clenching in his gut as he realized that this woman was his. That she was here in his bed.

He lowered himself next to her on the bed and kissed her, caressing her through her clothing. Rubbing his hands down her back, slipping his hand inside her dress to feel the smooth silk of her skin.

He traced her spine down to her buttocks and cupped both cheeks in his hands, drawing her closer to his body. Her legs shifted, one of them draping over his hips so that he could get closer to her. He pulled her more fully against him and felt the warmth of her center through her skimpy thong.

He slipped his hands lower, dragging her panties down her legs. They tangled in her shoes and he sat up, taking them off and then removing her shoes. He took one ankle in either hand and pushed her legs apart. She watched him and he waited to see her reaction.

She pulled her dress up to her waist and then opened her legs wider. "Come to me."

"Not yet." Starting at her feet, he traced the lines of her legs, all the way up the outside, skimming over the tight curls at their apex and then back down the middle. She had two serious scars on her left thigh, and he ached when he touched them and she flinched. One of them was longer and deeper than the other. That was the one that had given her the limp.

She rolled to her side, reaching for the bedside lamp. He caught her around the waist, holding her in place. He ached for her, for this woman who had lost so much of herself. He wanted to assure her that he'd just found her and he would shelter her. Even though those words felt foreign in his mind, he wanted to offer Roxy something he'd given no other woman. Not just in bed, either. In his life.

He bent his head to her thigh and traced those angry-looking scars with his tongue. She quivered under his touch. If she pushed him, he'd let her turn out the light. But he really felt that, tonight, she needed the light on. If he let her hide from him now, she'd never stop hiding. And that wasn't acceptable.

He slipped his fingers between her legs while he kissed her thigh. She moaned as he slipped a finger into her body.

He levered his body up until he lay behind her, her naked back to his naked chest. Her dress still covered her in the areas that he knew she didn't want him to see.

He slid his free hand under her body and rested it over her stomach, then gathered the material of her dress in his hand and tugged until it slid downward, slowly revealing her full breasts encased in pink silk and lace.

As he kept his fingers moving between her legs, her hips picked up his rhythm, rocking in perfect counterpoint. He shifted her in his arms until she lay on her back.

She reached up and held his head, brought her mouth to his as he continued touching her deep inside until he felt her start to tighten around his fingers. He thrust deeper inside her, petting her until the orgasm had rocked through her.

Then he reached into the nightstand and took out a condom, putting it on with the same hand he'd just had in the warmth of her body. Her dress was bunched around her waist and he reached under her to undo the clasp of her bra. He pulled it from her body and tossed it aside.

Her nipples were hard and red, begging for his mouth. He leaned down and suckled her while caressing her entire body and building the fire between them again. He pushed her dress down her body and she kicked it to the floor, her eyes closing as soon as she realized she was naked.

He pushed her thighs apart and settled himself between her legs. The primitive beast deep inside he tried to always ignore roared in his head, demanded that he make Roxy his completely. That she acknowledge she belonged to him.

"Open your eyes, Roxy."

She did, looking up at him and waiting. "Watch me take you this first time. Watch me make you mine and know that there is no one in the world who's more beautiful to me."

He shuddered as her eyes met his, their gazes locked, and then slowly her eyes slid down his body. If possible he hardened even more as he watched his body slowly sink into hers. Felt her legs tighten around his, moving higher so that he could slide all the way home.

He joined his hands with hers, stretched them over her head and started to move between her legs, thrusting into her again and again, making her completely his and giving himself to her. Needing to hear her soft cries. He moved both her hands into one of his and with the other caressed her entire body, pinching her nipple while he thrust even deeper than before. She made a sound in the back of her throat and then he felt her tighten around him as she cried out with her release. He let go of her hands and held her hips, thrusting into her two more times before he joined her over the edge.

He rolled over, wrapping his body around hers, telling himself that nothing had changed. But inside his soul, he knew it had.

Eight

Roxy waited until she was sure that Max was sleeping before slipping from the bed and turning off the light. She hurried into the bathroom, gathering her clothes as she went.

What had she done? She'd let him see her and now he knew. This man in his perfect world with his perfect life. She wasn't a mass of fears during the day, but tonight she felt so vulnerable, so alone. She was supposed to be in charge, dammit. This night had been for her, to reclaim her shattered femininity. Instead she found that she wanted to stay in the shelter of his arms. To find a way to make him stay in hers, and she wasn't one of those dependent women.

He'd touched her. And she'd forgotten about them. Forgotten for a while that she didn't know what she wanted anymore. In his arms it was easy to pretend that nothing had changed and that the changes that had happened didn't matter.

She sank to the marble floor of the bathroom, sitting in the dark with her knees drawn up. The door opened and light from the bedroom spilled into the room. She glanced up at Max.

"Blondie, what are you doing?"

He leaned against the counter—long, lean and perfect in his nudity. She was afraid to glance up at him. Afraid to reassume the role she'd assigned herself when they came into his hotel room. Fiercely sexual and in control…but she wasn't and she couldn't pretend any more.

"You wouldn't understand, Max."

He gave her a really sweet smile and she felt it all the way to her toes.

"Midnight is the time for regrets," he said.

If he only knew. Midnight was only the beginning. She hadn't had a good night's sleep in a long time. And she wished she'd been able to relax and sleep in Max's arms. But her own fears of what her body would look like in the morning, of his revulsion when his lust had passed…

"What do you regret?" she asked. Anything would be better than dwelling on her own insecurities.

He hunkered down on the floor next to her, cupping her face in those big hands of his. "That the woman I just made love to is sitting on the floor in the dark."

She held on to his wrists, looked him straight in the eye and said, "It's not you."

"It's not you, either," he said, kissing her tenderly. Drawing her up off the cold marble floor and into his embrace. In bed he'd been dominating, making sure she reacted to every move he made, but now he was gentle. She kept her eyes open, afraid to close them and find out that this was all a dream.

She realized something important about Max that she'd never noticed before. He really saw past all the things she used to keep most people at bay.

He lifted his head, rubbing his thumb over her bottom lip. She shivered in reaction to his touch, but he pushed to his feet.

He took one of the thick terry robes from the back of the door and wrapped it around her, then pulled her into his arms. She leaned against him, very much afraid that this was becoming a habit and one she'd never want to break. But she couldn't force herself away.

She'd been on her own since she was twelve and it was nice to have another person really care for her. Even if it was just a sexual thing, or temporary. For this night she didn't have to lie alone in her bed with only her thoughts for company.

"Will you stay with me until morning? Or would you like me to take you home?" he asked.

"I don't sleep. I haven't since…"

"No problem. What do you usually do?"

"Exercise. Watch TV. Sometimes I try to read."

"How does a bath sound?"

"Naked."

He arched one eyebrow at her. "Do you bathe with clothing on?"

"I usually bathe alone. I have body issues," she said, knowing that he must have realized it before this moment.

"I noticed."

"Hey, that's the first unchivalrous thing you've said to me. So the real Max isn't as nice as he pretends to be?"

"The real Max…are you sure you're ready for this?"

"Yes." More than he could understand, she needed to see his vulnerabilities.

"The real Max is a little spoiled, mean and determined."

"I'd say a lot determined."

He smiled at her. "I'll give you that."

He pulled her closer in his arms and she settled there. "I have issues with your body, too. You are too sexy. Every time we're out together, other men keep checking you out. It makes me want to do something to stake my claim. To make sure those men know you belong to me."

"Do I belong to you?" she asked. For most of her life she'd belonged only on the stage when she was dancing. Off the stage the competitive nature of her career had prohibited any deep and lasting bonds from forming.

"I don't know," he said, honestly. "I'm not entirely sure how to deal with you. But I want you in my life."

"For how long?" she asked and immediately wished she hadn't.

He rubbed her back, leaning against the countertop. She liked how well they fitted together physically. If only she'd get over her body issues, they could both relax together skin-to-skin.

"I think if I said forever we'd both be scared," he said at last, watching her reaction carefully.

He was right. Forever did sound scary, since she'd only known him two days. Two days…but it felt like a lifetime. Too much was happening too fast and it was easy to let Max sweep her along in whatever he had planned because it gave her the freedom of not being responsible for the choices she made. *He swept me off my feet.* Even as she said the words in her mind, she felt disconnected.

For the first time in her life another person was

asking her to make a decision that affected them. Asking her…oh, man what was he asking her? Forever? That was something that she'd never believed in. Her earliest memories were of being alone. Forever with another person—she simply didn't buy into that.

"You can't fool me. Nothing scares you," she said, trying to keep the focus off herself.

He hugged her tightly to him and bent his head so that he spoke right into her ear. "I'm afraid that I won't be able to keep you."

"I'm not a Learjet, Max. I'm not a possession."

"But I want to possess you," he said, shoving his hands through his hair. "I know that I sound…well, not exactly rational. But I *am* rational. If you know nothing else about me, Blondie, know that I'm the kind of man who thinks every decision through."

She didn't know how to respond to that. No man had ever wanted her, her father had left before she was born, no boy had asked her out in high school and once she'd started dancing the men who'd asked her out had always left. All except Alan, who'd scared her with his possessiveness.

She wanted to tell him that she'd be his. "I'm not ready for you."

"No? What about physically?"

She shrugged. Every time he touched her she felt the bonds between them strengthening. She tried to tell herself it was just sex but she was beginning to believe it was so much more.

"I bet you are."

He lifted her in his arms and carried her into the bedroom. That lamp on the nightstand was on again and she knew that this time he wasn't going to let her slowly remove her clothing and pretend that he wasn't seeing the scars.

And she didn't want him to have to treat her as though she was fragile, to have to factor in how to get her out of her clothing without her flinching like some frightened virgin. So she took a deep breath, untied the belt of her robe and slowly let it drop to the floor.

Max appreciated the strength it took for her to stand there in the lamp's light and drop her robe. He had to be honest and say that once she was naked he wanted to forget about everything except making love to her again. But he couldn't ignore the sadness in her eyes. This was a woman who had once felt pride in her body, and he wanted her to again.

"I thought I was supposed to be convincing you," he said, moving toward her.

She held her hand up and he stopped when less than a foot of space separated them. "You already did. Now, I want to do something for you."

"I think we've covered that. Why don't we do something that's for each other?"

"That's why I'm standing here naked. But first I want you to look at me. Really look at me."

"I am."

"Not my breasts."

"Well, they *are* gorgeous."

She stared at him for a minute and then smiled, her expression so tempting that he felt his erection twitch in reaction to it.

He took her hand in his and led her to the mirror that stood embedded in the wall in the dressing area. He hit the light switch.

Roxy wrapped her arms around her waist and tried to shrink her body. He stood behind her, pulling her arms from her body and holding them out to her sides.

"Look in the mirror."

She hesitated for a second and then looked up. Their gazes met in the mirror and he bent and kissed her shoulder. Drew his mouth and teeth along the expanse of skin there until she shivered in his arms and tipped her head, offering him the long column of her neck.

He nibbled at her neck, working his way up to her ear. He sucked the lobe of her ear into his mouth and bit it delicately. "Look at your body."

She shook her head. Max wondered if he was pushing too hard. If he should just back off. But he didn't want Roxy in his bed feeling as though she had to hide part of herself. He wanted her free of her inhibitions.

"Then I'll look at you and tell you what I see."

He cupped her shoulders and she lowered her arms to her sides. "Your arms are so feminine yet at the same time muscled and strong. I like the way they look in those sleeveless tops you wear. I can't resist reaching out and touching you."

He ran his hands down both of her arms, slowly taking his time to make sure that he didn't miss a single inch of skin.

"I like my arms, too," she said quietly.

He tipped her head back and kissed her. She opened her mouth for him, angling her head the way he liked her to, and teased his tongue to come deeper into her mouth. When he lifted his head they were both breathing more heavily. Her lips were wet and swollen from his kisses and her eyes were slumberous.

He skimmed his hands over her breasts. He cupped the full weight of them, and felt her nipples tightening under his touch. "You have gorgeous breasts."

Her eyes were on his hands, his tanned skin a contrast against her pale white flesh. Her body, so delicate and pink and feminine, contrasted with the masculine strength of his. She put her hands over his as she undulated against his entire body, her buttocks rubbing over his erection, her shoulder blades rubbing over his chest, her long silky hair brushing his neck and shoulder.

"Can we stop now?" she asked, her voice low and

husky. She turned in his arms, her hands roaming down his chest. Fingernails scraping over him. "I really like your body."

"I know you do," he said, kissing her harder than he intended because he really couldn't resist her. He turned her back in his arms and held her firmly against him. One hand at her waist, the other right beneath her breasts.

"This is the part you don't like," he said, caressing her stomach from her ribs down to her belly button and stopping before he reached the curls between her legs.

"Yes," she said her voice breaking.

He kept touching her there, stroking over her skin until she relaxed against him. He took her hand in his and moved it over her own body. Sensitive to her reaction, he stopped when she lingered over the first scar. There were seven in total, all varying in length, the longest of them no more than three inches.

It was a miracle to him that she was here now in his arms—whole and complete. He had to batten down his own rage at what she'd been through. He vowed she'd never be that vulnerable again.

"I was very vain, Max. I think I hate these scars because they are proof of that vanity. Proof that I liked my body too much."

He hugged her tighter to him. Words were impossible at this moment. He just rubbed their joined hands over her body. "You are a dancer, your body is your work. It's how you express your art."

She turned in his arms again. There was a sheen of tears in her eyes and another emotion he couldn't define. "Make love to me."

He lifted her and carried her back to the bed. He settled her in the center and then slowly lowered his body over hers. He rubbed his torso against her. Felt the humid warmth at the center of her body. He liked the feel of being totally naked with her. He slipped just a little into her body just to tease them both.

"Yes, that's it. Take me and make me yours. Make us one," she said.

He was tempted to do it like this, with no protection, but he'd made a life of being responsible, so he sighed and pulled back. Their hands met at the box on the nightstand and she took the condom from him. She rolled it onto his body and then pulled him back to her. He slid into her body and she held him with her arms and legs. He moved slowly, rocking them from side-to-side and thrusting leisurely into her body until they were both consumed by waves of pleasure.

He rolled to his side, disposed of the condom and then pulled her back into his arms. She reached out and flicked off the light on the nightstand, then turned to him, resting her head over his chest, and went to sleep.

* * *

Roxy woke up to the smell of coffee and the low rumble of Max's voice. She rolled over and glanced at the clock, surprised to see that it was almost ten. She'd slept the entire night in his arms. This morning she was determined to face what she'd put off last night.

She got out of bed and put on her robe, walking into the other room where Max was on the phone at his laptop computer. He smiled when she entered, reached for the carafe of coffee and poured her a cup. She added cream and then sat down on the settee that faced the windows overlooking the city.

This was his world. She'd glimpsed it more than once. He worked all the time, his job was demanding…it was his life.

She'd expected to feel different this morning. Somehow, her outlook should have changed in a significant way. But aside from some aches from having had sex for the first time in a year, she didn't feel unusual.

He finished his call and came over to her. Bending, he kissed her and then sat down next to her.

"Thanks for the coffee," she said, feeling shy and a bit unsure. She had nothing to wear but last night's dress; she'd bared her soul to this man last night. She wasn't sure she wanted him to realize how much of herself he'd seen.

"I would have had breakfast for you, too, but Hayden didn't know what you liked to eat. I'll order that now."

"Why would Hayden know that?" she asked, sensing there was more to this than breakfast. She'd noticed how Max liked every detail to be perfect. Why?

Max put his arm along the back of the couch and drew her closer to his side. "I know my employees' preferences."

"All of them?" she asked, because from what she understood he ran a huge conglomerate.

He squeezed her tight. "No, smarty, not personally, but I have a file and my secretary accesses the information when I need it."

She was amazed at the amount of detail that implied. Why did Max do that? She tipped her head back to study him more carefully. She sensed there was something underlying here. What was she missing? "Why would you keep a file like that?"

"People like it when you remember little things about them."

Details were the things most easy to forget, Roxy thought. She knew that because, in the group home she'd lived in as a teen, she'd been one of three blond girls. No one had bothered to remember any of their names, just called them all "blond-girl." A name was an important detail, and she'd made sure as an adult that everyone remembered hers. But Max was going beyond that. He was remembering things that sometimes even spouses and parents didn't know.

"What are the details about you? What are the things that make you happy?" she asked, hoping he'd reach out and show her some part of himself that no one else knew.

"That's not important. What do you like for breakfast?"

She sighed. Max wasn't going to reveal anything intimate to her. She'd bared her body to this man and he wanted to know what she liked for breakfast. When was she going to learn? "I like toast with blackberry jelly and coffee."

"That's not breakfast. That's what you eat when you're in a hurry."

He wasn't going to let this go. There was more to this than breakfast. From growing up in the system, she knew that everyone, no matter how normal they seemed, had some kind of issue to deal with. This need for facts was Max's way of building a relationship.

"Why are you looking at me like that?"

"I'm trying to figure out what makes *you* tick."

"What you see is what you get. Tell me about you and breakfast."

"What's to tell? I've never had a leisurely breakfast. Mornings aren't really a time to hang out for show dancers." When she was younger, she'd spent all of her time at the dance studio before and after school. Food had just never seemed that important, mainly because it had been scarce.

"Now that you have the gory details about my morning eating habits…what about you?"

Max stared down at her, his hands moving slowly over her shoulder, caressing her as they talked. She settled deeper into the curve of his body.

"I'm usually the one who makes the arrangements, so no one needs to know my preferences."

"What if I'm the one ordering?" she asked. She could never tolerate a relationship that was uneven. She wanted to take as good care of him as he did of her. She was going to make this relationship with Max work. She didn't want it to end when he left, and that meant really getting to know him. She'd shown him way more of herself than she'd meant to, something she'd never done before with anyone. So there was more to Max and her than she'd initially thought.

He arched one eyebrow at her. "In that case, I like poached eggs and Canadian bacon."

"Was that so hard? I'm not going to leak the information."

"You might be the first person to ask what I liked," he said, leaning her head back against his shoulder. He kissed her slowly and with great tenderness.

"I'm sure that's because most people already know." The kind of man he was, he'd surround himself with like-minded people. Hayden might not know what she liked to eat, but he treated his staff like family and she knew he was one of Max's closest friends.

"They don't."

"That must be your fault then."

He waited for her to continue, and she felt as if she might have blundered into something that she didn't mean to say. But she'd noticed that Max took care of the people around him, and not vice versa.

"You don't give anyone a chance to know you. You keep the spotlight focused on them."

"Them, or you?"

"Well, me, and it's very flattering but I forget to ask about you. I want to know *your* secrets."

"I thought Hayden gave you a file on me?"

"That only included your gambling habits. I want to know the real secrets. The ones that no one else knows."

"There are no secrets, Roxy. What you see is what you get with me."

He pushed to his feet and went back to his computer. He lifted the phone and made a call to room service, ordering breakfast for both of them. "I have to work after breakfast for a few hours."

She put her coffee cup down and walked slowly toward the bedroom. Then she realized she was running, the way she always did when things got a little sticky emotionally. She had no idea how to treat Max. But she knew that they both had to be able to pry into each other's lives. It was unfair that he'd seen her in all her imperfection and was unwilling to give her even a glimpse at the inner man he carefully hid.

"Did I offend you?" she asked.

"No, you didn't. I'm not a secrets kind of guy. This really is all I am."

There was a sadness in his eyes, and Roxy knew that there were secrets inside Max but sensed they'd been buried too deeply for him to tell her easily what they were. She'd find them out on her own.

Nine

Roxy wiped her sweaty palms on the legs of her pants and walked into the lobby of the Chimera one week later. Suzi Yuki, the high-stakes gambler whom Roxy had started hostessing for after Max, was a lot of fun. And she needed little encouragement to stay in the casino. Her game was craps and she was a phenomenal player. When Roxy had left Suzi a few minutes earlier she'd been up almost fifty thousand dollars.

Of course, she wasn't nervous at all about being a hostess. That job was turning into something she could definitely get used to doing, even though it didn't hold the same luster that dancing always had.

But she'd realized that dancing would never be the center of her life again.

Max was slowly becoming that focal point, which bothered her because she wasn't sure how she fitted into his life. One on one, they meshed, mainly because Max made sure that they did. He really listened to her and understood the things she wanted, as well as things she was afraid to ask for.

And that made her nervous, because she didn't know what to do for him. Of course, when he'd asked her to join him at a business lunch, she'd said yes.

Now she was having second thoughts. She'd never gone to college, hadn't even graduated high school. Her birthday was in March, so she'd become an adult before she was supposed to have graduated. Having no place to stay she'd started working in clubs instead of staying in school.

What if she embarrassed Max? What if she said something that was—

"Hey, Blondie, I've been waiting for you," Max said, slipping his arm around her waist.

She tried to relax against him and couldn't. "Hey, yourself. Where is everyone else?"

"We're meeting them upstairs in a private dining room. I wanted a chance to talk to you first."

She took a deep breath. "You don't have to worry, Max. I won't embarrass you."

He furrowed his brow. "What are you talking about?"

"Just that I know I don't know anything about your business. I'll keep quiet and just smile. I won't say anything—"

He put his finger on her lips, stopping the flow of words that was growing out of control. In her mind she wanted to apologize for everything she'd ever done and she didn't like that. She didn't like feeling discomfited by the life she'd led when she compared it to his.

"What are you talking about?" he asked quietly. "I know all I need to about business. I need you here to keep me from saying something I shouldn't."

"That doesn't sound like the man I've come to know," she said. She'd observed Max on the phone and he was always unfailingly polite and to the point. The ultimate professional.

"Well, MacNeil is seriously pissing me off," he said, taking her hand and leading her out of the lobby and into the courtyard that led to another tower of the hotel.

"So what am I supposed to do?" she asked as they walked.

"Just be yourself. He's bringing his wife as well. That's his way of calling a truce."

"Are you sure you want me there?" As soon as she asked she wanted to kick herself. What was wrong with her that she had to doubt her own worth? "Forget I said that."

"I will. Don't be nervous. Harron is a nice man when he's not trying to keep me dangling. And his wife, Sheila, is a huge patron of the arts in Vancouver, especially local dance."

She relaxed a little, thinking that maybe this lunch wouldn't be as bad as she feared.

But Max still seemed tense, and she wasn't sure how to help him out. "Are you nervous?"

"No. Why?"

"You seem edgy."

"Edgy?"

"Don't take this the wrong way…but you remind me of a predator on the hunt."

He laughed. "Good. I want MacNeil to understand exactly how I feel about this delay of his."

"Isn't this just part of the way acquisitions work?" she asked. Max had explained that he was in the process of buying out MacNeil's family-owned travel agency, the third largest in North America.

"Sometimes, but I'm on vacation and I'd rather be in my suite making love to you. Yet duty calls."

"If you hadn't invited me to lunch you'd be in your suite by yourself," she said, because she didn't want him to be too confident in his hold over her.

"You think so?" He pulled her off the walkway and behind a hedge.

There was a fountain gurgling in the middle of an oasis. The Chimera prided itself on its romantic ambience, and this particular fountain was a well-known wedding proposal spot. In fact, it was hidden so that a couple could have privacy and still have a photo souvenir. There was a small area behind the garden area where a photographer could be stationed.

"I know so. There's no way I could have asked Hayden for a long lunch to meet you in your room. Why are we here?"

Max led her to the bench in the middle of the garden. "Please have a seat. I have something I need to ask you before we join the MacNeils."

Anxiety slithered down her spine. "Do you want me to pretend I wasn't a topless dancer?"

He cupped her face in his hands, his long fingers sliding over her cheeks to the back of her neck and holding her so that he could stare down into her eyes. He lowered his head and brushed his lips over hers.

"I thought we already covered this. I want you to be yourself. I like the woman that you are, Roxy."

She swallowed, unsure how to respond to that statement. Sometimes he made her feel too much. A swell of emotion that she was unprepared to handle welled up in her throat. His hands dropped to his sides and he gestured toward the bench again. She sat down, crossing her legs and waiting for Max to join her. When he didn't she tipped her head back to look up at him.

* * *

Max straightened his tie and glanced around to make sure the photographer he'd hired was in position. He'd planned every detail of this proposal carefully. It had been a tight timetable to make sure he was ready for the MacNeil meeting and get the ring he wanted flown in before lunch. But he was used to juggling several projects at the same time.

And this thing with Roxy needed to be settled. He wasn't going to be happy until he'd put his mark on her so that every man she encountered knew she was his. Last night when she'd contemplated going home instead of coming up to his suite, he'd realized that he needed something permanent between them. A bond that even Roxy couldn't deny.

He patted his pocket again and rehearsed the words he'd planned to say.

"What are you doing?" she asked.

Great. First she thought he was nervous and now she probably thought…ah, hell he had no idea what she thought. He only knew that he'd been on his own his entire life and finding Roxy was like finding a piece that had been missing.

"Making sure every detail is right," he said, leaning to the left and finally spotting the pedestal ice-bucket and the bottle of champagne in it.

She raised both eyebrows at him. "For what?"

He took a deep breath and sat down next to her on

the bench. He took her small fine-boned hand in his and traced the veins on the back of her hand. She twisted her hand and slid her fingers through his.

"These last few days have been incredible," he said, not really sure where those words came from. Though they were the truth he didn't want her to know how he felt.

"I feel the same. I never thought that I'd meet someone like you." She smiled at him, her expression so tender that he knew he'd made the right choice. Knew there was no way she'd deny him.

"I think Hayden's finally found a way to pay me back for befriending him all those years ago."

"I don't like the sound of that. I told him I wasn't interested in being set up with you."

"You did?"

"Yes."

"Well my considerable charm must have worked on you."

"Not your charm, Max. Your attention to detail."

Max wasn't sure how they'd strayed onto talking about Hayden and knew he didn't want to discuss his friend. He wanted to discuss them. "Hayden has nothing to do with this."

"With what? You're being vague and that's not like you."

No it wasn't like him. His normal mode of operation was just to take what he wanted and keep moving forward. To acquire businesses, homes, cars, friends. He knew how to do that. But a wife…that was infinitely harder. They'd share everything—a home, a bed, their lives—and he'd never in his forty years shared all that.

Even his childhood home had been a series of empty showplaces that his family members had moved between depending on the season. His father always remarried in June, his mother always retreated to Aspen in November. But he wanted more with Roxy. He wanted to have something—someone—who could be with him all the time. He wanted a person to fill the void his career had always filled.

"I've never done this before."

"Done *what?*" she asked, putting her hand on his thigh.

All his thoughts faded. He wanted to move her hand higher. To bend and take her mouth with his and then make love to her. To reinforce the physical bonds that were between them.

"Done what, Max?" she asked again.

"Asked you to marry me," he said, biting out the words in a way he hadn't planned on them sounding. Dammit, he always screwed up the romantic fantasy when left to his own devices.

"What?"

"Marry me, Roxy."

He stood and pulled the velvet box from his

pocket, snapping it open as he dropped to one knee in front of her. He took her hand in his and looked up into her eyes. They were cloudy with doubts and he understood that. Everything had happened so quickly between them…too quickly, it might seem, but Max had learned long ago to trust his instincts and the way he reacted to Roxy was totally instinctive.

He took the platinum marquise-cut aquamarine-and-diamond-encrusted ring from the box and slipped it onto her ring finger. She didn't say anything, but goose bumps spread up her arm.

He heard the sound of the photographer snapping the pictures. The sound of people on the path that lay beyond the hedges. The soft sound of her every inhalation of breath, but he didn't hear the one word he waited for.

"I have a bottle of champagne and some glasses over here. We'll have a toast and then after lunch, I'm taking you away for an afternoon of pampering."

"I can't go."

"Why not?"

She pushed to her feet, wrapping her arms around her waist. She started when the ring scraped the skin of her arm. She looked down on the large ring and pulled it from her hand.

"Thank you for asking me to marry you, but I can't."

She held the ring out to him, but he didn't take it. He knew she'd change her mind. He just had to find the right words to say. The correct argument to use.

"Why can't you marry me?"

"We hardly know each other, Max. We're still practically strangers."

"No, we're not. We know a lot about one another. I know you inside and out, Roxy. Don't deny that."

"Maybe you know my vulnerabilities, but that doesn't mean we can live with each other day in and day out. I'm still adjusting to my new life, and it's hard. I don't know that I'm ready to become your wife and change my life again."

He crossed to her, taking her chin in his hand and leaning her head back. "Those are excuses."

"You might be right, but I can't marry you now."

He let go of her chin and stepped back. No one had ever told him no before. That wasn't true, he thought, his mind racing to accept the fact that she'd really said no. He forced back the momentary anger that had risen when she'd taken his ring from her finger. Roxy just needed to be persuaded, he thought.

He'd studied the details around Roxy. He knew things about her that few others did. What had he missed? Somehow this wasn't about marrying to make Harron get off his back anymore, but about making sure she stayed in his life.

He didn't say anything, just kept looking at her with a mixture of anger and resolve. Roxy didn't know what to do. Only knew that saying no was the hardest thing that she'd ever done. But she was only just figuring out this new life she had, this life away from dancing, and marrying Max after knowing him for such a short time wouldn't be fair to either of them.

She didn't want to face the truth, but in her soul was the fear that the home she'd felt in Max's arms might disappear if they lived together.

She took his hand in hers and pressed the ring into the center of his palm. She knew he wouldn't beg her to reconsider and she admitted to herself that was the problem. It was almost as if Max knew those details of her life and that he'd figured she'd say yes because acceptance had been so rare for her.

She turned on her heel and walked away, struggling not to limp but so agitated she couldn't keep her gait smooth. Her legs trembled. She didn't know if she'd make it back to some private place before she gave in to the tears she felt welling up behind her eyes. Because for a minute there she'd wanted to give herself to him cheaply. To trade her life for a ring. And she'd always believed she'd never do that.

"Roxy?"

She paused but didn't turn to look at him. She couldn't see him again, knowing she was just the right face at the right time, not the love of his life.

Why did that matter?

Her mind didn't know the answer, but her heart

did. She was falling for him. Heck, she'd fallen for him that first morning on the beach. Saying no was the only way she knew to protect her heart from breaking once again.

"Yes?"

"Where are you going?" he asked in a gruff voice that gave her a spark of hope that maybe he wasn't as unemotional as he was pretending to be.

She pivoted on her heel to face him. The midday sun slanted through the canopy of tree branches in the garden, falling over him, leaving him mainly in the shadows next to the fountain.

He looked so alone and determined that her heart ached. He still stood next to the bench. The ring and its box had been tucked away somewhere.

There was no hint of vulnerability in him, and she wondered for a moment if he'd really just asked her to marry him, because he didn't look like a man who'd had his proposal turned down.

"I…I was going back to work. I didn't think you'd still want to have lunch."

"You thought wrong. I misjudged you, but I won't do it again."

She didn't like the way that sounded. He was focusing on her the same way he was his merger. She bit her tongue before she could ask him if he was going to draw up a statement about the pros and cons of her marrying him. "I'm not a business you are trying to acquire."

"I know that. Companies are a lot easier to get a handle on. All I have to do is look at the P and L and then figure out if I can turn a profit."

"What's a P and L?" she asked to distract herself.

"Profit and loss statement."

"Kind of like pros and cons?" she asked.

"Kind of."

"How'd I stack up?"

His expression lightened as he skimmed his gaze down her body. "Better than I did, obviously."

She couldn't help but laugh at him. She slapped him on the arm. "That wasn't very sophisticated."

"Who said I was sophisticated?" he asked.

"No one had to. You exude breeding and culture with every movement you make. Unlike me."

"Is that why you said no?" he asked.

She wished it were something easy like comportment so she could take a class and fix it. But she knew it was more complex than that. She needed more from Max than a proposal after a few days. She needed emotion, and the man she'd come to know wasn't that open with his feelings.

"I'm going to ask you again, and the next time you will say yes."

"Do you have any idea how arrogant that sounds?" she asked, trying to change her mood and get past the emotions that weighed so heavily in her throat.

"Yes."

She had to laugh at the totally unrepentant way he said it. She knew she shouldn't encourage him because marriage wasn't in her plans, but there was something that felt so right about slipping her arm though his as they walked. "We'll see."

He stopped walking and turned to her there on the path, and there was emotion in his eyes this time. Real emotion that made her hope that he might feel more for her than he did for his business merger. "I want you in my life. If you're not ready for marriage then I can wait."

It scared her how important he'd become to her in such a short time. He was making her change and she knew she'd needed that impetus to start changing, but at the same time she was afraid to trust.

"I'm sorry."

"Don't be. I misjudged something. I'll figure it out and ask you again when the time is right."

"Part of the problem is you thinking that you have to figure this out by yourself. A relationship involves two people."

He scratched his chin. "I'll try, but honestly, I'm not sure I can do what you ask. I'm too used to operating on my own."

"What about your family? Don't you compromise on stuff like where you have holiday dinners and vacations?"

"We're not a close family. My schedule is always available to them, but they are busy."

"That's not what family is supposed to be. Is that how you envision marriage to me?"

"I'm not sure what you're asking."

"I'm asking if I'd get a copy of your schedule and then have to decide when I wanted to see you."

"From your tone, I think my answer better be no."

"We still have a ways to go, Max. We're not ready for marriage yet."

"What do I have to do? I'm good at achieving objectives."

She shook her head at him. "Stop acting like I'm a company you're trying to acquire. And you're going to have to compromise."

He arched one eyebrow at her in that arrogant way of his. "I'm sure you can be very persuasive if you put your mind to it."

"Are you talking about sex again?"

"I listen to you when we're not in bed."

He led the way into the tower building, holding the door for her to enter. She thought about how different Max was from every other man she'd ever been involved with. He did listen to her, and he heard things she wasn't even aware she wanted or needed. But he kept his own dreams and desires hidden away, and she really needed to know him to feel safe spending the rest of her life with him.

Ten

The next two weeks were hectic as Max divided his time between Vegas and Roxy and business trips to Vancouver and his corporate headquarters in Atlanta. He was tired, he missed Roxy and he wanted nothing more than just to hold her in his arms.

The second day in Vancouver, he'd invited her to join him for a mini-vacation while he closed the deal with MacNeil, but she'd refused. She had a job to do and she hadn't yet earned vacation time. Max had made a call to Hayden and asked him to free Roxy from her schedule.

Hayden had refused and Roxy had called Max,

livid that he would try such a thing. It had not been the smartest move on his part.

He'd showered her with gifts, but she'd told him to stop trying to buy her. She didn't need anything, and it made her uncomfortable to receive pricey gifts. Max *had* stopped, but it hadn't felt right.

From his mother's knee he'd learned that women wanted trinkets and baubles, and Roxy's disinterest in them was just another thing that set her apart from every other woman he'd ever known. She'd also told him that he better get used to her working, because she'd never be a lady of leisure.

Tonight she was working until nine o'clock, when her gambler was leaving for the airport. So he went to the poker room to play a few hands. Hayden was there talking to two Japanese men whom Max recognized from his own deep play. They were both whales, big-time gamblers who spent weeks at the casino several times a year. Hayden waved him over but Max didn't feel like socializing so he declined with a shake of his head.

He still had Roxy's ring in his pocket, and he wanted it on her hand. He hadn't asked her again, but had made love to her as often as he could. He'd also taken the time to ask about her dreams and where she saw her future. She wanted to open a small dance studio and pass her love for dance on to others.

She had an idea for opening a showgirl college of

sorts in Vegas and Max had already done some research into what that would take. He wanted to talk to Hayden about space for the facility in the hotel.

He'd called her every night, at first hoping to make her realize how much she needed him in her life. In his arrogance, he wanted to remind her of what she'd said no to.

But instead he'd found that he was the one who needed the conversations. And because dependence wasn't something he could tolerate, he'd deliberately stopped talking to her every day, calling her when he knew she wouldn't be there to prove to himself that he didn't need to hear her voice before he went to bed. He'd have her in his arms for the next four nights. That was the longest stretch of time they'd been together.

Arms snaked around his waist and he felt the cool press of Roxy's lips against his neck. "Hey, there!"

He turned in her embrace and kissed her with all the pent-up emotion that had been bottled inside him for the last five days. "Damn, I missed you."

Her lips were wet and swollen from his kiss. "I missed you, too."

"Are you ready to go?"

"Yes. I just got back from the airport."

"You took Suzi to the airport?"

"She asked me to ride with her. She's really nice and she gave me a huge tip. Dinner tonight is on me."

"No way." No woman of his was buying him a meal. He knew it was an archaic attitude, but he wanted to take care of her because no one else ever had. She'd been working and providing a shelter for herself since she'd turned eighteen, and now he wanted to spoil her. "I'd rather you buy something for yourself."

She shook her head. "I want to do this, Max. You're always showering me with gifts and stuff. And you have everything…"

He started to argue but she put her fingers over his lips. "Compromise."

When she put it that way, he understood where she was coming from.

"Great. Do you have a favorite restaurant?"

He had several and he tried to pick one in the moderate price range. He wanted her to feel good about buying him dinner but not stretch her budget. "There's a nice sushi place near the hotel. I'll have my secretary make us a reservation."

Over the last few weeks he'd come to realize that when she'd stopped headlining, her income had been cut in half. And he admired the way she'd been careful to make sure that she was still able to make ends meet by adjusting her lifestyle.

He kept his hand at the small of Roxy's back as they walked to his limo.

* * *

Two nights later Roxy put the finishing touches on her makeup in the luxurious suite that Max used whenever he was at the Chimera. Max was at a meeting, but they were having dinner with Harron MacNeil and his wife, who had flown to Vegas for the weekend.

Ever since she'd turned down his wedding proposal, Max had been going out of his way to learn to compromise. She knew it was a struggle for him.

"Roxy?"

"In here," she said. She blotted her lipstick and turned as he came in, shedding his jacket. He tossed it on the edge of the bed and crossed the room to kiss her. She loved that he did that.

"I'm sorry, Blondie, I thought I'd have you to myself for a few days but sometimes duty calls." He undid his belt and tossed it on the bed and then went to work on his shirt.

"Sometimes? It calls you all the time." She opened the closet and took out a fresh shirt for him while he went into the bathroom and freshened up.

"This is my life," he said, poking his head around the door and holding his hand out for his shirt. She handed it to him and he shrugged into it.

"I know. When I used to dance I was the same way about my career." She understood Max's dedication and didn't resent it. He always made time for her. The reality was, he was the CEO of a huge company, and there was no way he'd be able to step away from that.

He pulled a new tie from the drawer and put it around his neck, leaving the tails dangling while he buttoned his shirt and tucked it in.

"This should be the last dinner with them. I think MacNeil is ready to sign on the dotted line."

"What's been the hold up?"

"The company has been in his family for the last three generations and he wants to make sure that I don't change the essence of what they do."

"And that is?"

"Cater to families. They pride themselves on their wholesomeness."

"You're not exactly virtuous."

He gave her a wicked grin. "Ah, you know you like that about me."

He pulled her into his arms, leaning back against the vanity table. She rested her hand on his bare chest. "MacNeil is finally convinced that I will keep my word. I told him he could have an opportunity to meet the woman I'm planning to marry."

"Max, I haven't said yes."

"I know that. I was upfront with Harron, told him you were dragging your feet."

She shook her head. Sometimes he was outrageous. She honestly thought that the reason Max was so successful in business and in life was that he simply never gave up. "Harron thinks I'm the key to you keeping your word."

"He does. Dinner tonight is just a formality. Thanks for doing this."

"I don't mind. I really liked Sheila when we met them for lunch. I want to talk to her more about the dance studio she and her daughter own." She liked being a part of Max's business life. Since that was a huge part of who he was, it gave her another glimpse into the complex man she cared for. She stepped away from him so he could finish dressing.

"I've done some preliminary research into starting a showgirl dance college, if you're interested," he said, tucking his shirt in and knotting his tie.

She leaned over his shoulder, catching his eye in the mirror to make sure he saw that she was serious. She'd mentioned her dream of opening a school during a late-night conversation. If she didn't put up some stipulations, he'd use his money to make the showgirl college a reality before she had a chance. "Really. I don't want you to buy it for me. Plus I'm not sure I have the right personality to teach."

"Somehow I knew you'd say that. I ran the idea past Hayden, because it makes sense to have a central training area. Even if you decide not to teach, the idea should still go forward and you should be a part of it."

She shook her head. "I'm going to do this research, not you."

"Did you just tell me no?"

She bit the inside of her cheek to keep from smiling. If only he were as arrogant as he thought he was, it would be easier for her to resist him. Easier for her to pretend this was just an affair. Easier to sleep when they were apart.

"Yes, I did. You can't keep buying me things all the time. You make me feel like a kept woman."

He shrugged into his suit jacket, checked himself one more time in the mirror before turning to her. "Not a very well-kept one. You work as many hours as I do."

"And your problem with that would be?"

"Absolutely nothing, Blondie."

He mixed them both a vodka martini, shaking it perfectly, and handed her the glass.

"To us," he said.

"To us." Their eyes met as they clinked their glasses and even though she knew she wasn't really part of this world—his world—for once she felt as if she was exactly where she belonged.

Their dinner was nice but Max wanted to be alone with Roxy.

For the majority of his life, work had been his number-one priority and it was unnerving to find that a woman was now edging business out. It was early and he should suggest something like dancing or drinks, but all he really wanted to do was get back to his suite and make love to Roxy.

He shook hands with Harron and watched as Roxy and Sheila said goodbye. Niceties over, be guided Roxy back to his limo as quickly as possible without seeming to rush.

He wanted to ask her again to marry him. The words had been on the tip of his tongue every time they spoke, but he knew he only had one more shot to get it right. He couldn't keep asking her without making himself look like a desperate ass, an image he never wanted to cultivate.

"You're quiet," he said as the city lights flashed into the back of the limo.

"So are you."

He raised both eyebrows at her tone. "What's up?"

"I've been thinking about our relationship. I don't see how we can go on this way. I miss you a lot when we're apart."

He pulled her into his arms. "Good."

She punched his shoulder lightly but didn't leave his embrace. Instead she settled back against him as he wrapped his arm around her.

"I don't think so, Max. I'm not sure we can keep on the way we have been."

Finally, he was going to be able to have what he wanted. What they both wanted. He couldn't explain the bond between them. It was like nothing he'd ever experienced before. He only knew that his life paled when he was away from her.

"I agree."

"You do?"

"Of course, I do. I'm not any happier with the way things are. I want to sleep with you every night."

She tipped her head back and he lowered his mouth to hers, sipping from her. Tasting her with long sweeps of his tongue. The brief taste he'd had of her passion earlier wasn't enough. He needed more. He needed it now.

He shifted her in his arms until she straddled his lap. Her hands on his face, her breasts resting on his chest.

"I don't see how that's possible unless you move your headquarters to Las Vegas."

He skimmed his hands over her back, tracing her spine and shifted under her until he had them both as close as they could get.

"I'm afraid I can't do that. Too many jobs are at stake. Why don't you quit working for the Chimera and travel with me?"

She shifted off his lap and to the rear-facing seat. She crossed her legs and wrapped her arms around herself. "I can't. I can't stop working to be with you. I wouldn't be able to live with myself if I did that."

"Compromise, isn't that what you're always telling me?" he asked.

"Yes, I am. But—"

"What?"

"I'm not sure what I want to do," she said.

"I'll support you until you figure that out. You can try whatever you like."

She gave him a hard glare. "I promised myself I'd never live on charity again."

"There's a big difference between being charity and living together with a man you can't get enough of." Even now he couldn't make himself talk about emotions. Hers or his. He wanted her, he could vocalize his attraction for her body and late at night he could admit to himself that he needed her in his life. But he couldn't make himself that vulnerable to her.

"That's really not for me."

His anger bubbled over. He couldn't believe they were having this conversation. He felt like a heel for suggesting that she live with him. *He* didn't want a mistress—he'd wanted a wife. "I asked you to marry me and you said no. So tell me what will work."

"When you say it like that—"

Immediately he regretted his outburst. Eye on the prize. He was focused on getting her into his life. Making her his wife. "Sorry, my temper got the best of me. I know you need time to see for yourself what I already know about the two of us."

"What do you know?"

"I know that we fit together."

"Physically, we sure do. But our lives are very different."

"Variety is the spice of life, isn't it?"

"Yes, it is. But what if this is just the newness?"

"I can't make you any promises for what the future holds, I'd be lying and we'd both know it. But I can tell you that I can't imagine a time when I won't want you by my side."

She shifted in his arms, leaning closer to him. Her head on his shoulder. "I'm so tempted. But reality is hard on those kinds of fantasies. And I'm falling for you, Max. Really falling for the man you are in a way that has nothing to do with sex. Relationships are built on more than what we have."

Fear gripped him by the throat. He knew sooner or later this would come up. "I'm giving you all I can."

She swallowed. "I've always wanted a different kind of relationship."

"What kind?" he asked, knowing that this was the key to Roxy. The key to really understanding her.

"The kind I've never had. That perfect dream family I wanted as a child, the kind that I'd look at when I was at a shopping mall and long to be a part of."

"There's no such thing as perfect," he said. He cradled her closer, wanting to undo all the wounds that life had dealt her in the past. He would give her this if that's what she needed to be happy with him. "This isn't a fantasy or a dream. I'm a real man and I want you in my life. I want you to marry me so that everyone who sees us will know that you belong to me."

She took a deep breath as the car pulled to a stop in front of their hotel, then put her hand on his arm as the driver came around to open the door. "I want that, too."

Eleven

Max lifted her into his arms when she stepped out of the car and carried her through the lobby, drawing the attention of everyone they passed. But he didn't linger or say anything except to tell her to push the elevator button when they arrived at the bank.

She did, and then hit the button for their floor. Max lowered her down his body, his mouth finding hers. She wrapped her arms around him and clung to him, a feeling of complete rightness swamping her, making her feel like the choice she'd made was the right one.

The car stopped on their floor and Max lifted her into his arms again. She'd been carried before in a couple of shows and in ballet class, dancing a pas de deux. But this was different. Max's mouth was on hers, his arms tight around her, and even though he hadn't spoken of love or affection, she felt the commitment in his embrace.

"There isn't going to be champagne or photographers. You caught me by surprise," he said, setting her on her feet to open the door.

She remembered how much effort he'd put into his first proposal and knowing him as she did, she knew he liked every detail planned. It said something to her that he'd kept pursuing her even though she'd turned down his orchestrated proposal. "I don't need those things. I just need you."

"Me neither. I need you, too, Blondie."

He carried her over the threshold and kicked the door closed behind them. A lamp from the living area of their suite was lit and the room was cast in its soft glow. The drapes were pulled back and the lights of Vegas were spread out in front of them. And she felt like this time she'd get the emotion she'd been wanting from him.

"I know I should take this slow, give you a romantic evening to remember, but it's been too long since I've had you."

He found the zipper at the back of her dress and lowered it. She caught his hands and waited for him to look at her. No man had ever looked at her with as much passion as Max had in his eyes at that moment. "Every moment I spend with you is one to remember."

He twisted his hands in hers until he held both of her wrists in his grasp. "Me, too. I don't have the words I know you'd want to hear. Let me show you how happy I am that you've finally agreed to become my wife."

A feeling of joy and playfulness filled her. Nothing in her life had prepared her for the depth of her feelings for Max. She wanted to be with him more than she'd ever wanted to dance and be on stage. She wanted him more than she'd craved a family as a child or security as an adult.

He was an all-consuming passion that welled up inside her and spread everywhere. But he was also a soft and gentle breeze that brought peace and acceptance to her, something she'd never had before him. Sure the other girls in the show had accepted her, but they were all struggling the same way she'd been.

Only Max saw her, flaws and all, and accepted her. She hugged him tightly, her emotions bubbling over. She was so afraid to let him see how much she needed him in her life. Afraid to trust him with the depth of her love.

She bit her lip realizing the truth she'd stumbled on. She was marrying Max but letting him believe that she really wanted just this picture-perfect life when what she was afraid to ask for was his love.

He brought his mouth down hard on hers, his hand tangling in the hair at the nape of her neck, forcing her head back as he plundered her mouth in a kiss that left no doubt in her mind that he was staking his claim on her body. But what about her heart?

She stretched her fingers in his grasp and felt the fabric of his shirt. She skimmed her fingers over it until she could slip her fingertip under the button and feel his warm flesh.

He inhaled sharply, his hand leaving her neck and unknotting his tie. She watched him as he brought her hands up to his mouth and kissed each palm. "Take your dress off."

Was this the way to win him? What if this backfired on her?

She took her dress off and felt so naked with her newly acknowledged emotions flowing through her. She hesitated as she stood in front of him in the lamplight wearing only her panties and strapless bra.

"Turn around," he said, his voice gruff and commanding, sending shivers down her spine. She loved the way he sounded when his civilized demeanor dropped away and left behind just the man.

She pivoted on her heel, glanced over her shoulder at him. And felt a moment of intense pride in the body that she'd thought was flawed. Because the look on his face was a combination of lust and awe. Where was the love? And was she asking for too much to expect that?

He reached out and touched the skin of her back. "Lace your fingers together."

She didn't want to play sex games with him. She wanted him to drop the facade and show her what he really felt. "What are you doing?"

"Making you behave."

She shook her head. "I can't do this, Max."

Immediately he pulled her into his embrace. His hands rubbing down her back as he held her tightly to him. "What's the matter, Blondie?"

"I don't want to be an object to you. I need to know that I'm more than sex."

He framed her face in his hands and looked down at her. "You are."

"It doesn't feel like it."

"You are my life, Roxy."

He kissed her deeply, arousing her to the point where she stopped thinking. He finished undressing her.

He unbuttoned his shirt and tossed it on the floor on top of her dress. He pulled her into his arms, the hair on his chest abrading the tips of her nipples. She tried to shift in his arms, to move her aching breasts against him, but he held her still.

His mouth moved down her neck, suckling at the

pulse point. She shifted her legs, wrapping one around his thigh, trying to get closer. She needed him. She needed to believe that this was an expression of his affection for her.

He reached between them, lowering his zipper and freeing himself. She shifted against him.

He grabbed her waist and lifted her up. "Wrap your legs around my waist."

She did and felt him slide into her body. He cursed and pulled out. "Forgot something."

She held on to his shoulders, nibbled at his neck while she felt him reach into his pocket. He ripped the condom packet open with his teeth and sheathed himself with one hand.

She looked down into his eyes as he positioned himself and slid into her body, taking her deeply and completely. His gaze held hers as he leaned back against the wall and used his hands on her hips to control both of their movements. She rocked harder against him until she felt everything in her body reaching for her climax.

She fought it off as long as she could, waiting for him. He thrust harder and quicker and then leaned down and bit the tip of her breast as they both came together. She clung to him, holding him tightly.

But as their breathing slowed and he carried her to bed, she realized that she might have taken a high-stakes gamble that she wasn't ready to pay out on when she'd agreed to marry Max. Because she knew without a doubt that she loved him—and she had a hard time believing he felt the same.

Max had an early-morning meeting and got out of bed before Roxy. He left her a note telling her to be ready to make wedding plans that afternoon. He wanted to marry her before she had a chance to change her mind.

He glanced down at her sleeping in his bed. Damn, he wanted to see her in his bedroom in Dunwoody, not in a hotel bed. But the ring on her left hand reassured him that she was his. *His.* He knew she'd object to that statement, but it felt right in his soul.

He left their suite a few minutes later, getting on the phone to start making arrangements. His dad was in Napa visiting his family there and his mother was in Beverly Hills, but both would be in Vegas tomorrow for the wedding. Hayden was happy to make all the wedding arrangements. Duke had agreed to be his best man and was flying out with his wife Cami and their two children.

Max felt like all the pieces of his life were falling into place. He had a full day ahead of him and wanted everything cleared from his agenda so he could take the next two weeks off and fly to Hawaii with Roxy. Spend time, just the two of them in the same time zone. For a minute last night he'd felt her slipping through his fingers. He wanted to make sure she didn't.

His phone rang as he was walking through the lobby. "Williams."

"Hey, it's me," Roxy said, her voice soft and deeper than usual. He had no trouble picturing her sexy body in bed.

"Hey, you. What's up?" he asked.

"I'm trying to figure out what part of 'I don't want to sit around and wait for you' you didn't understand. Hayden just called and gave me the next few days off."

He should have guessed she wouldn't like the way he'd handled this morning, but to be honest, he couldn't concentrate while she was around. He needed to be one-hundred-percent at work.

"Blondie, I heard you, but I have to finish a few last-minute things. I thought you could use the time to get ready for our wedding."

"Are we really going to get married tomorrow?" she asked.

He exited the hotel into the sunny Vegas morning. His driver, Carl, pulled the rented limo up to the curb and got out, opening the door for him.

"Yes. I asked Hayden to make sure Tawny and Glenda are off the schedule for tonight and tomorrow. You should pick out dresses that you'd like them to wear. Let my assistant know and I'll make sure they get the sizes they need. Can you hang on a second?"

"Sure."

He pressed the mute button on the phone and turned to Carl. "I'm going to MacNeil's hotel—he's staying at the Golden Dream. While I'm there, I need you to go to the airport and pick up a package for me."

"No problem, boss."

Max slid into the car and opened his briefcase, pulling out his laptop to start downloading the numbers and e-mails that had come in the night before. He un-muted his phone.

"Sorry about that. I'm back now."

"You're doing too much."

He heard the concern in her voice and it warmed him. Even his parents never said anything about his work schedule. But then Roxy noticed things about him that no one else ever did. She noticed the details.

"This is what I get paid to do," he said lightly, not wanting her to realize that she'd touched on one of his weaknesses.

"Then do what you're getting paid for—running Pryce Enterprises. Let me handle the wedding details. You concentrate on finishing whatever you need to at the office."

"I want you to enjoy this wedding," he said, carefully. It was a character flaw of his that he hated to let go of any part of a project. And he knew he could make the wedding a fantasy dream come true for Roxy. It was that important to him. He knew her life had been hard and she'd worked hard for everything she had. He wanted to surprise her with a complete dream wedding. Although, to be honest, he had no idea what a woman dreamed of for her wedding.

"It's your celebration, too. I can take care of this. I want to do this for us."

"Thank you," he said.

"Silly man, we're in this together. This is what I was talking about. Compromise, remember? We're stronger when we both work together."

"I know you're right, but if you are struggling I can't promise not to step in and make things easier for you."

"That's one of the sweetest things anyone has ever said to me, Max."

"I'm glad." They hung up a few minutes later and he got out of the car at MacNeil's hotel with a lingering fear in his gut that he hadn't covered all the bases he needed to with Roxy.

Her wedding day was picture-perfect. Her dress was a lovely white creation that she never would have chosen if she wasn't marrying Max. It was slim-fitting and formal. The neckline plunged low between her breasts, but covered her entire back.

She'd looked at several lovely gowns that had low-cut backs but in the end she still wasn't ready to appear in public with too much skin showing. She was nervous about walking down the aisle and having her limp observed by everyone in attendance. Yet she hadn't found the words to tell Max.

She'd had barely three hours of sleep the night before and hadn't had a minute alone with him. Max's friends had thrown a party in their honor and she'd learned a lot about her soon-to-be husband. Especially that he was the solid one in his group, the man they came to when they needed anything.

It had amazed her, all the different things he was to so many different people. It was clear they all liked him, but just as clear that Max had carefully manipulated the relationships so that they all owed him a favor. He was never in anyone's debt.

She wanted to be his partner in that. She liked the man he was and realized that he had created his own family from his friends. His parents were more concerned with their own worlds than their son's. Roxy had been surprised, because as a child she'd always imagined that having two parents would fix all of her problems.

"Gosh, girl, you look good."

"Thanks, Tawny. Thanks for agreeing to be my maid of honor, too."

"It's my pleasure. I'm just glad to see you smiling again."

Roxy appreciated her friend's comments but they made the doubts plaguing her more real. Gave them more substance, because a part of her wondered if she was simply marrying Max because he'd helped her get past her scars.

But she knew she loved him. The depth of the emotions she held for him scared her sometimes. Last night she'd been unable to sleep, afraid if she closed her eyes she'd wake up and find that Max, and her relationship with him, was only a dream.

She swallowed hard as Tawny moved off to check her makeup one last time. As Roxy sank down on the padded chair in the dressing room, her hands were shaking.

Who would have thought a wedding would be so nerve-racking? She'd seen many pictures of brides and newly wedded couples at the hotel, and they'd seemed so blissful. But then from Roxy's point of view those brides had been living the charmed life she'd never had.

"You okay?" Tawny asked.

She thought about the fact that things in her life never stayed good for the long term. The bubble always burst and she was left standing on the outside looking in. And she really didn't want that to happen with Max. "Yes. No. I don't know. I've only known him a few weeks."

Tawny put her arm around Roxy, and she leaned on her friend, needing the support of someone who really knew what it was like to have come from nothing.

"I've never seen you like this with any other guy," Tawny said.

"Like what?" Roxy asked in a whisper, afraid to confess her own fears out loud.

"Like you're in love. Before, no man could compete with dancing in your life."

"Would I be in love with Max if I was still dancing?" Did Max love *her?* That was the biggest fear she had.

"I don't know, sweetie, but I really don't think that matters. You're not dancing anymore, and Max is your life."

"That totally scares me."

"It would me, too."

Someone knocked on the door.

"Come in."

Hayden walked in, dressed in his tailored tuxedo. He'd agreed to walk her down the aisle and Roxy was glad to see her friend. "Hi, Hay."

"Hey, Rox. You ready to do this thing?"

"Gosh, boss, did you woo your wife with romantic lines like that?" Tawny said.

"She likes it, says it's part of my charm."

"I think she might be prejudiced in your favor."

Hayden laughed and Roxy started to relax. She was getting married to Max.

"Thanks, Hay."

"For what, Rox?"

"Introducing me to him."

"No problem. A little of the good life is what you both needed."

"I don't know how Shelby lives with your ego."

"She has this way of deflating it," he said with a sardonic grin.

She checked her veil one last time, adjusting it before she took Hayden's arm. Tawny led the way out of the dressing room and they entered the chapel at the Chimera. She stumbled on her first step but Hayden just slowed his pace.

Glenda went up the aisle first, followed by Tawny, and Roxy kept her gaze trained on her friend's back until Hayden tightened his arm around hers and they started walking. She glanced up then. All the way to the front of the chapel. Past the rows of her friends and the rows of Max's family and friends.

There he was. Watching her with a look that was a combination of pride, lust and possessiveness. Her footsteps seemed a little lighter as she moved toward him. She knew that there was more to their relationship than sex and commonality. She saw a deep emotion in his eyes that he couldn't hide from her today.

Suddenly she was at his side and Hayden was placing her hand in Max's. His big hand was warm against hers and he brought her chilled fingers up to his chest, rubbing them against his shirt.

He leaned down to kiss her and whispered in her ear. "You take my breath away."

She didn't know how he knew the right thing to say. Or why it mattered that he had. She could only smile at him as the minister started the ceremony. She wasn't aware of the words she said or the other people who witnessed her vows. All she was focused on was Max and the way he watched her.

He put the wedding ring on her finger and leaned down while the minister was blessing his ring.

"Now, you're mine."

Once she slipped his ring on his finger, she said, "And you are mine."

"Forever," Max said.

Twelve

Max stepped out of the bathroom and found their suite empty. Candles still flickered on every surface in the room. Rose petals still littered the floor. The sheets on the bed were still rumpled from their love-making but his bride was gone.

All night he'd fought against the feeling that she wasn't really his. That the whirlwind romance he'd swept her up in wasn't overwhelming her. But there had been that almost panicked look in her eyes, and he'd sensed that she wasn't comfortable.

He cursed under his breath and grabbed his pants from the floor, pulling them on. He'd given Carl the night off, so his driver wasn't available.

That meant no one had been out front to see when or how she left.

He'd have to call Hayden and ask to see the security tapes. To track her down…oh, man, how the hell had he come to this? He was back in the exact same place he'd been when he was twenty-one. Chasing after a woman who didn't want to be caught.

He left the bedroom and walked into the living room. He was halfway across the room when he realized the balcony doors were open. He turned and saw the silhouette of Roxy. His racing heart slowed, and he moved toward her with a measured stride that should have calmed his temper.

But didn't. Why was she out here hiding from him? He stopped on the threshold. "I thought you'd left."

She had both hands braced on the wrought-iron railing. The lights of the strip were bright and colorful, an illusory background behind this woman who'd become the center of his life in such a short time. And he felt his hold on her was no more secure than a "sure thing" hand at the poker tables.

She glanced over her shoulder at him, an aura of sadness wrapping around her that made him feel as though all of his carefully ordered plans were falling apart. Getting his ring on her finger had been his focus, but now he knew the other details were going to haunt him.

"Did that bother you?"

"No, it pissed me off."

"I didn't think you got pissed, Max."

"I do. I just don't show it."

"Like all of your emotions."

Please don't do this, he thought. Just once in his life he wanted his failings to be overlooked. Rationally he knew they couldn't be. That she was entitled to have everything she wanted.

"This isn't about emotion, Blondie. This is about trying to find my wife of less than—" he glanced down at his watch "—five hours."

She wrapped her arms around herself. "Why would my being out here bother you? We had a quickie courtship, why not a quickie wedding?"

"I thought I made it clear to you how I felt."

"No, you didn't. And lying in bed, I started thinking about how much I needed you—emotionally—and I realized that you didn't have that same need."

He needed to distract her. To find a way to make her realize what he felt without having to say it. Because even though Roxy would never understand or believe it, she was the stronger of the two of them. She allowed him to see her flaws and vulnerabilities.

"You don't need anyone. You're this great tower of strength and you take care of everyone around you. I'm sure you realize that."

"Yes, I do realize it."

"Why? Why do you do that?"

He didn't want to tell her, but maybe an explanation would be enough to appease her. To get her back into his arms. "I'm trying to make sure that they never leave."

"Who left you, Max? I never realized you were vulnerable until tonight."

"Uh..." He didn't want to tell her. Didn't want to share that intimately embarrassing part of his life. The impetuous young man he'd been was a faint memory. Max had buried that part of his soul a long time ago.

"I stood naked in front of you. You forced me to look in the mirror and see this scarred body of mine through your eyes. Tell me, Max. Tell me so I can believe that I didn't just buy into the Vegas illusion."

He took a deep breath and stepped out onto the shadowy balcony with her. He hoped that somehow in the dark the words would be easier to say.

"I was twenty-one when I thought I'd fallen in love. My parents of course said I was too young. My father wanted me to get established in Williams & Co., the family business. But I wanted...it's hard to remember what I wanted and why, but I definitely wanted Jessica."

"Did she want you?"

"She seemed to. We had a quick engagement, and then the night before our wedding she disappeared. I thought...she'd been kidnapped because of my family's money."

Roxy left the railing and came to sit down next to him on the other balcony chair. "Oh, Max. You must have been terrified for her safety."

"I was. We started searching for her and found her back at college in the apartment she shared with two of her friends. Her parents were angry, I was angry."

She tilted her head to the side, studying him and he was afraid that she might see all the way to the truth. He hadn't been angry. He'd been scared that Jessica had finally seen the same thing in him that his parents and everyone else in his life had. That thing that made them want to leave before he got too close.

"We talked, she gave me back my ring and I left. My dad sent me to Japan to oversee a new operation for Williams & Co."

"Is that when you started channeling all your energy into work?"

"I guess. I didn't do much work then. I partied every night and got myself into a dangerous situation. That's how I met Duke—he saved my ass."

She sat down on his lap, pulling him into her arms, so that his head rested against her breasts. "And since then you've found a way to make sure no one can leave you…everyone in your life owes you something."

"Not you," he said between clenched teeth, knowing the truth of his words and the very real fear in his heart.

"Especially me. I love you, Max. I haven't said

those words to anyone since my grandmother died. You gave me a home here," she took her hand and placed it over her heart. "Where I've been longing to find one."

"Thank you for loving me, Blondie."

"You don't thank me, Max. You tell me that you love me, too."

He stared down into her face. "I'll never leave you."

She pushed herself to her feet. "That's not enough, Max. I need to know how you feel."

"That's the one thing I can't give you."

She backed away from him. He knew he couldn't make her stay. She dressed and quietly left their honeymoon suite.

Max woke the next morning feeling more alone than he ever had before. He'd followed Roxy to her home outside the city limits and made sure she was safely inside before he came back.

Maybe he was just one of those guys who couldn't be married. But in his gut he knew that wasn't true. He wanted Roxy—he was just afraid to tell her how much.

Roxy took her time getting dressed and slowly drove back to the Chimera. She shouldn't have left last night without hashing everything out. Max was the one person she wanted to spend the rest of her life with. The only person who'd ever wanted her for herself, not because she was a good dancer but because of who she was inside.

She had to find a way to his emotions. Had to figure out the details he needed to feel secure enough to tell her how he felt.

She called Max and left him a voice mail asking him to meet her in the atrium café for breakfast. She drove to the hotel and went directly to the restaurant to wait for him.

The hostess told Roxy her table would be available in a few minutes. Roxy sat down on the bench to wait. Trying to gather her thoughts. She heard someone approach the table and glanced up expecting to see Hayden.

Instead, she was surprised to see Harron MacNeil standing there, a concerned look on his weathered face.

"Good morning, Harron. What can I do for you?"

He stood still, towering over her. Roxy pushed to her feet.

"Where is Williams?" he asked. He held a newspaper clutched in his hand and wouldn't look her in the eye.

"In his room. He'll be down in a few minutes," she said, hoping that was true. "Why don't you have a seat?"

He nodded stiffly. But instead of sitting he paced around her. She caught the hostess's eye. The woman gestured for them to join her and took them to a table at the back of the restaurant.

"Is Sheila okay?"

"What? Yes, she's fine. This is about our merger."

"What's the matter?"

"Nothing I want to discuss with you."

Roxy pulled back from Harron. She was surprised by the way he was behaving, had thought they'd become friends after sharing several meals together.

"Harron, whatever it is, maybe I can help you."

He pulled today's newspaper from his briefcase and tossed it on the table. The picture of herself stopped her.

The paper had been folded to the society pages and the headline would have been visible even half a room away. The Billionaire and the Showgirl.

She picked up the paper, reading quickly.

Billionaire Max Williams got lucky at more than the poker tables in Las Vegas, where rumor has it he walked away a big winner. He also found himself a bride—the former headliner at the Chimera's famed revue, *Chimère.*

"I don't care how much it costs. I'm going to stop the merger now," Harron said. "Our image isn't about gamblers and showgirls. Topless dancers turned trophy wives are not what my family has spent the last three generations building our reputation on."

She gasped out loud, realizing that she was going

to be responsible for Max losing this new piece of business. A piece he'd worked really hard to acquire.

"I'm sorry you had to hear that," Harron said, shaking his head.

"I'm sorry you *said* something like that. Obviously this paper was looking to stir up some trouble and you are playing right into their hands."

"Don't make this about anything other than what it is. You took your clothes off for a living. I thought you were a dancer."

Did he feel duped? Was that what this was about? "I am a dancer. I was the headliner in *Chimère*. I worked long hours to get to that point. As many hours as you and your father and grandfather worked to make the travel agency one of the top three in this part of the world. How does hard work not fit into your ethics?"

He said nothing to her, and she thought maybe she was getting through to him. She wanted Harron to understand that dancing, topless or not, was just as hard as running a business. Maybe even harder. The struggle, the competition was fierce.

"I started training to be a dancer when I was a little girl, Harron. My entire life was dedicated to dance until I was injured. There is nothing sleazy about what I did. Not in my mind. Not in the minds of the people who came to the shows I performed in.

"We've gotten to know each other over the last few

weeks and the man I've come to know isn't going to let the society pages dictate his business decisions.

"Pryce Enterprises is the kind of company you want to trust your business to, because Max cares about his workers. He remembers their birthdays and little things like what they like to eat at catered meals."

"That's about employee retention."

"It's about a lot more than that. Max actually cares for his workers and treats his employees the way he does his friends."

Max was ready to meet with Roxy and give her whatever she needed to stay with him. He exited his suite and got on the elevator, noticing he had missed a call from Duke. He dialed the callback number.

"It's about damned time." Duke greeted him. Max heard the sound of a computer keyboard in the background and knew that Duke was on his laptop.

"Skip to the good part. I left you in charge for less than twenty-four hours and already you're calling me."

"Actually, there's no good part to this. I wouldn't have called unless I thought you needed to handle this. Have you seen today's paper?"

"No. Why?"

"Because instead of running a bridal portrait of Roxy, they have her publicity photo from *Chimère*."

Max cursed succinctly under his breath. "Where is MacNeil?"

Max didn't have time to deal with this. Roxy was his first priority and he couldn't afford the time away from her. He was fighting for his life with her and he needed to make sure she understood how important she was to him. More important than Pryce Enterprises. Without her, nothing else mattered.

He almost dropped the phone as he realized he loved her. It wasn't supposed to happen like this.

"He wants to call off the merger regardless of what it costs him. He said, and I quote…topless dancers turned trophy wives aren't the image we want at MacNeil Travel."

Max couldn't believe Harron had had the gall to say something like that. Max was sick of this merger anyway. They'd wanted a nice profit-maker for their company and to expand into a line of business they hadn't dabbled in before but honestly, at this point, he didn't want to do business with MacNeil. "I can't deal with MacNeil this morning. I have another fire that needs to be put out."

"What fire? I haven't heard any rumblings from anyone. Is it that damned hockey team you bought?"

"No, Duke. This one's personal. I don't need your help with it."

"You always need my help."

"Not with my wife."

"Oh, you have a point there. What do you want me to do with MacNeil?"

"Let him back out of the deal. We'll do it the aggressive way. We're still going to acquire his assets."

"Are you sure about that? We have our reputation to think of, and we don't do hostile takeovers."

Max closed his eyes. He wanted MacNeil's heart for his angry words about Roxy. He didn't care that he'd built Pryce into the kind of company that everyone respected and admired. Right now he wanted revenge. He wanted to take MacNeil's company and break it into pieces while the man watched.

"You're right. I'll deal with MacNeil later. In the meantime make an offer to Trans/Time Travel. They are MacNeil's chief competition, right?"

"I'll pull together the numbers and information we have. But we don't have to move on the travel company acquisition until you're back from your honeymoon."

"Are you managing me, Merchon?" he asked, because though the two men were friends, Duke had never told him what to do in his personal life before.

"Yes, Williams, I am. Enjoy your new wife and forget about business for a while."

"I don't think I'm going to be able to do that until I take care of the newspaper people and MacNeil."

"Pryce Enterprises has already sent a letter and wedding photo from yesterday's event. I personally sent a letter expressing my outrage."

"You were outraged. I'm touched."

"Yeah, well, I don't have many friends, you know that. When they strike at you, they strike at me, too."

Max was a little humbled by Duke's words. "Thanks, man."

"I think I owed you."

"No you didn't. Touch base with MacNeil later, will you?"

"No problem," Duke said, before disconnecting the phone.

Max rubbed the back of his neck, hoping that MacNeil hadn't said anything to Roxy about the photo the paper had run. Harron and Sheila were staying in the Chimera for a few days gambling. She might not want to be reminded of a career she no longer had.

He entered the restaurant—and saw Roxy talking to Harron. Anger began a slow burn in his gut as he crossed to the corner table where they were sitting. Roxy had her back to him, but he could see that she was sincere in her words.

"Max actually cares for his workers and treats his employees the way he does his friends," Roxy said.

He was humbled to hear her defending him. She'd come to his rescue, even though he'd let her down. Taken what she had to offer but been unwilling to give her what she really needed in return. Not gifts or money or a new career, but love. Even though she'd walked out his door last night, here she was defending him.

The press had portrayed her in a bad light, but she wasn't slinking away from Harron in embarrassment or regret. She put her hands on the table and leaned forward.

"You should be happy to merge with Pryce Enterprises because Max is the kind of man who never rests on what he's accomplished. He's going to take your number-three travel company and make it number one. I know the fact that I was a Las Vegas showgirl doesn't sit well with you, Mr. MacNeil, but I'm willing to bet any profits you'd see from Pryce would go a long way to making you feel better."

"There won't be any profits from Pryce," Max said, crossing to Roxy and MacNeil.

"Now see here—"

"No, MacNeil, you see here. No one insults my wife."

"I didn't mean those insults. I've got a quick fuse and this morning I was surprised by what I read in the paper."

"So surprised that you had to track down my wife to confront me?"

"Yes. We spoke at length about the client base that MacNeil Travel draws from. We once lost ten percent of that base when Sheila's dance studio put on a show from Mikhail Baryshnikov's White Oak Dance Project. And that's a legitimate ballet. Can you imagine how this would affect business?"

"Maybe you don't want those people as your clients. Dance is an expression of emotion, Harron. I'm confident Sheila wasn't embarrassed by the ballet they did."

Harron flushed. "No, she wasn't. And she wasn't too happy with me this morning when I got angry over Roxy's picture."

"I'm not happy, either. Duke will be calling you this afternoon and we'll stop the merger."

Harron started to leave but Roxy stopped him with her hand on his arm. "Wait. I think you two can work something out. You've both worked so hard on this."

Max waited to see what Harron would say. Finally the older man nodded. "I'll talk to Duke this afternoon and we'll work the details out. You go enjoy your honeymoon."

Harron left the restaurant. Roxy faced Max, and he didn't know how to thank her for what she'd done. Nor how to tell her how much she meant to him. He wanted to make sure she realized that Pryce Enterprises wasn't the most important thing in his life anymore…she was.

Max pulled her into his arms as soon as she was close enough. "I'm sorry."

"For the picture? Don't worry about it."

"No. I'm sorry I was too stubborn to tell you how I feel."

"How do you feel?"

I love you. The words were in his head but he couldn't force them out. Not now, not here.

"Did seeing it make you regret not dancing? If you decide you want to dance again…I can open an office here."

"That's a sweet offer, but I think my headlining days are over."

"What about your days with me? Are they over?"

He wrapped his arm around her and led her from the restaurant to the private bench in the maze where he'd first proposed to her. "I was surprised when I heard you defending me."

"Why surprised?"

"I'm used to being the one who makes everything right."

"Well, you've got me now."

"Yes, I do," he said, holding her closer. He kissed her, but now there was something more than passion in his embrace. He should have known when she turned him down the first time he asked her to marry him and he'd decided he had to have her that there was something more than comfort in his mind. Something more than sex and things in common.

She put her hand on his jaw and looked into his eyes. "No matter what happens between us, Max, I'm not going to let anyone hurt you."

He squeezed her even tighter. "I love you, Roxy."

Max's words were like magic wrapping around Roxy and clearing out the hurt that had lingered after Harron's callous words. She relaxed against him and remembered how little she'd had to like about her life just a few weeks earlier before he'd swept into her life and changed it.

Finally, she felt like she found the home she'd never had here in his arms.

"They got one thing right in the article," Max said, picking it up and skimming it.

"What?"

"I did get lucky in Vegas."

"At the tables?" she asked, teasing him.

"When I met you."

* * * * *

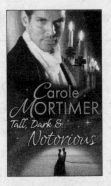

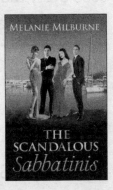